THE PREROGATIVE OF KINGS

ROBIN MACKENZIE

Published by

MELROSE BOOKS

An Imprint of Melrose Press Limited
St Thomas Place, Ely
Cambridgeshire
CB7 4GG, UK
www.melrosebooks.com

FIRST EDITION

Copyright © Robin Mackenzie 2011

The Author asserts his moral right to
be identified as the author of this work

Cover designed by Jeremy Kay

ISBN 978 1 907732 05 8

Printed and bound in Great Britain by:
CPI Antony Rowe. Chippenham, Wiltshire

For Daphne and the visit to Franschhoek
that inspired me to write this story

Introduction

MY FAMILY MAY WELL THINK THAT THIS is a story of *What Might Have Happened,* because there is no doubt that one of our great great great great grandfathers was indeed a page to Marie Antoinette and there is a family rumour that he was also her lover.

There is no real evidence to support this belief other than the fact that he was suddenly banished to Pondicherry in French southern India and when the British took over France's Indian colonies he changed sides, moved to Calcutta, and was given a senior position in the Bengal Cavalry. He married an aristocratic Frenchwoman whose family had been in India for several generations and one of their daughters duly married an influential member of the Bengal Civil Service. It is on this couple and their descendants that I have based the story of *The Prerogative of Kings.*

The idea came to me while on a trip to South Africa during which I visited a number of museums and also many of the well-known vineyards and wineries of the Cape. I heard stories of British, Dutch and French settlers and also of British visitors who had stopped at Cape Town on their way to govern our fast growing empire in the East, and I wondered if any of my ancestors, on their way to India, might have been one of such visitors. I don't know; but the idea did seem to offer potential for a story.

However all the happenings in *The Prerogative of Kings* come entirely from my imagination as do the people, with just one exception. The vineyards, houses, hotels and other buildings, with two exceptions, are also imaginary being combinations of places I have been to, but if anyone feels their property has been unfairly used, I hope they will forgive me.

I must thank Daphne Mackenzie for introducing me to the wonderful scenery of the Cape winelands and also for acting as navigator on an exploratory drive that encompassed almost the entire length of England and Scotland. My thanks are also due to Brigid Martineau for endlessly driving me round East Anglia in a search for suitable locations, and to several friends and family members for reading the many versions of the manuscript and providing constructive, and occasionally destructive, criticism.

Robin Mackenzie
Ampfield
September 2010

PROLOGUE

PART 1
1792

THE SIX MEN CROUCHED UNDER THE TREES by the shore of the loch, shivered and pulled their cloaks closer round their shoulders as an icy wind ruffled the surface of the water. A February afternoon was no place to be in this weather, thought the men, but then on this particular late afternoon in 1792 they were awaiting the arrival of a foreign ship, a ship that was carrying a valuable cargo, and the reward they were promised for unloading and disposing of that cargo was well worth their present discomfort.

"Look yonder, what's that out there?" one of the men said in Gaelic. "Aye, there she is. You can just see the loom o' the sails against the hill. Wait you here while I see what's happening," and he slipped down the bank and walked along the tideline.

"Here, Rorie Mor," a voice said. "Can you see? They're lowering a boat, I can hear the splash of oars; aye, and here they are." Then the boat grounded on the shingle and a voice hailed them.

"Monsieur Macrae?" it said in French, and Rorie answered in the same tongue.

"Monsieur le Commandant, you have the cargo? Oui, c'est bien, then we should start work at once, for all should be finished by daybreak and you must be away by then."

And then, and for the next several hours, the loch shore and the hillside behind were the scene of frantic activity until finally, in the early hours of the following morning, Rorie Mor turned to the Frenchman.

"C'est fini," he said, "the job is done."

"Excellent! So now you will come on board and take a cognac, oui?"

"Non merci, mon Commandant. I still have work to do here, but you will, perhaps, on your way, take my men to Skye where they live?"

"Of course, mon ami, it's a pleasure; so now it's au revoir," and the captain shook Rorie's hand, stepped aboard his barge and gave the order to cast off.

Then, as the rest of the men were boarding the brig's longboat, one of them turned and looking up at Rorie Mor, waved his arm and said in a shrill voice: "See now, Rorie Mor Macrae, I hae the stane in ma hand and I lookit in it, and ye ken what that means. It means I see things – aye, terrible things – deaths! Many deaths! And some soon to come; soon I tell ye, verra soon."

"Ach, away wi' ye, Seumas," one of the other men said and hauled him aboard as the longboat pushed off and rowed out to the brig.

Rorie Mor stood for a while on the shore watching the brig and considering Seumas's forebodings. The more he did so the less he liked them, for the lad was well known for having the second sight. Then, seeing the brig had reached the open waters of the Sound, he turned and called to the two boys watching the horses to follow him up the hill.

An hour later he returned alone and loosed the horses, except for one, which he mounted and trotted slowly back towards the head of the loch. Then, after about a mile, something made him look back. What it was and what he saw no one will ever know but it caused him to break into a headlong gallop and never to ease until he reached the inn by the bridge. Minutes later, when the innkeeper came out, the horse had vanished and the body of Rorie Mor Macrae lay lifeless by the doorway.

It seems that the brig never reached Skye and no trace of her, of her crew or her passengers was ever found. There was, however, one man who might have thrown some light on the fate of both the brig and Rorie Mor Macrae, and he emerged from the woods above the lochside and gazed down the track after the fast disappearing horse and rider.

"If I know Rorie Mor, that'll be the end o' him. The bogies fair put the fear o' God into him," he muttered and vanished back into the wood, to emerge a few minutes later further along the shore where a small sailing boat was beached in the shadow of the trees. He unhitched a rope, threw the bundle he was carrying into the stern and dragged the boat out into the loch, clambered in and rowed out until he caught the tide, then raised the sail and set off for the far shore.

"Yon was a good night's work. His lordship will be gey pleased – if only this weather will let me to Inverness to tell him," and he looked up and felt the first flakes of snow on his face. Half an hour later, with the ferocity of the blizzard increasing, he brought the boat into the lee of a rocky bluff. There he hauled it ashore, made fast the painter and climbed up the hill to a cottage by the side of the old drove road. Once inside, he made up the fire and from his pouch he took a black, leather-covered bottle and put it to his lips. "Aye, a good night indeed," he thought.

Six months after the events detailed above, on the evening of the 9th of August 1792, Louis XVI, King of France, his Queen and the rest of the Royal Family left their palace of the Tuileries and took refuge within the Assembly.

"Oh, why did we not leave France when we could?" Marie Antoinette asked her husband. "You told me the Scottish nobleman had everything prepared for us."

"I know, I know," the King replied, "but after the failure of the last attempt, I could not go through with another. That is my weakness I fear – always to bow to the inevitable. Now we must await our fate." And they did not have long to wait before they were moved to the ancient Tower of the Temple and from there, on the 20th of January 1793, Louis XVI, King of France, went to the guillotine.

The night before his execution, Louis was permitted a last meeting with his Queen and his children. There, despite the close attention of the gaolers, he managed to pass to Marie Antoinette a small wooden box and a leather pouch, and as she slipped them beneath her dress, he whispered, "For Antoine, if you have a chance."

In due course Marie Antoinette was moved from the Temple to the prison of the Conciergerie and there one last attempt was to be made to rescue her. By arrangement with a friendly guard, a certain gentleman was admitted to her presence with the final details of the plan and before he left she managed to give him the box and the pouch that the King had given her.

"For Le Chevalier de la Tour du Lac," she said, and he nodded. By chance, as he left the prison, he saw the Chevalier, once the Queen's faithful page, waiting by the gate but unable to enter and without a word passed him the box and pouch. The rescue attempt was betrayed and on 16th of October the Queen followed her husband to the guillotine.

PART 2
1835

THE CHEVALIER SURVIVED THE TERROR AND WAS eventually banished to the French colony of Pondicherry in Southern India where he took the name of Dulac, married the daughter of another émigré gentleman and subsequently enjoyed a successful career as a merchant.

During this time, he made many contacts in the British East India Company and became particularly friendly with Arthur Kingdom, an influential Bengal trader, who persuaded Dulac to move to Calcutta where, in due course, he married Dulac's daughter, Camille.

Some years later Antoine Dulac, as he was now universally known, retired and moved up country. The Kingdoms meanwhile had become people of great influence in Calcutta, and in 1839 their daughter Julie married Mr Thomas Saddler, a member of the Council of India and scion of a wealthy Suffolk family.

Shortly after the wedding Antoine, having retired, now gave considerable thought to what should be done about the royal mementos he had brought from France all those years ago. Finally, he decided that he should hand them over to his granddaughter and her distinguished husband. Therefore, a short time later, when he knew that Thomas Saddler was staying with them, he paid a visit to the Kingdoms in Calcutta.

"I have often told you about my life at the Court of Louis XVI, where I was a page to Queen Marie Antoinette," he said one evening after dinner. "Well, now I am going to tell you about things I have never spoken of before; things that happened in the early days of the Revolution."

Then, for the next hour, he told of the events leading up to the execution, first of the King and then, six months later, of Marie Antoinette. He spoke of the failure of the final attempt at escape and of how, shortly before her death, the Queen had managed to get two small packages passed to him. And here he produced the box and the leather pouch and handed them over to Thomas.

"This pouch contains some of the Queen's jewels which she wished me to have as a reward for loyal service and the box contains instructions on certain actions I was to take in the event of the worst happening. Well, it did, but I was never able to take the action. I believe you, Thomas, with your connections, will be able to. I therefore give them to you, and I want your promise that they will never go out of the family."

Three weeks later, his business in India completed, Thomas took passage to England and on the long voyage home he had plenty of time to look at what the Chevalier had given him and to think what he should do about it. The jewels, he realised, must be deposited in a secure place until he could establish who actually had a legal right to them. The contents of the box were more difficult; they had proved to be a metal trinket and a paper, in the Queen's handwriting, instructing the holder to visit an address in London. This he put aside to discuss further with the Chevalier on his next visit to India.

On his arrival back in England he told Julie about the jewels, and they agreed that he should deposit them somewhere safe, but not, she felt, in a bank, where someone might talk. He agreed that this would be sensible and so, having made his report to the Council, he paid a visit to his family in Suffolk, taking with him a locked steel box containing the jewels. This he hid in a place where he thought no one would think of looking and, for the present, kept the location to himself.

The following year Thomas again sailed for India, taking with him the Chevalier's trinket and paper. On this voyage, however, when the ship stopped at the Cape, he travelled up country to visit two friends; first a Huguenot, Peter Jordaine, at his farm of Oude Klippen and then they both went on to the du Toit family at the nearby property of Blouberg.

It was while at Blouberg that Thomas realised that he was in for a bad bout of the fever that had troubled him for many years. This worried him, as he had been warned in India that another serious attack could prove fatal.

"What if it should?" And the thought made him realise that in such an eventuality the knowledge of the whereabouts of the royal treasures would die with him. He therefore wrote a letter to his father in Suffolk explaining about the jewels. This he was just able to do before delirium overtook him.

An hour later, in an interval of consciousness, he thought, "What to do about the other things?" His friends, he knew, were out, so whatever he did, he would have to do alone. "That thing we saw this morning – there's a place to hide them there, and I'll just about manage to get to it."

When he got back, he felt the tremors returning and realised he had not much more time. He picked up a notebook and started writing, but gradually slipped into a coma from which he would not recover, and when they returned to the house, his friends found him lying on the floor of his room. Some ten minutes later, he was dead.

Part 3
2000

Queen Marie Antoinette of France, a member of the Court of the Honourable East India Company, a farm in the Cape Colony and an address in eighteenth-century London. It was inconceivable that there could be any connection between them, but there appeared to be; and it was this fact that was going round and round in Andrew Henderson's head as he dozed in his seat on an overnight flight from Cape Town to London. Was chance stranger than coincidence? Or was it the other way round?

It was chance that he came across the book, but it was coincidence that it was he, possibly the only person in the Cape to whom it made sense, who found it. It was chance that he was staying near the farm, but it was coincidence that he had the knowledge that enabled him to see that it was an address that was referred to and where that address would probably be.

Chance and coincidence, coincidence and chance. It was like an endless dance. Marie Antoinette and her page in a graceful minuet; Marie Antoinette and her page in bed, first in a farmhouse then in an inn. In and out, round and round, until with a start he awoke to see a smiling stewardess offering him a glass of orange juice.

"I hope your dream was as good as it looked," she said. "I was really sorry to disturb you, but we'll be in London in an hour."

Was it all chance and coincidence, he wondered, or was there something more to it? "Soon we shall find out," was his final thought as he stepped from the plane into the terminal building.

CHAPTER 1

THERE ARE FEW THINGS MORE PLEASANT THAN to be awakened by the late summer sun striking the walls of your bedroom. Such were exactly the thoughts of Andrew Henderson on that March morning, as he turned over lazily and gazed out of the window.

It had been a hard few days, he thought, but well worth it. The contracts he had concluded with the two wineries should be of great benefit to his brewery's expanding wine trade. And now he had a week's holiday with Jenny at the Stanleys' farm in the hills behind Paarl.

Andrew Henderson was an interesting character. At school he had been both a scholar and a fine all-round athlete, qualities which had subsequently resulted in his leaving Cambridge with an Athletics Blue and a more than adequate degree.

After a short spell in the army, where his quick brain and natural fluency in languages had led him into the mysterious world of Special Operations, he decided that the time had come for a proper career.

Now, some twenty-five years later, he had just passed his fifty-second birthday and was chairman of the family business, Henderson Braithwaite Limited, brewers of fine beers, of Gunnersbury, West London. The firm was one of the most successful privately owned breweries still in existence and, under Andrew's direction, had recently acquired a small chain of high-class retail shops. It was his intention, through these shops, to introduce to a discerning public the joys of top-quality New World wines, and it was this that had brought him to South Africa.

But wine buying was not his only reason. Two years ago, he had been hit by a tragedy which had nearly ruined his career and had even threatened

1

his sanity. His wife had suffered a stroke while shopping in London and died two days later, aged only forty-one. For several months, he had shut himself away, seeing no one and neglecting the brewery, until finally his cousin, a fellow director, had told him he must either pull himself together or resign. His behaviour was strangely out of character for such a capable and determined person and, in later years, he himself was unable to account for why he had behaved so. But realising he could not go on as he was, he started once again, albeit somewhat reluctantly, to attend the office and to accept the occasional social invitation.

It was on one of these occasions that he met Jenny Stanley, a slim South African girl with sparkling grey eyes and a mass of closely waved auburn hair. She was not someone who could be easily overlooked, but his present mood was such that he hardly noticed her; she, on the other hand, was greatly taken with this good-looking but somewhat morose man. That he was highly intelligent she realised at once; but why, she wondered, was he so obviously unhappy? After dinner therefore, she sat herself next to him and gently but firmly persuaded him to talk about himself. Bit by bit the story came out and finally, to his great surprise, he found himself saying:

"So you see Alice was no longer with us and our only child had died three years before, so what had I to live for? Sure, my friends have persuaded me to try being more active, but what's the point? For two pins I'd give up again and go and hibernate in the country."

"But what good would that do?" she asked. "You're quite young still. Yes, you know you are," she said with a smile, when he attempted to demur. "I don't know how old you are, but I do know you are quite young enough to re-create your career. You have a family business – you are the boss – and what you need is a new interest, perhaps a new direction for the firm. You told me it's a brewery. Well, what doesn't it do that your competitors do?"

"I don't know," he replied. "We brew very good beer, we own very good pubs, mostly in our own area; almost a captive market, I'd say. There are families that have drunk in our pubs for three generations or more. What else do we need?"

"Oh come off it, Andrew – can I call you Andrew? Well I will anyway. That's the typically English attitude to almost anything – it's there, it's perfect, therefore leave it alone. And in the case of a business what happens next? You fall behind and along comes a big bad predator and you're taken over. Then you watch the new owners making a bigger success – and a bigger profit – than you ever did. No, you can do better than that, my dear."

"You really are quite the little business woman, aren't you?" Andrew said smiling and then adding, "So tell me, just where did you get this commercial ambition?"

"Oh, from my father. He was in steel, and then became a partner in a bank in Johannesburg," she said. "I was brought up thinking business and would like to have tried my hand at it. But I'm just old enough to be of the generation where well brought up girls, particularly in Johannesburg, did not do anything as vulgar as work. Then Father bought an estate near Paarl. That's down in the Cape, where the wine comes from. He revolutionised vine-growing on the estate, built a winery and brought in a first-class wine maker. My brother has carried on the good work and is now one of the most important producers in the country. You should come out and see it sometime."

"I could just do that," he said; then after a pause, he went on, "do you know, you've given me the beginnings of an idea." And for the first time she saw a glimmer of enthusiasm in his eyes. However, at that moment their hostess came up and put an end to the conversation.

"Come on, you two," she said, "you've been together in that corner for long enough and I particularly want Andrew to talk to our Belgian friend."

The next morning when he arrived at the brewery, he jumped from his car, threw the keys to the commissionaire with the request, "Tom, you park her please," and ran up the stairs to his office. Such was his energy and enthusiasm that the commissionaire, having parked the car, came into Reception and with a broad grin, said to the girl at the desk, "It's a while since we've seen Mr Andrew like that; I wonder what's got into him!"

"Perhaps it's love," the girl replied, "or maybe he's gone back to having good ideas like he used to. Anyway, I don't mind as long as he doesn't go back to his rages."

3

Once in his office, Andrew asked his secretary to find his cousin Tony and also Frank Walker, the Finance Director, and ask them to come and see him as soon as possible. When they appeared he waved them to the chairs usually reserved for distinguished visitors, and himself stood with his back to the magnificent oak fireplace that had been a feature of the Chairman's office since the days of the founding Hendersons in the eighteenth century.

"Now listen," he said, "I met someone last night, a girl if you must know, and she has given me an idea. No, not what you think! And Tony, I'll thank you to be serious, for this could mean big business for us."

Tony Henderson tried to look suitably contrite, but felt he was not very convincing. Andrew, however, appeared not to notice and continued to elaborate his idea.

"Now I'm sure I saw somewhere that Webbers are thinking of parting with that funny off-licence chain they have. What do they call it?"

"The shops are called The Sommelier," Walker said, "the idea was that they would be an upmarket operation selling, primarily, quality wines in pricy locations. They've never really taken off. The idea may have been good, but it doesn't seem to have worked."

"Silly name for a start," said Tony, "and wrong focus. People buy quality wine from a wine merchant. Off-licences are where they buy variety, anything from plonk to Veuve Cliquot. If you want your chain to have some sort of speciality, go for saki or Polish vodka or New World wines or something like that."

"Exactly," replied his cousin. "Now the girl I met last night is South African and, what's more, her family own one of the biggest wine estates in the country. Apart from that, she lectured me on everything from my personal life to competition in the drink trade. And the more I think about the latter, the more I think she has a point. We need something new, so what about high street wine shops – speciality, inter alia, New World wines. I don't think it's being done."

"No it isn't, not really," said Tony, the marketing man, "but it will be, so if we want that niche we'd better get in there fast; and I agree we really should be thinking of some new investment. What about it Frank?"

The finance man, as always when asked a question involving spending money, looked cautious.

"It's certainly a possibility, but it will need a lot of looking at," he said.

"Right, gentlemen, let's start now," said Andrew, who had got to his present position by always pressing home any advantage gained and never allowing time for doubts to creep in. It being a moment to apply these principles, he immediately started issuing instructions.

"You, Tony, get going on the market. Find out what has been done and who the competition will be. Then I want an analysis of countries, quality, prices and who we should be seeing. Shippers or deal direct and so on. Frank, a business plan please, with source of funds, method of acquisition etcetera. I myself will get hold of that man at Webbers – Spears, Charles Spears, that's his name. I was at school with his brother. Now let's see about timing. Assuming Webbers are interested we must alert the Board, and then go for a full presentation in September. I think we should be aiming for a deal by the year end."

And that was just about how it turned out, Andrew thought. For by the end of the year several things had happened. Henderson Braithwaite had acquired the Sommelier chain and renamed it World Wide Wines. An expert on Australian and New Zealand wines had been hired and had already negotiated some useful contracts. Tony Henderson, a fluent Spanish speaker, was out in Chile and was more than enthusiastic about the UK market potential for the many excellent Chilean wines.

But for Andrew, by far the most important thing had been his blossoming friendship with Jenny Stanley. Within a week of their first meeting she had dined with him and thereafter had been his constant companion, persuading him to get out and about and, more importantly, ensuring that his enthusiasm for World Wide Wines did not flag. Then in the New Year, she had suggested that he should visit South Africa.

"I must go home for a bit," she had said, "so why don't you come out too? I know my brother would be delighted to arrange for you to meet the top wine people in South Africa. In fact, what you must do is to come for the Nederburg auction. You'll learn more about our wine there than anywhere – and meet more people."

So that was what had happened, and most successful it had been; and now he was looking forward to a short holiday and being shown that most beautiful of landscapes, the mountains and winelands of the old Cape Province.

When, some thirty minutes later, he came downstairs to the dining room he found Ann Stanley pouring herself a cup of coffee.

"Good morning, Andrew," she said and waving to the table added, "help yourself to fruit and cereal, it's all on the table. Eggs and bacon coming up shortly."

Then, as he sat down, Jenny appeared, put her hands on his shoulder and kissed the back of his neck.

"Did you sleep well, darling? Most people do here." Then turning to her sister-in-law she said, "Where's David, and what are we planning for today? Must be something good for Andrew's first day here."

"Didn't you say Andrew, that you had Huguenot relations or connections or something?" Ann asked. "Well, we thought we'd go over to Franschhoek. It's the Huguenot town, you know, and has a wonderful museum."

"That's right, Andrew, isn't it? Didn't you tell me that your mother's family were Huguenot?" Jenny asked.

"Yes," he replied, "my mother was a Jordaine. They came to England in 1690 or so, at the time when the French were becoming anti-Protestant again. Franschhoek and the museum – yes, I think that sounds a great idea. We might even find that some of the relations came here, as well as to England!"

"It's possible," Ann said, "because that, I think, is about the date when many of the Huguenots came out to the Cape, bringing with them their vines and wine-making. Isn't that right, David?" she added as her husband came into the room.

"It is," he said, "and there are still a lot of vineyards known by the names of the original French families, although the present owners may be no connection. I thought we might visit a couple, as well as going to the museum. I rang Freddie Voss and he would be delighted to see us. An unusual man and makes some unusual wines. You'll like him – and, what's more, he also runs a splendid restaurant and we'll have lunch there. Now, I've still got things to do, so Jenny, why don't you and Andrew go on? Go to the museum and then meet us at Freddie's – the farm, not the restaurant – at, let's say, midday."

From the Stanley estate of Neder Paarl to Franschhoek is about twenty miles, mostly through flat, rather uninteresting country. However, the town itself, parts of which still retain the appearance of a frontier outpost, is ringed on two sides by jagged mountains and, for the rest, is surrounded by the gentle hills of the winelands. The Huguenot memorial area is dominated by a tall, three-arched monument set in a semi-circular cloister and to one side across a well-kept lawn is the neat, white, Dutch style museum.

At the counter, Jenny introduced Andrew as an English visitor of Huguenot ancestry who was interested to know if any of his family might have gone to the Cape. The lady in charge suggested that they should look in one of the inner rooms where there were lists of all the early Franschhoek settlers and Jenny went off in search of this.

Andrew, however, was more interested in the history of the settlers and spent some time studying the early documents and maps displayed on the walls. It was as he was tracing the route they had taken through the mountains that an excited Jenny came up and took his arm.

"Darling, you must come over here and look. I've found that several families of Jordaines settled round here. I wonder if any of them had any connection with your lot?"

"Let's have a look and see if there's anything that might strike a chord, a Christian name or something," he said. "I have an Uncle William and I believe there has been a William in every previous generation. Here we are," he added, scanning a list of names, "now what about this G. Jordaine?"

"Yes, but you said William."

"Come on, my dear, where's your French? G is for Guillaume, and Guillaume, you may remember, is the French for William. Guillaume Jordaine, Oude Klippen 1696. Let's go and ask if they know anything about him."

"It's strange you should ask about Jordaines," said the lady at the counter; "we had someone else asking the same question a week or two ago. A man it was; he said he'd come back, but he never did. I did have a look though and I found a box labelled Oude Klippen. I kept it out for him," and she rummaged under the counter and produced a dirty cardboard box. "Here it is. Do you want to have a look? Sorry it's so dirty, I think it's been here for a hundred years or more. We get these things from time to time, usually from a lawyer when someone dies or a farm changes hands."

Andrew took the box, and walked over to a bench, sat down and took off the lid. Inside was a mass of papers and a black, leather-covered notebook. He opened this and gave an exclamation of surprise; then he turned over a few pages, shut and put it back in the box.

"What's so interesting?" Jenny asked.

"I'll tell you later, when I've had a better look," he replied. "Let's go and ask if we can borrow it."

Andrew was nothing if not persuasive, and in no time he had got permission to take the box home provided he brought it back the next day.

"In case the other people come back," said the lady in charge, "and also provided you tell us if you discover anything of historical interest."

Andrew glanced at his watch. "Come on," he said, "or we'll be late for Mr Voss. I know you're dying to know about the box, but all will be revealed later and it could be quite interesting. For in that little notebook there was a name I recognised. Nothing to do with Huguenots, but it intrigued me."

CHAPTER 2

THE VISIT TO THE VOSS ESTATE WAS a great success and, having shown them round; Freddie proceeded to conduct a tasting of some of his more unusual wines. Finally, in honour, presumably, of Andrew's considerable interest, he himself entertained them to lunch in his restaurant.

When they got back to Neder Paarl, Andrew excused himself and retired to his room to study the contents of the box.

"Give me an hour or two, and I think I may be able to tell you quite an interesting story," he said with a smile.

Once in his room, Andrew closed the door and pulled up a low table on which he placed the box. The contents, in addition to the black note-book, consisted of a mass of papers, the property of a Mr Thomas Saddler, a member of the Court of The Honourable East India Company, and it was this name that had aroused his curiosity when he first looked into the box. The majority of the papers concerned a forthcoming visit to India, and these he put aside for later examination.

There was, however, one paper, a letter addressed to Mr Daniel Saddler of Passford Hall in Suffolk, which he read immediately and when he had finished, he lay back and gazed at the ceiling.

"Very interesting," he said to himself, "so the stories were true. I only wish I could remember them better. I shall have to consult Cousin Wilfred when I get home. For now though, let's see if this little book tells us any more." And he picked up the small, leather-covered volume.

At first glance it appeared to be a diary; a record of day-to-day happenings which, it seemed, Mr Saddler kept as a form of aide-memoire for both business and personal matters.

Looking again at the letter, Andrew noted that it was written 'as from Oude Klippen' on the 15th of March 1843. So he looked for any diary entries for the early part of that year and found a mention of a voyage to India, during which he had broken his journey at Cape Town, and travelled up country to visit a friend, Peter Jordaine, at his farm of Oude Klippen.

During the next two hours, Andrew read the rest of the diary entry for the visit to Oude Klippen and a most extraordinary story it told. Then he re-read the letter several times, had a quick look at the other papers in the box and finally went through the black book from cover to cover.

"An incredible story," was his conclusion, "but there are some odd things about it. Why, for instance, are these papers here and not at Passford?" And he stood up and closed the book at the precise moment that Jenny's head appeared round the door.

"How are you getting on?" she asked. "And why on earth are you being so secretive? Anyway, dinner will be in half an hour, and we'd love to see you – if, that is, you can drag yourself away from your researches."

"Of course I can," he said, taking her face in his hands and kissing her lips. "Now if you'll allow me time for a quick bath, after dinner I'll tell you a remarkable story. And then we can decide what we do about it."

Andrew came down to find the rest of the party sitting out on the covered terrace drinking champagne and watching the orange flames of sunset fade from the jagged peaks to the east, and the sky change from the pale, translucent light of evening to the deep-blue velvet of the African night.

David Stanley welcomed him and handed him a glass. "As it's your first proper evening here, I thought we should open a bottle of this – I think it's the best sparkling wine produced in the Cape and it comes from right next door," adding with a smile, "When you've tried it you'll probably want to meet Carl. It would be a great triumph for Three Ws to get an agency. But no business tonight. All we want to hear is the secrets of your Huguenot past!"

"All in good time," a laughing Andrew replied. "For now I just want to enjoy your excellent wine."

Dinner was accompanied by further tastings and once it was over, they moved to a small comfortable sitting room, and while Ann poured the coffee, Jenny turned to their guest.

"Now, darling, you can't put it off any longer. What have you found in that box that is so interesting?"

"Before I do that," he replied, "I'll tell you what it was that first attracted my interest and made me ask if we could borrow the box. It was a name, two names to be exact, two names that had nothing to do with my Huguenot ancestry but which interested me considerably. They were on this letter which was the first thing I saw when I looked in the box. There was the name of a person – Mr Daniel Saddler – and an address in England – Passford Hall, Suffolk. Now finding these two names was a quite extraordinary coincidence. First, because Saddler was Alice's, my late wife's, maiden name and secondly, because she used to stay with cousins in Suffolk at a house called Passford Hall."

"But Andrew, when was all this and who was Daniel Saddler and why was someone writing to him from South Africa, and come to that, why is the letter still here?" Jenny asked.

"As to why the letter is still here I'm not sure, although we can probably make a guess. As to the rest, I'll explain as briefly as I can," and Andrew paused, holding up the letter and the diary.

"The box contained a mass of papers including this letter and this little book, and they are the only items that concern us. The letter is from Thomas Saddler to his father Daniel, and the book is a diary in which, it seems, Thomas noted significant happenings he wished particularly to remember. However, before I go any further I had better tell you one thing I know to be true, for the whole story depends on it. One of Alice's ancestors was a French aristocrat, the Chevalier de la Tour du Lac, whose granddaughter married Mr Thomas Saddler, who was pretty high up in the British East India Company. The Chevalier was one of Marie Antoinette's pages, possibly even her lover. He was with her right up to the time she was imprisoned and family history has always said she left him a legacy, but there has never been any sign of it. Anyway, he escaped the Terror, but for his pains was exiled to, I think, Pondicherry."

"Where is Pondicherry?" Jenny asked.

"It was part of the old French Empire in India," her brother said and then, turning to Andrew, asked, "Do you know what the legacy was, and have any efforts been made to trace it?"

"Legend says her jewels, or rather some of them," Andrew replied, "and as it has always been treated as a legend, I think the answer is no. Wealthy Suffolk squirearchy were not given to romantic flights of fancy. However, you will see how wrong they may have been. For, according to the letter to his father, Thomas seems to have suffered an attack of fever while visiting friends north of Cape Town, where he had stopped on his way to India. The attack he says, is the worst he has ever had and, fearing he may die, he goes on to tell his father several things. The first is that the story of Marie Antoinette, the Chevalier and the jewels is true, and on a previous visit to India, the Chevalier gave him a package and asked him to keep it safe. He apparently hid it at Passford and now feels he must tell his father where it is. It is, he says, 'Where poor Toby died – Eliza will know what I mean.' It then all becomes a bit rambling, for he is obviously very ill, but he finishes by saying that there are other things to tell and he will write again from India when he has talked to the Chevalier."

"What an extraordinary story. Who was Eliza? And what happened to Thomas, do we know that?" Jenny asked.

"Eliza was Thomas's sister, that I can tell you," Andrew replied. "I have an idea that Thomas did die abroad, but whether here or in India, I don't know. Remember, it's not my family. When I get home I will have to talk to Alice's cousin, Wilfred Saddler, the present owner of Passford, and see what he says about poor Toby and what happened to Thomas."

"If Thomas died in South Africa, he's probably buried here," David said, "unless of course they sent him home pickled in brandy. They did that you know! If he is here, he's likely to have been buried in either the cemetery at Paarl or possibly at Franschhoek. We can do a bit of checking tomorrow."

"I still don't really understand why he was here," Ann said. "Presumably he was on his way to India on Government business and his ship stopped in Cape Town. They all did in those days, but why was he up in the winelands?"

"I don't know. The letter says he was just visiting a friend and had been taken to stay on a neighbouring property, which is where he became ill."

"Is there anything more in the book? Come on, darling, let's have the rest of the story," Jenny said.

"Well, it's very odd and I don't know quite what to make of it," Andrew replied. "It starts by giving a bit more detail than the letter. The friend he was visiting was called Peter Jordaine, no relation of mine as far as I can tell, who had a farm at Oude Klippen near Franschhoek and who took him to stay at another farm called Blouberg belonging to someone called Carel du Toit."

"Blouberg's just down the road. It still belongs to the du Toits," David said. "I don't know about Jordaine. Oude Klippen did you say? Well we can probably find out."

"That could be helpful; but it's Blouberg that concerns us now," Andrew continued, "for it was while at Blouberg that Thomas was taken ill and thought he might be dying, so wrote to his father about the jewels and, if you remember, mentioned another thing that he needed to talk to the Chevalier about. The black book tells us about this other thing but does not say what it is."

"Why did he not tell his father?" Jenny asked.

"Before I answer that, let me tell you what's in the diary. It's the final entry and it's not dated. It's in a very shaky hand and all the lines fall away to the right, but I will do my best to read it to you exactly as it is written here. This is what he says:

> *'The fever is worse than I have ever known it before. If it stays like this I cannot last the night. I wrote to father – hope it reaches him. Did not tell him about the King, just that I want to talk to them in India. May not get there so if you want to know, the Scotsman's porter will help you. Oh God, the pain, I can't... and the light... ah, blessed darkness. Tell Julie...'*

And that's it, for presumably at that point he lapsed into delirium."

"To go back to Jenny's question. Why didn't he tell whatever it is to his father?" David asked. "And how in heaven's name did these papers and things fetch up in the museum?"

"I can only guess," Andrew said, "but I think that when the Chevalier gave him the jewels and whatever else was involved, he did not explain the import or significance of it. Thomas was therefore taking it to India to get more information from the Chevalier or possibly Julie's father who, I think, was also in India; but it seems the fever overtook him. How did they get to the museum? The lady there thought they may have come from lawyers, but a long time ago. Perhaps someone died; someone who, had they lived, would have dealt with Thomas's effects. It could have been Jordaine himself. One could also ask why the Chevalier and others in India did not enquire if the family had indeed received the jewels. Perhaps they had all died. In the days of slow communication, a great deal of information just vanished between destinations. And Julie, who knew about the jewels, why did she apparently do nothing? I don't know."

"Your family did seem to like riddles," Ann said. "You say we will have to wait till you get to England to know about poor Toby. So what about the Scotsman's porter? If we knew what that meant, maybe we'd find out about this King business."

"I've no idea what it means," said Andrew. "Is there a place round here called Scotsman's something? Or is there something called a Scotsman's Porter? You know, like a Scotch Egg or a Welsh Rarebit."

"Or a French Letter perhaps," suggested David.

"Oh shut up, David, and don't be vulgar," said his sister. Then after a pause she looked up and said, "I think, you know, I may be able to help here. Darling, you accused me earlier of forgetting that Guillaume was the French for William. I'm now telling you that you are forgetting a well-known theatrical maxim. When I was at drama school – you didn't know that, did you? Well I was, and to us the words Scotsman, the Scotch King, the Scotch play had only one meaning – Macbeth – for you must never mention that actual name in the theatre. It's very bad luck. Ann, have we got a Shakespeare?"

"I think so, in that bookcase there." Jenny walked over and, after a moment's search, pulled out a book.

"Yes, here we are. Now let's have a look and see if there's a quotation or anything that might have a bearing." She sat down and started turning

14

the pages saying, "I've got an idea that a porter appears just after Duncan's murder. You know, when there's all that knocking."

"I'm sure you're right, my dear, but you're way ahead of me," was Andrew's comment, and before anyone else could speak, Jenny startled everyone with her excited shouting.

"Eureka! I knew it," she cried, leaping to her feet. "Just listen to this and I'll quote:

'*Enter a Porter. Knocking within.*

Porter. Here's a knocking indeed... *[Knocking.]* Knock, knock, knock. Who's there, i' the name of Beelzebub? Here's a farmer that hanged himself on the expectation of plenty...' and so on."

"Now that bit about hanging rings a bell, but I can't think why." Nor, it appeared, could anyone else.

Suddenly David brought his hand down on the table, setting the coffee cups rattling. "Of course," he cried, looking round triumphantly, "of course – Jenny, you remember the old story that maid, I've forgotten her name, used to tell us to frighten us into being good. About the old man, an early settler he was, who hanged himself, I forget why. 'Served him right, he took our land,' she used to say."

"Yes, I remember the old mammy," and there was excitement in Jenny's voice, "she used to point over there saying, 'Don't you go that way or he might come back and get you.' And that's towards Blouberg, isn't it?"

"It is indeed," said David, "but whether it was on du Toit land or not, I'm not sure. I think it may have been somewhere near that old monument, so if it wasn't du Toit's when he did the deed, it is now. But why was old Saddler being so secretive?"

"Suppose as his condition worsened he realised that he might not live to get to India," Andrew suggested. "I think he did what you or I would probably have done and hid whatever this other thing was. Then in a lucid moment, he realised that if what he had hidden was ever to be found, he must leave a clue. The letter was written and sealed, so he made this entry in his diary. It seems he is telling us that somewhere on the Blouberg estate something is hidden. The question is, how on earth are we to find it? Incidentally, Thomas must have been some Shakespearian scholar!"

CHAPTER 3

S OME MONTHS BEFORE THE EVENTS JUST DESCRIBED, a clerk in an obscure government department in Paris was sorting through drawers of ancient documents, preparatory to their destruction or transfer to the Special Archive, when, in a box marked 1792, a bundle of faded papers tied with ribbon caught his eye. 'La Reine et l'affaire Dulac' he read on the first paper and, realising the significance of the year, he read on.

When he finished he sat back, an amazed expression on his face, and thought for a good ten minutes before folding the papers again and carefully retying the ribbon. Then he took them upstairs to his superior.

"I think, monsieur, you should look at these," he said, putting them on the desk.

Monsieur Dindon was a pompous and choleric little man who disliked intensely being interrupted by his juniors. He looked down at the papers and then up at his clerk.

"Yes, yes," he said testily, "l'affaire Dulac. I know all about it. It is not of significance."

"But I think if you read those papers you may change your mind," the other said. "I believe they contain important matters of state, even though they may be two hundred years old."

"Very well, I will look at them later," Monsieur Dindon said, pushing the papers into a drawer, "but woe betide you if they are rubbish. Now run along, I'm busy."

The clerk left the room, shaking his head. "Wait till he reads them," he thought, and left for home. There, although he knew he should keep the matter confidential, he could not resist telling his wife everything he'd read that afternoon. Now his wife, with a peasant eye for a bargain, took the matter rather more seriously than did Monsieur Dindon and so wasted no time in telling her lover the whole story when they met the next morning.

Thus it was that, after two expensive trips to India and several unrewarding interviews, Jean Lemaître found himself lying on his bed in a small hotel in Franschhoek wondering what his next step should be.

What Thérèse had told him that morning in Paris had rekindled his interest in the stories he'd heard about certain royal treasures, reputedly taken from Paris at the time of the Revolution, and never subsequently found. His belief in the possible truth of these stories was strengthened when he read the documents that she had, with great difficulty, persuaded her husband to copy and smuggle out of the office.

It seemed that around the time of their imprisonment, the Royal Family had managed to arrange the removal from Paris, and probably from France, of some unspecified items of the royal treasure. Where they went was unknown except, apparently, to a certain Monsieur Dulac. According to the papers, Monsieur Dulac was an erstwhile courtier, the Chevalier de la Tour du Lac, who had been banished to Pondicherry and had never returned to France. As far as was known, he never referred to the treasure and it seems all knowledge of it died with him.

Lemaître had subsequently found out from his mistress that, as a result of the discovery of the papers, the government was starting to take an interest in the matter. This news confirmed his opinion that, whatever form the missing property took, it was of very considerable value.

He therefore went to see Le Grand Homme, a gentleman who specialised in handling the proceeds of large-scale robbery. After explaining his ideas and emphasising the need for speed and secrecy, the government and possibly others being already involved, he persuaded the master to finance an investigation which, so far, had not gone well.

A trip to Pondicherry, where he posed as an agent of the French Government, had yielded nothing. In Paris, as an author researching a treatise on French colonial influence in eighteenth-century India, he visited endless government departments, libraries and museums with little success. Monsieur Dulac seemed to have vanished into the vastness of the sub-continent.

Just when he was beginning to feel he would have to confess to Le Grand Homme that he had failed, a meeting which promised to be somewhat uncomfortable, an official in the Foreign Ministry whose hobby was eighteenth-century India suggested he should try the Sorbonne, and it was there that he had his first bit of luck. While discussing his problem with one of the librarians, he mentioned the full name of the Chevalier but it was to no avail. She did, however, produce a book which she thought might help, but after spending an hour going through it and finding nothing, he handed it in and left the building.

As he stepped onto the pavement, he paused and someone behind him put a hand on his arm.

"Un moment, monsieur," a voice said. "I heard you mention a name in there, a name I know, and I think I may be able to help you."

He turned and saw a good looking, well-dressed woman of about fifty with just a suggestion of grey in her fair hair and what might be called a comfortable figure.

"What name was that, and how do you think you might help me?" he asked.

"The Chevalier de la Tour du Lac," was the reply.

"Yes – so what?" he said in a voice heavy with suspicion.

"I see the Brasserie Fabrice over there," she said, looking across the road. "Their coffee is quite good. If you will buy two cups I will explain."

The café was almost empty and smelt faintly of coffee and stale Gauloises. They sat themselves at a corner table and when the coffee arrived, she looked across at him.

"Tell me why you are interested in the Chevalier de la Tour du Lac," she said, "and don't tell me you are a researcher or an academic because you're not. I could tell that by the way you handled the book."

"Who are you and why should I tell you?" he asked.

"My name is Annette Barry," she replied, "and, as you will realise, I am French. My husband, however, is English, and is a great great-great-great-grandson of the Chevalier. The Chevalier's daughter married an English merchant in Calcutta. Now about you?"

18

Lemaître paused, toying with his coffee spoon, then made up his mind. This was the first sort of clue he'd had and he couldn't let it go. He'd have to tell something near the truth and he must find out what her interest was.

"I am Jean Lemaître and I work for the government – the Finance Ministry, in fact – I'm a sort of undercover agent," he said. "Papers have come to light suggesting that Dulac, that's the name we know him by, was involved in the disappearance of valuable property, royal property, actually, at the time of the Revolution. We have no idea where it is. We also have no idea whether Dulac left any information about it and we know little or nothing about him. The Ministry, however, is anxious to trace this valuable property."

The woman seemed in no hurry to answer, for she felt in her handbag and took out powder and lipstick. By the time she was satisfied with her make-up, she too had decided how to play her hand.

"I won't pretend I know nothing of your story," she said, "for it is common knowledge in my husband's family that Marie Antoinette was fond of the Chevalier, maybe even in love with him, and so entrusted him with some secret; whether about valuables we do not know, but it seems probable. There is even a rumour that she gave him some of her jewels. My husband, who I no longer live with, is from a junior branch of the family, but that doesn't prevent me from being interested in anything, particularly anything of value, that may have been given to them. I cannot find out anything here in Paris; I believe, therefore, that if the Chevalier did have something, or knew something, then it is to India, to Bengal, in fact, that one will have to go to find out about it. I can't do that, but you, as a servant of the state, perhaps can." Here she paused, then looking him straight in the eye, continued, "Now I have told you what to do, in return you will tell me anything you find out. OK? And please, monsieur," she said, holding up her hand, "please don't put on that righteous face with me. I can tell from your eyes it's share and share alike – we both take our cut and France can have what's left. Here's my card. Let me know what you find out and don't forget you will still need me to help with family information."

Then, before he could say anything, she got to her feet and picking up her handbag, left the cafe and disappeared into the crowd.

Now, some weeks later, and on his way back from a second trip to India, lying on his bed in a Franschhoek hotel, he thought that this second trip had been rather more productive than the first. One of Lemaître's assets was that he spoke fluent though somewhat ungrammatical English, and while in Calcutta, he had discovered that a relation of the Chevalier, a Mr Saddler, had sailed from India for England in 1841. He had left the ship in Cape Town and spent some time there, apparently with friends.

Then, in Cape Town, a helpful person in a shipping office told Jean that some two years later a passenger of the same name had left an Indiaman and journeyed up country, possibly to visit a family called Jordaine in or near Franschhoek.

Lemaître's trouble was that he could not decide how to proceed. He knew of Saddler's visit to Franschhoek, but more than that he did not know. The local authorities had no records that could help and suggested the museum. There he was told that many Jordaines had settled in the area. The name Saddler, however, meant nothing to them but they said they would have a look and if they found anything they would let him know the next day, but he had not bothered to go back.

After a further fifteen minutes of fruitless consideration, he got up, looked at his watch and, seeing it was after midday, decided to find somewhere for lunch. His problem was that Annette Barry, whom he had kept informed, was now on her way from Cape Town to join him and would be hoping he had made some progress. He could only hope for another lucky break.

He walked over to the mirror, struggled into his shirt and put a comb through his straight black hair. Jean Lemaître, a second-rate criminal aspiring to a higher level, was a fairly unprepossessing person. Slim and of medium height with a thin wedge of face, unsmiling black eyes and a cruel slit of a mouth, he nevertheless, like many of his kind, had no difficulty in attracting women. Satisfied with his appearance, he checked that he had money, then walked out into the bright sunshine and made his way to the cluster of shops that formed the centre of the town.

There, in a little square set back from the road, was a restaurant with a trellis over the door covered in bougainvillea and with pots of flowers on either side. He had noticed it before and thought it looked promising, so decided to try it. He went in and the first thing he saw, at a table against the far wall, was a party of three, a man and two girls, one of whom he had met the week before in Cape Town.

As he was being shown a table by the door, the girl looked up and seeing him, beckoned.

"Jean," she said, "what a coincidence! Come and join us and I'll tell you something that will interest you."

CHAPTER 4

Early on the morning following the discovery of Thomas Saddler's papers, David Stanley took Andrew to his office and arranged for copies to be made of the letter and the relevant pages of the diary. The copies Andrew put in a folder which he locked in his briefcase, the originals he replaced in their cardboard box and took both back to the house. Then he went to look for Jenny and found her just starting breakfast.

"Where on earth have you been?" she asked. "Ann's had breakfast and is going in to Cape Town for the day, so we're on our own. What do you want to do?"

"I have been making copies of the letter and the black book in David's office and he suggested we take a car and do whatever we like. There are several things I want to do and I'll tell you about them in a moment, but first I'm going to have breakfast."

"You do that," Jenny said, "while I catch Ann before she leaves. I know she wants me to do some domestic shopping."

Ten minutes later Jenny returned, saying that they could do all the shopping in Paarl or Franschhoek, and had he decided what he wanted to do.

"Yes," Andrew replied, "I'd like to have a look at this Blouberg place; just a quick one now to see what it's like. Then we ought to have a look at the two cemeteries and see if we can find Thomas's grave. We must return this box to the museum and I think we ought at least to look at Oude Klippen, although I don't think any answers lie there. Much more likely at Blouberg, where he died."

"Well that's all quite easy. Let's start in Paarl. While I shop, you can look for the grave. Then we'll come back here, leave the shopping and go

22

and have a look at Blouberg. That's easy too, as it's more or less on the way to Franschhoek. Do you want to call on the du Toits?"

"No, I think we'll leave them for the moment. Maybe I'll need to meet them later. All I want today is to get the lie of the land."

"Fine. We can do that easily without going onto the property. So then we go on to Franschhoek and have a look at the graveyard and take the box back to the museum. That'll about take us to lunch and there's a couple of decent places to eat there. Then we can finish by having a look at Oude Klippen. I'm not absolutely sure where it is, but that's easily found out."

A search of the Paarl cemetery yielded nothing. So after a brief stop at the house, they drove for a few miles in an easterly direction and then turned off the main road towards the mountains. After a mile or so Jenny slowed down as they passed some gates and pointed up a drive towards a clump of trees.

"There's the Blouberg house," she said, "you can just see it beyond the trees. It has the most wonderful views and the rose garden is unbelievable. But if I go to the top of the next rise – yes, here will do very well – now you should be able to get a good idea of the layout of the estate."

They left the car in a patch of shade and walked across the road to a low mound, which gave a panoramic view of all the ground to the northeast. From the road, the rows of vines stretched away to stop just short of a small lake, beyond which a lawn led up to the house. With the aid of his binoculars, Andrew could see, to the left of the house, some of the famous roses. To the right, clumps of agapanthus lined a road leading to a group of neat white outbuildings. Beyond them were more vines, divided into sections by earth roads.

One of these roads led through the ranks of vines to an open space, beyond which was a small wood. In the middle of the open space was the monument. As far as Andrew could tell this consisted of a stone pavement some ten feet square, in the middle of which was a massive plinth and a slender, pointed column.

He turned to his companion and pointed to the column. "You say you're not sure what this commemorates. Could it be the hanging?"

"No, I don't think so. If I remember rightly it has something to do with one of the treks," she replied. "Our old maid used to point in this general direction when frightening us about the hanging, but I don't think that meant anything. The du Toits would probably know all about it."

Andrew nodded vaguely and continued scanning the area around the monument through his glasses. Assuming this was the farm where Thomas Saddler had hidden something before he died, the monument seemed a good place to start searching. It would have been there at the time, it was a useful landmark and, as it was a little way from the house, something buried there would be reasonably safe from accidental discovery. It was certainly worthy of closer inspection and he already had an idea how this might be done.

"I think that's all we can do here for the moment," he said, getting to his feet and holding out a hand to the girl. "Let's go and get rid of the box."

The woman in the museum was busy with a whole stream of visitors and when Andrew held up the box, she nodded and pointed to the end of the counter. He smiled an acknowledgement, put it where she indicated and they walked out without having to discuss what they had found.

"That," he said, "was very convenient. It's better she knows as little as possible about us and our interest in those papers. Whoever else it was who enquired about Jordaine or Oude Klippen could well return. Now, what about lunch, or is it a bit early?" And when Jenny nodded, he agreed, saying, "Yes, perhaps it is; in that case let's go and look at the cemetery."

"This is the place I told you about," Jenny said some thirty minutes later, as they stepped under the bougainvillea and into the cool of the restaurant. It was still early for lunch and as yet not many tables were occupied, but just along from where they sat were three young people, a man and two girls, one of whom was holding forth on her recent adventures in Cape Town, most of which appeared to be of an amorous nature.

"What it is to be young," he sighed.

"Oh come off it," was the reply. "I'm not going to have this old man business here. You're young and fit; you've had a successful week as far as business is concerned, and now you are going to have another one investigating your family history. And, what's more, you have the invaluable help of a most attractive young lady who would, if and when you have time, like to be bought a drink and made a fuss of."

"Yes, darling, of course," he said with his most dazzling smile, something he knew she could never resist. "And I shall start now as I mean to go on, with a kiss," and he raised her hand to his lips, "a bottle of wine and the best lunch Franschhoek can offer. I feel like a really good bottle of white wine, so with your local knowledge, go ahead and choose."

When the wine arrived and the food had been ordered, Andrew looked across at his companion and raised his glass.

"An excellent choice," he said, taking a sip, "so let's drink to the success of World Wide Wines coupled with the name of Thomas Saddler. We've found his grave, and with any luck we may discover what it was he was trying to tell his relations all those years ago."

"And how do you propose to do that?" she asked. "You've been lucky so far. You've found the monument and you've found the grave, but I don't see that either have been very helpful. Will Oude Klippen help?"

"I doubt it, but we'll have a look at it this afternoon. Now, let's leave further discussion until this evening and concentrate on lunch. Meanwhile you can tell me a bit about your African childhood."

The rest of the meal passed pleasantly enough with Jenny describing her early days in Johannesburg and then producing a series of improbable stories of her school days there and of university life in Cape Town.

"Then, of course, there were wonderful holidays by the sea near Hermanus and what I enjoyed most, visits to the cousins in what's now called KwaZulu-Natal. They have an estate and stud farm north of Durban, between the Drakensberg and the sea, with a small game reserve nearby. It's a pity you can't stay longer because I'm going up there for a few days the week after next."

The conversation then moved on to other more general matters, until Andrew glanced at his watch and called for the bill. While he was paying, Jenny took the opportunity to ask the proprietor the best way to Oude Klippen, and was not only given directions, but also a commentary on the owners, the beauty of the estate and the excellence of its vineyards. As they were escorted to the door, such were the expressions of goodwill on all sides, that they failed to notice the slim, dark man who edged past them through the door.

Jean Lemaître, however, noticed them. It was not difficult, for they were a striking couple, just the sort his background had trained him to notice and store for future reference. As he stood by the door allowing his eyes to adjust to the cool shade of the restaurant, he heard someone calling his name and looking round, he saw a girl on the other side of the room waving to him. He said something to the waiter who was showing him to a table, and walked over to where she was sitting.

"Jean," she cried, "you remember me, surely. Pauline. We met last week in Cape Town," and waving towards the other two at the table, added, "and these are the friends I told you about. I wanted you to join us but we've had lunch and they want to go. Look, I've got something to tell you. It's about that man Saddler you said you were looking for or wanted to know about or whatever. Well, that couple who just went out were talking about someone called Saddler. Said they'd found his grave."

Now this interested Lemaître greatly, and he realised that he must talk to her as soon as possible. He vaguely remembered her, and as she was an attractive blonde with a well-rounded figure, he was certainly not averse to renewing their acquaintance.

"Yes, of course," he said looking down at her, "and I should very much like to know more about what you heard. Can you not stay and tell me and join your friends later? No? Well what about dinner tonight?"

"Jean, I'm sorry but tonight's no good either, but tomorrow's OK. Look, we're staying in a friend's flat in Stellenbosch. Here's the number, ring me tomorrow morning. Now I must go." With that she picked up her bag and joined the others, who were waiting outside the door.

Lemaître smiled to himself as he returned to his table. "That could make for an interesting evening," was his thought.

CHAPTER 5

THE ESTATE OF OUDE KLIPPEN IS A little way out of Franschhoek, and lies in a gently rising valley, surrounded on the north and east by the steep cliffs and jagged peaks of a range of mountains.

Andrew had little hope that a visit would tell them anything new, for the people in the restaurant had said that it had recently changed hands and the new owners were doing a lot of modernisation and new building. However, when they got there they found that the winery was open to visitors, so they went in, and when Jenny explained who they were, the winemaker appeared and offered to show them round.

He had been with the estate for many years and gave them the history of the place back to the early nineteenth century. The founders, the Jordaine family, had sold up in 1922. However, during all the subsequent changes of ownership the estate had continued to produce quality wines, and now there was a new proprietor who was investing in modern equipment and had started planting some of the higher slopes.

Everything he heard and saw there confirmed Andrew in his opinion that Thomas Saddler was not referring to Oude Klippen, and that therefore they should concentrate their efforts on Blouberg. However, the visit proved useful for a completely different reason. After tasting some of the wines, particularly some very promising reds, Andrew said that he would arrange for his agent to get in touch with them with a view to doing business.

When they got back to the house, as there was no one about Jenny decided that a little exercise would be a good thing and suggested a walk in the woods that separated the farm from the mountains. The way led them up a stony track, and when they had gone about a mile Jenny turned up a narrow path covered in pine needles, and taking Andrew's hand steered him to where a gap in the trees gave a view over the whole estate. There she stopped and, linking her arm in his, pointed to the endless panorama of vineyard, wood and mountain.

"Isn't that a breathtaking view? My father had a wonderful eye for country. He saw a great many places before he settled on Neder Paarl, and wasn't he right?" she said. Then taking his two hands, she looked up into his eyes. "Tell me, darling, what do you think of my country? With our climate, our scenery and our quality of life, don't you envy us living here?"

"Yes and no," he replied. "Yes, because of everything I've seen in the past week. No, because I wonder just what the future holds. At present, everything is turning out better perhaps than could have been expected. But what if it were all to turn sour?" and he paused to let the idea sink in. Then he went on, "Yes, today it's still a wonderful country. Built up by wonderful people and I am out to win the love of one of the most wonderful."

"You already have, darling. You know, I think you had from the moment I met you; and now, before your vanity gets the better of you, I think we'd better go back." She kissed him lightly on the forehead and turned and ran down the path, with Andrew following at a more sedate pace.

Needless to say conversation at Neder Paarl that evening was almost entirely devoted to Thomas Saddler and his secrets. The Stanleys wanted to know how they had got on and had they discovered anything new; David particularly wanting to know what Andrew proposed to do next, if anything.

"No, I wouldn't say we found out anything we didn't already know, or at least guessed," was Andrew's reply, "but having seen both Blouberg and the place at Franschhoek, I am sure that if Thomas did hide something it will be at Blouberg that we'll find it. Even if I'm wrong and we should be looking at Oude Klippen, I don't believe we'd find anything there. There have been too many changes of owner and too much new building."

"OK, so you think Blouberg's the place," said David Stanley. "What then are you going to do about it?"

"I'm going to have a closer look at that monument," Andrew replied. "I just have a feeling about it. If I'd been Thomas wanting a hiding place, I think I'd try to keep clear of the house, but knowing I was in for a bout of fever I would not want to go far, so I think of the monument. I'd know it was a convenient distance, for I would have already been taken to see such an interesting landmark."

"Could I ask how you propose to get your closer look?" David enquired.

"Well, I noticed this morning that it is easy to reach the monument from the road, and for most of the way you are out of sight of the house. I therefore propose to visit it tomorrow night."

"You're mad," David said. "You'll be caught and then I'll have to explain why I have friends who trespass on my neighbour's land."

"I will not be caught," Andrew replied, "and for this reason. The latter part of my time in the army was spent on undercover work in the Far East and then seconded to MI6, so I know what I'm undertaking, but first I do need to have a better look at the ground. Therefore tomorrow morning, I'd like to borrow a car and do a bit of reconnoitering."

When, at lunchtime the next day, Andrew returned from his reconnaissance, he went straight up to his room and dropped the parcels he was carrying on the bed, then turned to find Jenny watching him from the doorway.

"Why on earth are you looking at me like that?" he asked. "I'm not going to commit murder. All I'm planning is a little mild trespass."

"A little mild trespass!" she cried. "You realise, don't you, that some vineyards have guards, and possibly dogs. What are you going to do about them? And what have you got in those parcels?"

"Come in and sit down," he said, "and I'll tell you what I'm going to do and how I'm going to do it." Here he opened the various packages and laid out the contents on the bed. First a large square of black muslin, then a pair of thin rubber gloves, and finally a small electric torch. "The muslin, with suitable eyeholes, covers the face; the gloves, now they were a problem: they had to be dull enough not to show up in the dark, thin enough to allow a sensitive feel and big enough to fit me. Not what the average housewife wants, but I eventually found them. The torch with a bit of paper over the lens will be fine. The only other thing I need is a black or dark blue jersey, and I hope your brother can supply that."

"I expect he can. So then what?" Jenny said.

"Well, I have done a bit of checking and found that the moon sets at half after midnight, so for the next two or so hours after that the night will be pitch dark. At that time, therefore, someone – you or David – will drop me about a mile beyond where we stopped yesterday and then come back here, for I daren't risk leaving the car there. I've had a good look and from where you drop me I can go through that little wood almost up to the monument. By the way, I understand there are no guards, except at the house, and I assume I won't meet any African wildlife?"

"I don't think so," she answered, then added brightly, "unless, of course, you tread on a snake. You might startle some birds, which I suppose could give you away."

"I'll have to risk that," he said. "I reckon that to get to the monument, look at it and then get back to the road will take me just over an hour. It should still be dark at two o'clock. So at two exactly, one of you will come back to the same place and pick me up. I'll be at the edge of the wood. If I'm not there, give me a quarter of an hour and then come back home and wait for the storm to break! Now, can I have a drink and some lunch? I've had a hard morning."

At fifteen minutes after midnight, Andrew came downstairs to the hallway. The muslin mask covered his face and was held in place by a baseball cap, property of one of the Stanley sons. A black polo-necked jersey of David's, dark grey trousers and desert boots completed his outfit.

"Hm, James Bond would be proud of you," was David's comment. "To be serious, though, got your gloves and torch?" Andrew held them up. "Good! By the way, are you armed?"

"No, and I'd rather not be," Andrew replied, "but I've got this," and he held up a short, but heavy, rubber truncheon. "Quick and silent; I never travel without it."

"Okay then, so let's go." David had firmly vetoed the idea of Jenny taking any part in the operation and said that he would do all the driving.

As Andrew had predicted, the moon had set, and a thin cloud cover made the night even darker. They met no other vehicle along the way, but to be on the safe side, just before they reached the brow of the hill, David switched off

30

his lights. Then, as they came into the shadow of the trees, Andrew signalled him to pull in and stop.

"I'll help you turn round," he said, "so don't switch on the lights till you're well back down the hill."

He watched the car disappear, then pulled his mask down and tucked the ends into the neck of his jersey and put on his gloves. He took a compass from his pocket and checked his direction, then moved cautiously down into the trees. He already knew that there was little undergrowth, so that even in the absolute darkness of the wood, he should be able to move quickly and silently. In fact it proved easier than he had thought, and some fifteen minutes later he was close to the edge of the trees.

Luckily, he had arrived at a point slightly below the monument, so could just make out its outline against the sky. He crouched down behind the trunk of a tree and looked towards his objective. There was just enough light for him to see that there were about thirty yards of open ground between the wood and the monument, and while crossing this he would be in view of anyone on the road or coming down the track. Once in the shadow of the monument, however, he reckoned he would be safe. There was nothing for it but to crawl, and he was about to set off when he heard voices and saw two figures silhouetted against the sky, coming in his direction. He moved cautiously back into the wood and lay flat on the ground in the shelter of a low shrub.

"I'm sure there was a car up there," a voice said, "twenty minutes ago, when I was up where the two tracks meet."

"Alright, let's walk up the edge of the wood there and see," another voice replied, and the two men moved off up the hill.

They had gone barely thirty yards when the first man stopped and seized his companion's arm. "Quick, into the wood and out of sight. I can see someone coming down from the road and as soon as he's near enough I'll put the lamp on him, so be ready to grab him." Then after a short pause he cried out: "There he is, Jan – get him." And the beam of the powerful torch showed up a short, thick-set man with a heavy black moustache holding, on a chain, a snarling Alsatian.

"What the hell's going on here?" the man said, shielding his eyes against the light. "What do you boys think you're doing?"

31

"Sorry, Chris. We were doing the rounds and we thought we saw a car stop up on the road, and were going to investigate when we heard you. We thought we had intruders. Did you see anything up there?"

"No, and I can't think why anyone should be around this end of the place. There's nothing here but vines and that bloody statue thing. Did you see anyone?"

"Can't say we did," said Jan, and the other man shook his head.

"Well then," the man called Chris said, "if there was anybody they must be in the wood. Come, we'll go round that way and back by the top path. If there is anyone about the dog'll find them, and I wouldn't give anything for their chances if Fritz gets his teeth into them." He bent and unfastened the chain. "Go on, boy, find 'em."

"Just as I thought," Chris said when they emerged from the far end of the wood, "nothing there. You boys have got intruders on the brain. If there was a car, it was probably a young couple having a go. We're wasting time here, but just to make sure, you go back to the end of the wood and I'll take the dog round the top."

Andrew listened to their retreating footsteps, gave them ten minutes, and then slipped down from his tree. "Close shave," he thought, "and I didn't like the look of Fritz. He sniffed around a bit but the tree foxed him." And with that he set off on hands and knees towards the monument until he was in the shelter of the mound, when he took the last ten yards in a crouching run.

Kneeling in the shadow of the monument, he waited another five minutes but could see and hear nothing, so risked using his torch. Set in the centre of the plinth and immediately below the column was a bronze plate with an inscription in both English and Afrikaans. The lettering had suffered with the passage of time and his torch gave only an indifferent light, but as far as Andrew could make out the important part of the inscription was as follows:

> *This stone marks the place where Jan du Toit and his*
> *friends settled in 1806 in the hope of starting a new*
> *and thriving community...*

There then followed a brief description of the hardships of the journey from the Cape and what they hoped to do in this new settlement.

Andrew switched off the torch and sat for a moment on the stone pavement. "A new and thriving community," he thought. "Of course, that was the 'expectation of plenty'. Clever chap, old Thomas. Now I really believe we're getting somewhere, but I need to have a closer look in daylight – and with the owner's permission."

Then he looked down at his watch and realised that if he was not to cause an emergency, he must get back to the road. Not wishing to take any more risks, he crawled the whole way back to the wood. Once under cover he walked briskly up the hill and onto the road, and just over the crest found the car hidden in the shelter of the trees. As he approached, David emerged from the shadows and minutes later they were on their way home.

CHAPTER 6

THE BUILDINGS OF THE UNIVERSITY OF STELLENBOSCH take up much of the centre of the town, but further out, surrounded by the famous oak trees, are substantial houses, many belonging to members of the academic staff.

On the same evening that Andrew Henderson was preparing for his visit to the monument, Jean Lemaître made his way to one of these houses. Earlier in the day he had telephoned Pauline and been greeted with enthusiasm.

"Jean," she had said, "I hoped you would ring. Look, my friends are out this evening, so why don't you come round about seven and I'll tell you what I heard yesterday in the Franschhoek restaurant."

When he suggested that they should go out to dinner she had told him quite firmly that they would stay in. "I will cook for you," she had said, "and don't worry. I think my cooking is well up to French standards!"

He found the house without difficulty, a typical whitewashed building in the Cape Dutch style, standing in well-kept grounds. He left his car in the road and walked up the drive. As instructed, he avoided the front door and walked round to the right side of the house, across a shaded courtyard to an inconspicuous side door and rang the bell. Moments later Pauline was welcoming him and leading him across the hall to a spacious sitting room, comfortably furnished in modern style and with a number of brightly coloured scenes of African life on the walls.

Pauline, who had no illusions about Jean Lemaître, had already decided that it would be fun to seduce this rather seedy little Frenchman, and had dressed for the occasion in a dark blue skirt and green and white-striped blouse, and had her long blonde hair held back by a black-velvet band. Jean, who equally had no illusions about what he intended to do, was nevertheless astonished by what he saw. Despite his upbringing in one of the meaner

34

quarters of Paris, his profession had taught him to recognise, and appreciate, quality when he saw it.

"How do you have friends with apartments like this?" he asked. "I thought you said you were a secretary?"

"And so I am," she replied with a smile, "but my father is a professor at Cape Town University and has friends at the University here. When the Cronjes heard that my friend Patti's boyfriend was coming out from England, and that I had promised to show them the country, they said why not base yourselves in our apartment for a week while we're up in Johannesburg. So here we are."

While she was talking, she had poured out two glasses of wine and handed one to Jean.

"This is one of my favourites. It comes from the Stellenbosch area. I think you'll like it," she said.

"It is indeed excellent," he said, taking a sip. "And now tell me what it is you have discovered."

"All in good time, my dear; we have the evening before us," the girl said seating herself on a stool, and then, indicating a chair, added, "Sit yourself down and tell me again why it is you are interested in the name Saddler. When you have told me that, we'll have dinner and then I'll tell you what the people in the restaurant said."

Jean thought for a minute or two before replying. His naturally suspicious mind warned him not to say too much, but he realised this was an intelligent woman and if she was to tell him anything, his reasons for wanting the information must have a ring of truth.

"Eh bien," he began, "I think I already told you that I work for the French Government. Now the Government has found that certain papers of great importance, concerned with the Revolution and particularly the last days of the monarchy, are missing. It seems that these papers may never have been registered, and that one of the Queen's servants, a Monsieur Dulac, who had been banished to India, may have taken these papers with him. It is now my job to locate the missing documents."

"Then why are you in South Africa and not India and what has the name Saddler got to do with it?" the girl asked.

"Ah, but you go too fast," Jean replied. "I have already been to India and there I found that the man Dulac gave something to an Englishman named Saddler. I have also discovered that in 1843 Saddler was in Cape Town and travelled up to somewhere in this area. It seems he was on his way back to India, but he never rejoined a ship, so it is possible he died out here. What I need to know is where he went while he was up country."

"Well there I may be able to help you," Pauline said, "but now let's eat. Help yourself to some more wine, give me five minutes, and then bring yourself and the bottle through to the kitchen."

Pauline was indeed a good cook and had prepared a meal, which she considered must tempt the palate of even the most particular Frenchman. Then, when she had served the main course and poured some red wine, Pauline thought the time had come to tell her guest what she had heard in Franschhoek the previous day.

"You remember, Jean," she said, "that as you came into the restaurant another couple were just leaving. Now they had been sitting quite close to us, and even though we were all three talking continuously, I could hear a good deal of what they said. Not that I listened particularly – that is, until I heard them mention the name Saddler – when I definitely pricked up my ears. As far as I could make out there was some sort of family connection between the man and Saddler, but whether their interest in him was just this connection or something more I can't tell you. All I do know is that they spent the morning trying to find where he went and what he did while he was up here."

"And were they successful?"

"Depends what you mean by successful. What they did discover is that he died and is buried somewhere round here. I heard the girl say something like 'you've found the monument and you've found the grave, not very helpful I know, but what about Oude Klippen?' The man replied to the effect that they'd have a look at it in the afternoon. That is all I can tell you about Saddler, for after that they started talking about her life in South Africa and I lost interest."

"Well that's a start," Jean said, "but where was the grave, and what's this about a monument? Is it part of the grave or something else? And what's Oude Klippen?"

"I'll tell you in a moment," was the reply, "but now let's leave all this and go next door. You go on in and I'll be with you in a moment with the coffee."

It was almost dark in the sitting room, and rather than search for light switches Jean walked over to the window and looked out at the garden, but with daylight failing fast he could see little, so he fell to thinking about the evening.

Lemaître was a man with few illusions about himself; so why, he wondered, do girls like Pauline, well educated and from well-to-do backgrounds, hanker after common criminals like himself? That they did he knew from his own experience, and he had no doubt that Pauline would be true to form, for his instinct told him that helping him with information was incidental to her plans. It was him and his body that she wanted. That her information was what he had been seeking for the past several months was his good fortune, and there were still some other facts he hoped to get from her.

Then the lights came on and he turned from the window to see the girl putting the coffee tray on a low table by the sofa.

"Come and sit here, Jean," she said, pointing to the sofa, "while I draw the curtains, and I think we'd do with a little less light. That's better – now how do you like your coffee?"

She had left them with just one standard lamp and the picture lights lit, and he knew that if he was to get his last few facts, he must do it quickly.

"Now, chérie," he said stretching out and gently stroking the back of her neck, "just tell me about that monument they mentioned. Do you think it was part of the grave?"

"I don't know, they didn't say. It could be, or it might be something quite different. The Huguenot Memorial, perhaps – have you seen it?"

"Did they say where the grave was? And what about that place – Oude Klippen, was it not?"

"No," she replied, "the girl just said they'd found the grave and there was no mention of why they were interested in Oude Klippen. However, I can tell you that it's a farm and winery just outside Franschhoek. You can visit it, and we did yesterday. Now can we stop the interrogation? I've given you a lovely dinner and I want a little romance in my evening. I don't want to think of other people, I want to think of you and me. I've given you lots of information, and just to show what a clever girl I am, I'll tell you one more thing, something you haven't asked for. This morning I was in Franschhoek and I popped into the restaurant and asked them if they knew anything about the couple. The man they had never seen before, but the girl's name is Stanley. Her family own a famous winery near Paarl and her brother is a big noise in the wine business. The estate's called Neder Paarl, and that's all I'm going to tell you."

"Ah, ma petite, but it's quite enough; and now we have the reward, is it not so?" And he moved his hand from her neck and softly massaged her right ear, while turning her face towards him. She smiled up at him, and he bent over and kissed her lips while his other hand undid the three buttons of her blouse and slipped it off her shoulders. Then, with an ease born of long practice, he undid the fastening of her bra and moved over to kiss her nipples and run his hand up her thighs.

She sighed, moving her legs gently. "I've done my best for you, my love, and now you're doing all I hoped for and it's wonderful," she said. Then she reached down and took his hand from between her legs, kissed it and got to her feet. She picked up two cushions and dropped them on the floor, at the same time wriggling out of her skirt; she then stood over him while he deftly removed her knickers.

Some three hours later, leaving the girl asleep, he slipped out of the house, walked to the car and drove back to his hotel in Franschhoek. The guard who let him in gave a broad grin and hoped he'd had a good evening. Guests returning well after midnight are uncommon in a place like Franschhoek. While this exchange was taking place he failed to notice a red Toyota saloon drive slowly past the hotel. In fact, that same Toyota had followed him all the way from Stellenbosch, but so preoccupied had he been with the evening's happenings, he had failed to notice it.

Since her meeting in Paris with Lemaître, Annette Barry had been living in London, in a flat off the Bayswater Road belonging to her estranged husband.

This flat she was currently sharing with a retired naval officer; at least that was how Caspar Boscawen described himself.

In fact, after reasonable success at a famous public school, he had joined the Navy, where his pay failed to match his preferred lifestyle. In order to make up the difference he resorted to embezzlement, was duly caught and dismissed the service, but just avoided a prison sentence. Thereafter his career went from bad to worse. As a result of defrauding a second-rate book-maker he was forced to take part in a series of doping affairs, but this time his luck ran out, and when Annette met him he had just been released after serving eighteen months of a two-year sentence. The very person, Annette thought, to help her in her quest for the Tour du Lac legacy.

So now, as a result of a fax message from Lemaître telling her what he had been doing, she and Boscawen had flown out to Cape Town where she had found a further message. This said that he was going up to the wine-growing area as he had discovered that Saddler had visited friends there on his way back to England in 1843.

There being no further information on where exactly Lemaître had gone, after looking at a map, they decided to base themselves in Stellenbosch, at least to start with, and a fortunate choice that was to prove. For on the evening of their arrival they were walking from the hotel to their car, when Annette happened to look round at the passing traffic.

"Quick, Caspar," she yelled, "that blue car, that one stopped at the lights. I swear that was Jean in it." She already had the keys in her hand when she reached the car and moments later, they were off after the blue car.

"It went straight across," Boscawen said. "That's it there, and now it's turning right – there, down that wide road with the dead end sign, and that's a bit of luck, for he'll have to stop somewhere there. Slow now, don't get too close – yes, he's parking just beyond that white house. And now he's walking back to it – and he's going in."

"It's him alright. I wonder how long he's going to be?" Annette said. "Tell you what, we'll give him fifteen minutes. If he's still there after that, then we'll decide what to do. First, though, I'll turn round."

"OK, and then just go up to the road junction," Boscawen agreed. "I thought I saw a restaurant up by the traffic lights... Yes, I did. You hang on here and keep an eye on Jean while I go and investigate."

On closer inspection the restaurant, as Caspar had thought it would, proved ideal for their needs. It was quite small and had a place where they could park the car, but its main asset was the front window. This gave a view of the road and the junction where Annette was now parked, and although he could not see Jean's car, he reckoned they would have enough warning of his departure and would certainly see which way he went. He therefore booked a table close to the window and said he would be back in twenty minutes.

"Any movement?" he asked when he got back to the car, and when Annette shook her head he said, "Here's what we'll do then. He's obviously having dinner in that house and I suggest we do the same. I've got a table in that place across the street from which we can watch this road. But from what you've told me of our friend, dinner may not be the only reason he's at the house so he may be there for some time, and as we can't stay in the restaurant for ever, we'd better find somewhere where we can continue our watch without arousing suspicion."

"Well I can solve that problem for you," she replied, "for while you were over the way I did a little recce. At the end of this road, beyond the houses, there's a bit of a park with a lake and a place for leaving cars. There's a couple there now. If you are prepared to do your tough guy act if we're molested, I think it would be ideal."

And that was how it turned out. They had a very good dinner and left the restaurant at about midnight. As there was still no sign of Jean, they drove down to the end of the road and parked by the lake. It was some ninety minutes later, during which time they had seen no one, police or muggers, that Caspar sat up.

"Here he comes... Follow, but not too close. He's turned left on the main road. OK now... get after him... Not too quick, though. Good... there he is, going over those lights. Now all we need to do is to keep him in sight."

It was obvious that Jean Lemaître was not staying in Stellenbosch, for they were soon clear of the town and driving fast along a wide highway.

"Damn the fellow," Annette said, "we seem to be in for a long night. I think this road said Franschhoek, and that's some twenty miles. I suppose that's where he's staying, so let's hope he's discovered something."

Thirty minutes later they came to Franschhoek and watched the blue car turn down the main street and stop outside a small hotel.

"'The Peaceful Dove' – curious name!" Annette said as they drove past. "Anyway, we'll ring him there tomorrow – early – that'll teach him to keep us up!"

"The dove, and you as a Frenchwoman ought to know this, is the Huguenot emblem, and Franschhoek was – and still is – a Huguenot town," Caspar said, then added, "Now for God's sake, let's go home!"

CHAPTER 7

O<small>N THE MORNING FOLLOWING HIS VISIT TO</small> the monument, Andrew was late down to breakfast and found the others had almost finished.

"What have you been doing, darling?" Jenny asked. "We're all dying to know what you discovered. I gather you told David nothing on the way back."

"Well, that's not quite true, for I did tell him roughly what happened."

"Yes, and I've already told them of your little adventure with the guards and the dogs," David interjected.

"Anyway," continued Andrew, "the main thing that came out of my night's work was that I must visit that monument in daylight and that, as you can imagine, presents some interesting problems."

"And what more is it that you hope to get from this daylight visit that you didn't get last night?" David asked.

"Well, let me tell you a little more about this monument," Andrew said. "Let into the plinth below the column is a metal plate with an inscription in Afrikaans and English. It's quite worn and was hard to read in the dark and, because of the guards, I had to be careful with the torch. But as far as I could make out the monument commemorates the arrival, in 1806, of Jan du Toit and others, and the hope that they would start a new and thriving community in the area. 'A thriving community' it says, and doesn't that tie up nicely with 'expectation of plenty'? So I think Saddler not only wanted to draw attention to the monument, but more specifically to the plaque. And I want to see it in daylight and with the owner's permission."

"And how do you propose to do that?" Jenny asked.

Here David interrupted the proceedings by glancing at his watch and getting to his feet. "Sorry, but I must leave you now," he said. "I've meetings all day and won't be back till dinner and I'll look forward to hearing your plans then."

After David left, Andrew was allowed to finish his breakfast in peace while the women went about their household tasks. Then, at about eleven o'clock, Ann suggested that they move out to the verandah and hear Andrew's suggestions for visiting Blouberg.

"From what you said earlier, I gather you want to meet the du Toits," Ann said.

"Yes, and that's the problem," Andrew replied, "for we must not forget that we are not the only people with an interest in Oude Klippen. Remember somebody else made enquiries at the museum. Up to the time that we returned the box they had not been back, but they may have been since. If they have, we don't know what the museum may have told them, so it's just possible they may know about us."

"Does that matter?" Jenny asked. "We don't know what their interest is. Maybe they are just interested in the Jordaine family."

"Possibly," Andrew replied, "but we can't assume that and my suspicious mind says suppose they are on the same quest as we are? Don't ask me why – just let's assume they are. If that is the case, I don't want to be seen anywhere near the monument, nor do I want the du Toits to see Andrew Henderson."

"You do make things difficult, my sweet – or perhaps you just like playing Boy Scouts," Jenny said. "So what do you propose to do? Disguise yourself as the British Ambassador?"

"Disguise myself yes, but I don't aspire quite as high as that. No, I intend to be the sort of person who is likely to be interested in a monument."

"And who might that be?" asked Ann. "Someone like an archaeologist, I suppose."

"Exactly," Andrew answered, "an archaeologist perhaps, or what about an historian? Well I've plumped for the latter. Thinking about it this morning I suddenly remembered my old history tutor at Cambridge, Sidney Cooper. Mad on the Boer War, he was. He's been dead for years so I thought I might borrow his identity, or rather his name. I can't believe the du Toits would have heard of him, and I'll take that risk."

"But how are you going to make yourself look like him?"

"I'm not. I said I would borrow his name. What I will look like is as unlike myself as possible. I had in mind a flowing grey wig and a heavy moustache – and that, Jenny, is where you and your theatrical training come in."

"And where precisely am I going to get wigs and moustaches in this part of the world?" Jenny asked. "Make-up I can do, but I don't go around with a complete dressing up box!"

"If that is really what you want and you think it will work, I can probably help," Ann said.

"Well I can't think of anything better."

"OK then, let's see what we can do." Then, turning to her sister-in-law, Ann said, "Jenny, do you remember the Hendricks? He was some sort of professor at Stellenbosch, but his wife had a lot to do with drama at the University. I see her quite often and could easily ring up and ask if they could help. Don't worry, I'll think of some story to account for the request."

"Well that would be marvellous," Andrew replied, "but I'm afraid there's something else I'll have to ask."

"Yes, darling, and I know what. You're going to need us to fix a visit to Blouberg. Can we do that, Ann?"

"Tomorrow morning, if possible," said Andrew, interrupting.

"I'm sure we can fix something. Now you two run away and play and I'll see what I can do. See you for lunch." And Ann got up and went into the house.

"Come on, Andrew," Jenny said, "we've got an hour and a bit. I'll show you some more of the countryside."

When they returned from their expedition, they found that Ann had been more successful than they could have hoped. If they went to the Hendricks' house, Mrs Hendricks would take them to someone who should be able to provide all the disguise they wanted. And as for Blouberg, the du Toits would love to see Jenny and Dr Cooper at about eleven tomorrow and would show him the monument and tell him a bit about its history.

The Stanleys were not the only people occupied that morning in making plans. Annette Barry and Caspar arrived at the hotel in Franschhoek sharp at nine o'clock and found a surprised and bleary-eyed Lemaître just starting breakfast.

"How did you find me here?" he asked. "For I was just thinking to myself 'Now how do I find Annette – has she come yet to South Africa and has she got my message?' And then I realise I have not given any place to find me up here. Then in you walk. How did you do it?"

Annette sat down at the table and waved to a waitress. "Bring us some coffee," she ordered. "No, nothing to eat – just coffee. And now, Jean Lemaître," she went on, turning to him, "you weren't thinking anything of the sort. What you were thinking was 'I have discovered something. She doesn't know where I am, so I'll keep it to myself and she can whistle for me.' That's right, isn't it? Well, you're out of luck, for we just happened to see you in Stellenbosch last night and we followed you back here. What the hell were you doing in that house? And you'd better have a good explanation, for my friend here, Caspar Boscawen, can be a real bastard if he doesn't like you."

"Now wait a moment," said Lemaître, looking just a little scared. "First, I was not trying to avoid you. I would have left another message for you at the shipping office. And then what, you ask, was I doing in that house? Well, I was working for France and for you. I told you that a man called Saddler, a relation of the Chevalier, had gone from India to Cape Town, so I did the same. When I got to Cape Town, I discovered that Saddler had only made a brief stop there. I also discovered that some eighteen months later, he was back in the Cape, this time on his way to India, and had stayed there to visit friends, possibly in the Franschhoek area. So I thought that's where I'd better go. What could I discover? Nothing! That is until I met a girl. That was why I went to that house. She knew I was interested in the name Saddler and she promised, if I went to dine with her, that she would tell me something of significance about that name."

"She took a hell of a time to tell you," Caspar said. "Now you'd better tell us a damn sight quicker, and make sure it's the truth."

Lemaître half smiled, half leered. "My friend, when you dine with a beautiful woman in her house, there are other things to do than talk," he said.

Boscawen, who was a big man, well over six foot and heavily built, started to rise from his chair. Annette laid a hand on his arm.

"Calm yourself," she said. "Let's hear what he has to say." Caspar subsided onto his chair while Lemaître, who had no love for the English, continued to smile superciliously.

"Yes indeed, you must keep calm while I tell you what you want to know. This girl was lunching with friends in a restaurant across the road here and there was another couple in the restaurant and she overheard them mention the name Saddler. Then they talked about a grave, a monument and a place called Oude Klippen."

He then went on to explain that it appeared that Saddler had died, probably while visiting Oude Klippen and that the couple had found his grave. Oude Klippen, his girl had told him, was now a well-known winery. The location and significance of the monument, if it was known, was not divulged. It could be at the grave, it could be at Oude Klippen, or it could be nothing to do with either. He himself had already discovered that in Saddler's time, Oude Klippen had belonged to a Huguenot family called Jordaine, but that had led him nowhere. The only other thing of interest was that the girl had been back to the restaurant and enquired about the couple. It appeared that the woman was called Stanley and lived near Paarl. The man they did not know.

"I believe," Jean said in conclusion, "that if Saddler brought anything from India, he hid it before he died, and that the monument holds the secret of where it is to be found."

"You have done well, mon cher Jean. Better – much better – than I thought you would," said Annette, smiling at him. "So now let us see what we know. First, we know that Saddler, a relative of the Chevalier, visited him in India and then, after a couple of visits to the Cape, finished up in Franschhoek, where we believe he died. Secondly, the French Government believe the Chevalier went off with important state papers; my husband's family history suggests he went off with something far more valuable."

Ever since they had arrived at the hotel, Caspar had been watching Lemaître closely. Five years on the fringes of the underworld and almost two years as a guest of Her Majesty had given him plenty of time to study criminals and the criminal mind. Furthermore, on a number of occasions during his naval career, he had had dealings with the civil servants at the Admiralty, and he knew how government departments worked. It seemed to him highly unlikely that any government organisation, let alone the elite French Civil Service, would employ anyone like Lemaître, and even if they did, they would hardly send him on expensive trips to India and South Africa in search of documents, particularly if they concerned events that took place over two hundred years ago. This, together with everything he'd seen and heard of Lemaître in the past twenty-four hours, suggested the petty criminal on the make.

"And I believe the family history," he said, "Monsieur Jean's government papers are a figment of his imagination. Aren't they, little man? You're not working for France at all, are you? You're on the track of valuable goods; jewels, bullion or whatever. Yes, and I expect there's some mastermind behind you paying the bills – and who you are probably planning to double cross."

"Is this true, Jean?" Annette asked. "And if it is, I hope you weren't planning to double cross me as well. I don't think Caspar would like that at all."

"No, no. I wouldn't have told what I have if I'd had that in mind," Jean said, then, giving Caspar a wary look, he went on, "I will be honest. What Monsieur Boscawen has said is almost true. What I originally told you in Paris was that papers had been found suggesting valuable royal property was missing. That is true, and the information came from the department – through a friend's husband to be exact. I work for myself, but certainly there is one who finances me. This one indeed believes the missing property is part of Marie Antoinette's jewellery and will expect his cut from anything found. There, I have told you the truth and I hope we may continue to work together."

"I'm sure we can," said Annette after a nod from Caspar, "but remember what I told you in Paris – with us it's share and share alike. We take our cut before anyone else gets anything. Right? So now, what are we going to do?"

"What I want to know," Caspar said, "is who are these other two, what are they after and what do they know?"

"No idea," said Annette, "so we'd better find out. The name Stanley means nothing to me. What about the man? Perhaps he too knows about the Saddler history – must do in fact. We could try the museum. See if he's been there and if they know who he is, or we could go to Oude Klippen. You say, Jean, that they went there? Well then I think that's the better bet. What about you, Jean?"

"I want to know about the monument. So I shall hang about Paarl and see where they go. Perhaps they will lead me to it."

"Very well, you do that," Annette replied. "Meanwhile, we'll have a look at that winery place. Ring me tomorrow evening at this number; it's our hotel in Stellenbosch."

CHAPTER 8

Early the next morning Andrew Henderson's bedroom was a scene of considerable activity, resembling nothing so much as the principal actor's dressing-room before an important first night.

Mrs Hendricks had been as good as her word, and had arranged for one of the University's theatrical societies to lend them all the items Andrew needed for his disguise. So now he was sitting before a mirror in a positively Einstein-like wig, while Jenny put the finishing touches to a thick grey moustache.

"There, that's fine," she said, "and I promise it won't move."

"You don't think we're overdoing it, do you?" Andrew asked. "The wig looks almost too much."

"I'm just going to trim it a bit, then it'll be fine," Jenny replied, "and I must make you a little paler and your eyes a bit older. Can't use too much make-up in this weather, but we must age you a bit."

"There you are; the very model of a Cambridge historian," Jenny said some twenty minutes later. "I'm sure Sidney Cooper would be proud of himself if he could see you now!" Then she added, with a barely suppressed giggle, "All I beg of you is, whatever the temptation, please don't mop your brow or blow your nose or I won't answer for the consequences."

Andrew got up and put on a blue and white bow tie and a slightly stained linen jacket, both borrowed from the drama group's props, then his own rather scruffy suede shoes completed the outfit.

"Excellent," he said looking at himself in the mirror, "just what I wanted. Darling, you've done a wonderful job. Indeed, the elderly Cambridge don! A little overdone perhaps, but certainly nothing like me! Come to that, nothing like Sidney Cooper either. He was small, gingery and very short-sighted!"

As they got down to the hall, Ann and David emerged from the kitchen and immediately burst out laughing. When they had recovered, they both agreed that the disguise was excellent, and no one who knew Andrew could possibly recognise him.

"One thing," said David, searching in a cupboard and emerging with an old Panama hat, "I envisage the professor as coming from the generation that took sunstroke seriously."

Andrew put it on and walked over to an elegant gilt-framed mirror. "Yes, that definitely completes the picture," he said.

"Come on, darling, let's go before anyone thinks of something else," Jenny said, taking him by the arm and dragging him to the car. "Bye, and see you all later."

At Blouberg they were greeted warmly by Jan du Toit and his wife and ushered into a comfortable sitting room containing some fine examples of early Cape Dutch furniture.

"Very nice to see you, Jenny," du Toit said. "We have this pleasure all too rarely." Then turning to his other guest, he added, "And it is a great pleasure too to meet you, Dr Cooper. I understand you are interested in the history of the Dutch settlements in the Cape and of the Boers' journeys through the mountains."

"Indeed, sir, that is so," the scholarly gentleman replied. "I am currently working on a book tracing the history of the wine-growing areas and their colonisation by both the Dutch and the French. My research has been greatly helped by my very good friends the Stanleys. We have looked at the Stellenbosch and Franschhoek areas, and now I hope to find out more about the origins of the vineyards around Paarl."

"Well then let me explain a little of our history," du Toit said. "As you will have realised, the cultivation of vines has gone on in parts of this countryside for some three hundred years. We, the du Toits, only arrived here at the beginning of the nineteenth century. When my ancestor, Jan du Toit, and his companions reached this area it was largely unexplored, and as it was admirably suited to their requirements, they immediately set about developing it. There is a monument on the estate commemorating their arrival. I'll show it to you if you like."

"That would be most interesting, but first can you tell me something of how development progressed?"

"Of course," Jan du Toit said, then proceeded to give a most interesting and knowledgeable talk on the history of the Paarl area and his family's association with it during which Andrew took copious, and he hoped scholarly-looking, notes. Then at the end of an hour du Toit paused. "I think that's enough talking," he said. "Now let's go and have a look at the estate."

They were shown the winery, the gardens with their famous roses and hibiscus, the existing vineyards and the new plantings extending high up the surrounding hills.

"You see, nothing stands still here," their host said. "For two hundred years we have been improving and expanding, and it is my intention to continue doing so. Despite everything, I believe South Africa is still a country of opportunity. And now here's the monument."

Then, just as they were about to get out of the vehicle, there was a loud ring from his mobile telephone. After listening for a moment, du Toit turned to them and said, "Look, I'm sorry but I must go back to the office. Why don't you have a look at the monument and read the inscription? Then if you walk back along that track there, past the lake and up through the garden, you'll arrive at my office and we can have a little tasting."

After watching the vehicle out of sight, Andrew and Jenny walked up the slope to the base of the plinth and Andrew bent down to look at the bronze plaque. "Doesn't tell us much, I'm afraid," he said, and after a quick look, Jenny nodded her agreement.

"However, our host being called away is a bit of luck, so let's make the most of it," said Andrew, looking down at the stone pavement, then up at the slender column and finally letting his gaze rest on the plinth. "Now, supposing you had something to hide, and you felt a severe bout of fever coming on, where would you look for a hiding place? Not too far away, I guess, so you might think of the monument, somewhere in or on it perhaps. So – are there any loose flags, I wonder?" And he crouched down and felt around the edges of the pavement. "Nothing there," he said, getting to his feet and fanning himself with his hat. "God, this wig's hot. I'm sure the make-up must be running!"

Jenny, who was fiddling with the plaque, looked up and said it appeared okay to her and then pointed at two little emblems on either side of the plaque.

"What do you think these are?" she asked. "They look like birds, and one of them is loose; I think it unscrews."

"They're doves. Huguenot doves; probably the du Toit crest," Andrew replied, then moving her hand, said, "Here, let me have a go. Yes, it does unscrew, and what's more there's a sizeable hole behind it – and what about this?" he added as he withdrew a small copper tube some six inches long from the hole.

"Is there anything inside?" Jenny asked. "Can you open it? Good old Thomas, I bet he's hidden something in it."

After a bit of a struggle Andrew managed to unscrew the top of the tube and when he shook it, a small metal object fell into his palm.

"What on earth is it?" Jenny asked. "And is there anything else?"

"At a guess it's a seal; a rather unusual one, for it's quite heavy. And yes, there's a piece of paper," Andrew replied, feeling inside the tube, "but I don't think I can get it out without damaging it. Also I think we ought to be getting back before they start wondering where we are – and before I really do start melting! Look, I'm going to take the tube home. I reckon they don't know about it," and he put the seal back in the tube and slipped it into his pocket, then screwed the dove back in position. "Come on now, let's get back. I find the idea of a little wine-tasting definitely attractive!"

Early that morning, Jean Lemaître had driven over to Paarl determined to try to find out more about the girl called Stanley and her companion. Tactful enquiries at the Post Office resulted in a series of cautious replies: "Yes, of course everyone knows the Stanleys at Neder Paarl," and "No, we don't know if there's anyone special staying there and we wouldn't tell you even if we did. Besides, it's a huge operation and there are always people visiting. The wine trade, you must realise, is very important to us. Why don't you go and ask at the office? Neder Paarl is easy to find, take you ten or fifteen minutes to get there."

The estate office were equally non-committal, although they did let slip that they believed Mr Stanley had been visited by an important client from England. A brewer they thought; a name like Anderson or Henderson. Deciding not to push his luck any further, he went back to the main road and drove slowly in the direction of the house. As he was approaching the main entrance a car emerged and drove past him in the opposite direction, and the driver was the girl he had seen in the restaurant in Franschhoek. Sitting beside her was an elderly white-haired man whom he had certainly not seen before.

Not that he thought that it would get him anywhere, but for the want of something better to do, he decided to see where they went. So he turned and followed them until, about twenty minutes later, they turned into a driveway with a sign saying Blouberg Estate. Not knowing what he might find at the end of the drive and not wishing to meet the girl in case she might recognise him, he drove on down the road hoping to find somewhere he could park and keep watch.

The left of the road was all vines, presumably belonging to Blouberg, but on the right was an area of uncultivated scrub. Finding a track, he drove off the road and parked in the shade of some trees. He got out of the car, found a place from which he had a good view of the vineyard and the first thing that caught his eye was a slender stone pillar.

"The monument!" he thought to himself. "So this is the place. Let's wait and see what, if anything, happens."

Nothing did happen for a long time, and he was just beginning to wonder how much longer he could stand the heat, when a vehicle appeared driving down a track between the rows of vines and stopped just below the monument. After a few moments, two people got out and the vehicle drove off in the direction of the farm.

Unfortunately for Jean he had not got binoculars, but he could see that there was a man in a Panama hat and a girl. "Must be them," he thought as he watched them walk towards the monument. Then he saw them fiddling about at its base, but without glasses he could not see what they were doing.

After about ten minutes the man straightened up, slipped something into his pocket and motioning to the girl to follow, the two of them walked up the slope behind the monument and disappeared over the crest.

Reckoning there was nothing further he could do at the moment, Jean returned to his car and drove slowly back to his hotel. But he decided that a visit to the place, in slightly less conspicuous circumstances, was called for.

CHAPTER 9

"WELL THAT WAS PRETTY SUCCESSFUL," ANDREW SAID as they drove back to Neder Paarl. "Not only have we found that someone has indeed hidden something at the monument, but we've also tasted some distinctly promising wine. Now I'll have to find some way of doing business with them without giving away my alter ego, for I feel they might not take kindly to my little deception."

"Do you really think that tube was put there by Thomas Saddler?" Jenny asked.

"I don't know, but tomorrow we'll see if we can find out. I've done enough detective work for the time being, so let's give it a rest for tonight."

Having made that decision, Andrew determined to stick to it, so despite the pleading of the family he did no more that evening than describe their visit to Blouberg and the discovery of the hiding place in the base of the monument.

At dinner, with the wine-tasting at the du Toits as an excuse, he turned the conversation to his plans for World Wide Wines, the success of his negotiations with the various vineyards he had visited in South Africa and how the whole scheme was due to Jenny's inspiration and determination.

"It's very sweet of you to say so, darling, but you're dodging the issue. What we all really want to know is what's in that funny metal tube," was Jenny's reply to the compliments.

"That, as I've already said, is for tomorrow," Andrew replied, getting to his feet and looking round the room. "Tomorrow I promise all will be revealed – that is if there is anything to reveal. So now, if you will excuse me, Ann, I'm going to have an early night."

Once in his bedroom, Andrew took off his jacket and then collected his leather toilet bag from the bathroom. From a zipped inside pocket, he retrieved the copper tube. He unscrewed the top and gently tipped out the seal and studied it carefully.

It was, as he had originally suspected, somewhat unusual. The upper part was the normal patterned and engraved brass with a handle and ring, but the base was definitely peculiar. Instead of the symbol or crest being cut into coloured glass, the base was a shiny metal, hard and quite heavy. The symbol, which appeared to be a hound, was cut deeply into the metal. The animal was strangely angular and the edges of the cut were straight and sharp.

"Very odd," he thought. "I wonder whose it was and what it was used for? Not just sealing letters, surely. Well, maybe the paper will tell us. Let's see if we can get it out."

He put the seal down on the bedside table and switched on the light. The paper had been rolled up and dropped into the tube, but was now tight round the inside and no amount of shaking would free it. He picked up his jacket, felt in the pockets and took out a small penknife. He inserted this gently between the paper and the side of the tube and managed to free a centimetre or so all round, but the blade was too thick and short to do more.

He looked vaguely round the room for inspiration and eventually reached for his briefcase. In one of the pockets, he found a brochure for a car hire company with a shiny and remarkably stiff cover. To cut a strip of this was the work of a moment, and it proved to be ideal for what he wanted. After some thirty minutes of gentle prising and teasing with his plastic strip and a pair of tweezers, he was able to ease the paper from its hiding place.

Unrolling it proved almost more difficult than extracting it, for it was extremely brittle. However, using the back of his comb, warmed by soaking it in hot water, he gradually smoothed it out, and after an hour he found himself with a sheet of fine paper, about six inches by four, covered in writing and still fairly legible. It was in French, a language which Andrew spoke fluently, and although the writing was somewhat old-fashioned, after another hour's painstaking work he had made himself a fair and reasonably complete copy, which he then settled down to translate. This proved easier than he expected.

The writing may have been old-fashioned but the language was quite straight-forward, and when he had finished the translation he found himself regarding a most extraordinary document.

> *A.*
>
> *It is finished and we are prepared for whatever may come, even the guillotine. His Majesty commands that you take this seal to The Sign of the Stag in London. The rich Englishman will tell you what to do and may you live to enjoy the rewards of your faithful service.*
>
> *Ever your friend,*
> *MA.*

Andrew turned and looked out of the window at the darkening landscape. "Now I wonder just what that means," he thought. "A message from someone acting on behalf of a king, someone who signs MA – and MA with a considerable flourish. Fits in rather nicely with Thomas's other papers, doesn't it, and indeed with the family history." Here Andrew paused and gazed at the seal, at the paper and at his translation. "Addressed to A – Antoine, I'm sure the Chevalier was Antoine. Signed MA – Marie Antoinette, surely. Well, the signature's easily checked. But what the rest means, heaven knows. Obviously the next step lies in London. But now, I think, it's bedtime."

He picked up the tube and the seal and replaced them in their hiding place; the two pieces of paper he placed carefully between the leaves of a book on the bedside table, and five minutes later was in bed and asleep.

The next morning he was down early and found David just finishing breakfast.

"Have you looked at your finds?" he asked.

"Yes, and what they disclosed was very interesting indeed. I'll tell you all about it later," Andrew replied.

"Look, I've got to go over to the office for a couple of hours but I can be back for an hour just after ten. Can you leave it till then?"

"Yes of course, David. I'll be ready at ten and I'll make sure the others are too."

Ten o'clock found an impatient family party drinking coffee on the verandah while they awaited the arrival of David Stanley.

"No, I'm not going to tell you anything until he arrives," Andrew was saying when a somewhat breathless and apologetic David appeared.

"Sorry I'm late. Slight crisis back at the ranch! But all is now well, so fire away, Andrew."

"Let me tell you first," Andrew began, "that I was quite right not to involve you lot last night. Extracting the contents of this tube," and he held it up, "and trying to make head or tail of them took me rather over three hours. Even now, I only know what they are and why they are where we found them. I don't really know what they mean, although I can make some sort of guess."

"Well come on, tell us all," said the ever impatient Jenny.

"The first thing that came out of the tube was this," and he showed them the seal. "Jenny has already seen it, and I said then that it was probably a seal. Well, I'm now sure that it is. It's a very unusual one, so I think it has some other use than just sealing, but I've no idea what that may be. The base on which the symbol is engraved is not the usual glass, but an extremely hard steel. The other thing the tube contained is this paper. Don't touch it. It's very brittle and I had the devil of a job getting it out. It's a message – in French – and here's the translation. Have a look at it."

"Who is 'A'?" Jenny asked. "And His Majesty – a king! – what on earth does it all mean?"

"And who is 'MA'? Seems to me we've got yet another riddle here," was David's contribution.

"Come on, darling, where's your memory and your imagination?" said his wife. "Surely you remember Andrew talking about his ancestor and Marie Antoinette. It's a message from her to her page – I think that's what you said your ancestor was – and I presume he's 'A'. That's Royalty for you. However selfish her life may have been, she and the King, when facing death, still found time to think of a faithful courtier. That's my interpretation, Andrew."

"And very good too," Andrew replied. "Yes, I think this is a message from the Queen; or really, I suppose, from the King, to the Chevalier de la Tour du Lac, whose name I think was Antoine, asking him to carry out some task which would be of ultimate value to him. What it might be, I can't imagine. I can only guess that the contents of the tube came into the possession of Alice's family at the same time and by the same route as the Queen's jewels. They, we know, or think we know, are in England. The paper and seal therefore must be what Thomas was going to ask his father-in-law about when he got to India. That's about as far as I've got, and I don't think I can go any further without talking to the family in Suffolk and also making some enquiries in London – in the City to be precise."

"Tell me," said David looking across at Andrew, who had settled back in his chair, "when you say you can't go any further, does that mean that you are intending to pursue the matter? That you believe there is something in all this that merits investigation?"

"Yes indeed," was the reply. "Having found out what we have, in fairness to the Saddler family, I must find out if there really is some sort of Bourbon legacy."

"What are your plans then?" asked Jenny. "Are you intending going back to England immediately, like tomorrow? Remember, I'm going to stay with the van Stadens and I rather hoped you would come too. They have a stud farm and a small private reserve on the edge of the Drakensberg. You haven't seen anything of our wildlife yet and this would be a marvellous opportunity."

"I know, but I don't think I should delay that long. If I'm going to try and solve these puzzles we seem to have collected, I want to make a start as soon as possible. Don't forget that the lady in the museum said that someone else had been asking questions, so we may not be the only ones interested in Thomas Saddler."

"Well, I'm going to leave you lot to sort out your plans," said David Stanley, getting to his feet, "for I must get back to the office. See you this evening."

After he left there was a long discussion on how to proceed and eventually it was agreed that Andrew would return to London in two days' time.

"Apart from investigating the Saddler saga, I do have a brewery to run," he said. "I must get people working on all the contacts I've made out here, to say nothing of making sure nobody's done anything terrible since I've been away!"

It was also suggested that Jenny should go and stay with her friends as planned, and then join Andrew in England in three or four weeks, by which time he should have made some progress in following up the various clues left by Thomas Saddler.

"We can go up to Passford. I'd like you to meet Cousin Wilfred, he's a very interesting chap and definitely the authority on the Saddler family history. He was given Passford when his uncle, my Alice's grandfather, went to live on his wife's vast acres in Northumberland. However, of more immediate importance is the copper tube. I must put it back in that hole in the monument, but I'd better leave it empty. I don't think anyone other than us knows of its existence; however, if someone else were to discover it, I would rather it told them no secrets."

"When are you going to do this?" Jenny asked.

"Tonight. And no, you can't come with me. Far too dangerous. If David agrees we'll repeat the procedure of the other night. He can drop me off and collect me later." Then turning to Ann he added, "I wonder if I'm now entitled to a drink? All this talking is becoming hard work!"

It was just after midnight when David stopped the car near the wood leading down to the monument. Andrew got out and picked up his torch and truncheon and slipped them into his pocket, then he turned to David.

"This is fine," he said. "I'll walk from here. After last time I'm taking no chances. We're below the crest here and we've had the lights off for the last half mile, so I should be OK. Same drill as before and see you in an hour." With that, he pulled the mask down over his face and set off down a grass slope towards the edge of the wood.

This time he followed a slightly different route, for instead of entering the wood at once he continued down the edge on the side away from the monument. It was in deep shadow and he was able to move both quickly and silently until he reckoned he was about level with his destination.

He had guessed correctly, for when, on hands and knees, he reached the opposite edge of the wood, he found himself at the bottom of the slope leading up to the monument. Carefully parting the branches of a bush, he saw to his considerable surprise a figure approaching the top of the slope. This was no guard, for when he reached the platform he produced a torch, and with little regard for caution proceeded to study the plinth and its surroundings.

So occupied was the man with his investigation that he never heard Andrew's approach. The first he knew was a voice in his ear saying, "Don't touch!" With a startled oath he swung round, and as he did so, Andrew hit him hard on the point of the jaw. Catching him as he fell, he lowered him onto his back and then, shielding the light with his body, shone his torch briefly on the man's face.

"Now I wonder who you are," Andrew said to himself, "and just what you are doing here." Then looking closer, he thought, "I've seen that ferret face somewhere before. I can't remember where for the moment – but I will, and another time I shan't forget it."

Crouching down by the plaque, Andrew took a quick look round, but despite the lights and other activity, all seemed to be quiet. However, feeling that this was no place to hang about, he unscrewed the dove and replaced the copper tube in its hiding place and, with a last look at his victim who was breathing heavily but otherwise seemed unharmed, he returned to the wood. Once in cover, he waited for five minutes, but no one appeared and the man did not move. Then, with a quick look at his watch, he moved quietly up the hill, but now keeping well inside the wood.

Once at the road, he used the cover afforded by a low bank to make his way back to the rendezvous point, and five minutes later David pulled up beside him.

"Just as well I decided to leave the tube empty," Andrew said as he got into the car, "for there was a man sniffing round the monument. Who he was I don't know, although I've a funny feeling I've seen him somewhere before. No, he never saw me, except in the split second before I knocked him out. Obviously I had to leave him there, but whether he'll discover the hiding place, I don't know. Won't do him much good if he does! Anyway let's go home. I'll tell you all a bit more tomorow."

CHAPTER 10

ON THE MORNING OF THAT SAME DAY Annette Barry had gone into the hotel dining room and found a bad-tempered Boscawen just finishing breakfast.

"Let's face it," he said, "we're getting nowhere fast. Sure, from that little creep Lemaître we've discovered that a man called Saddler, on his way to India, stopped in South Africa and visited farms in the Franschhoek area where he probably died. We think, but we don't know, that he possessed something valuable that he hid here before he died – perhaps in or near a monument. Oh yes, and there appear to be two other people around who are also interested in his doings. An odd coincidence, I grant you."

"You bore me, Caspar, when you go on like this," Annette replied. "You mentioned an odd coincidence. Well, to me the odd coincidence is that Saddler's actions fit so neatly with the family history." Here she paused, expecting a reply, but when Boscawen remained silent, she continued.

"So what are we going to do? Well, today we are going to try and find out about this other couple; who they are, and why they are interested in Saddler. So let's follow round where we know they have been, starting with the farm called Oude Klippen. Then there's also the possibility that Jean will find out more about the monument."

At Oude Klippen they parked in the shade of a jacaranda tree and walked towards the office. Avoiding a group of people listening to someone explaining the workings of the estate, Annette went into the office and straight up to a young man, who looked up enquiringly.

"You seem rather busy today," she said, "but I hope you may be able to help me."

"Do my best," the young man replied. "What is it you want?"

"I am a French journalist," she said, assuming an exaggerated French accent, "and I am writing some articles on what happened to certain Huguenot families who left France in the seventeenth and eighteenth centuries and went, some to England, some to Canada and some to the Cape. Now, I have been told that this estate was once in the ownership of the Huguenot family Jordaine, but I think no longer. Perhaps there is someone who can tell me of the history of Oude Klippen?"

"You need to talk to Jonty Clark," was the reply. "He's the winemaker and he's been here for ever. I've only been here since my father bought the estate a couple of years ago. That's Jonty outside, talking to those French and Italians." Here the young man looked up at a clock. "He must be nearly finished, for my father and I are due to take them round the vines at eleven o'clock. Hang on a moment while I find out what's happening."

And he left the office to return a few minutes later with the tall man they had seen outside.

"Jonty, this lady's a French journalist. She's interested in the Huguenot history of Oude Klippen. I've said you can tell her all about it."

"Well, that's rather a tall order," the winemaker said as the younger man left to join the group in the courtyard. "Take about two hours and I can only spare ten minutes. Any specific questions I can answer? And perhaps you could come back some other time?"

"I believe the farm originally belonged to the Jordaine family," Annette said, "and I have a particular interest in them."

"We believe they were the first owners. Certainly they arrived from the Cape in the early seventeen hundreds and it was they who planted the first vines. They remained here for over two hundred years." The man paused and glanced at Annette with a slight air of suspicion. "It's curious you should ask about them. We had someone else in quite recently enquiring about the Jordaines – a man who was with the Stanley girl from Neder Paarl it was – said he was of Huguenot descent; some Jordaines who went to England, I think he said, and he wondered if there was any connection. He was also interested in an Englishman who visited Oude Klippen in the last century. Don't remember the name, I'm afraid."

"How interesting," Annette remarked. "Was your visitor called Jordaine?"

"No, no. The Jordaine was on his mother or grandmother's side. I can tell you his name though – Andrew Henderson it was. A brewer in London, and we had a most interesting talk."

"Now look," said Annette glancing at her watch, "we mustn't keep you. You've been most helpful, and perhaps we could come back another day?"

"Yes, but ring first. Here's a brochure with the number. Pleased to have met you." And he shook hands and escorted them to the door.

"Well that was a bit of luck," Annette said as they got into the car, "but now let's go back to the hotel and get a drink and some lunch and then I'll tell you why. It's all to do with the name Henderson. Then we'll ring Jean and decide what to do next," and she bent over her companion and kissed his cheek, then clapping her hands, she added, "Eh bien, Caspar, I think at last we make some progress."

Back at the hotel in Stellenbosch they found a table in a quiet corner of the dining room and Caspar ordered a bottle of white wine, and putting the menu aside, waved away the waiter saying they would order later.

"Now what's all the excitement?" he said to Annette. "What's so interesting about the name Henderson?"

"You remember that I told you that my husband was descended from the Chevalier de la Tour du Lac," she said, "from a granddaughter I think it was, and I believe it was her sister who married Saddler. Now, what is much more interesting is that one of my husband's Saddler cousins had a daughter who married a London brewer whose name I'm sure was Henderson. I've been a bit slow in working this out, but it all fits together, so I think I must be right. This Henderson, like us, must be following the trail of the Chevalier and I just wonder what he has found out. Incidentally, I think I heard that the wife died quite recently."

"So what next?" Boscawen asked.

"I think we see what, if anything, Jean has discovered," Annette replied.

This, however, proved easier said than done, for Lemaître was nowhere to be found, and it was not until the next morning that they tracked him down and he was able to explain what he had been doing over the previous two days.

First, he had gone to Paarl to see if he could find out more about the girl called Stanley. The people in the Post Office had been non-committal, and suggested that if he wanted to find out about the Stanleys he should go to Neder Paarl. This he had done.

There, on the pretext of finding out about wine-tastings, he mentioned that he had recently met someone, he couldn't remember the name, who said he had been invited to stay at Neder Paarl and wondered if he was still there.

"Oh, I wouldn't know about that," the girl in the office had said. However, wishing to prolong her conversation with the charming Frenchman, she had added that she did think there might be a man staying at the house, a friend of Miss Stanley she believed, with a name like Henderson or Anderson. And that was all he had found out at the farm.

"I knew it! I knew our luck was changing," Annette cried in French. "There's the name Henderson again. We must be on the right track." Lemaître looked at her in amazement and was about to say something, when she held up her hand. "I will tell you about it later, Jean, but now you tell us what else happened yesterday."

"Wait a moment," he said, continuing in French but glancing at Boscawen who indicated that he understood, "I haven't yet finished with the day before." And he went on to describe how he'd followed two people from Neder Paarl to another large estate apparently called Blouberg. One, he guessed, was the daughter; the other was an elderly man whom he had never seen before.

The couple had turned into the Blouberg drive, where he obviously could not follow, so he had driven on and eventually found he was looking across acres of vines to a tall stone pillar.

"C'est le monument!" he thought to himself. "They must be going to visit the monument. But why? Well, let us wait and see." So he found a convenient place to park the car and settled down in the shade to watch.

"I waited a long time," he said, "and it was hot, very hot, even in the shade and I wondered how long I could stand it. Then suddenly, driving down a track between the rows of vines, a vehicle appeared. It was one of those cross-country things and it stopped just below the monument."

He then described how two people, who looked like the girl and her elderly companion, got out of the vehicle which, after a few minutes, drove back the way it had come. The man had a quick look round, then said something to his companion and both of them walked up to the stone pillar.

"This was where I cursed myself for not having the spy-glass with me," Jean said, "for the man bent down to look at something at the base of the pillar. After some minutes he straightened up and appeared to put something – I could not see what – into his pocket. Then he had another look round, as if to check that they were unobserved. He appeared to be satisfied for he took the girl's arm and the two disappeared over the crest."

"If he put something in his pocket he must have found it there. What was it, do you think?" Annette asked.

"I told you, I had no glass so I could not see, but it was quite small," was the reply, "and now let me finish my story. I decided I must have a closer look at that pillar and its surroundings, but it had to be at night, so I could not be seen."

Back at his hotel he had decided to leave further investigation until the next day. So the following evening he had driven out to Blouberg and parked in the same place as before. Then, under cover of a small wood, he managed to approach the monument unseen.

"I saw that there was a metal plate with writing at its base and I bent down to look at it. Suddenly there was a voice in my ear – an English voice. I don't know what it said, but I turned to look – and someone hit me very hard and very expertly. The next thing I knew, I was lying on a stone pavement looking up at a pale blue sky."

He had struggled to his feet, gingerly feeling his chin and cursing himself for a careless fool. Then, seeing there was no one about, he decided to take a closer look at the monument and the metal plate, but could find nothing of interest. So, with a ringing head and an aching jaw, he had returned to the car without any further mishaps.

Caspar, with his ever suspicious mind, looked round at the other two. "The man you saw on the first day must have been Henderson or whatever he calls himself. But why was he in disguise? What, if anything, did he find and put in his pocket? And why did he go back last night? Because it must have been him who knocked you out."

Annette's suspicions were of a different kind and centred on whether Jean was telling all he knew, but she decided not to pursue them for the moment and to concentrate on Caspar's comments.

"To find out the answer to your questions, Caspar, or at least some of them," she said, "you and I, mon cher, are going to visit the Stanleys at Neder Paarl. It will be no problem, for I shall say that I have heard that they have a Mr Henderson visiting them, and I just thought that he might be a connection... I'll think of how to put it. Yes, and I think we'll do it this afternoon. You, Jean, you must see if you can find out anything more of interest in Paarl or Franschhoek."

At lunchtime that same day, Jenny was lying by the edge of the pool. Through the surrounding screen of trees, she could just see the jagged semi-circle of mountains that framed their valley, and she thought, as she had done so often in the past, that in spite of everything, there were few better places to live than South Africa. Could she ever, she wondered, give it all up for that cold, damp, overcrowded island that was her view of England? Then, realising where her train of thought was leading, she pulled herself up abruptly. "Why am I thinking like this?" she wondered. "Am I really seriously assuming that I'm going to spend the rest of my life in England and, what's more, married to an Englishman?" She gazed at the sky and a smile flickered across her lips as she thought, "Yes, that is exactly what I am doing – and the man hasn't even asked me yet!"

"Jenny! What on earth are you thinking about? I've already asked you three times if you know where Andrew is." Her sister-in-law's voice finally impinging on her consciousness, Jenny scrambled to her feet.

"Sorry, I was miles away. I've no idea where Andrew is. I thought he was in the house. Isn't he?

"No, and lunch is ready and David's coming back specially."

"OK. I'll just go and put on a dress. Won't be more than a couple of minutes," Jenny said, "and I'm sure Andrew won't be long wherever he is."

Andrew was, at that moment, striding down a path through the trees above the house. Kidding himself that he must take some photographs of the countryside before he went home, he had set off soon after breakfast and climbed up above the trees until he reached the bottom of the cliffs. There, in the shade of a boulder, he sat down to think.

Two subjects dominated his thoughts. What was he to do about Thomas Saddler, and the new light his papers had thrown on the Bourbon legacy story? A story which had always been taken with a grain of salt by the family, but now perhaps should be revisited in a more serious vein; and that, he decided, after an hour's thought, was exactly what he would suggest to them.

His second problem was more serious and, he thought, more difficult to solve. It was what to do about his relationship with Jenny? That he was in love with her there could be no doubt and as he pondered this point, it suddenly came to him that there was only one thing to do, and that was to marry her, and the details of how this was to be achieved could wait. So, having reached decisions on both his pressing problems, he picked up his stick and set off briskly down the hill towards the house.

A short while later Jenny, now wearing a white skirt with a red and white striped shirt, walked into the hall and found a scene of considerable activity. David, very smart in tan suit with collar and tie, was trying to urge people towards a table that had been laid in the shade of the inner verandah.

"Come on," he was saying, "no time for a drink. Have to make do with a glass of wine with lunch. Ann, are we ready?"

Ann at that moment was trying to talk to Andrew who, having run the last five hundred yards down the hill, was hot and out of breath.

"Yes it's all on the table," she said. "Go ahead and help yourselves. Andrew will join us as soon as he's got his breath back." Then to Andrew she added, "Don't bother about David, he's always like this before an important meeting. Have a wash and I'll get you a proper drink. Go on, before they all start asking where you've been."

"Well I like that," said Jenny. "Not a word to anyone except you. Where had he been?"

"Don't know. Didn't ask him, but no doubt he'll tell us when he's ready." And sharp on his cue Andrew re-appeared, to be handed a glass of something long and cool by Ann. He looked at her with a twinkle in his eye.

"Why all this spoiling?" he asked, noting Jenny's glare.

"Oh, I think you deserve it," Ann said. "This is supposed to be your holiday, and yet you've been working harder than anyone. Then as soon as you sit down, the vultures come crowding in wanting to know where you've been and what you are going to do next."

Before he could reply, Jenny burst out, "Well, what have you been doing? And why didn't you tell me you were going out? I might have liked to come with you."

"Just let me finish my drink and I'll tell you everything," he said. Then, putting down the empty glass, he went on, "Now I know David's in a hurry, so I'll start with last night, for I never told him the full story."

"Good man," David said, "and for that you deserve a glass of wine."

Having tasted the wine and made a suitably appreciative comment, Andrew started his story by describing how he'd looked up at the monument from the edge of the wood and had seen a man studying the plinth. Somewhat taken aback by this, and knowing that he must not be discovered, he decided that the man, whoever he was, must be got out of the way with minimum fuss. He therefore worked his way through the wood until he was above the monument and then, with the aid of a convenient ridge, he was able to get within a foot of his victim.

"I tapped him on the shoulder and said 'Boo' or words to that effect. He gave one yelp and turned, then before he could make any trouble, I hit him hard, and that was him out for the count! I risked the torch to make sure I hadn't damaged him too much, and also to replace the tube in its hiding place. Then I turned him over and had a good look at his face. As I had no idea how long he'd been there, whether he had an accomplice or whether he might have disturbed anyone or set off any alarms, I didn't hang about. I beat a hasty retreat to the wood and made my way, keeping under cover, back to the car."

"Have you any idea who he might be?" asked David. "You were very non-committal last night."

"Last night I had no idea who he was. All I knew was that I had a lurking suspicion I had seen him before, and this morning I realised where." Turning to Jenny he said, "Do you remember almost bumping into a man as we left that restaurant in Franschhoek? Well, I am sure it was he that I saw at the monument last night."

"But why was he there?" Jenny asked.

"Well I think we must assume he was after the same thing as we are, though who he is and how he knows, I've no idea."

"And what were you doing this morning? Why didn't you tell me you were going out?"

"I wanted to do some quiet thinking and I wanted to do it alone." And before a furious-looking Jenny could interrupt, Andrew held up his hand and said, "Now just calm down and listen. I had to decide whether to go on with this treasure hunt and to consider what that may entail, particularly now that there appears to be a rival party interested. Then, having decided one way or the other, I had to think about my next move. I wanted to do all this free from interruption and that was why I took off into the hills. And now let me tell you my conclusions."

The appearance of another party with an apparent interest in his doings, he decided, left him with no alternative but to follow up the clues they already had and to see if there really was a Bourbon legacy. To do anything else would be less than fair to his late wife's family who, if Thomas Saddler was to be believed, were the heirs to this legacy.

"If this legacy, jewels and whatever else there may be, really does exist," he concluded, "we cannot allow it to fall into the wrong hands."

"Agreed," said David, and Jenny, who had recovered her equanimity, nodded.

"So what is your plan?" she asked.

"There doesn't seem to be anything more to be done here," Andrew replied, and went on to say that he had definitely decided to return to England in a couple of days' time. Apart from the need to attend to his business, he was certain that it was in England that the solution to the various clues would be found.

"I must go to Passford and talk to Wilfred and see if he can make sense of the reference to Eliza and 'poor Toby'. Then we've got the Marie Antoinette note. The mention in that of The Sign of the Stag and a rich Englishman smacks to me of eighteenth-century bankers, so I must consult my City friends."

"And what about me, darling?" Jenny asked. "Am I now out of it, doomed to watch the story unfold from six thousand miles away?"

"Well, it's rather up to you what you do, but it would be helpful if you stayed on here for a bit, for we need to know if our unknown friends take any further action. Also, why don't you to go ahead with your visit to Natal? Then, depending a bit on how I get on, why don't you come over to England in three or four weeks' time?"

"Sounds good sense to me," said David, "but I must leave you to decide. Duty calls, so see you this evening."

After David left, Ann also excused herself, and beckoning to Jenny, led her from the room.

"Look it's not for me to interfere," she said to her sister-in-law, "but if I was you I think I would agree with Andrew's plans. I realise how you feel about each other, but you must bear in mind that he's a busy man with much to think about. Apart from the Saddler thing, as soon as he gets home he's going to have a lot to do at the brewery. He's been away for a month and, apart from that, he'll have all the business he did out here to deal with. When he's got that cleared, he'll need some time with the Saddler relations. Then, when he's ready, I'm sure he'll be in touch with you. That's the time to go to England." Finally, after another half hour of discussion, Ann made her point, and Jenny agreed that she would stick to her plan to visit the van Stadens.

Andrew, meanwhile, had retired to a more comfortable chair, and after an unsuccessful attempt to read a magazine, had fallen fast asleep and that was how Jenny found him some two hours later.

"Come on, wake up," she said shaking his shoulder. "We've got visitors – a man and a woman. She asked for you. Says she thinks you're some sort of relation. Can't say I care for the look of the man – the sort my father would have called a bounder!"

Andrew struggled to his feet, straightened his hair and tried to adjust his mind to a strange woman seeking him out in the Cape wine country.

"Can't imagine who she can be," he said, "so we'd better go and see. Where are they? In the hall?" Jenny nodded and they walked through to where the couple were standing, looking out at the view across the fields of vines towards the distant mountains.

At their approach, the woman turned and held out her hand. "This is the most beautiful place you have here," she said.

Andrew took the hand and said with a smile, "Indeed it is, but I'm afraid it's not mine." Then looking at Jenny, he went on, "I think you have already met Jenny Stanley and the farm belongs to her brother. I'm Andrew Henderson, and I gather that you think you know me."

"Well, not quite know you, rather I've made a guess as to who you are," the woman said, and Andrew noticed the faint trace of a foreign accent. "My name is Annette Barry and my husband James, from whom I'm parted, is a distant cousin of Wilfred Saddler."

"I see," Andrew replied cautiously. "Well, since you've guessed who I am, you probably realise that Wilfred is a cousin of my late wife. I never knew James Barry, but I think I've heard the family mention him."

"So you are the Andrew who was married to Alice? Yes? Ah, we wondered that when we heard the name at one of the places down the road. Oh! And I'm so sorry, this is my friend Caspar Boscawen." The heavily built man with the red face came forward and shook hands.

At that moment, Ann came in, and after introductions, led them all out onto the terrace. "Tea is just coming," she said, "so please find yourselves a seat."

During tea, Annette, with some skill, led the conversation to other members of the Saddler family who'd been to the Cape. Andrew, who was now definitely suspicious of the visitors, refused to be drawn but did some-what mischievously ask Annette whether they had any special reason for visiting South Africa. "A family search party, perhaps?" was how he put it.

"No, not really. My friends in Cape Town have been asking us for some time when we were going to come out and see them," Annette said, "so we spent some time with them, and then I had an urge to find out about the

72

Cape vineyards. I'm French, you see, and come from the Loire Valley. Then I suddenly remembered my husband talking about a family story. Something about jewellery from India that was being taken back to England and was lost on the way, possibly out here. Were you ever told anything like that?"

"No, but I do remember Wilfred saying something about heirlooms in India. If my memory serves me right, he said they had been left to some relations in Hong Kong. I believe there are some of that family now living in Scotland."

After another half hour of family conversation, Andrew turned to Ann and said that they ought to be thinking of changing if they were going out to that drinks party and then to dinner. Annette took the hint, and amid general expressions of goodwill Andrew saw them out to their car.

"Well, at least we now know who the enemy is," Andrew said when he rejoined them on the terrace, "and I'll bet the chap at the monument is part of them. They were obviously fishing for information but fortunately the mention of James Barry made me suspicious from the start. He was indeed a cousin, but was something of a black sheep and certainly not a friend of Wilfred's or of father-in-law's. Also I must admit I didn't take to Mr Boscawen.

"By the way, what I said about Hong Kong is partly true and I rather wish I hadn't mentioned it," he added, getting to his feet, "for there are still connections living in Scotland. Strangely enough, I once worked for one of them, and I think he might be able to give us quite a bit of help; I must talk to him." Then, with a grin, he said, "Now having told a whopping great lie to get rid of them, suppose I was to salve my conscience by taking you all out to dinner?"

CHAPTER 11

TWO DAYS LATER ANDREW WAS SAFELY ENSCONCED in a window seat in the upper cabin of a British Airways 747 on the night flight from Cape Town to London Heathrow, enjoying a quiet drink and catching up on the news in the previous day's English papers.

The flight had proved entirely uneventful except for that extraordinary dream; and after the stewardess had woken him with the glass of orange juice he tried to remember it, but it was no good, it had gone. All that remained was a hazy picture of two people kissing and one wore a crown. Could the Queen of France be trying to tell him something? He was still thinking about it when they landed at Heathrow, but then the business of passport, luggage and Customs put the whole thing out of his mind.

At the barrier his chauffeur greeted him and took the luggage, saying, "Nice to have you back, sir. You're right on time so I guess you had a good flight."

Then, once the bags were stowed in the car and with Andrew in the passenger seat, the chauffeur turned and asked, "Where to, sir? The flat?"

Now one of the advantages of a brewery in Gunnersbury is that it is only a short drive from Heathrow, and if you happen to be the Chairman there are some additional benefits. You have a dressing room and bathroom, and if you are sensible you keep a change of clothes there.

"No, Jim, let's go straight to the brewery. I can have a bath and change there and then have a few minutes to collect my thoughts before everyone arrives. Anything exciting happened while I've been away?"

"Not really, sir," the chauffeur replied. "Mavis in Accounts, that's her with the red hair, she had twins. Bobby Winslow scored a hat trick in the match against Fullers. Oh yes, and one of the lads in the boiler house won

74

a thousand quid in the Lottery. Cheesed off he was – thought it should have been a million!"

And so the list of trivial, but to the staff important, happenings went on until they reached Gunnersbury, by which time Andrew felt he was well briefed on the social and domestic affairs of his employees.

At the brewery he was welcomed by the commissionaire, who had just come on duty.

"Yes, Tom, it's good to be back," he said in reply to the greeting. Then in response to various requests for instructions, he added, "Tom, if you'd take the small suitcase up to the office – no, leave the briefcase – I'll take that. And Jim, I'm not sure yet when I'll need you again, but leave the rest of the luggage in the car. Angela will let you know when I want you."

Once up in the directors' area, he retired to the dressing room and having bathed and changed into a clean shirt, suit and well-polished black shoes, he emerged into his office to find that his secretary had arrived.

Angela Richardson was a good-looking woman of about forty-five who had been with Henderson Braithwaite since she was seventeen. She had been secretary to Andrew's father for his last two years as Chairman, and she had met his grandfather, old Sir James, as he was known, when he used to visit the brewery after his retirement. Not surprisingly, she knew as much about the workings of the company as anyone there, and ran the Chairman's office, and indeed Andrew himself, with a calm efficiency.

"'Morning, Angela," he called. "You got my e-mail, I hope; so, what have you organised for me today?"

"Good morning, Mr Henderson. I hope you had a really good holiday, although judging by all the messages you sent us, you seem to have spent most of the time working." All this was said as she walked across to stand by his desk, then taking her seat beside him, she went on: "Yes, I got the e-mail and I've warned Mr Tony that you'd want to see him first thing. Then Hedley Strawson wants to see you as soon as possible, and Frank Walker. I also think you should see Personnel today. They have one or two problems which Mr Tony will tell you about. Here's the provisional programme I've arranged for you," and she laid a sheet of paper on the desk. Andrew read it through, made a couple of pencil notes and then looked up.

"Fine, except that I think we'll have to put off Personnel until after lunch," he said. "Now, let's get Tony in, and I'd like you to stay. Before we get down to business I've got a rather extraordinary story I want you both to hear. After that Tony can bring me up to date, and then I'll see the others. Hedley first, then a quick word with Frank," he added, naming the technical and finance directors. "After that you and I should look at any important papers awaiting my attention. Oh yes, and I assume there's a Board Meeting on Thursday, so tomorrow I'll need to spend time with Jason." Jason Porter being the company secretary and a lawyer.

"I have provisionally fixed that, and I think you'll need him this afternoon when you see Personnel."

At that moment there was a knock and Tony Henderson put his head round the door. "Welcome back to the travelling man," he said, "and you certainly have been a busy little bee while you've been away."

"Come in, Tony, and sit down. There's something I want to tell you and Angela before we get down to business."

"Oh Lord! I suppose you've got yourself into trouble with that girl. Going to marry her, are you?" Tony asked, and got a disapproving glare from Angela.

"Really, Mr Tony! That's no way to talk to the Chairman," she said.

"No, nothing like that," Andrew replied, disregarding the potential argument. "It concerns Alice's family and the story of a secret legacy, a story that up till now has always been taken with a considerable pinch of salt. Well, quite by accident I have discovered evidence that makes me think the story is true. If it is, it seems we may be dealing with a legacy of considerable value, and in fairness to the family, the evidence must be investigated further, and I propose to do just that."

Tony Henderson raised his eyes to the ceiling and let out a groan. "Buried treasure we're into now, are we? Where will this man's ambitions end?" he said.

"Shut up, Tony! Just be serious for a few minutes while I tell you the story," Andrew replied. "No, it's not buried treasure," and he paused, "although on second thoughts it just might be, so listen to what I have to say."

For the next twenty-five minutes his audience listened with interest and increasing astonishment while he told them about what had happened during his stay at Neder Paarl.

"So you see," he said in conclusion, "I have two lines of enquiry to pursue. First, where are the jewels? It sounds as though they are at Passford, or somewhere near, so I shall have to go and talk to the family. Secondly, there is the paper I found in the tube. The only real clue it contains is this address: 'at The Sign of the Stag', and to find someone who can make sense of that I'll have to visit our friends in the City. Now all this is going to take time and I have no idea what it may lead to. It could be that over the next month or two, I shall need to be away quite a lot. When I can, I shall continue to come into the office. When I'm away you, Tony, will be in charge but I will always be accessible and will communicate through you, Angela. I don't want anyone else to know what I have just told you. Remember, there appear to be other people interested, so just let's say I have a tiresome problem concerning Uncle Edward's estate in Lincolnshire."

"Fascinating," said Tony, "and I wish you luck, but I think you've got quite a problem. When are you going to start?"

"I'll be in the office for the rest of this week, for I'd better be up to speed on what's been happening here. Also there's work to be done on the South Africa contracts. I'll go to Passford at the weekend and I'll ring you at home, Tony, and let you know my plans and you can tell Angela. Then I'll see you both some time on Monday. Now let's get to work. Tony, you tell me all that's happened since I've been away, and Angela, let Hedley know I'll see him in fifty minutes."

By half past six that evening, Andrew, feeling that he was now back in control of his business, rang Security and asked them to warn his chauffeur that he would be leaving in ten minutes. Then, as he walked down the passage, he met his cousin emerging from his office.

"Look, Andrew," he said, "why don't you come round and have a quick supper with us? I know Phyllis would love to see you and hear all about South Africa." An offer which Andrew accepted with alacrity as, not knowing what time he'd be home, he'd told his housekeeper that he'd look after himself. He did, however, smile to himself over the idea of Phyllis wanting to hear about South Africa, for he knew perfectly well that what she really wanted to hear about was the state of play between himself and Jenny.

Living in Chelsea and working in Gunnersbury means that you are normally going against the main commuter traffic. So barely twenty minutes later, Jim was helping Andrew take his luggage up to his third-floor flat.

"That'll be all, Jim," he said. "I'll get a taxi to Mr Tony's. Seven forty-five tomorrow – to the brewery, yes – and then I've a lunch at the Savoy. Good night."

Andrew Henderson had what house agents are pleased to call a luxury flat in a nineteen thirties block just off the King's Road. The furniture was a comfortable mixture of modern and antique, but what distinguished it from the homes of many other rich and successful men was his renowned collection of modern English landscapes.

Having shut the door, he looked round with that sense of satisfaction that comes with finding oneself home after an absence of several weeks. He unpacked only what he knew he needed and left the rest in the hope that Marg, his Austrian housekeeper, would deal with it in the morning. Then he had a quick shower and put on blazer and flannels and sat down to ring Wilfred Saddler.

After giving a very brief account of his doings in South Africa, as they concerned the Saddler family, and listening to Wilfred's surprise, he suggested that he should go up to Passford for the weekend.

"Delighted to see you," was the reply, "although I'm not sure what you can achieve here."

"Just wait until you hear the full story. I don't want to tell more on the telephone for reasons which will become clear when we meet," Andrew said. "What I shall really need, I think, is a much better idea of the history of the Saddler family and also a feel for the topography of the Passford Estate."

"Well none of that should be difficult. See you then on Saturday in time for lunch."

Andrew replaced the receiver and looked up at the clock above the fireplace, decided he hadn't time to make any more calls, so went down and took a cab to his cousin's house off Kensington Church Street.

At the door, he found himself entwined and kissed extravagantly by Phyllis. "Andrew, darling, how are you?" she said in her high-pitched drawl. "Come up and tell me all about what you've been doing down in the Cape. Tony says you've been having a wonderful time."

Andrew, used to Phyllis's exotic ways, gently disentangled himself, and followed her upstairs to the drawing room. There he found Tony standing ready by the drinks tray.

"Whisky?" he asked, and Andrew nodded, took the glass and perched himself on the club fender and for the next twenty minutes conversation was fairly general, until Phyllis got to her feet.

"Come on now," she said, "dinner's ready, so let's eat," and led the way down to the kitchen.

As Andrew had suspected, it was not long before Phyllis turned her large expressive eyes on him.

"Now, darling," she said, "tell me all about your doings in South Africa. Not that boring detective work that Tony hinted at or all the marvellous deals you completed. Tell me about Jenny and her family. What's their farm like? And are they very rich?"

"Really, Phyllis!" her husband said; even after twenty years, he was sometimes surprised by his wife's lack of tact. "You can't expect Andrew to answer that."

"Nevertheless, I will," Andrew replied. "I don't know exactly how many hectares they have, but as vineyards go it's large. As to wealth – well, they have a wonderful state of the art winery and extensive cellars, and are probably in the top six of Cape wine producers."

"So she'd make a good wife for you. I like the idea of a vineyard in the family. So much more romantic than a boring old brewery."

Her husband cast a despairing glance at the ceiling and Andrew smiled. "My dear Phyllis," he replied, "whoever said anything about marriage? Jenny is South African and I've no idea whether she'd want to leave the country. It's a wonderful place to live, despite its problems."

"There you are, I knew it," Phyllis said triumphantly. "First it's the country. It won't be long before it's Jenny."

"Well, she will be coming over here in a month's time. So let's just leave it at that."

Realising that Andrew wished to put an end to Phyllis's speculation, Tony seized on the subject of South Africa as a place to live and got Andrew to give his opinion of the current political situation out there. This, together with some purely family chat, lasted until Andrew, who was beginning to yawn, said he must go.

Despite the exhaustion of a night flight and a full day's work, he lay awake for some time thinking about what Phyllis had said. He finally fell asleep having concluded that when Jenny arrived in England in a few weeks' time, he would have some important decisions to make.

CHAPTER 12

TWO DAYS BEFORE SHE WAS DUE TO leave for Natal, Jenny had reason to visit Stellenbosch, and as she was about to enter one of the University buildings, she heard her name called. She turned and saw Annette Barry.

"What a pleasant surprise," Annette said. "I thought you'd gone back to England."

"No, Andrew's gone back and I may join him later. I'm off in a couple of days to KwaZulu-Natal to stay with my cousins."

"Ah yes, I remember now that you said you were. I've never been up there. Where is it you're going?"

"Mooi River. We have extensive farming interests in the area," Jenny replied. "But look, I must fly now. I've got an appointment in here and I'm already late. Nice to have seen you, and perhaps we'll meet again sometime." And she vanished into the building.

Finding out where Jenny was going was something of a lucky break and Annette determined to take advantage of it. Back in the hotel, she toyed with a number of possibilities and finally decided, despite certain misgivings, to get Caspar to follow Jenny and see if he could discover what she and Andrew had found out. So after dinner, having settled him down with a glass of brandy, she put the idea to Caspar.

"Look," she said, pointing to a map, "here's Mooi River. Go up there and find out where she's staying. She said she was going to see her cousins who have an extensive property. If that is so, and the owners are cousins of the Stanleys, somebody's bound to know where they live."

"Sure, I've no doubt I can find the place quite easily," Boscawen agreed, "but why don't you go yourself? You're far better than me at getting information from people."

81

"Because I have other things to do," Annette replied, "including having a serious talk to our friend Jean. Like you, I don't entirely trust him, and I believe he's holding back information. No, I think it will have to be you who goes and you shouldn't have much of a problem. Once you know where she's staying, watch where she goes – what she does – then surely you can organise an accidental meeting; in a local shop perhaps. Invite her for coffee or a drink and get her talking. Use your charm – you've got plenty – and you use it well when you want to. But hold off the blustering bully act. She's not a fool and she'll see through that. And I wouldn't get too close to her friends."

"Okay, okay, but just remember I'm not a fool either," Boscawen said. "I'll do it but I'll do it my way, and I promise you'll get results. I'll need to get a car though, and I'll need to stay somewhere. You'll have to give me some money, for I'm running a bit short."

"That's alright. You get the car tomorrow and I'll get some money," Annette said. "Now, I think she's leaving the day after tomorrow. I don't know how she's going, but you'd better start tomorrow afternoon."

The van Staden estate consists of some five thousand hectares of rolling grassland. To the west are the foothills of the Drakensberg and the southern part of the estate is bisected by the Mooi River, the wooded banks of which are home to a wonderful variety of bird life.

The house stands at the top of a steep slope some way back from the north bank of the river and some two hundred yards below, on the edge of a bluff, there is a small wooden building with a wide verandah making it an ideal place from which to watch the endless wildlife activity of the riverbank. Jenny, who was sitting in the deep shadow at the back of the verandah watching the antics of the weaver birds on an overhanging bush on the opposite bank of the river, had just put down her binoculars and picked up a book, when she heard footsteps crossing the room behind her and an obviously English voice asking to come in.

She turned to see a man who seemed vaguely familiar standing in the entrance to the verandah.

"I'm sorry to intrude on you like this," he said, and added, "I'm Caspar Boscawen. You may remember we met at your home last week. I was with Annette Barry."

"Yes, of course. I remember she had some family connection to Andrew Henderson," Jenny replied, remembering only too well that she had told Annette where she was going when they met in Stellenbosch. She hadn't cared much for the look of the man when she saw him at Neder Paarl, and now she felt a definite revulsion. However, feeling she must keep up her original air of surprise, she went on, "How on earth did you find me here? And how did you get in? My cousins are away for the day and the boys should not have let anyone in." And as she said that, she realised it was probably a mistake.

"If you really want to know, I saw you in the town yesterday and thought I recognised you. When I asked in the hotel, they said you were Miss Stanley who often came here to stay at the van Staden place. Then they obligingly told me how to find it."

"Yes, but then how did you find me down here?"

"Ah, that was easy," Boscawen replied. "I left my car up that side track short of the house and walked down towards some wooden buildings where I found one of your boys. 'Quick!' I said, 'I have an urgent message for Miss Stanley. Where is she?' Then for good measure, I added that I was her brother. The boy looked at me a bit strangely, but pointed to this building and I walked briskly down here."

Fear now began to take the place of revulsion, for she realised that he was lying. For a start, many of the boys spoke only Zulu and if it had been one who understood English he would have referred any stranger to the house.

"What would you have done if they'd said I was in the house?" Jenny said, trying not to show her fear. "And anyway, why are you here? I should hardly have thought we were on social calling terms, so what do you want?"

Boscawen pulled up a chair and sat down, adding as an afterthought, "May I?" and when Jenny nodded he continued, "I was very intrigued with the story that your friend and Annette were discussing. You remember – all that business about the French and jewels and India. I've always been interested in family histories and I wondered if you could tell me any more about it, particularly how South Africa comes into it, and wasn't Hong Kong mentioned? Annette seemed interested in that part of the story."

Jenny looked at the florid face, the close-set eyes and a mouth which was both mean and lascivious. Not the face of a man who has ever been interested in family history, she thought, and decided that he'd been sent by the Frenchwoman to see if he could find out any more about what Andrew might have discovered. She was also beginning to think that he had other ideas of his own and that she was some way from any help. Well, there was nothing for it; she'd have to play for time.

"You realise it's not my family," she said, "so I can tell very little. In fact, I've heard little more myself than you and Annette did that afternoon. But can I ask why you are interested? Do you think there's some truth in these stories?"

"Of course there's bloody truth in the story," he almost shouted, leaning towards her, "and you damned well know it. You and that boyfriend of yours, you've been searching for something and I'm going to find out what."

"Mr Boscawen, please do not shout at me," Jenny answered, jumping up and reaching for the rope on a large brass bell. "I have already told you I know little of the story you are talking about, and I have not been searching for anything – and even if I had, I would not tell you about it. Certainly not while you're in this mood." And with that she rang the bell violently. Boscawen left his chair and lurched towards her, grabbing her arm to try to stop the furious clamour.

"Stop that row," he said quite quietly now, "and don't shout either. Not that I think anyone would hear. I did a careful recce before I came out here and there didn't seem to be anyone about. Now don't struggle or you might get hurt more than necessary," and he brought up his right hand and she felt the blade of a knife against her left cheek. Against his strength, she could do nothing, and so she let herself go limp and hoped that the boys had come back with the horses and had heard the bell.

He let go of her arm, and still keeping the knife at her face he pushed her back into the chair and leaned down towards her. Putting his free hand inside her shirt, he ripped it open down to the waist. He was now breathing hard and he pushed his face towards her.

"That stupid bitch sent me to ask you questions, and she believed I would do just that. Yes, she's after the jewels – and something else, she thinks. She's guessed lover boy has found out something and she wants to know what. Perhaps I'll find out for her," he said and then continued in a kind of hissing whisper, far more frightening than his shouting, "but I had other ideas in coming here. Ideas that came to me when I first saw you. I've been watching you and I saw you come down here. Yes, I did meet one of your boys and I'm sorry, but I had to dispose of him. So you see we're all alone and no one knows I'm here."

He reached down and she felt the knife cut the waistband of her shorts, then he straightened and felt for the buckle of his belt, and as he did so his foot caught in a gap between two of the floorboards. He staggered and raised his arms to regain his balance. Jenny's foot caught him fairly between the legs, and even without shoes it must have been agonising. He gave a gasping moan and doubled up clutching himself, the knife clattering to the floor.

Jenny screamed for help at the top of her voice and went on screaming hysterically. Boscawen struggled up and reached for the fallen knife, when there was a loud shout – "Alright, Miss, I'm here!" – and the powerful figure of Mzumi, the head boy, vaulted over the side rail of the verandah. Caspar turned, and as he leapt towards Mzumi his knee caught the edge of the table and he crashed into the front balustrade. Not meant for that sort of treatment, the flimsy woodwork gave way precipitating Caspar head first into the river.

"Oh my God, Mzumi!" Jenny yelled. "We must get him out! I saw that big croc down there half an hour ago. Please, please do something. We can't leave him to die like that."

But from the river there already came the sound of a large body thrashing about, a terrified screaming and a final despairing shriek.

"Miss, I think we're too late," said Mzumi, peering down at the river, where a red stain was spreading across the surface of the water. Then moments later, with a final lash of the tail, the crocodile emerged onto the far bank with an unspeakable bloody mess in its jaws.

Even Mzumi, who in his life had seen nearly every kind of savagery that men and animals can inflict on each other, was shaken by the terrible fate of Caspar Boscawen and, for a moment, leaned weakly against the rail.

"Induna, what... Oh no, not that!" Jenny's faint voice roused him and as he turned towards her, her legs gave way and she fell unconscious to the floor. In one stride he was at her side. She was deathly pale but he could see she was breathing. She was also half-naked from Caspar's mauling, something which offended his sense of propriety. Looking round, he twitched the gaily-coloured cloth from the table and wrapped it round her. Then he picked her up and carried her from the hut and up the track to the lodge as though she was a baby.

As he walked through the open french windows he shouted, "Mama, come quick!" and moments later the van Staden's nanny, who had served them for over thirty years, came through from the back quarters. As soon as she saw Jenny she unleashed a volley of Zulu at Mzumi and he replied in the same tongue. Finally she turned and led the way down a passage and into a bedroom. Mzumi laid Jenny on the bed and was then subjected to a further series of instructions, before being chased from the room by Mama.

It was some fifty minutes later that Jan and Betty van Staden returned to find the house in a state of chaos. Mama was weeping and saying Miss Jenny was dying and they must get the doctor. The big Zulu head boy, who had now got himself completely under control, was leaning against the wall saying that there had been terrible happenings and he must talk at once to the Master, and they would maybe need the police.

"Betty, go with Mama and see what's happened to Jenny," said Jan, taking instant control of the situation. "I'll talk to the Induna and find out what this is all about." Then turning to Mzumi he told him to go to the office and wait.

"God knows what's happened," he added to his wife. "You'd better ring the doctor anyway, even if he's not needed. Then I'll come and see you as soon as I've got some sense out of Mzumi."

In the office, Jan found an unhappy-looking Mzumi standing by the window and waved him to a chair. Knowing the boy would be more likely to talk if he kept the interview informal, he sat himself on the edge of the desk.

"Now," he said in Zulu, "tell me exactly what happened to Miss Jenny this afternoon. I gather there was some sort of accident at the river hut?"

Bit by bit and with much prompting Jan managed to extract the following story: after lunch, about one-thirty, he thought, Mzumi had heard Miss Jenny say she was going down to the river hut. About an hour later, one of the boys had told him that he had seen a strange white man behaving suspiciously.

Mzumi himself was busy and so told the boy to find out what the man wanted. Some time later – he was not sure how long – he heard a commotion from the direction of the hut, and then Jenny screaming. He had raced down the path and jumped onto the balcony.

"There was a big white man there, bending over Miss Jenny, and her clothes were all undone. I think he was going to rape her. As I landed on the verandah he jumped at me, tripped and went through the railings into the river. Miss Jenny shouted that she'd seen a big crocodile there earlier. She was right, for almost at once I heard its tail thrashing and the man screaming. Then the croc came out on the far bank. It had part of a body in its mouth."

"What happened then?" Jan asked.

"Miss Jenny fainted. I carried her to the house and left her with Mama. I myself took two boys and the rifle and went down to the river. No sign of the crocodile, but we found the body. The man was already dead and the beast had taken his legs. We brought the body back and it is in one of the sheds."

"We'll have to get the police – and try to find out who he is and why he was here."

And before Jan could say more, Mzumi interrupted. "That's not all. When we got back with the body, I was told that one of the new boys was lying dead in the trees behind the sheds. It was the boy I'd sent to find the man. The bastard must have killed him."

"Have you dealt with the family? Good man. Well, see what else you can do. I'll have to tell Captain Hansie and he'll want to see you no doubt. Then I must see how Miss Jenny is and whether she can tell us anything about the man."

Having phoned the police, Jan walked back to the main part of the house where he found his wife in the hall.

"Jenny's conscious," she said, "but in no state to tell us anything. She's obviously had a terrible shock. Keeps saying 'don't let him near me' and 'oh no... not that. Mzumi – Induna, the crocodile – do something.' She must have a sedative or a sleeping pill or something, so I've sent for Doctor Matthews and he's promised to come as soon as he can."

Jan gave her a brief account of what he'd learnt from the head boy. "I've sent for the police," he added, "and Hansie will be along directly. He can talk to Mzumi and deal with the bodies. He'll have to come back tomorrow to talk to Jenny. Let's hope she can throw some light on this very nasty affair."

Some three hours later, the big fair-haired police captain, who'd once played rugby for the Transvaal, having finished his investigations walked up to the house.

"Come in, Hansie, come in," Jan said, ushering him into the sitting room, "and tell us what you think happened."

The policeman greeted Betty, who pointed to a chair. "Yes, Hansie," she said, "what do you think it's all about?"

"What it's about I can't tell you, not at least until I've talked to Miss Stanley."

"That won't be until tomorrow afternoon at the earliest," Betty said. "She's heavily sedated and Doctor Matthews said she's not to be disturbed until he's seen her again."

"Well, let's hope she can throw some light on the matter," the captain said. "Anyway, as far as I can establish, here's what happened. This man parked his car back down the road sometime in the morning. He then discovered, I'm not sure how, that you were away and Jenny was alone. I think he knows Jenny, for he spent a long time watching her movements. This is partly conjecture, for the boy who saw him is the one who's dead. He's the one your Induna sent to find out what the man wanted and who was killed, presumably to prevent him raising the alarm. The rest you know from Mzumi. What we don't know is whether the man was there purely to rape Jenny or for some other purpose to which the sexual assault was incidental. Now, if you'll excuse me, I have many administrative details to attend to; one of which is to identify the white man and find out about next of kin. Perhaps Miss Stanley may be able to help."

The policeman got to his feet, and refusing a drink, said goodbye to Mrs van Staden and walked out to his car, accompanied by Jan.

"I'll ring you in the morning," the latter said, "and let you know when you can come and see Jenny."

By ten o'clock the next morning Jenny had recovered sufficiently to talk to her host and hostess, which she did sitting up in bed.

"Look, I'm sorry all this should have happened," she said, "and yes, I can tell you who the man was and why he was here. You remember I told you about Andrew Henderson and the papers we found in the museum at Franschhoek and the family stories of legacies and treasure. Well, the man who attacked me was called Caspar Boscawen and was a friend – lover, probably – of a Frenchwoman, Mrs Annette Barry, who is also somehow connected with the family. She sent that man up here to see if I would tell him about the papers and anything else we found. When I refused, he attacked me, hoping I would tell rather than submit, or maybe he just intended to rape me. If he hadn't slipped and the Mzumi hadn't come back and heard the bell and my shouts, that's what he might have done. I'd rather not talk about the rest if you don't mind."

"Poor darling," Betty said, "it's for us to be sorry it should have happened here on our estate. Do you know where that man was staying, because that's what the police want to know?"

"Yes, I think so. I saw the woman come out of the big hotel in Stellenbosch, the Dorp Street I think it's called."

"Assuming the doctor agrees when he sees you, do you feel well enough to talk to Captain Hansie this afternoon?" Jan asked. "He'll want to know about the man and about Mrs Barry. He'll have to break the news to her, I suppose. I think you'll also have to tell him how you come to know Boscawen. I shouldn't be too specific. Just say you think he wanted some family information that he thought you had. Then, if you can bear it, I would say something like 'If you really want to know, I think it was me he wanted.' As the poor man is dead, I don't think the police will pursue the matter any further. They have better things to do."

CHAPTER 13

ARLY ON THE DAY AFTER BOSCAWEN HAD gone to the van Staden Estate, Annette Barry, who had spent two days with friends in Cape Town, finally got around to visiting the Huguenot Museum in Franschhoek to enquire if they had any records of a family called Jordaine.

"What is so interesting about this family?" the woman behind the desk said. "You're the third person to ask about them in the last ten days. In fact, I've still got the box here. Haven't had time to put it away. Do you want to have a look at it? I've no idea what's in it, but the last man took it home."

"What was he like, this man?" Annette asked.

"Oh, tall and rather good-looking, and he had a girl with him. He was English but she was local, I think," the woman replied and then asked, "Are you French? Huguenot perhaps?"

"Française, oui, mais Huguenot, non," Annette said with a smile, then reverting to English added, "But the couple you were describing and I both have an interest in certain Huguenot families and Jordaine is one. May I have a quick look at this?" and she picked up the box and walked over to a chair.

After a brief shuffle through the papers, she pulled out the letter with the Saddler name and address and read it. Then she flipped through the black leather book; finally she put the box aside and lay back with her eyes half closed.

"Well that's interesting," she said to herself. "So a Saddler was in this part of the world, apparently visiting a friend called Jordaine, and these papers of his have been lying around here for the last hundred and fifty years. Andrew must have found them by accident, realised their significance and has obviously learnt something of interest from them. Well, since he's done all the work, I guess I don't need to do anything except follow him and see what he does next. I think that will mean a return to England; but first I must see Jean and find out what he knows and hasn't told."

She reached down, picked up the box and took it back to the entrance desk. Then, having thanked the woman in charge and said that what she had seen had been most helpful, she walked to the car park and, noticing that it was lunchtime, drove to Jean's hotel where she found him just about to go out.

"Come on," she said, "jump in and I'll take you out to lunch. There's a small restaurant about two miles out of town which will do nicely."

Over lunch she told him about her visit to the museum and the Saddler papers she had found.

"So you see," she said, "we're on the right track. Thomas Saddler was in this area back in the middle of the last century. I only had time for a quick look at the papers but there was a sort of notebook, and also a letter to his father in which he said he feared for his health and must tell him about the jewels. I also got the feeling that he had hidden something out here. What it might be I don't know, but I believe Henderson did find out what it was, and may even have discovered it. You said you thought he picked up something at the monument and put it in his pocket. Are you sure you don't know what it was?"

"Absolutely sure," Jean replied with some vehemence. "I told you I had no binoculars, so I could not possibly see. Well, now that you seem to be satisfied that we're not on a wild goose chase, what are we going to do? Remember there is another besides yourself who finances me. I must report to him and he's a bad man to cross."

"We're going to wait and see if Caspar has found out anything from the girl," Annette said, "then we're going back to England to find Henderson. It shouldn't be difficult as we know where he works, and anyway, I'm sure he'll make for the family home. Then we shadow him. He's done all the work so far, so let him continue."

"That's all good, but what shall I tell Le Grand Homme?"

"Just say that you now know that there is truth in the story and you are following up a clue to the whereabouts of what you believe to be jewels, and you are going to England." Here Annette paused and looked thoughtfully at the Frenchman. "I think, Jean, it might be an idea if you moved to our hotel in Stellenbosch. I'll ring and see if there's a room."

Five minutes later, she was back saying that was all fixed. "So you can check out of your hotel. Oh, and where did you get your car? Cape Town – OK, then you'd better keep it and hand it in at the airport. You go along now. I'll pay and see you later in Stellenbosch."

When he got to the hotel, Jean found a note from Annette saying she had met a friend and would not be able to have dinner with him but would see him the next morning.

It must have been well after midnight when Lemaître awoke to hear someone knocking on his door. He turned over and grunted and then he heard Annette's voice asking in French if he was awake, and could she come in and, if so, would he please hurry up?

"Un moment," he said, rolling out of bed and searching frantically for something to put on, for he slept naked. All he could find was a rather dirty waterproof, and wrapped in that he walked over to the door and opened it, keeping a foot firmly against it, but she pushed him unceremoniously aside and slipped in. She was wearing one of the hotel's towelling bathrobes and stood looking at him with a faint air of disgust.

"Don't stand there like an idiot," she said. "Shut the door, and for God's sake take off that revolting coat."

"I can't. I've got nothing on underneath."

"That's your worry," she said. "I don't mind; but if you want to save your modesty, why don't you get back into bed."

Turning his back on Annette, he slipped off the waterproof and dived beneath the sheets. "For all the world like a rabbit down a hole," she thought.

"Comfortable?" she asked, walking over and sitting on the bed. "So now, my Jean, you and I have got to have a little talk."

"Why?" he asked. "And why now? Can't it wait until morning?"

"No it can't. You see, I don't think you are playing fair with me." She got up and leaned over the bed, her robe fell open and her hand shot under the sheet and squeezed hard. He gasped and tried to pull her hand away, but she only squeezed harder. With his other hand he grabbed at her throat, but she caught his wrist.

"Now shall I castrate you or break your wrist?" But this time it was Jean who was too quick. Before she could do anything, he pulled his hand from under the bedclothes and hit out at the triangle of thick light brown hair at the base of her stomach.

She staggered back, gasping for breath. Jean leapt from the bed, but she recovered her balance, put her head down and caught him right in the solar plexus. She pushed him back onto the bed and lay on top of him, her knee in his groin.

"Mon Dieu, but she's strong," he thought as he struggled to free himself.

"Yes I am," she said, reading his thoughts, "and you haven't felt half of it yet." And, as her knee pressed harder, he could barely suppress a scream.

"So now shall we talk?" she asked. He nodded, and the pressure relaxed. "That's a good boy," she said. "If you tell the truth there'll be no more; in fact there might even be a little reward. You went back to the monument, didn't you?" He nodded. "And what did you find?" And he felt her knee press down again.

"OK, OK," he said. "Yes I did go back – and no, nobody saw me. There are two ornaments; like birds they are. One of them unscrews and there's a hole. There was a copper tube in it. Sort of thing you could hide a rolled up piece of paper in, but it was empty."

"So that's it," Annette said. "What Henderson slipped into his pocket must have been whatever was in the tube. And it must have told him something. What we have to do is find what. There, my Jean, I knew you'd be a good boy in the end, and now for some fun." And she pulled away the sheet, slipped off her robe, swung her legs onto the bed and once more lay on top of him with her legs apart and her knees well clear of his groin.

When it was all over, Jean looked down at her. "Who are you?" he asked. "Yes, I know you are Annette Barry who was married to an English aristo. But who were you in France? You know tricks that only a gamine would know."

"Careful, my little man," she said, "we don't want any more pain, do we? And I might have other tricks. Yes, I will tell you, but then you must forget it. You might have heard of me. I was once known as La Chérie."

Jean Lemaître shivered and thought what might have happened if he'd resisted. Yes, he had heard of La Chérie and he didn't like what he remembered, so he made a mental note to be careful in future.

These unpleasant thoughts were thankfully interrupted by the unexpected ringing of the telephone. Jean reached over and picked up the handset and listened.

"Oui, un moment, s'il vous plaît – hold on please," and putting his hand over the mouthpiece, he whispered to a surprised-looking Annette, "It's for you. The hotel say they can get no answer from your room and wondered if I knew where you were. They say it's urgent."

Annette sat up, swung her legs off the bed and reached for her robe. Then she took the telephone and listened for a moment.

"Yes, this is Mrs Barry," she said, "and yes, I know a Mr Boscawen." Then she listened again for a long time, while Jean watched her changing expressions. First shock, then horror, followed by a brief flash of anger, and finally her face softened and she searched for a handkerchief to wipe her eyes.

"How terrible," she said, "and thank you for telling me... Yes, of course I will let you know what is to be done about the remains. I'm sure you understand that this has been a great shock and I must have time to think. I will try to contact his relations... Yes, I will get back to you and, if necessary, I will come up. Good night, and thank you again."

She replaced the receiver and stared into space for a moment, then turned and buried her face in the pile of bedclothes at the foot of the bed. After five minutes, Jean bent down and put a hand on her shoulder.

"Hadn't you better tell me what's happened, ma petite? It's Caspar, isn't it?" he said in a surprisingly gentle voice.

She raised her head and turned towards him, wiping her eyes with the back of her hand.

"Yes, it's Caspar," she said, looking down and twisting the handkerchief in her hands. "He's dead." She remained staring at her hands for a good five minutes. Then she stood up, smoothed her robe and appeared to regain control of her emotions.

"It was my fault," she said. "I should never have trusted him," and with a sudden burst of anger she beat her hand on the back of an armchair. "Fool, fool, fool that he was. All he had to do was to get some information, and what does he do? He tries to rape the girl and finishes up in the river where a crocodile got him. Served him right! I was fond of him you know, but I don't like being let down. So now he's dead, I forget him. Now can I use your bathroom for a moment?"

When she returned, Jean asked her what she proposed to do, and in particular did she mean to continue with the search for the jewels.

"Indeed yes," she said. "We will go to England as we discussed and we will find and follow Henderson. To tell you the truth, I had in mind to drop Caspar, and now that idea has been decided for me. Pity though that we didn't get any information from the girl." Then she glanced at the clock by Jean's bed. "I'll go and lie down for an hour or two and then have a bath and dress," she added, "and by that time I can ring England and break the news to his family and find out what they want to do."

CHAPTER 14

THE SATURDAY AFTER HIS RETURN TO ENGLAND found Andrew Henderson driving through London's East End on his way to Suffolk, something which, because of the crowds and the endless series of roundabouts, required considerable concentration.

However, once he reached the A12 driving became easier and he was able to turn his mind to the conversation he'd had with Jenny on the previous evening, during which she had said that, for the first time ever, she was finding life at Neder Paarl trivial and boring. When he asked why, she had replied that she thought it was partly that there now seemed to be no place for her in the family business. Much more important, though, was the fact that he was no longer there.

"I had no idea," she had said, "how much I would miss you, and I'm almost counting the days until I can come to England. Thank heavens I'm off to the van Stadens tomorrow. Perhaps that will give me something else to think about."

That she was in love with him he now had little doubt, and in considering the many possibilities conjured up by this thought, he failed to notice that he had passed Colchester and so almost missed the turning which took him north along a river valley and then west into a country of prosperous-looking farms and gently rolling woodland.

When, after another twenty minutes, he reached the gates of Passford Hall and turned into the famous avenue of lime trees, he thought how little it had changed since his last visit over three years before.

The house is Georgian; the front door is guarded by a pillared portico and the windows on either side are framed by magnolias.

On the south-east side of the house a flat sweep of lawn leads down to a ha-ha, beyond which fields stretch away to a stream which feeds the lake, the main feature of the park. To the west of the house are the stables and from the yard a path leads to a small wood and eventually on to the lake.

Andrew parked in the shade on the right of the drive and walked slowly over to the front door and rang the bell. Almost immediately he heard footsteps and the door was opened by a surprisingly young-looking manservant.

"Good afternoon, Mr Henderson," he said, "and may I say welcome to Passford, for it's a long time since we last saw you here."

"Indeed it is, Steven, and I'm very happy to be back," Andrew replied, and looking round the hall added, "I must say little seems to have changed – and you don't look a day older yourself. And how is Mrs Jenks?"

"Ah, sir, nothing much changes hereabouts," the butler said, "and thank you, we're both keeping well. Mr Saddler is in the drawing room and said you was to go straight in. Don't worry about your case, I'll see to that." And he led the way across the hall, and opening one half of a double door announced, "Mr Andrew Henderson."

"Come in, come in, my dear Andrew," said the tall man who rose from a chair by the fireplace. Wilfred Saddler had the stooped shoulders and high forehead of the scholar, which indeed he was. However, his clear eyes and ruddy complexion displayed his other side, countryman, farmer and one of his county's most respected landowners.

"Thank you, Wilfred. And how are you?" Andrew asked, as he shook hands with his host. "I must say you look marvellous. And you too, Mary," he said, bending over and kissing an attractive white-haired woman. "But then, as I said to Steven, you keep things on an even keel up here. The whole place looks exactly as I remember it before Alice died."

"Well, we do our best, but even here things are beginning to change. Colchester is crawling ever nearer and has already swallowed up parts of some estates that are not so far away," he said as he walked across to a side table and picked up a decanter. "Sherry?" he said, filling two glasses and carrying them over and then pouring one for himself.

"Come and sit by me," Mary Saddler said, shoving a King Charles spaniel off the sofa.

"And what brings you here?" asked Wilfred. "You said something about wanting to know about Thomas and the India connection."

"Yes, and what's all this about Jenny someone or other?" Mary added. "And don't look so surprised. I had Phyllis on the phone the morning after you saw them, saying I might get more out of you than she could."

"No doubt," said Andrew with a laugh, "but that can wait."

"But lunch can't," said Wilfred, leading the way to the dining room. "Come on in, and no more business while we eat. That can wait till afterwards."

During lunch, in accordance with Wilfred's suggestion, the conversation remained general. In response to a question from Mary, Andrew told them about World Wide Wines and this led conveniently to his visit to South Africa.

"And now, Mary," he said, "I'll satisfy your curiosity. The idea for World Wide Wines came from a girl I met at a dinner party. She's South African and her name is Jenny Stanley. The family own large wine estates in the Paarl area and as the purpose of Three Ws is to introduce the English wine drinker to the delights of the New World, she suggested I go out and visit them and learn a bit about their wines."

"And did you?" Mary asked. "Or was the attraction your new girlfriend?"

"Come now, that's a bit unfair," Andrew replied with a smile. "Yes, the visit was a commercial success and I made a lot of useful contacts – and yes again, Jenny and I are now firm friends. Let's leave it like that until you've met her, when you can form your own opinion. But now what I really want to tell you about is a rather odd thing that happened during the visit."

"Then let's go through to the drawing room," Wilfred said, and turning to his wife added, "Perhaps they could bring the coffee there."

"My story starts with a curious coincidence," Andrew said when Mary had finished pouring the coffee. "You probably remember that my mother was a Jordaine and the Jordaines are, of course, of Huguenot descent and came to England at the end of the seventeenth century. At the same time a lot of Huguenots went to the Cape and settled at a place that came to be known as Franschhoek. There's a very interesting Huguenot museum there and Jenny took me to see it. For fun, I asked if any Jordaines had come there and we found a Guillaume Jordaine of Oude Klippen, and to cut a long story short, the museum people produced some papers. I had a quick look at them and the first thing that caught my eye was a letter addressed to Daniel Saddler of Passford Hall. How's that for a coincidence?"

"Extraordinary," exclaimed Wilfred. "And did you look further?"

"Naturally," replied Andrew, "and what did I find? I found a lot of papers belonging to Thomas Saddler. Exactly how they got there is not clear, but their content is more than interesting and I'll tell you about it later. Before I do, however, I want you to give me some information."

"OK. What do you want to know?"

"I want you to tell me all you know about the Chevalier and his life at the Court of Louis the Sixteenth," Andrew said, "and I would also like to know about James Barry. I think he's some sort of relation and he has, or rather had, a French wife called Annette."

"Let's deal with the last question first," Wilfred said, "for the story of what the family calls the Bourbon legacy will take some time. James Barry is, I think, my fourth cousin. However, during the war the children of all branches of the family tended to congregate at Passford, so your father-in-law and I got to know James quite well, and I have to say we never liked him. He grew up to be something of a black sheep, and eventually got himself prosecuted for fraud. After that, although he escaped prison, we rather lost track of him, and he made no attempt to keep in touch. Yes, he married a Frenchwoman and, if I remember right, there was something a bit, shall we say, fishy, about her. Why do you want to know about James Barry?"

"It's not James, it's the wife who features in my story, and what you've told me fits in very nicely, but more of that later. Now what about the Bourbons?"

For the next hour, Wilfred Saddler recounted the family history from the time of the Chevalier de la Tour du Lac up to the end of the Second World War. Andrew, who in the past had only heard parts of the story, for neither his wife nor his father-in-law were particularly interested, was fascinated and wished that he had understood it better when he was in South Africa.

"So the Chevalier really did receive a reward for his faithful service?" Andrew said.

"Yes, Julie told her son – my great grandfather, that is – that Thomas had been given the jewels by the Chevalier when on a visit to him in India and had brought them back to England and hidden them. In fact, there is a letter from Julie's mother Camille confirming this. Where they were hidden Thomas apparently would not say, but we have always understood that it was somewhere on this estate. Then of course he died unexpectedly, and so whatever it was he did remained a mystery. His death also is a bit of a mystery. It was known that he died in the Cape, for that is what a friend, who was also on his way to India, told Camille. This friend also arranged that someone who was returning to England would tell Julie. But we actually know very little about what really happened, for neither Julie nor anyone else seems to have tried to find out."

"Well, let me tell you a story," Andrew said, "and when I've finished you will know what happened to Thomas. It's rather a long story, I'm afraid."

"In that case I think we've talked enough for now," Wilfred remarked, getting to his feet, "so I suggest we leave your story till after dinner." Then turning to his wife he said, "My dear, I think Andrew and I need a little fresh air," and to Andrew he added, "Come on, we'll have a short tour of the estate."

When Andrew came down to dinner that evening he found his host talking to a slightly built, fair-haired man who came straight across to him and shook hands.

"Simon, how good to see you," said Andrew in some surprise. "And what are you doing here?" Simon Manningham and Andrew had been at Cambridge together and for some time after had been close friends; but following quite different careers, they had gradually drifted apart.

"Simon is the agent for the Passford estate," Wilfred said, "and as his wife is away and I knew you were friends, I asked him to come over for dinner."

Dinner was a most enjoyable meal and enabled the two friends to catch up on each other's lives. However, as soon as they had finished their coffee, Simon got up and made his apologies, saying he had an appointment with a tenant and hoping it would not be so long before he saw Andrew again.

"Now, Andrew," said Wilfred some fifteen minutes later, "let's have your story."

"You remember that I told you about my visit to the Huguenot museum," Andrew began, "and that there I found a bundle of papers which had obviously belonged to Thomas Saddler. Well, I asked to borrow them so I could study them in detail, and the two items of most interest in the box were a letter from Thomas to his father, written while he was suffering a severe bout of fever, and a sort of notebook or diary."

Andrew then went on to explain about Thomas's visit to his friend Jordaine, who had taken him to stay with a Carel du Toit at Blouberg and how, while there, he was struck down by the fever. Such was the severity of the attack that Thomas feared he was dying. Realising that if the worst happened, no one would know where the jewels were, Thomas wrote a letter to his father explaining how to find them.

"But it seems the jewels were not the only thing the Chevalier had given him," Andrew continued, "for there was another item, the meaning of which he did not understand, and so he was taking it back to India to consult his grandfather."

From the notebook, it appeared that Thomas had told no one in England about this item and, furthermore, seemed unwilling to leave it with his friends in South Africa. Despite his failing strength, he managed to hide it and to leave a clue to its whereabouts in the notebook. Andrew then described how they had deciphered the clue and how, after various adventures, they had found what it was that Thomas had hidden all those years ago.

"And here it is," he said, and from his pocket produced a box, from which he took a piece of paper and the royal trinket and placed them on the small table in front of the chairs. Wilfred reached over and looked at the paper.

"It's okay, you can pick it up," Andrew said. "It's a copy – the original is locked in my safe."

"Do you know what this means?" Wilfred asked. "I realise it's from the Queen to Antoine Tour du Lac – old TDL as we call him – but what's all this about The Sign of the Stag?"

"I don't know for sure," Andrew replied, "but it sounds to me like the London address of an eighteenth-century banker or merchant; but that, I'm sure, can be found out."

"And this funny little thing – what do you think it is?" Mary asked, picking up the trinket and weighing it in her hand. "A seal? But it feels rather heavy for an ordinary seal."

"Indeed it does. For all that, I think it is a seal," Andrew said, "but it obviously had another use for, as you say, it's heavy – made of steel, in fact – and also the symbol is very deeply incised, but what that use was I can't imagine."

"Something to do with hunting perhaps? Louis was a keen hunting man and the symbol is a hound," Wilfred said. "Now tell us about Thomas and how these papers and things came to be in a museum in an obscure town in South Africa."

"Thomas is buried in the Franschhoek Cemetery. That I can tell you for sure, because we found the grave," Andrew said, "so I think we must assume that he died of his fever while at Blouberg. Why did the papers appear in the museum? We shall probably never know. Perhaps his friend Jordaine, a Huguenot, took them and for some reason they turned up in the museum. I seem to remember something was said about a lawyer."

"Well, at least we can now add his death and burial to the family archives," Wilfred said, "but what comes out of all this and where do we go from here? In fairness to old TDL and to Thomas, we ought to try to solve some of these riddles."

"What I suggest," Andrew replied, "is that you try to find out who Toby was and where he died. If Eliza was supposed to know perhaps there may be something in the archives. For my part, I will get hold of some of my City banking friends and see if The Sign of the Stag means anything to them. Give me a couple of weeks and I'll get back in touch."

CHAPTER 15

I<small>T WAS HALF PAST SEVEN IN THE</small> morning, on the Tuesday after Andrew Henderson returned from Suffolk, that the telephone in his flat rang. He had a busy day ahead of him and was particularly anxious to get to the office early, so it was with a certain irritation that he picked up the receiver.

His irritation, however, quickly vanished, to be replaced by a worried frown, as he listened to David Stanley's voice telling him about the attack on Jenny and the death of Caspar Boscawen.

"Yes, yes I understand what happened," Andrew snapped, "but for heaven's sake tell me, how is Jenny? Is she badly hurt and should I come out?"

"I realise your concern, but calm down and listen," David replied. "No, she was not hurt, thank God, just badly shocked. She's now back here, but both Ann and I think she should get away and to be with you seems like the best therapy. Also she could be in some danger. The police have interviewed the Barry woman but are uncertain whether the attack was her idea or a personal effort of Boscawen's. The problem is that, having dealt with his family and the funeral arrangements, she has now vanished, as has a Frenchman whom the police also talked to. Incidentally, he sounds very like your friend at the monument. The police think it's possible they might still try to get hold of Jenny."

"I agree with them," Andrew said, "but just hang on a moment while I stand down my driver. He'll be wondering what's happening."

"Right, that's done," he added on his return, "and yes, I think she'd better come to England as soon as possible. With great respect to your police, I think it will be easier to protect her in England; and that could be true even if the opposition are now over here."

"Sure," David replied, "but now I'm going to hand you over to her. When you've talked we can get down to arrangements."

It took Jenny a good quarter of an hour to convince Andrew that she had come to no harm and that all she wanted to do was to get away as soon as possible.

Eventually in a burst of exasperation she said, "Look, for heaven's sake, I'm not a child. I've had a nasty experience, but if I now tell you I'm alright, you'll damn well believe me. Now do you want me to come to London or not?"

Then it took a further twenty minutes of discussion for them both to calm down and to agree that Jenny would fly to England in two days' time.

As he put down the telephone Andrew glanced at his watch, swore mildly, then grabbed his jacket and briefcase and almost ran into the hall.

"Come on," he said to the patiently waiting Jim, "the brewery, quick as you can."

Because of the delay caused by the telephone call, by the time he reached his office he found himself involved in a prolonged round of meetings and discussions. This was followed by a session with his secretary, so it was well into the afternoon before he found a moment to make a couple of telephone calls. The first was to his flat to tell Marg to prepare for the arrival of Jenny, and he had to admit that he was a little nervous as to how this piece of information would be received. However, in the event all was well. Marg had already met Jenny and approved of her and appeared to be quite prepared for her to stay in the flat.

The second call was to a Jordaine uncle, a recently retired solicitor, who was now occupying himself in preparing a new edition of the Jordaine family pedigree. Andrew asked him if he knew of any English branch of the family who might have had connections with Jordaines in South Africa.

"When I was out there recently," he said, "I discovered that some Jordaines went to South Africa about the same time as our lot came to England... Yes, they moved from the coast up to a farm called Oude Klippen... That's right, but what really interests me is that in the eighteen forties the incumbent of Oude Klippen appeared to be friendly with a Thomas Saddler... Yes, I did say Saddler... That's it, an ancestor of Alice's."

Although his uncle promised to look into it he was not hopeful, saying he had never heard of a South African connection. "Bang goes another lead," he said to himself. "I must say, it would have been nice if my family could have told me something about Peter Jordaine and how the Saddler papers came to be in that museum."

The next couple of days were a rush of business commitments, many concerned with the official launching of World Wide Wines, and it was only by the skin of his teeth that Andrew managed to get to Heathrow to meet Jenny off the overnight SAA flight.

"Look, darling," he said when they were settled in the car and Jim was weaving his way through the morning rush hour, "I'm taking you to the flat and I'm afraid I've got to desert you for the rest of the day but Marg will look after you, and anyway, you know your way around."

"Just like a man!" Jenny said, smiling to herself. "I arrive jet-lagged and after a series of traumatic adventures and what does he do? Dumps me in his flat and then retires to the office." Then, squeezing his hand, she added rather more gently, "Of course, darling, I understand. Anyway, before I do anything I want to get rid of the jet lag; but don't be too late back for I've a lot of important things to tell you."

"Right – I'll do my best to get back by five so we can have a good two hours' talk, then I'll take you out to dinner – a nice peaceful dinner I promise, for tomorrow we've got a major cocktail party at Brewers' Hall to launch Three Ws."

True to his promise, it was some two or three minutes after five when Andrew unlocked the door of the flat to find Jenny in the kitchen pouring boiling water into a teapot.

"You have great faith in my punctuality," he said with a smile, kissing the nape of her neck.

"There now," she said, "you can take the tray in. Marg's been marvellous. Sorted out all my things and installed me in the spare room. I have to admit that she eyed your bed rather dubiously, saying, 'I hope the spare room will suit you.' I said it would be fine. I've told her we'll be out to dinner, so she's gone home. Now sit down, for as I said, I've important things to tell you."

"Yes but first, if you can bear to, tell me about that dreadful man Boscawen."

"Of course I can bear it. God knows I've told it often enough – every bloody policeman, lawyer and doctor in the Cape seemed to need to know!" And she told him the whole story, from meeting Annette in Stellenbosch through to the various meetings with the police. "It's not what happened to me that I mind, because I came to no harm, other than severe shock. No, it's the feeling that I was responsible for his death. Yes, yes! It's all very well saying self-defence – and I know it was Mzumi he was going for when he tripped, but I can't help feeling..." and she left the rest of the sentence in the air and laid her head on Andrew's shoulder.

"Now listen," she said a few minutes later, "there's something you must know. When I was talking to the Barry woman before I went to the van Stadens she muttered something about Scotland. Said you'd mentioned some other relative there or something. I'm afraid I wasn't really listening because I was already late for my appointment."

"Yes, the trading associates in Hong Kong," Andrew said. "Their descendants now live in Scotland; but I only mentioned them to try to put her off the idea that we knew anything."

"Well," Jenny continued, "when she was interviewed by the police and they asked about her future movements, she apparently said that if and when she got back to the UK she was thinking of visiting Scotland. She also said the same to Jan van Staden, who went to see her, as I had refused point blank to talk to her."

"All that presumably means that she's been doing some research and has found out about Norrie. Norman Colquhoun, that is – Brigadier Norman Colquhoun of Barrs to give him his full title," Andrew explained, rubbing his chin thoughtfully; then after a few minutes he added rather more briskly, "I'd better warn him. In fact, I think I may have to go and see him. He could be very useful."

"Who exactly is he?" Jenny asked. "And why are the others so keen to see him? Come to that, what makes you think he could be useful? Stop talking riddles and explain."

"Sorry, darling. As I said, I only mentioned the Hong Kong connection on the spur of the moment to try to put Annette Barry off, though funnily enough I almost know more about the Hong Kong side than I do about the Indian."

"How come?" Jenny asked.

"That's just what I'm about to tell you," Andrew said, "so keep quiet and listen. Arthur Kingdom, Thomas's father-in-law, had a business associate called Colquhoun in Hong Kong. In those days the China trade – and that's the polite name for it, drug trade was probably a truer description – was dominated by the Scots. Like many others, the Colquhouns, having made their very considerable fortune, then invested part of it in a Highland estate called Barrs where their descendant, the aforementioned Norman still lives. Now Norrie, as he's always been known, had a long and distinguished career in all sorts of secret military and civilian organisations, and no one knows more about the seamier side of international crime than he does. It therefore occurs to me that he might know, or be able to find out, about Annette and her friends, for I don't think she's as innocent as she'd have us believe. Also there just might be something in the Colquhoun archives about their dealings with Arthur Kingdom which could be helpful."

"So what are you going to do?" Jenny asked.

"The first thing I'm going to do," Andrew replied, "is to get us a drink and then we're going round the corner to dinner; a nice little Italian restaurant called Il Bersagliere which is just a two-minute walk away."

"You asked me what I'm going to do," Andrew said as they awaited the arrival of the first course. "Well tomorrow we can't do much because we've got this party in the evening. It's a nuisance it's on Friday, and that hasn't pleased the Brewers' Company, but it was the best day for getting all the people we wanted. I will, however, get hold of Norman Colquhoun and try to arrange to go up and see him on Monday. On Sunday, I'm going to take you to Passford. I'm sure they'll be delighted to have you and I think you'll be safer there until I return. You can also do some research on Eliza and poor Toby!"

"Fine – and then what?" Jenny asked.

"That depends on what I find out in Scotland and what you discover in Suffolk; but above all, it depends on where Annette Barry is and what she decides to do," Andrew replied. "My guess is that her strategy will be to let us do the work, and when she thinks we've found out something, to try and get in ahead of us. Now shall we leave the Saddlers and their legacies and talk about something more interesting. Us maybe?"

That interesting subject kept them occupied throughout dinner and on the short walk back to the flat. There Andrew poured himself a whisky and soda and asked Jenny what, if anything, she'd like.

"Darling, don't put it like that," she said. "You make it sound as though I wasn't old enough to drink! I've never been a great one for whisky; but if, as seems increasingly likely, I'm going to spend more and more of my life with you in this wretched damp climate, perhaps I'd better try to acquire the taste."

"Now, Andrew Henderson," she said as he handed her the glass, "bearing in mind what I've just said, I find it odd that although I've told you a good deal about my life, you've never asked about boyfriends or affairs."

"I suppose I didn't think it necessary," he said. "After all, if you'd wanted to tell me, I imagine you'd have done so."

"Another lovely Englishman's remark," she said with a barely suppressed giggle. "You are very sweet, but I think you should know about the one love of my life. It's something I never talk about and I think you'll understand why."

"So," she said some ten minutes later, "there we were, all ready for the wedding. He had just been made Finance Director of Incorporated Computers and business was looking up. Everything seemed wonderful until that terrible evening when the car thieves struck. They forced him off the road, pulled him from the driving seat and shot him three times in the head; then they drove off in the car, leaving him lying in the road. It's a quiet area and it was ten minutes before one of the neighbours found him."

"I'm sorry," was all he could think of saying, but after a moment he added, "Were the gang caught?"

"No, they never are. The car was probably shipped straight to Europe. That's what they do," she said and added, "Like your problems when Alice died, it took me a long time to recover and that's why I was determined to put a stop to your nonsense."

"Come on now," she said taking his hands in hers, "bed, for we've all had a long day. Oh yes, now what about Marg if I come and kiss you goodnight? Do you realise I've never been able to do so?" Then she added mischievously, "Or won't your conscience let me?"

"I daresay it will, and I can't imagine how you think Marg will know," he said, pulling her towards him and kissing her lips.

Ten minutes later, she came into his room to find him reading. Seating herself on the edge of the bed, she gently removed the book and turned off the light. "Move over, darling," she said, slipping in beside him and putting her arms round him. "It's obviously been some time, so we've both got a bit to learn!"

CHAPTER 16

A s soon as Andrew got to the office the next morning, he explained to his secretary what he proposed to do over the next four or five days.

"I've got Mandertons the sugar people this morning, haven't I?" he said.

"At nine thirty," Angela Richardson replied, pointing to the day's agenda. "Then Frank, with Mr Johnson from the auditors at eleven, and in the afternoon you're going to the Brewers to check that you are happy about the arrangements for this evening."

"Right, Angela; so it seems that you'll have to get hold of Mr Saddler and Brigadier Colquhoun, give them my apologies and explain what I want. Assuming we can organise the brigadier, then book me on a flight to Edinburgh on Monday morning – from Stansted if possible – and back again on Tuesday afternoon."

The World Wide Wines party was a great success. Agents from all the main exporting countries were there, together with quite a few vineyard owners. Wine merchants, owners of rival off-licence chains and brewers also came, curious to see what it was all about, and most were highly complimentary. One or two elderly brewers muttered about cobblers sticking to their lasts, as did a couple of pompous city wine merchants. The Press – popular, serious and trade – were there in force making sure they got their fair share of the entertainment. To give them their due, they did Three Ws proud; several of the Sundays mentioned the party, and some of the weekend supplements had prepared articles commending a really worthwhile venture. So it was a very satisfied couple who finally got back to Andrew's flat well after midnight.

"You realise, darling, don't you," Andrew said, closing the front door and taking Jenny in his arms, "that this is all your doing. It was your idea;

it was you who kept me to it in the early stages; it was you and your family who got me really enthusiastic about wines from outside Europe." Then, after a long pause for kissing, Andrew raised his head and added, "I suppose we must give young Tony some credit. He ran with it from the start. Of course, it did give him a chance to exercise his Spanish!"

"Fool!" she said. "But it was a lovely party, and I've definitely fallen for the English drink trade, particularly Tony. I think he's sweet, but his wife's a handful, isn't she? She wanted to know all about me and kept interrupting when I was doing my South African marketing bit!"

While they were talking, Andrew had led them through to the kitchen, and a bottle of Champagne and two glasses had now materialised.

"Come on, one last drink," he said, raising his glass. "To World Wide Wines, and to Jenny Stanley whose idea it was." Their glasses touched, they smiled at each other and drank.

Then Andrew put down his glass, turned and put his hands on her shoulders and whispered in her ear, "But perhaps not Jenny Stanley for too much longer." He raised his head and looking into her eyes, said in a voice that brooked no denial, "Darling Jenny, will you marry me?"

Jenny reached over and put her glass on the table, then gently removed his hands from her shoulders and stepping back, looked up into his eyes and said, "I expect so, my angel, but I don't think either of us can decide that now. It's very late and if you want to tour your shops tomorrow we must go to bed."

With that she dropped his hands, kissed him gently and slipped quickly into her bedroom. Andrew smiled to himself, turned out the lights and walked towards his room humming quietly the old Doris Day song, 'Che sera, sera'.

At ten o'clock the next morning Jim appeared with the car, and the morning was spent in an almost royal progress round north and west London, with visits to four of the Three Ws shops which were fully up and running. Then in the evening the directors of Henderson Braithwaite, their wives and, of course, Jenny dined at Claridge's. But there was no further mention of marriage; that had to wait until Sunday when they were driving up to Passford.

A fine spring Sunday is not a time to drive east out of London. The traffic, Andrew decided, was even worse than it had been the previous Saturday, so it was not until they were well clear of the suburbs that Jenny was able to get his attention.

"That question you put to me the other night," she began, when at last she thought he was listening. "I suppose you do remember, don't you, that you asked me to marry you? Well now, darling – and please, just keep looking ahead and your hands firmly on the wheel – for I'm going to tell you that the answer is yes, I will marry you. However, before you get too excited, I'm going to make one condition and that is that we do not tell anyone else until we have resolved this treasure hunt business. This will not only avoid possible distraction, it will also avoid announcements and having to listen to people making plans for us."

Andrew, who had held his breath waiting for this mysterious condition, was relieved to find that it was something he was himself intending to suggest, and so he readily agreed to it.

"Dear Jenny, thank you – thank you from the bottom of my heart. And yes, for the present let it be a secret between us. Watch out for Phyllis, though," he said with a smile. "If she possibly can she'll wheedle it out of you!"

The rest of the drive passed mainly in silence, both of them being busy with their own thoughts, until some forty minutes later, they reached the Passford gates.

"Just look around you," Andrew said as they turned into the drive, "for you're now driving down one of the finest lime avenues left in East Anglia. There was a time when every major country house had its avenue of trees, – beech, elm or lime – but now many have gone, the victims of gales and disease."

"It's beautiful," Jenny said, "and so's the house. What a setting; and look at those magnolias."

This time it was Wilfred himself who greeted them at the front door, and after Jenny had been introduced, led them through the house and out onto the terrace.

"It's such a mild day, and we're so sheltered on this side of the house that we thought we might have drinks here before lunch," Wilfred said. "And now, Jenny, if I may call you that, let me introduce my wife. Mary, this is Jenny Stanley."

Andrew was amused to see how quickly Jenny fitted into the Saddler household. "Why did everyone used to talk about gauche colonials?" he wondered. "They are so much more at home in strange places than we are. Americans, Australians, South Africans, they're all the same. I suppose that if you and a few others found a new country you can't afford to be shy or standoffish."

During the rest of the day, Andrew explained what Jenny had found out since his last visit, while she gave a brief description of her adventure with Caspar Boscawen.

"So you see," Andrew said when they'd finished telling their stories, "it seems to me that I must go and see old Norman before the others get to him. Anyway, as you know, I served under him at one time and I want some advice. This sort of thing is right up his street."

"Well, give him our regards," Wilfred said. "Now I'm afraid we haven't made any progress. My fault – been very busy, but now we've got Jenny here we'll have a real go at Eliza and Toby. Yes, and we'll see Jenny comes to no harm. Strangers are easily identified round here."

"I'm sure she'll be as safe here as anywhere," Andrew said. "I'm afraid, though, that I've got a terrible confession to make. My plane tomorrow morning is seven fifteen from Stansted. So I suppose I ought to leave at six."

"Or even a little earlier," Wilfred said. "I suggest Steven brings you tea at five. No, don't worry, it's better if he lets you out anyway. The alarms are quite complicated."

"And, darling," Jenny added, "don't expect me to come and wave goodbye at that hour."

Just after eight-thirty the next morning, Andrew's plane touched down at Edinburgh Airport, and ten minutes later Norman Colquhoun was greeting him as he emerged onto the main concourse.

"Good to see you, Andrew. Aye man, and how are you keeping these days?" he said, leading the way to the main exit. "Car's just outside." Which indeed it was, parked right next door to a sign saying STRICTLY NO WAITING and guarded by a member of the airport police.

"Thanks, Alick," Norman said as they got in, "most helpful. Saved us a lot of time."

"Ach, Brigadier, it's no bother!" Alick grinned. "Glad to help you. Aye, and just watch your speed. The traffic boys are out today between here and the bridge."

"Lost none of the old persuasive power I see, Norrie," Andrew said as they threaded their way through the traffic making for the Forth Road Bridge and the industrial estates of Fife. "If I'd tried to park where you were, I wouldn't have survived five minutes."

"It's all a matter of knowing your men," the brigadier replied. "Take Alick Winchester now; he was a Lomond Highlander, my batman out in Borneo in fact, before he joined the airport police. Happy to do anything for me, or if he's not available there always seems to be one of his friends about! May be considered questionable these days, but I'm a great believer in oiling the wheels to keep life running smoothly. Too many simple things are made difficult nowadays by this political correctness lark! Political correctness? Nonsense! More like busybodies delight, I'd say."

Andrew smiled to himself. Age, it seemed, had not changed his companion one little bit. Norman Colquhoun had always been an achiever and could not stand anyone getting in his way and preventing the smooth completion of the task in hand.

Once they crossed the bridge, however, the commentary on life eased a little, since the road from Dunfermline to Crieff requires considerable concentration on the part of the driver, so allowing the passenger a chance to enjoy the scenery.

"Well now, what's all this about Bourbon jewellery and mysterious Frenchwomen in South Africa?" he said when, at last, they had passed Gleneagles. "You said it was all mixed up with old William's dealings in Hong Kong and India. Pretty dubious they were too. Problem of our family – dubious dealings. Barbara always said I had a dangerous affinity for them myself!"

"It's a long story," Andrew replied, "and I'd rather keep it until we get to the house. When you hear it, you'll see that it could be useful to know something of any dealings, dubious or otherwise, William Colquhoun may have had with a Bengal merchant called Arthur Kingdom. You'll also see that there are a number of pretty unsavoury characters involved, and as I have a reputation to consider, before things get out of hand I need professional advice, and you're the man to give it."

"Not so sure of that, Andrew. I'm not so young as I was and, rather surprisingly you may think, I too have been persuaded to have a care with my reputation. Anyway, let's leave advice until I've heard the whole story."

The estate of Barrs lies at the foot of the high ground west of Crieff, and is now considerably smaller than it was in 1850 when William Colquhoun bought it, though the house remains largely unchanged.

"Forgot to tell you, Barbara's away. She sent her love and is sorry not to see you," Norrie said as they walked into the hall with its massive oak table, still bearing a brass tray for calling cards, and its walls adorned with stags' heads and other trophies. "Just leave your bag there; we'll deal with it later. And don't worry about Barbara's absence. Mrs Fleming – you remember Jeanie, I'm sure. She'll look after us."

"Now," he went on, leading the way down a passage to a comfortably furnished business room with a breathtaking view of the distant hills, "I suggest you tell me what this is all about. Then, after lunch, I've got to go and see Colin Watson at the distillery. We're doing some work on the river and they're feared for their water supply. That won't interest you particularly but I'm sure they'll give you a tour of their state of the art operation, and I'll bet it's better than your little brewery, eh? Then we're going to have a drink with your old flame Angela Armstrong, and after dinner we can discuss what to do with your problem. Okay?"

"Sounds fine," Andrew replied. "Always pleased to see a brewery or distillery and compare notes. And heavens, I'd forgotten Angela lived up here. He died, didn't he?"

"Yes, fell two hundred feet off a ledge while stalking. Bit careless I thought, but didn't like to say so. Now hang on while I organise coffee," and he went to the door and shouted, "Jeanie, coffee in the study, could we, please."

Then for the next hour, Andrew described in detail the whole story from the visit to the museum to Boscawen's attack on Jenny and Annette Barry's stated intention to visit Scotland.

"When Jenny told me that," Andrew said, "I had to assume that the Barry woman knew of the association between Kingdom and Colquhoun and had decided that there was truth in my remark about the jewels having gone from Hong Kong to Scotland. The first thing I had to do therefore was to warn you. That done, I thought I ought to see if you had any correspondence or other records which might help."

"I've no idea, but let's have a look," was the brigadier's initial comment; and then, after a moment's thought, he added, "Now you may just be in luck, for a couple of months ago we had an old boy up here – used to be an archivist with the Service, and he's put old William's papers and other family and estate bumf in proper order. Let's go and see what we can find."

In the passage outside the study, Norrie unlocked a heavy steel-lined door and fastened it back against the wall, and then led the way into a large windowless room containing racks of shelves with roller doors, several filing cabinets, a steel gun cupboard and a massive safe.

"Genuine Victorian strong room," he said. "Very useful. Built into the walls of the house. Need to be careful not to lock yourself in, though!" Then he bent down and unlocked one of the roller doors and pushed it up, disclosing rows of neatly tied and labelled documents.

"I think these are what we want. Here, take these through to the study while I lock up," and he gave Andrew several bundles of papers.

"Now let's have a look," he said as he came back into the study and walked over to the table where Andrew had dumped the papers. "Yes, we'll start with these: 'Wm Colquhoun, correspondence 1838/40' – sounds about right, don't you think?" he said, picking up a bulky folder.

Half an hour later, having found nothing of any interest, Andrew left his host to continue searching through the letters and turned his attention to some of the other papers he'd brought in. One item that he thought might be of interest was an account book with details of transactions with various trading houses in Calcutta. Looking through it he could find no specific mention of Arthur Kingdom, but he did find, pinned to one of the pages, what appeared to be a letter. "Hullo, what's this?" he said to himself, unfastening the three thin sheets of paper covered with rather faded writing.

"Listen to this, Norrie," he said a few minutes later. "It's a letter from Arthur Kingdom to William dated October 1842. There's a certain amount of business and social news of no interest to us, but then he goes on:

> *'You remember when you were last here*
> *you met my son-in-law who was about to sail*
> *for England with certain family heirlooms,*
> *and in your last letter asked if they'd arrived*
> *safely. Well, I have now heard from Thomas*
> *saying that the jewellery has been safely stored*
> *on the icy shores of Ithaca! I have no idea what*
> *he means by this, but I hope he will explain on*
> *his next visit...'*

Now what do you make of that?"

"Me personally? Well I have to admit it means nothing to me, nor, I suspect, to you," he replied, "but it is obviously worth following up. Perhaps it will mean something to old Wilfred. Didn't you say there was some other evidence that the jewels were hidden at Passford?"

"Yes – but Ithaca, surely that's an island somewhere off Greece. Hardly icy, I'd have thought."

"Might be in winter," Norrie replied, grinning. "Anyway, I think that's enough for now. Let's have a drink and lunch."

The rest of the day was spent on other activities, including a visit to the very modern distillery, which Andrew found extremely interesting, although he felt it made his brewery look somewhat old-fashioned. The drink with Angela Armstrong was, he felt, not so successful. While it is always interesting to renew old friendships, in this particular case it only served to strengthen his view that the romance of thirty years ago is best kept in the mind – the present reality can so often be disappointing.

It was not, therefore, until after dinner that they returned to the subject of Thomas Saddler's legacy.

"Well, you've got some further information on where the jewellery may be hidden, provided that is that Ithaca means something to Wilfred," the brigadier said, "but I'm afraid I've been no help on the things you found in that copper tube, although I will have a further search through William's papers."

"Let me know if you find anything, but don't let it take up too much of your time."

"Don't worry about that. I'm beginning to get interested. Quite like the old days, and I was needing something to exercise the brain." Norrie paused and gazed into the fire. Then he turned to his companion and said, "I've been thinking about those two characters – the Frenchwoman and her companion. I'd take a bet that she is Annette Duvalier, known throughout the French underworld as La Chérie. A very dangerous girl, so watch your step. The other I'm not so sure about, for we haven't that good a description. His real name may or may not be Lemaître, but I think he might be a small-time thief called Pascal Nero. The gangs called him Don Juan for obvious reasons."

Then he opened a drawer in his desk and took out a cardboard box. "I think you may find this useful," he said. "It's the latest in tracer bugs. The makers kindly sent me a couple to try out and you could be an ideal test bed. Very useful if you want to keep track of a car."

Andrew arrived back at Passford the following afternoon at about half past five, to be assailed immediately by Jenny and the Saddlers wanting to know how he'd got on and whether he'd discovered anything new.

"Yes and I'll tell you about it later," he said, moving in the direction of the stairs, "but first I must have a bath and change, for I've had a somewhat exhausting day. Yesterday was alright, for we spent our time between the Colquhoun archives and a visit to a distillery, but today was a different matter. I knew we had a problem when Norrie announced that after breakfast we'd have a short tour of the estate. The first part was okay. We drove round in the Land Rover looking at woods and sheep, but then Norrie decided he wanted to look at a loch way up in the hills. So we abandoned the transport and walked about five miles up some pretty steep slopes. Then to cap it all he gave me a lecture on how he was restocking the loch, and I'm afraid nothing bores me more than your enthusiastic fisherman. As a result of this little expedition we only just caught the plane. I've had no lunch and didn't have time to change!"

An hour later, bathed and changed, Andrew was seated in front of the drawing room fire with a large whisky and soda, and once again under pressure to tell how he'd got on.

"Eventually I found this account book," he said, after he'd described the search through the archives. "The book itself didn't tell me much, but pinned to one of the pages was a letter from Arthur Kingdom. Now, William Colquhoun must have been in Calcutta when they were discussing the jewels, because in the middle of the letter Kingdom suddenly mentions them and says that he's heard from Thomas that he's hidden them on the icy shores of Ithaca. Now what on earth does that mean? Any idea, Wilfred?"

"Ithaca? Yes, it's an island in the Ionian Sea," Wilfred said, then held up his hand for quiet when this remark was greeted with howls of protest. "Now just calm down and give me a chance to continue. Ithaca is also what we call that small island in the lake. I think it was Daniel, Thomas's father, who gave it the name. He was something of a classicist and his wife was called Penelope, and so Ithaca it's been ever since. But why the icy shores, I've no idea."

"I walked down there this morning," said Jenny. "There's a bridge over to the island but I didn't go across it. How exciting! Do you suppose that poor Toby died or was buried on the island? I must go and look tomorrow. Oh, sorry, darling," she added, seeing Andrew's puzzled look. "We have confirmed that Thomas's sister Eliza had a dog called Toby, but we don't have a clue about its death."

Any further discussion was halted by the ringing of the telephone. Wilfred picked up the receiver and listened for a minute or two, occasionally making a remark. Then he turned and said to Andrew: "It's Norman Colquhoun for you, says he's discovered something that may help."

Andrew took the instrument and listened. "Yes, I've got that," he said. "Murray, did you say? ...Yes, a banker in London, got that... Both Arthur Kingdom and Colquhoun used them, originally Arthur's idea... Yes, and there's some evidence, you say, that it dates back to the Chevalier and a man called Necker... OK, Norrie, and thanks, could be very helpful, and thanks too for last night... No, I won't write. Bye."

"Now we really are getting somewhere," Andrew told the others. "Norrie's found some papers relating to a bank in London called Murrays which was used by Arthur Kingdom on the advice of his father-in-law, and also by Colquhouns. The Chevalier must have heard of the bank during his time at the French court, for apparently Jacques Necker, the King's finance minister, also had dealings with them."

"What next, then?" Wilfred asked.

"I must go back to London tomorrow first thing. I must see what's happening at the brewery and then I'll get hold of one or two people in the City who may be able to help with Murrays Bank."

"Leaving me alone again, I suppose," said Jenny with a mock pout. "Well, we'll have a bet. I'll find Toby and the jewels before you find your old bank."

"Right, but just take care," Andrew said. "Remember that there are others who just may think of making a clandestine visit to Passford in search of Toby, and they don't seem to be too particular in their behaviour."

CHAPTER 17

A S SOON AS ALL THE ARRANGEMENTS FOR the return of Boscawen's body to England were complete, Annette Barry flew to London, taking Lemaître with her. The South African police had decided, somewhat reluctantly, that the rape attempt was entirely Caspar's idea and therefore there were no grounds on which they could be detained.

They had arrived in England some three or four days before Jenny and were now ensconced in Annette's flat off the Bayswater Road. The flat, together with its contents, had been part of her divorce settlement from James Barry, and amongst the contents were a number of books, including some relating to the Saddler family.

Annette had never paid much attention to these, but now she hunted them out to see whether there was anything in any of them about Thomas Saddler's wife and her relations in India.

Most of what she found related to the Suffolk estate and the family's part in the official and social life of that county, but hidden between the pages of 'The Pedigree of the Saddler Family' was a pamphlet entitled 'Arthur Kingdom and the Calcutta Traders'. Glancing through the index, she noticed that there was a chapter on Arthur's links both with the Dutch East Indies and with other British Colonies; notably Hong Kong where he had developed a close friendship with a Mr Wm. Colquhoun.

On turning over a page, Annette found a pencilled note saying that the Colquhoun family had moved to Scotland, the writer adding that he or she had spent a pleasant week, in September 1928, visiting their place near Crieff.

"That is where we must go. They must be the people Mr Henderson referred to when he talked about Hong Kong and Scotland," Annette said, putting down the book and turning to face Jean.

Jean, who had been reading a newspaper article which was highly criti-cal of France, threw the paper aside and said in French, with an air of disgust: "Why are the English always against France? There is not a good word in this journal."

"Mon cher Jean," Annette said, "surely by now you have realised that, ever since Waterloo, Englishmen have considered that all foreigners should be kept in their place, and that this applies particularly to the French; but forget all that and pay attention. Did you hear what I just said?"

"Yes," he replied, "and I did not understand a word. You speak riddles. Where is it we must go and who are these people?"

"I have just found out from this booklet that the father-in-law of Thomas Saddler had a friend in Hong Kong who retired to Scotland," Annette said. "There is also a note that someone visited them in their castle seventy years ago." Jean was about to protest but was stopped by Annette, who held up her hand and added, "Yes, I know that is a long time ago, but if that remark by Henderson is to be believed they are still there. That is what we are going to find out."

"And how will we do that?" Jean asked.

"We will go to Crieff, wherever that is, and we will make enquiries. I don't believe Crieff is very big and everyone is sure to know who lives in which castle."

While she was saying this, Annette was searching through the drawers of her desk and eventually, under a pile of old fashion magazines, found what she was looking for, a road atlas of Great Britain. A quick scan of the index indicated that Crieff would be found on page forty-eight.

"Here it is," she said, putting the atlas down on the table and pointing, "north-west of Edinburgh. I think we should go by train. Railways are more anonymous than airlines. Yes, we'll go to Edinburgh and I expect we can hire a car. Now, mon Jean, hand me that AA book and we'll find a suitable hotel. I think we are a honeymoon couple, don't you!"

The train journey to Edinburgh was a revelation to Jean Lemaître, for although well travelled, his visits to England had been mainly to London and he knew little of the rest of the British Isles. He watched with interest as they passed through the rich farmlands of the East Midlands, the pastures of Yorkshire and Durham and the bleak moorlands and rugged coastline of the Borders.

"It is true, isn't it," he said to his companion, "that in France we think of England as a small country of endless dirty towns. But here we have travelled through beautiful scenery, tidier perhaps than France, but just as varied. We have seen towns, yes, but they look clean and prosperous."

Renting a car had proved no problem and an hour and a half later, having taken a couple of wrong turnings, they had reached their hotel. Small and comfortable, it stood on the outskirts of the town in the shadow of the famous Hydro.

The barman was both welcoming and a mine of information. Even before they had ordered drinks, he was extolling the glories of the Perthshire countryside.

"Colquhoun?" he said in answer to Annette's question. "Aye, that'll be the brigadier you're wanting. Brigadier Norman Colquhoun of Barrs. Barrs, that's the name of the house – they don't like it called a castle. Built by some rich ancestor, I believe. That was the thing in those days: the younger sons of the lairds, aye and sometimes just ordinary laddies wi' a taste for adventure, they all went off to the army or to be traders – or sometimes both – in what they called the East India Company. Make your fortune there and then back to Scotland and build a mansion house."

"And what about this Norman Colquhoun?" Annette asked. "What does he do? Do you know him?"

"Aye, I ken him fine. I'm often there at the beating. That's for the grouse, ye ken. But you'll not be having grouse in France, I expect. He's a grand man. He was in Korea and later in Borneo, where I was mysel'. And they do say he was in the Secret Service or such like. But here's the major, he'll tell better than I can. Evening, Major!" he said to the slight man with thinning ginger hair and a fierce moustache who, despite the warmth of the bar, was wearing a thick jersey and a heavy tweed jacket. "This young lady is from France and is enquiring about Norrie – some kind of cousin, did you say?"

Major Duncan, for that was his name, took his large tumbler of whisky and smiled at Annette.

"So you want to know about Norman, do you? Well, let's go and sit down," he said and walked over to a table by the fire and settled Annette in a chair. He glared at Jean, who had followed them over, and when introduced favoured him with a somewhat distasteful nod.

"Now, what is it you want to know?" he asked. "And you say you are a cousin of his?"

"No, I don't think there is any relationship, but I believe that an ancestor of my first husband was friendly with a Mr William Colquhoun," she answered. "This was in India some hundred and fifty years ago. I am doing research for a French University into British and French trading houses in India and China, and if Brigadier Colquhoun is of the same family he may be able to help me."

"Certainly sounds as though it's the same family," Major Duncan replied. "I'm a bachelor, you know, and ever since I retired as Secretary of the Golf Club I've lived in this hotel. Very comfortable, but a bit lonely, and Colquhoun and his wife have been very kind to me. Dinner, bridge and the occasional round of golf – you know the sort of thing – so I think I know him fairly well."

"But what makes you think he is of the family that interests me?" Annette prompted him.

"Ah yes! Well now, Norman's great-great-grandfather, I think it was, came back from Hong Kong about the time you say and it was he who built the house. But why don't you go and see Norman? You'll find him an interesting character and he'll put you right on the family. Clever chap; was a Lomond Highlander – that's our local regiment – and finished up in MI6. Worked closely with French intelligence on atomic secrets, I believe. Should interest you!"

"Thank you, I'll do that," Annette said.

"Good luck then," the major said, finishing his drink. "Now, if you'll excuse me I must go. Out to dinner tonight. Oh, and I'd ring before you go to Barrs. Make sure he's in."

"I don't like it," Jean said once they were alone. "I remember that atomic secrets business. An Algerian gang working for the Libyan Gaddafi it was. I'd been involved as a drug runner by some Algerians once, so army intelligence had me infiltrate the gang. Dangerous, so I ran away! But there was a formidable British officer sent to help our people. I saw him once and I think he may be notre gentilhomme écossais. Be careful what you say to him, he is a professional."

"Indeed I shall be," Annette replied. "All I shall say is what I've already told you: does he have any papers relating to his family's doings in the Far East which might help in my research?"

Having been forewarned by Andrew Henderson, Brigadier Colquhoun was not in the least surprised to get Annette's telephone call and said he'd be delighted to see her and her new husband about three o'clock the next day.

"Should be interesting," he said to his wife, "that was James Barry's ex. The woman Andrew was talking about. Says she's now doing research for a French University and have I any papers that could help. She knows James's family and mine had trading links in India and China. What she hopes, I expect, is that I'll tell her what I told Andrew. What I shall do is find out what she already knows and also who she and her boyfriend really are. Incidentally, she's now passing him off as her new husband."

When Annette and Jean arrived at Barrs the next afternoon, they were met by Norman Colquhoun himself and taken straight to his study.

"Now if I understood you correctly," he said to Annette, "you were married to James Barry. I never knew him well but I remember he had a French wife. You say you are now doing research into English and French involvement in the Indian and Chinese trade in the eighteenth and nineteenth centuries. So how can I help you?"

Annette then explained that she had discovered that in the early nineteenth century one of her husband's ancestors, a Calcutta merchant, had dealings with a Mr William Colquhoun in Hong Kong. She knew all about the Indian side but was short of information on Hong Kong traders.

"Do you have any family papers that could help me?" she asked. "And if so, could I look at them? I am particularly looking for information on the trade in gemstones and precious metals between India, the Dutch colonies and China. This was not a usual business for the Bengal merchants and I wondered if you could throw any light on it from the Colquhoun end?"

"I wish I could help you," the brigadier replied, "but in the early twenties there was a bad fire here. A number of pieces of valuable Scottish furniture and several paintings, collected by my great grandfather, were destroyed, together with much of the family archive. I do seem to remember though, family stories of valuable cargoes falling victim to Chinese and Malayan pirates so there probably was such a trade, but I'm afraid we've no records that would be of use for serious research."

Here Jean, who had been staring out of the window, suddenly woke up and turned to Norman Colquhoun.

"Monsieur, I am an agent of the French Finance Ministry," he said, and received a surreptitious kick from Annette to which he paid no attention, "and we have reason to believe that, at the time we are talking about, a shipment of great value – jewels certainly, bullion possibly – was illegally exported from France and may have gone via India to the Far East."

While the Frenchman was talking, the brigadier had watched him carefully, and the more he looked at him and listened to him, the more sure he was that this was the stupid and cowardly spy, Pascal Nero, who had associated with Algerians. And now he was living up to his reputation by ruining his companion's carefully guarded questions. About Annette he was less sure. He had never seen La Chérie, although he had heard a lot about her. Her questions certainly suggested someone who knew what she was about and he had noticed her suppressed fury at Lemaître's intervention – not the reaction to be expected of an innocent researcher towards her husband.

"No," he said in answer to Jean's statement, "I have never heard of anything of that sort, and as I've already said, all the records of that time were destroyed in the fire. To find out more about the activities of William Colquhoun and his associates I think you may have to go to Hong Kong, unless of course your ex husband's family can help."

"That is a possibility," she replied. "I might certainly try them. But now we must say goodbye," she added, getting to her feet, "and thank you for your help. I fear it has not advanced my investigations very much, but I have to explore all possibilities."

Since there was nothing further for them to do in Scotland, when they got back to the hotel Annette suggested that they should return to London that evening. The hotel expressed disappointment that they were leaving so soon and hoped that it was nothing to do with the service they had received. On being assured that everything had been most satisfactory, the manager said that if they left at once they would have plenty of time to catch the evening train.

The train was a fast one, stopping only at Newcastle and Peterborough and after Newcastle, as they had their seats to themselves, Jean started grumbling about their progress.

"That meeting this afternoon was a complete waste of time," he said, once again relapsing into French, "and also unwise. I'm sure that man was the English officer in the Algerian affair; furthermore, I believe he was lying. A fire indeed! Far too convenient to my mind, that was. You made too elaborate a story. We should have followed my line and persisted in direct questioning about the jewels. He might have let something slip."

"Mon cher Jean, you have just said that Colquhoun is a dangerous professional," Annette replied. "He wasn't going to let something slip. But the time was not all wasted, for whether he was lying or not, I got the feeling that Scotland is not where we should be looking."

The arguments persisted after they got back to the flat and only ended when Annette sent her companion off to the spare bedroom.

"Get out of my sight," she shouted after his retreating figure, "and you can go off on your own for all I care. Go and find the Saddler family if you want to, but you'll get nowhere. No English gentleman is going to talk to a little Parisian apache, and that's what they'll know you are. I'm going to find Henderson and try my charms on him. He'll be out of his depth with me."

"Do that, and I wish you luck. I shall be gone by tomorrow morning," and he slammed the bedroom door.

CHAPTER 18

L EFT ALONE AT PASSFORD, JENNY HAD NOT wasted her time. First she borrowed a book called 'The Saddlers of Passford', a detailed history of the family from the early eighteenth century until the start of the Great War. This gave her a far better understanding of who was who in the family. Then she asked if there were any letters or diaries covering the Daniel and Thomas years and was shown a solid wooden chest with a massive lock.

"I'm afraid we've never been very good at looking after the family papers," Wilfred said as he unlocked the chest. "We have nearly two hundred years of farm and estate records, mostly on microfilm now. Personal papers, though, are another matter; all those that we have are in this chest but I'm afraid they've never been properly catalogued. The County Records Office are always on at me to do something about it, but there never seems to be time. Anyway, have a look through and see if you can find anything. Use the table in the study by all means for I shall be out for the rest of the day."

For the next two hours, Jenny sorted through bundle after bundle of letters, diaries and household accounts. All were neatly tied up, but in no sort of order and, in many cases, the various items in a package bore no relation to each other. Eventually, however, Jenny managed to abstract from the chaos almost everything that had been written by or referred to Eliza.

There were endless letters to friends and relations; there was a sketch-book with some very passable watercolours and a commonplace book with some fascinating entries, but what interested Jenny most was a collection of diaries covering the years 1835 to 1850. These she took to the study and sat down to read from beginning to end.

Toby, who appeared to be a terrier of some sort, featured regularly from about 1838 onwards. Then, in an entry for September 1841, Jenny found what she was looking for. Heavily edged and underlined in black ink was the sentence: 'Today poor Toby was killed. One of the farm horses kicked him and he died at once and without pain. This evening one of the gardeners helped me to bury him on Ithaca. I am going to mark the place with a stone.'

"So Ithaca is the place we want," she said to herself.

"Why do you want Ithaca?" Mary, who happened to be passing the study door, asked.

"Sorry, Mary, I didn't realise I'd said it aloud. Anyway, come and listen to this," Jenny said and read out Toby's obituary. "Doesn't that seem to confirm that Thomas hid the jewels somewhere on the island? After all, he's mentioned it in two separate letters."

"What are you going to do then?" Mary asked.

Jenny looked out of the window. The April dusk was falling, and a bank of heavy black clouds suggested it was about to rain. "I think it's a bit late now," she said, "but tomorrow morning I'm going to have a big explore of that island."

"Well, discuss it with Wilfred first and don't go there without telling us."

The morning after their row, a somewhat subdued Jean Lemaître, having made his peace with Annette, proposed that, as she had suggested, he should go and reconnoitre Passford.

"I borrowed this map," he said, "and look, here is the house – Passford Hall – and here is a small village – Oakover, I think you call it – and in Oakover, I have discovered, is the cottage of my English friend Mr Jonathan. He is an artist and also a dealer in stolen goods, what the English call a fence. He has helped me many times. I did not know he was so near this place called Passford. I suggest I visit him and see what happens there."

It turned out that Mr Jonathan was going away for a week and would be delighted to lend his cottage to Jean and, of course, should anything of value be found and there was a matter of disposal...

Annette, having agreed to the plan despite certain misgivings, provided him with the money to hire a car. So it was late that afternoon that Jean drove down to Oakover and, having established himself in the cottage, found he just had time for a quick reconnaissance of the area.

The cottage was some two or three miles north-west of Passford Hall, on the edge of a wood and set back a short distance from a minor road, on the other side of which Jean found an overgrown track which appeared to lead in the direction of the Hall. However, as it was now almost dark, he decided to leave further exploration until the next day when he would have had a chance to study a map.

The map showed that a mile or so down the track there was a building of some sort. Beyond the building the track petered out, although a dotted line suggested a footpath, which itself ended at the bank of a small river. Across the river was a considerable area described as ornamental parkland. At the far end of this, perhaps half a mile from the river, was Passford Hall.

"It seems," Jean said to himself, "that I can take the car as far as this building. If there is anyone there I can apologise and leave. If it is unused, or even a ruin, perhaps there will be somewhere to hide the car, for it looks like walking from there on."

At ten o'clock the next morning, Jean left the cottage, crossed the road and drove cautiously down the track until he reached a clump of trees just short of the building; there he was able to park the car out of sight and then work his way forward in the cover of a badly overgrown hedge.

He now realised that there was more than one building and, as the place appeared to be unoccupied, he emerged from his cover and walked slowly down the track. The ground was quite soft, and even his untutored urban eye could see that the track had not been used for some time. Nor, indeed, had the buildings, which he guessed were the ruins of what had once been a small farm. A large wooden shed, its doors hanging open on rusty hinges, caught his eye and he decided that it would provide perfect cover for the car.

With the car safely hidden, Jean walked through the farmyard to what had once been a cowshed, where a tumbledown wall provided an admirable place from which to spy out the surrounding country.

There was, indeed, a narrow overgrown footpath leading downhill towards the river. Following the course of the river, he realised that some three hundred yards to the left of where the path ended, the river widened into a lake. Taking out his binoculars, which this time he had made sure he had with him, he studied the lake carefully. Altering his position slightly, he realised it was much bigger than he had thought, and that what had appeared to be the far bank was, in reality, an island. Moving round even further he saw that there was a bridge from the bank across to the island, but there seemed to be no way of getting to it from his side.

On the opposite bank a grass field, dotted with small clumps of trees, climbed gently uphill to a group of buildings. Beyond these his glasses showed him much taller trees, through the branches of which he could just see the chimneys of what he judged to be Passford Hall. To his right an ornamental wood and shrubbery sloped down from the Hall buildings to the bank of the river, and when he studied this he realised that there was a path through the wood which led to what looked like a bridge, although it was not marked on the map.

While he was studying this, he became aware of a woman emerging from the wood. Turning his glass to look at her, he realised that she was the girl he had first seen in the Franschhoek restaurant.

"Mlle Stanley," he said aloud, and with a note of triumph in his voice, "so I was right to come here. Eh bien, ma chère, let us see what you do now."

Emerging from the wood, Jenny turned along the riverbank in the direction of the lake. Jean watched her until she was some hundred yards short of the bridge, then moved cautiously down the path until, on his right, he was level with a ragged plantation of poplars. This he had already noticed would take him to the unmarked bridge, and would also give him some sort of cover. A quick look back showed that Jenny was about to cross to the island, so he plunged into the plantation and ran as fast as possible towards the bridge, which, when he reached it, proved not to be a bridge but a massive concrete beam carrying a pipe across the stream. It served its purpose, however, and minutes later Jean was making his way along the path to the island. There was little cover on the path, and he just had to hope that Jenny would be so occupied with her own business that she would not notice him, and also that no one had followed her from the house.

When Jean reached the bridge, he paused behind the trunk of a convenient willow and looked across at the island. It was well wooded, with a thick undergrowth of osier and other shrubs, and as he could see no movement, he crossed the bridge and moved quietly up the slope in front. At the top, on hands and knees, he peered through the undergrowth to see the girl standing in an opening among the trees and staring down at a small gravestone. She was some ten yards away, but as far as he could see there was no chance of getting any nearer, for to walk quietly over the carpet of broken reed stems would be quite impossible.

Beyond the clearing where she stood the ground rose again, and Jean realised that the centre of the island was a mound, on the top of which he could see a ruined building. He also saw that between the mound and the water there was a path, and it was towards this path that, a few minutes later, the girl walked.

As soon as she was out of sight, round the left side of the rise, Jean slipped down into the clearing and peered at the stone. "Toby," he muttered. "A name surely, but of who or what?" He bent down and pushed at the stone but it appeared to be very firmly embedded. Then he heard footsteps behind him and realised that Jenny must have walked right round the island. He had just time to crouch behind a rather insubstantial alder, when sure enough she emerged round the right side of the mound.

Speed was essential, and here Jean's life in the backstreets of Paris came into its own. Three quick strides and he was beside her, one arm round her waist preventing movement, and the other hand over her mouth.

"Do not struggle or shout or I will kill you," he hissed in her ear, "believe me! See what I do to you now." Like lightning he moved his arm from her waist and she felt a hand on her throat – then she was gasping for breath and there was a roaring in her ears.

Gradually he released the pressure and she was able to breathe. Then once again she heard the voice in her ear. "No noise or I will do it again, and if I make a mistake and do it too long you will die. Comprenez?"

Jenny, who had sunk backwards against the bank, clutching her throat and trying to get her breath, could only nod. Apparently not satisfied, Jean stepped towards her and grabbed the front of her shirt, at the same time drawing from his pocket an open flick knife.

"Not a sound now, and do not attempt to run – say you understand." Again Jenny, who was far too weak and frightened to do anything, could only nod.

"Now listen," Lemaître said, pulling her towards him, "you come from that big house, yes? Passford, is it?" Jenny, who had at last got her breath back but was too confused to grasp what was happening, again nodded. "Then is anyone from the house likely to come down here?"

"No, I don't think so," she gasped. "Why do you ask? And who are you anyway?"

"You know perfectly well – and if you don't, the answer can wait; but for now, you do exactly what I say. Come here and stand beside me," he ordered, and when she hesitated he shouted, "Quick, quick!"

Then, when she was beside him, he put his arm round her and slipped his hand up the back of her shirt so that she could feel the knife against her bare back. "We are lovers see, and we walk like this. No shout, no escape or you feel the little prick," and he giggled and jabbed, and she gasped as the tip of the knife broke her skin. "Now walk."

They met no one on the way back to the car and as they approached it, Jenny felt the knife removed from her back, but before she could make any move a noose was slipped over her wrists and knotted. Lemaître opened the passenger door. "In," he commanded, and as she sat down, "Hold out your legs." Again a noose was slipped over her ankles and knotted securely. "I don't want any nasty kicks," he grinned as he started the engine and drove slowly up the track.

When they reached the cottage, Jean loosed the hobble and led Jenny into the kitchen and sat her in a chair to which he tied her ankles.

"Now, ma petite," he said, "you are going to answer some questions and if you don't, I am going to hurt you. Why were you looking at that stone? Is it a clue to the treasure then?"

With that last question Jenny suddenly realised where she had seen the man before. He was the man in Franschhoek who was a friend of the woman Annette, and who they thought must be the man Andrew had found at the monument. "So they really are after the French jewellery," she thought, "and they've tracked us to here."

"My neck is horribly sore and my throat hurts if I talk," she croaked, "so can I have something to drink?"

He looked down at her and decided he'd better not be too hard yet. "Yes, I'll make some coffee," he said, switching on the kettle and leaving the room. When he returned he was carrying a flat piece of wood about a quarter of an inch thick by an inch and a quarter wide and some eighteen inches in length. This he put down on the table and then made two mugs of coffee. He freed Jenny's arms and put one of the mugs on the table beside her. "No movement," he warned, "just drink your coffee."

Jenny massaged her wrists carefully, realising only too well that she was quite incapable of doing anything but drink the coffee and wonder, with a certain apprehension, about the piece of wood.

When she had finished her coffee, he once again tied her wrists together and fastened them securely to the back of the chair. He than walked round to stand staring down at her, and for the first time she began to feel real fear.

"Now we shall have a little talk," he said. "You know who I am, don't you? Don't you?" he screamed and he moved round behind her. Once again she felt the hands on her neck and the roaring in her ears. She felt tears starting from her eyes, which seemed about to be squeezed from their sockets.

"Stop! Please stop," she sobbed, hardly able to get out the words. Then, when the pressure eased, she whispered, "You were in South Africa with that woman."

"That's better," he said, "so then you know why I'm here."

"I've no idea," she gasped, then with a sudden access of courage added, "Now you must let me go. If I don't get back to the house soon, my friends will start looking for me."

"Possibly they will," he said, "but we're quite safe here; no one will think of looking in a respectable artist's cottage. We are even so safe we can try a little persuasion." And she felt his hands move down the front of her shirt and fondle her breasts. She tried to shrink away from him, but the cords held her secure. "Now, ma chérie, be sensible. Say you know why I'm here and what I want."

The ghost of Caspar Boscawen seemed to float before her, and this time there was no Mzumi to come to the rescue. The hands had now removed her bra, but she looked up at him and shook her head.

"I really have no idea why—" and the rest of her answer dissolved in terrified screams, as he pinched her nipples viciously.

"Now will you tell me why you were looking at that stone and who or what is this Toby?" and again she felt the agonising pain in her breasts. Her head fell forward but he pushed it back and slapped her face. "Answer!" he hissed.

"I can't, I can't. I—" she whimpered and then a grey mist seemed to cloud her eyes and she fainted.

When she came to, Lemaître was standing in front of her holding the wooden batten and slapping it against his left hand.

"Well now, you seem to know why I'm here," he said, "so you are going to help me – yes?"

"Help you – why?" She looked at him vaguely and her head lolled forward again. Then the next thing she knew was the shock of cold water hitting her face.

"Wake up, you little bitch," she heard him say, "and answer my question. What has Toby to do with this family legacy?"

The cold water had its effect; her mind cleared and somehow being called a bitch seemed to stiffen her resolve to say nothing.

"I don't know anything about legacies," she said. "I know Andrew found something in South Africa and got excited about it, but it's not my family so I know no more than that."

"Oh yes, I think you do," he said. "I saw you at the monument with that old man and we thought the jewels must be there. Annette knows your lover's family stole them from France. Then I find you here, where Annette says the family live, so I think you know something, and if you won't tell me, I shall have to make you."

"But I tell you, you can try what you like," she said with a bravado she was far from feeling, "but I can't tell you what I don't know."

"Well, we'll see about that. You felt what I did just now; this will be much worse. I have seen the strongest men in Paris confess after a taste of the baton," he said putting down the wooden instrument and moving towards her. Then he bent down and pushed up her skirt until it was above her hips.

He gazed down at her thighs which, because of the way her legs were tied, were slightly splayed.

"Very pretty," he said tapping her knickers with the batten. She closed her eyes; but what happened next was not what she expected, and again she screamed as he started methodically to beat her left thigh. It was quite gentle but the pain was intense. Up and down he went until she thought her leg would burst.

"Stop!" she cried. "I've told you I know nothing."

He smiled down at her. "Very well, we'll try the other leg," and he raised the terrible piece of wood.

"No," she gasped, "no, please stop," and the stick came down on her right thigh and she rolled about in the chair, screaming, until at last he stopped.

"Don't start again," she moaned and her voice was barely above a whisper. "Toby, the book said. Where Toby died in the cold. That's all." And she slumped sideways in the chair with such violence that Jean only just stopped it crashing to the floor.

CHAPTER 19

O<small>N THE PLANE FROM</small> E<small>DINBURGH</small>, A<small>NDREW HAD</small> found himself thinking, for the first time since Alice's death, that his life was back to normal, something his friends too seemed to accept. He'd set the brewery on a new course, he was going to get married and he was determined to solve the Saddler family mystery. It was this latter that really excited him; he'd always loved the world of secret intelligence and here was a chance to get back into it.

The next day, on the drive from Passford to London, his thoughts turned again to the Saddler family, and never a man to let matters rest once decisions were made, the first thing he did on arrival at his office was to arrange a meeting with his old friend Oliver Forbes, Chairman of Freeman Baxter, the brewery's stockbroker.

"Look forward to seeing you," Forbes had said. "One o'clock tomorrow at the Broad Street Club."

Realising that over the next few weeks other matters might take precedence, he devoted the rest of the day to the business of the brewery, not least with the first week's trading from World Wide Wines.

Now, if you want to meet anyone of significance in the City of London, even in these workaholic days, the Broad Street Club at lunchtime is not a bad place to start. Andrew Henderson, although not a City man, had been a member for many years. He had found that his customers and others who had business in central London appreciated a visit to the City, rather than trailing out to Gunnersbury or being taken to one of the well-known clubs around St James Street.

It was not surprising, therefore, that when he walked into the club the next day, the commissionaire greeted him with enthusiasm and with the news that Mr Forbes was in the bar.

Oliver Forbes was a very tall man with a somewhat serious expression, offset by a mop of unruly grey hair. When Andrew entered the bar he was talking to a stout, balding man, but immediately broke off the conversation and loped over to take Andrew's hand.

"Do you mind if we go straight in?" he said. "I want to give us plenty of time, and I have an appointment at two forty-five."

"Fine. Suits me," Andrew replied. "I've a lot to do at the brewery and I need to stop and see old Jenkins on the way back."

"Ah, Mavis, how are we today?" Oliver said to the attractive red-haired waitress. "And I'll tell you what, while we decide," and he tapped the menu, "could you bring us a carafe of the club white? Suit you, Andrew?" and his companion nodded.

"And now, gentlemen?" Mavis asked as she came back with the carafe of wine and filled their glasses.

"Right, I'll have the potted shrimps and the escalope of veal," Oliver said.

"I'll follow you with the shrimps," Andrew said, "but I'll stick with fish. The Dover sole would be fine."

"It's very good, this white," Oliver said. "Australian, you know. Good idea of the committee to have some of these new world wines. By the way, how's your new venture going?" And the discussion on the successful launch of World Wide Wines lasted until the first course arrived.

"Now you said, Andrew, that you wanted some information about eighteenth-and nineteenth-century banks in London. Am I allowed to ask why?"

"Yes indeed," and Andrew gave a brief outline of the discovery and contents of the Saddler papers.

"Now, as far as the jewellery is concerned, we know from the letter that it is somewhere on the Saddler estate, and we now think we know where. The contents of the tube are another matter. First there is the seal, and then the command to take it to the rich Englishman at The Sign of the Stag. The emblem on the seal is a dog, which could mean anything. A rich man at The

Sign of the Stag sounds like the address of one of those early City merchants, and we do have one other clue. We have now discovered that the French Court and Saddler's father-in-law dealt with a London banker called Murray. Any of that mean anything to you?"

"To be honest, no; but there is someone in the club who might help. Do you remember old Spottiswoode? Well, I saw him as I came in," Oliver replied, "and he is a mine of information on City history. If anyone can help, he can. He's sure to be in the Coffee Room after lunch. We'll have a word."

Old Spottiswoode was indeed ensconced in his usual chair at the back of the Coffee Room, and looked up as Oliver approached. "Hullo, young man. You seem to get taller every time I see you. And I know you, don't I?" he added, turning his gaze to Andrew. "You're Henderson, aren't you? Remember your grandfather – acted for him on several occasions. Well now, you look as if you were going to ask me something."

"Indeed," said Andrew. "Forbes said you might be able to help me with a little bit of City history. Does the name Murray mean anything to you? Probably a banker, possibly having connections with the Bourbons in the seventeen seventies or eighties."

"Murray – yes, Peascod and Murray – goldsmiths and bankers and, if I remember rightly, to be found at The Sign of the Stag in Poultry," the old man said. "Why do you ask?"

Andrew, who had nearly upset his coffee at the mention of the address, replied, "I recently found some family papers saying that some property might have been deposited with them, and I wondered if they still existed."

"Well, let me think," Spottiswoode said, stroking his chin; then after minute or two's silence he continued, "Yes, now I remember. About the time of Waterloo they became Peascod Brothers, and then Buller and Peascod. Then there was some sort of disaster and they did not survive the Boer War; swallowed up by the Middlesex Bank which, of course, is now part of United Counties and has been for fifty years. Would they have any records? Well, that you'd have to ask them. Get young Forbes here to introduce you to Brinsley Maufe. Sure he'll try to help."

"That was more than successful," Andrew said as he and Oliver stood in the hall, after thanking Spottiswoode profusely. "Brinsley Maufe? He's the chairman of United Counties, isn't he? I don't know him."

"I do," Oliver replied. "Tell you what... I'll ring his secretary and say you'll be in touch. Then you ring her tomorrow and see if you can get into his diary. Now I must fly. You OK for transport?"

"Yes, car's round the back of the Brewers. Jim has a secret place! Anyway, thanks for your help and I'll let you know how we get on."

The following day turned out to be rather busier than Andrew had expected. Apart from the normal business of the brewery, the Managing Director of Blundells, a small Essex brewery partly owned by Henderson Braithwaite, asked for an urgent consultation. Then, after lunch, he and Tony had a long and very interesting meeting with the owner of a Chilean vineyard. As a result, he had to leave it to Angela to contact Sir Brinsley Maufe's secretary. Now, arranging top-level meetings was one of Angela's strong points and she did not fail on this one, for during the meeting with the Chilean a note appeared saying that the Chairman of United Counties Bank would see him at two thirty the next day.

"That was very quick," he said to his secretary, when later she brought in the mail for signature. "Didn't expect to see the great man as soon as that."

"His secretary said that Mr Forbes had said it was a matter of some urgency," Angela replied, "and the fact that I know her quite well may also have helped. I got the impression, too, that Sir Brinsley was keen to talk to you anyway."

"You're a very shrewd operator, Angela, and you're probably right. I suspect he would like a slice of the business from one of London's largest brewers. Now, just let me finish signing these, and then get Jason and Frank so I can make sure everything's ready for tomorrow morning's Board."

That evening, for a change, Andrew had no engagements, so was settling down to deal with one or two personal matters when the telephone rang.

"This is Annette Barry," the voice at the other end said, "and I guess you must be surprised to hear from me."

"I am, and may I ask what it is you want?" Andrew replied somewhat coldly.

"Since I've been back in London, I've been looking at some of the books on the family that James left here," Annette said, "and I've become very intrigued by the story of the Chevalier and his life at the Bourbon Court, particularly his, how shall we say? His relationship – perhaps even amorous relationship – with Marie Antoinette. And I wondered again about that story of a gift, a gift perhaps of great value."

"I've already told you all I know is – and this is if there is any truth in the story – that anything of value went to a colleague of the Chevalier in Hong Kong," Andrew replied with a certain asperity in his voice.

"And I'm saying I don't believe you," Annette said. "I have a friend who works for the French Government and who knows that certain items of value left France illegally with the Chevalier and it is thought that they remained with his family. My friend knows an artist or writer or someone who has a cottage near the Saddler home – Passford is it called? And he's gone up there to see if the locals can tell him anything."

"I very much doubt that," Andrew said, making a mental note to warn Jenny.

"Me also," Annette replied. "What I think would be far more useful to us all is for you and I to meet and discuss our mutual information. So can we find a time when I can come and see you?"

"No, we can't," Andrew said, then added, "Look I don't mean to be rude, but I'm far too busy at present to waste time on something as trivial as this. I have meetings all over the country for the next three or four weeks. I have a very large business to run, you know."

Annette knew when she was beaten. "Alright then, but I shall try again. Meanwhile I shall continue to see if I can find anything in the books my husband left here. Au revoir, mon cher." And she rang off.

"I don't like it one little bit," Andrew, who was a very shrewd judge of character, thought as he put down the phone. "That's a dangerous woman and a determined one. She and that little French creep make a dangerous couple and they certainly seem to have decided that the Saddler legacy exists and mean to have part or all of it. Now I'd better warn them at Passford that the

Frenchman is somewhere around that area." As he reached for the telephone, and before he could pick it up, it rang.

"Darling," Phyllis's voice said, "Tony has just appeared with the wife of that Chilean wine man. He's been taken to some big dinner and she's all alone. Come and help entertain her." And she added mischievously, "She's very beautiful." So he never rang Passford, thinking that Angela could do it in the morning, but then he forgot to tell her.

Having just prevented Jenny and the chair crashing to the floor, Jean Lemaître bent down and listened to her breathing and then felt her pulse. Deciding that she was alive and in no immediate danger, he undid the ropes round her ankles and carried her upstairs and laid her on a bed. Then he got a jug of water and a glass and put them on the table by the bed, undid the cords around her wrists and went out, locking the bedroom door.

Outside the front door he stood for a moment looking at the car, and then walked round to the back of the cottage. In one of the two sheds there he found what he was looking for – a bicycle. It was old and somewhat rusty but he decided it would suit his purpose admirably. Much less conspicuous than the car, and easier to hide.

Making sure that there was no one about, he crossed the road and pedalled down the track until he reached the poplars. There he hid the bike under a bush, checked that there was nobody in sight on the other bank of the river, then made his way to the island.

He tried again to shift the Toby stone, but it remained immovable. He then walked to the top of the rise and examined the ruined building. Judging by the broken pillars lying around, it had once been a classical pavilion. Despite a careful search, Jean could find nothing that suggested a hiding place, and so he walked back down the slope towards the gravestone. Nearly at the bottom, his smooth leather soles lost their grip on the damp grass and he slid forward, tripping over some solid object. Scraping aside the grass and undergrowth he uncovered a stone slab, and above it, set into the hillside, what looked like a cast-iron hatch cover some five-foot high by three-foot wide. The stone slab was unstable when he stood on it, but he was unable to move either it or the metal cover.

As he stood considering the significance of his find, he heard voices from the direction of the bridge, and a man shouted "Jenny!" several times. He was now in something of a quandary. Where he stood in the dell, he was out of sight of anyone on the bridge and he would still be out of sight if he slipped out round to the left of the knoll. His problem was that he'd heard at least two people, and if they decided to walk round the island in opposite directions he would be trapped.

He would also be trapped if he stayed where he was, so bending low, he scuttled over the shallow bank and sank down behind a thick bush. The voices came nearer and he reckoned they were crossing the bridge. Then the man shouted again and he heard the footsteps move off to the right.

The back streets of Paris had taught him to think and move quickly, so as soon as he was sure there were no footsteps moving towards him, he was across the dell, down the bank, over the bridge and running towards the wood. He knew he had about three minutes before they would be round the island and could see him; less if they went up to the ruin.

He just made it. As he flung himself down in the edge of the wood and turned to look back, a man appeared among the broken walls of the pavilion, closely followed by a woman. He saw them talking and pointing until, after a few minutes, they moved down into the dell and back across the bridge. On the path, they hesitated for a moment, then moved off towards the far end of the lake and were soon out of his sight.

Jean moved cautiously from his cover and, seeing no one, ran back across the river to where he'd left his bicycle and rode off up the track. At the old farm buildings, he stopped to take stock of his position.

From his lookout point by the cowshed wall, he turned his binoculars in the direction of the lake and saw, in the distance, two figures moving up the hill in the direction of Passford Hall.

"Eh bien," he said to himself, "they don't seem to have seen me, but I'll have to be careful on future visits; although having found no sign of the girl there, they may leave it alone and try other places."

The more he thought of that loose slab and the metal hatch cover, the more he thought they were worthy of further investigation. Not tonight, though, he decided, for he must see about the girl; she was too valuable an asset to allow to come to any harm. Anyway, he would need tools, so he'd better see what there was at the cottage. Pushing the bike until he reached the top of the rise above the farm, he mounted and pedalled back to the cottage.

He found Jenny lying on the bed just as he'd left her, but when he approached her she opened an eye and, in a voice he could hardly hear, told him to go away.

"I have nothing to say to you," she whispered. "Now leave me alone," and she turned over and closed her eyes.

It was some three hours later that he went up again, and this time he found her sitting on the edge of the bed, looking at the bruises on her thighs.

"You must let me go to the bathroom and attend to these bruises," she pleaded. "They really need arnica or something, but at least cold water would help."

"No, you can't come with me," she added as he moved to follow her, "but I promise not to try to escape."

The owner of the cottage obviously looked after himself well, for although there was no arnica or embrocation, there was some antiseptic cream and plenty of towels, so she undressed, washed and then sat with a towel soaked in cold water on each leg for twenty minutes. Then, having applied the cream to the places where the skin was broken, she put on a dressing gown which was hanging on the back of the door and hobbled back to the bedroom, where she found Jean, who asked if she wanted any food.

"Just a cup of tea," she replied.

When, ten minutes later, he returned with the tea, he put a key on the table beside the bed.

"Here, you can take the key and lock yourself in," he said, "but don't try to escape. Your window is locked and so is the one in the bathroom, and I shall lock the door at the end of the passage, okay?" Jenny nodded.

"Tomorrow, in the morning," he went on, "I shall return to the island and if I find what I think I will find, then we will drive back to London and Madame Barry will decide what next. So now, bonsoir, ma chérie."

As she sipped the tea, she wondered what the Saddlers were doing. Had they told Andrew? They must have, she thought, but what could he do? He wouldn't have any idea where she was. What would that man do to her next?

She shivered at the thought and tried to put it out of her mind. Looking round the room, she noticed a chest of drawers and when she investigated it, in the second drawer was a pile of neatly ironed shirts, one of which she decided would make an admirable nightie. Then she locked the door and five minutes later, wrapped in yellow Tattersall check, she sank into an exhausted sleep.

CHAPTER 20

O N THE MORNING OF THE DAY THAT Jean Lemaître made his first visit to the island, Andrew Henderson got through the business of his board meeting in quick time and took his colleagues in to lunch sharp at one o'clock. As soon as the main course was over he excused himself, and at two minutes after half past two, he was shown into the Chairman's palatial office in the United Counties tower in Gracechurch Street.

"Very pleased to see you, Henderson, or may I follow the modern trend and call you Andrew?" Sir Brinsley Maufe said.

"Please do, Sir Brinsley," Andrew replied.

"You know, it's strange that you should have rung when you did," Sir Brinsley said, "for I've been meaning to get in touch with you for some time. As I'm sure you are aware, before the First War, the old Middlesex Bank did quite a lot of business with Hendersons Brewery, and we'd be very happy to renew the association. Perhaps we could arrange a little lunch here and discuss the matter?"

"I'd be delighted to discuss the idea, but obviously I can make no promises."

"No, of course, I understand that. My secretary will be in touch and we'll see what can be arranged. Now what is it that we can do for you today?" Sir Brinsley said.

"In the eighteenth century there was a bank in Poultry," Andrew said, "called Peascod and Murray. To be more precise they were goldsmiths, who also conducted banking business at The Sign of the Stag. After a good many changes of name and fortune they were finally swallowed up by the Middlesex sometime about the turn of the century. Whether Middlesex inherited any of their records I don't know, but if they did, would they have been passed on to you?"

"I remember my grandfather talking about Murrays and its various successors," Sir Brinsley said reflectively, looking out of the window. "Haven't thought of them for years. Buller and Peascod they were then. Old Sam Buller was a friend of his," and he swung his chair back to look at Andrew, "but whether we have any of their stuff I don't know. Jones would though, he's the archivist." He picked up the telephone and asked his secretary to get someone to find Leighton Jones and send him up. "Interesting chap, Leighton Jones – Jones the Archive they call him – if anyone can help, he can. But why do you want to know?"

"Way back some ancestors had dealings with them, mainly involving property," Andrew answered. "I won't bore you with the details, but something concerning this property has now cropped up and it would be immensely helpful if we had more details of the original transactions."

"Ah now, here's Jones," Sir Brinsley replied, as a small, grey-haired man slid through the door in response to the Chairman's brusque "Come in."

"Let's see if he can help us. Leighton, this is Mr Henderson of Henderson Braithwaite the brewers. He needs to know if we have any records of that bank, Murray and something, one of the ones that the Middlesex rescued."

"Buller and Peascod, do you mean, sir?" Jones asked and Andrew nodded. "Yes, I think we have. But whether they're here or out at Hayes I couldn't be sure. We'd have to go and look in the vaults."

"Could you take Mr Henderson down then and see what you can find? Andrew, would you be happy if I left you to Mr Jones?" Sir Brinsley stood up and held out his hand.

"Of course," Andrew replied, "and I'm most grateful to you and the bank for your help."

On the way down to the vaults, Jones remarked that it was a pity it was not the bank's dealings with the brewery he was interested in, for they'd had them out only a week ago. "So Sir B really is interested in our getting together again," Andrew said to himself.

"What we've got in London is in here, but most of the newer records are on microfilm in a warehouse out by London Airport," Jones said, opening a strong room door. "I don't think we ever filmed the Peascod stuff – too old – so we may be in luck."

The archivist walked to the far end of the room where there were racks of old-fashioned deed boxes.

"Yes," he said, "there are three here, all to do with Peascod and Murray or their successors. Now, sir, what about this? No 11, Peascod and Murray 1770–1810."

"Sounds promising," Andrew said.

"Well, let's see if we have a key," and Jones crossed to a tall metal cabinet. "Here we are, No. 11," and he carried the box over to a table and unlocked it.

In the box were bundles of documents tied with pink and red ribbon, the descriptions of their contents so faded as to be almost illegible. Underneath the bundles was a heavy leather document case with a brass label inscribed 'Mr Aeneas Murray'. The archivist looked at the lock and shook his head.

"Don't know if we've a key for this," he said, but when Andrew pressed the catch and lifted the flap, it opened. Inside were several sealed packages and a rather unusual-looking tin box.

Andrew sorted through the packages and finally put one aside. "It's difficult to read," he said to Jones, "but don't you think that looks like 'Bourbon correspondence'?"

"Indeed, sir, that's what it says," he said, studying it under a special bright light. "Would you like me to open it?" and he picked up a thin-bladed knife. "There you are. No damage, for age has hardened the wax and the seal hasn't even broken."

There were a number of letters from various members of the Court of Louis XVI, and also from the French Government, all concerning loans to the King. One, in particular, interested Andrew and he sat down to read it. It was not easy, for the ink had faded and the French was somewhat archaic, but eventually he decided he had the gist of it.

It was from Jacques Neckar to Aeneas Murray and said that all the arrangements were complete for their friends to travel to England, and funds for their stay would shortly be in the hands of Lord Strathconon. As regards the box, Murray was to keep this in a safe place. If someone came to claim it, he would know them because only they would have the key to open it.

The box was some eight inches long by two wide and two deep and made of steel rather than the normal tinplate. It looked like the sort of case that might contain a valuable necklace or possibly an important historic deed. The most unusual thing about it though was the keyhole. This was not in the expected place, but in the middle of the lid and protected by a sliding cover.

Andrew pushed up the cover, displaying a round hole, perhaps a quarter of an inch deep and with no shaft to take a key.

"Have you ever seen anything like this?" he asked Jones.

"Can't say I have," the archivist replied. "Doesn't seem that it's meant for a key. Shall we try pressing?" and he picked up a pencil and stuck it in the hole. "No give there, sir. Wait a minute though, when I put my finger in the base feels rough, almost jagged, as if you could grasp it with tweezers or pliers."

Andrew picked up the box and looked at the hole, then he too felt it and, using his latchkey, tried to turn the base, with no success.

"I think you're on the right track, sir. That base is meant to turn," Jones, who had been watching Andrew's efforts, said. "We just need something that fits the hole."

Andrew looked at Jones and put down the box. "Of course," he said, "something that fits the hole. Something that has indentations to fit over those jagged edges."

He felt in his jacket pocket and produced a cardboard box from which he took the Blouberg seal.

"Let's try this," and he dropped the seal into the hole, turned it and found he was pressing against a spring and with a click, the lid opened.

Inside were two sheets of paper, about the size of modern writing paper, and neatly folded to fit the box. Possibly because the box was airtight, both paper and writing were in surprisingly good condition.

"What do I do now?" Andrew asked. "Do these letters and papers belong to the family – after all we've identified ourselves by the key – or do they belong to the bank?"

"That, I think, you will have to ask Sir Brinsley," Jones replied.

When they rang her, Sir Brinsley's secretary said that he'd asked not to be disturbed but she'd see what she could do and ring back, which she did ten minutes later. The Chairman's view, it appeared, was that this was one for the lawyers. She had therefore asked Charles Beaman, the Senior Legal Adviser, to go down and discuss the matter.

Beaman turned out to be a brisk, no nonsense barrister who took a quick look at the letters and other papers, and then examined the box and the seal.

"I think I've understood the rough meaning of the letter," he said to Andrew, "but my French is not that good. If yours is, perhaps you'd translate for me. Then I think it would be helpful if you could give me a little background."

"Sure," Andrew said and gave a brief account of the Chevalier's connection with the pre-revolutionary French court, his assumed gifts from the King and Queen, and of the handing of them to the Saddler family. Finally, he described his discovery of Thomas's papers and of the seal.

"So you see, by a series of unlikely coincidences the Saddler family, in the form of my late wife and her cousin, have a chance of discovering the truth of this hitherto fabled royal legacy. We have not yet found the jewellery but we think we know where it is. To find out what else the King may have intended the Chevalier to have, I need these papers from the box, or at least copies of them."

"Yes indeed," the lawyer said. Then after a long pause, he picked up the seal and looked across at Andrew.

"It seems," he said, "that you have fulfilled the requirement of the letter to Murray, that the box and its contents belong to he who can produce the key. This you have done and we are aware of your personal standing and of your relationship to the Saddler family. My opinion is that, subject to the approval of the Chairman, you should be allowed to take copies of these two papers. The originals should then be replaced, the box locked and returned to us for safekeeping. Also, to keep matters reasonably official I think that I should have a word with your solicitors."

Sir Brinsley Maufe agreed to this plan, and half an hour later Andrew returned to the brewery with the copies and also the all-important seal. Everything else remained with the bank.

At the brewery, Andrew dealt with a couple of minor matters, then left and went straight to his flat. There he settled down to see what new twist to the tale of the Bourbon legacy the seal might have unlocked.

"More puzzles!" was his immediate reaction when he looked at the copies he had brought back from the bank. First there was a letter, apparently confirming some earlier instructions, which he translated without difficulty.

> *My Lord,*
>
> *The brig Candide has sailed with the cargo you are expecting. The Captain is confi-dent of finding the landing place and Rorie Mor Macrae and his men know the hiding place. Rorie Mor has arranged for the brig to founder and only he knows it is to happen. Should fate overtake our patrons, they wish their faithful page, the Chevalier Antoine, to be the beneficiary. He has a copy of this letter and a clue to guide him to the hiding place.*
>
> *Your servant,*
> *F Chisholm.*

Then there was a poem.

> *The ice cold maidens fearsome stand*
> *And look to confluent seas.*
> *Their western shore is where you'll land,*
> *On rocks beneath the trees.*
> *The monster's back you then must line*
> *With steps across the wave.*
> *The noble head up high's the sign*
> *That marks the mossy grave.*

Andrew sat for some minutes, gazing at the two documents. 'My Lord' he decided must be Lord Strathconon, and the letter was confirmation to him of the information Neckar had already sent to Murray. If the poem was intended as the clue, then as far as Andrew was concerned it could hardly be less helpful. He lay back in his chair and closed his eyes, his mind a jumble of frozen maidens, rocks and monsters.

He was almost asleep when the telephone rang. He reached over and picked up the receiver and heard Wilfred Saddler's voice. What he said drove all other thoughts from Andrew's mind.

"Oh God! You say Jenny is missing? And that bloody Frenchman's up there... Yes I understand, yes, and I'll tell you what I mean in a moment. You say she went out this morning and hasn't been seen since... Yes I'm sorry, I've been out all day and the brewery would not have been able to get me this afternoon. But listen, Wilfred, as I said, that Frenchman who's going round with Annette is somewhere in your part of the world... Yes, I meant to get Angela to ring and warn you, but I forgot. Have you told the police? ... Good; well don't. I'll come straight down now. We can't do much tonight other than think about the best way to proceed. Let's hope she's still somewhere in your neighbourhood or we really have a problem... Right, see you in a couple of hours."

Fifteen minutes later, having rung his secretary at home and given her some instructions and left a note for Marg, Andrew was threading his way east through the evening crowds.

CHAPTER 21

VERY EARLY THE NEXT MORNING, WELL BEFORE daylight, Jean Lemaître slipped out of the cottage and round to the sheds at the back. There, after a short search with the aid of a torch, he found exactly what he needed: a spade, and also a stout metal lever of the sort used for lifting manhole covers. These he tied to the bar of his bicycle, and having made sure there was no one in sight, pushed it across the road and set off down the track.

His objective was to get the tools as near to the island as possible in the dark and then hide them; for he reckoned that if he was found wandering about the Passford Estate, an apology in broken English would probably end the matter. However, to be found carrying a spade and a jemmy would take rather more explaining and might even involve the police. He would like to have done the whole job in the dark but that would have meant a torch, and even he knew that farm workers rise early.

Not wanting to risk a light, he pushed the bike as far as the poplars. There he hid it, untied the tools and stood for a moment listening. His luck was in, for it seemed that there was nobody about; so just ten minutes later, with the spade and jemmy safely stowed away close to the bridge, he was back and pedalling up the hill to the cottage.

It had been half past nine when Andrew reached Passford to find a very agitated household. Wilfred Saddler, usually so calm, was wandering around feeling he ought to do something but not quite sure what. Mary, unused to crises, and jolted suddenly from the normal gentle rhythm of the Suffolk countryside, had retired to bed. In fact the one person who appeared to retain a reasonable grasp of essentials was the butler, Steven.

153

"Bad business this, sir," he said as he greeted Andrew at the front door. "I've never seen Mr Saddler this upset, so I hope you'll be able to do something."

"So do I, Steven, so do I," he replied grimly. "The first thing to do is to talk to them and find out just what happened. Where are they? In the drawing room?"

"Mr Saddler is, but Mrs Saddler has gone up to her room," Steven said. "And you, sir, have you had anything to eat?" Andrew shook his head and the butler added, "Nor have they. If you'd like to go in, I'll bring some sandwiches, and there's a nice fruit cake cook's just made."

"My dear Andrew, I can't forgive myself for this," Wilfred said when Andrew walked in. "I should never have let her go to the island alone, but she'd done it safely on the previous two days. I can't think what has happened."

"I can," Andrew answered, "and I'm furious with myself for forgetting to get Angela to warn you about Lemaître. He's someone Annette Barry picked up – from the backstreets of Paris, I rather think. I've never seen him properly, but Norman knew about him and says he's a nasty bit of work. Now, before we decide anything, tell me – do you have an artist living round here?"

"An artist? Yes – why do you ask? But look, first let me get you a drink. Whisky?"

"Lovely, thanks. I'll tell you why I ask. The other evening Annette Barry rang up and tried to pump me, but I wasn't having any of it. Then she said that she'd had a row with Lemaître and he'd gone off on his own. Said he had a friend, an artist, I think she said, who had a cottage near Passford. He'd found out that that's where the Saddlers lived and that was the place where the answer would be found. And so that's where he was going. That's what I forgot to tell you! There can be little doubt that Lemaître has got Jenny. It's likely that he's found the island and may be ahead of us in discovering what's there."

"Looks a bit like it," Wilfred said gloomily, "but let me tell you about our artist. He's another dubious character, Jonathan Posgate by name; and it must be him your Frenchman is talking about. He lives at Oakover – Plumtree

Cottage – it's just outside the village, about a couple of miles from here as the crow flies. Up the hill beyond the lake. Of course it's rather further by road, four or five miles maybe."

"Sounds ideal for Monsieur Jean's nefarious purposes," Andrew said, "so what we must hope is that he's taken Jenny there and that she's still there. I rather think she will be, for I doubt Lemaître will realise we know about his artist friend, so he'll think she's safe there. Yes, Plumtree Cottage is where we'll start. You and I, Wilfred, will go there tomorrow morning and find a place for a good spy. We ought to be in position by seven or a little before."

It was just after six when Jean got back to the cottage, and he immediately set about making himself coffee and toast. Toast he considered an English abomination, but he'd not had time to buy rolls or croissants or even some decent bread. So toast, butter and strawberry jam, which he'd found in the larder, it had to be.

"It'll do for the girl, though," he thought as, having finished his own breakfast, he prepared a tray for Jenny, took it upstairs and knocked on her door.

"There's a tray outside the door," he said. "I'm going out, but you are still locked in so don't try to escape."

In the thirty-six hours he'd spent at the cottage he'd seen remarkably few people. There had been the odd car on the road, but no one had come to the house, and apart from the people searching for Jenny, he'd seen little activity in the surrounding fields.

"Yes, Plumtree Cottage suits my purposes very well," Jonathan Posgate had told him. "You get a few cars morning and evening making for the main road. As for visitors, well, the locals mostly leave me alone for I'm considered unfriendly, rude and even slightly sinister."

On the strength of this advice and his own experience, Jean reckoned that it was safe to leave Jenny in the cottage, and that at a quarter to seven in the morning there was unlikely to be anyone around the island. He therefore picked up his bicycle and pedalled down to the road, and promptly encountered the first setback to his plans.

As he neared the end of the path, he heard a vehicle approaching from the right, so he left the bike behind a tree and walked down to the roadside hedge. A cautious look showed him a car just rounding a bend about two hundred yards away. It was followed by a somewhat battered pick-up truck which stopped opposite the entrance to the farm track, and waited while a tractor and a string of cars passed. The last in the line was a Land Rover which stopped beside the pick-up; the drivers exchanged a few words, and then both vehicles drove off down the track for about two hundred yards, before turning right through a gate and vanishing from sight over the edge of a rise.

Jean now had two problems. First and most serious was that he had no idea where the two vehicles had gone. From the direction they took, it seemed likely to him that they would be in sight of his route to the island. This would mean that he'd have to proceed with care, and that would compound his second problem, which was the delay he'd already suffered due to the traffic, a delay which was to prove more serious than he realised, for his activities were now under observation.

At the edge of a wood, on the high ground a quarter of a mile beyond Plumtree Cottage, Andrew Henderson lowered his binoculars.

"A man just left the cottage and is bicycling down towards the road," he said to Wilfred Saddler, who was crouched down behind him. "I can't be sure whether it's Lemaître for I can't get a proper view of his face. Wait though, it looks as though something's happened," and he raised the binoculars again. "Yes, he's dropped the bike and he's peering through the hedge at what appears to be a sudden rush of traffic. Now there's a pick-up and another vehicle, a Land Rover I think, and they've stopped opposite the cottage."

Wilfred glanced at his watch, then moved forward and held out his hand towards Andrew.

"Let me have the glasses a moment," he said and had a long look at what was happening on the road. "That Land Rover is my farm manager's, so I think the pick-up must belong to the plumber. I'd forgotten he was coming to look at the ram. Yes, there they go across the field, and the ram's just at the bottom."

"What's the ram?" Andrew asked, taking the binoculars, and focusing again on the man by the hedge.

"A hydraulic pump," Wilfred answered. "It takes water from the river just downstream of the lake, and pumps it to a small reservoir which feeds a number of cattle troughs. Old-fashioned idea, but funnily enough they're becoming popular again."

"It's him alright," Andrew cried, lowering the glasses. "He's walking back to the bike and I got a good view of his face. Now he's riding off down a track on the other side of the road. Where does that go?"

"To some old farm buildings, and eventually down to the river. It's the way he'd go if he was heading for the island," Wilfred replied. "He'll have to be careful though if he doesn't want to be seen, for he'll be in view of anyone at the ram."

"So it may take him a bit of time," Andrew said, and his companion nodded. "Then if that's what he's doing, now's the time to investigate the cottage. I'll walk straight there while you go and get the car," and pocketing the binoculars, he set off down the hill.

Not knowing if there might be anyone about, Andrew approached cautiously via an overgrown shrubbery and the outhouses. There he paused and studied the back of the house with his binoculars. One particular window interested him, for there seemed to be movement in the room behind. Then his heart leapt, for suddenly a woman's figure appeared at the window, looked out briefly and then retired out of sight.

He couldn't be sure if it was Jenny and the only way to find out was to enter the house. So under cover of the shrubbery, he worked his way round until he reached the blank gable end of the cottage. He then carefully edged along the back wall, keeping below the level of the windowsills, rising only to peer into each in turn. He then repeated the procedure in the front, and nowhere did he see any sign of life. What he did see, however, was a window at the back which seemed to offer a means of entry.

It was a single casement window, probably the cloakroom was Andrew's thought, for it had a flap-type top section which, as is so often the case, had been left open. After a quick look to see that there was nobody about, Andrew heaved himself onto the stone ledge and reached inside the flap. Somewhat to his surprise the casement was secured only by a handle and, as far as he could see, there was no lock. With a silent prayer that there was also no alarm, he raised the lever and gently opened the window.

It was a tight squeeze, but he managed to slide head first through the narrow gap, finishing with an elegant forward roll over the lavatory seat. It was not exactly a silent performance and he stood for a moment listening, but all he could hear was the pounding of his own heart.

He opened the door and listened again, but as all seemed quiet, he went ahead and searched the ground floor. There was a kitchen with a pile of unwashed dishes, then a short passage leading to a hallway and the front door, opposite which was the staircase. To one side of the door was an untidy sitting room, and on the other a locked door. "Probably the studio," Andrew thought, remembering the large, north-facing window he'd passed.

At the top of the stairs, he found a landing with three doors. To the right a bedroom and what turned out to be a linen cupboard, and to the left a locked door. "Odd," he thought. Then he tapped on the door and called, softly, Jenny's name. When there was no answer he called again, this time much louder, and rattled the door, then stood listening. A woman's voice, very faint, said something but he could not hear what. That there was someone there, though, was quite enough for Andrew.

The door did not look that substantial and after two well-aimed kicks and the application of his shoulder, it swung open revealing a short passage. Someone was banging loudly on the door on the right and he heard Jenny's voice calling his name.

"Keep away from the door and I'll be with you in a moment," he shouted and applied the same treatment as before to the door. This one was a bit more rugged but after the fourth kick the lock gave, and moments later a sobbing Jenny was in his arms.

"What on earth has he been doing to you?" he asked, noticing her bruised throat.

"He nearly strangled me and then beat me. No," she added, seeing his worried look, "he did not rape me or even try. Can we go quickly? Now, before he comes back?"

"Yes, as soon as Wilfred gets the car here, but look you must put something more on," he said noticing the makeshift nightshirt. "Here, try this bathrobe while I bundle up your clothes. Now, the next thing is, can you walk alright?"

"Yes, but just help me down the stairs."

When they reached the bottom of the stairs, he asked her to wait for a moment.

"Try the sofa there," he said, pointing to the sitting room. "I won't be long but I must shut a few windows and doors so my break-in is not too immediately obvious."

"Now, let's see what we can do about the front door," he said as he came back down the stairs. "Oh dear, our friend really is rather careless. First the cloakroom window and now this," and he reached up and took a key from the ledge above the door. "Old country habit – spare key above the door. I bet this does the front door."

It did, and seconds later they were out on the path and Andrew was locking the door behind them.

"I think I'll keep this," he said, pocketing the key. "Now take my arm. No, on second thoughts I'm going to carry you. It's not far. Wilfred and the car should be there at the end of the path and I'm going to leave you in his care. I must follow Jean for I'm sure he's gone to the island."

"I'm afraid that's my fault," Jenny sobbed. "I had to tell him about Toby. I couldn't stand the pain any more. I'll tell you about it later."

"Don't worry, darling; you did all you could. It's our fault for not protecting you and from now on you'll never be left alone. Now here's Wilfred," he said as they reached the road and saw the car in the entrance to the track.

As soon as he saw them, Wilfred pulled onto the road and got out, and seeing Andrew with Jenny in his arms, he opened the rear door. Andrew gently laid Jenny on the back seat and then took Wilfred aside.

"She's had a rotten time," he told him, "so you'd better take her straight home, and I think you should get the doctor. He beat her up and nearly strangled her, and her legs and neck both look pretty nasty. I feel awful at leaving her, but I must go and find Lemaître. I'm sure he's on the island, and I want to see what he's doing. I don't like the idea of him being there on his own. I think he needs a little company. I'll see you when I do, and whatever happens don't let Jenny out of your sight."

"Don't you worry about Jenny," said Wilfred who, now Jenny was safe, had completely regained his composure, "we'll look after her. Now let's get going, for I don't think this is a good place to hang about."

As Wilfred got into the car, Andrew moved round to Jenny's side and said through the window, "I'll get back as quickly as I can, but I must find out what Jean's doing."

"I know," she said, fighting back tears, "and for God's sake take care. He's a very dangerous man."

He watched the car until it disappeared round the corner, then turned and walked slowly along the track until he found a place where he could spy the surrounding country, without himself being seen.

CHAPTER 22

A s soon as he was sure that the two vehicles were out of sight of the top end of the track, Jean had picked up his bicycle, and choosing a moment when the road was clear, had ridden off towards the farm, hoping that the hedges on either side of the track would give him adequate cover. Before he reached the buildings, he stopped in a ragged little copse and had a long spy.

There was no sign of activity there that he could see, and the track appeared to be clear as far as the edge of the poplars. What he could not see was what was happening to the right, in the direction the Land Rover and the pick-up had gone. Deciding that the bicycle would be a liability from there on, he hid it in the copse and moved down to the steading. He still could not see the bottom of the slope or the end of the poplar plantation, so keeping well below the top of the protecting hedge, he continued down the track until he reached the start of the plantation.

There his worst fears were realised, for when he peered round the edge of a thick tangle of thorns, he saw the two vehicles parked just beyond the pipe, and close by were two men, one lying full length and reaching into an open manhole, the other standing watching.

Realising that there was no way he could reach the bridge to the island unseen, Jean was resigning himself to a long wait, or worse still, the possibility of having to give up and return later, when the man on the ground looked up and spoke. The other bent down, listened and then nodded. After a minute or two he stood up and looked at his watch and said something which was acknowledged by a wave of some tool or other. He then turned, walked to the Land Rover and drove off up the hill.

Jean had watched this performance through his field glasses and noted that the Land Rover man wore a jacket and tie, whereas the other was wearing overalls and an open shirt. Now, with the boss away, Jean wondered if the workman could be bluffed. Worth a try, he thought, so walked back up the track and across the field to where the man was working.

"Pardon, monsieur, mais... non! Pardon, now I try the anglais," he said with an exaggerated accent. "I lose the way. Je veux aller – non, I want the château. You call it Passford, oui?"

"Oh, Passford 'All – you want the 'All, do yer, mate? Straight over there," the man said, pointing, "then up through the wood, can't miss it."

"Merci, monsieur," Jean said and passed rapidly over the stream and vanished into the wood. From what he could remember, he thought that if he went on up the wood a bit and then cut across the park to the bridge, he would be hidden from the plumber by a fold in the ground, and provided nobody else was walking in the park, he should be safe.

This indeed proved to be the case, and ten minutes later, having collected his tools, he was standing in front of the metal hatch.

Andrew had two big advantages over Lemaître when it came to moving around the Passford Estate: the conducted tour he'd had with Wilfred Saddler, and his own excellent eye for country. So, after a quick look at the ground in front, he left the track and made a big sweep round to the left so as to reach the lake at its upstream end. He was banking on the fact that Jean would have to cross the river somewhere other than by the bridge and would therefore be out of sight of the route he was taking.

When he reached the lake, he worked his way along the overgrown bank searching for a boat, for in his experience, every sheet of ornamental water had a boat, and sure enough, this was no exception. Having found his boat, he loosed the painter, and not wanting to risk the noise of oars, towed it quietly along the bank until he was opposite the centre of the island from where, with just an occasional twist of an oar at the stern, he let the current take him across.

At the island, he secured the painter, and crept quietly through the undergrowth. Before he left her, Jenny had managed to tell him the lie of the land round the Toby stone, so when he reckoned he was level with it, he eased himself up the low bank and peered through the osiers; there straight in front of him was the small memorial stone, exactly as Jenny had described it.

Far more interesting, though, was a narrow opening at the base of the rising ground on his left which was, as far as he could make out, the entrance to some sort of cave or grotto.

Wishing to get a better look at it, he was just about to move when, from the cave entrance, a hand appeared clutching a metal box wrapped in sacking, most of which was in an advanced state of decay. Then another hand grasped the side of the opening and, with a grunt, Jean Lemaître heaved himself out through the narrow hole and stood there, breathing hard.

After about a minute he put the box on the ground, reached up and slid an iron cover across the entrance then, picking up a spade, he levered a heavy stone slab into position against the base of the cover. Finally, by some judicious adjustments to the neighbouring bushes, he made a reasonable job of hiding the entrance to the cave.

While all this was going on Andrew lay absolutely still, wondering what was the best thing to do. If Lemaître came towards him he would have little alternative but to deal with him. If, on the other hand, he went up the bank opposite and left the island by the bridge, would it be best to stifle his desire to break the man's neck, and instead follow him to see what he did next?

On balance, he decided that the latter was the better policy, and it was not long before he had to put it into practice. For Lemaître, after a quick look to see that he'd not left too many signs of his activities, chucked his spade into a bush, picked up the box and disappeared up the bank opposite.

Andrew gave him two or three minutes then, after confirming that his man was moving downstream in the direction of the ram, he returned to the boat, rowed back to the mooring and set off rapidly up the hill.

At the top of the rise was a hedge from which he could get a good view of both the farm buildings and the track leading up to the road, and when he reached it he was just in time to see Jean retrieve a bicycle and ride off in the direction of the cottage. Andrew, with the aid of another hedge and some rather sparse clumps of trees, made his way to the road and crossed into the wood some two hundred yards from Plumtree Cottage.

As he neared the cottage, Jean was surprised to see another car, which he recognised as Annette's Mercedes, parked next to his, and Annette and another man, whom he did not know, sitting in it.

"What are you doing here?" he asked, as Annette opened the car door and stood up. "You could ruin the whole thing."

"We just thought we'd come and see what you were doing, and indeed if you really were here," she replied. "And this, by the way, is Marcel Masson. He's come from Le Grand Homme to see what you're up to."

"A pleasure, monsieur," Masson said, holding out his hand. "We had heard you were working with La Chérie and our master felt that with the two of you on the job, results should be forthcoming, and I have been sent to find out. When I arrived in London, I was fortunate, for I looked in the telephone directory and there is Mme Barry's name. So I ring and she is at home, and now we are here."

Jean grunted a somewhat disapproving acknowledgement and walked towards the door, taking the key from his pocket.

"Well, since you're here, you'd better come in," he said, leading the way into the sitting room. "At least I've got good news for you. I found the girl and she's locked in a bedroom upstairs. What happened after I found her is a long story and can wait. It is enough to say that after a little persuasion she gave me a hint as to where I might find something, but what it might be she did not say."

"And did you find anything?" Annette asked.

"Un moment, you must have patience," Jean said. "Again it's a long story, but yes, I did find something; I found this box which I believe may contain the jewellery."

Annette walked over to a window and opened it. "I find Marcel's tobacco offensive," she said, and then turned to Lemaître. "Good, so we may have the jewels. We'll have a look in a moment; but did you question her about anything else?"

"No, for my persuasion was a little painful and she needed time to recover. Also I wanted to check if what she'd told me was the truth," Jean said.

"We'll get her down in a moment," Annette said, walking to the table where Jean had put the box, "but first let's see what's in here."

Andrew, who was crouching outside the window, reckoned that they'd all be so occupied with the contents of the box that it would be safe to take a quick look. On a table he could see a rectangular metal box, and Annette and Jean Lemaître, whose voices he'd already recognised, were taking from it a number of soft leather pouches. Standing watching was a man he did not recognise.

"It's the jewels alright," Annette said, and Andrew hurriedly ducked as she turned towards the light. Then some fifteen minutes later, Andrew heard her say, "That's a tidy collection. It must be very, very valuable. Well, Marcel, that's something for Le Grand Homme, is it not?"

"I don't doubt he will be pleased," the unknown man said.

"Now, let's put these away... and you, Jean... go and get the girl," Annette said, then paused, adding more slowly: "No – hold on a minute. On second thoughts, I guess we need to get away from here. The girl's been missing for twenty-four hours, so the police may be searching for her and they could just think of trying here. We'll take her back to London and I think it would be safer to use my car. Someone may, probably will, have seen yours, so we'll just leave it here for the moment. OK? So collect anything that's yours, then bring down the girl."

As soon as he heard this, Andrew, who had already decided to leave the jewels with them and to concentrate on finding their base in London, felt in his pocket and took out Norman Colquhoun's bug which, having previously read the instructions, he knew to be a very sophisticated piece of equipment. About the size of a yo-yo, with a powerful magnet allowing it to be fixed to any metal object, it contained a transmitter, a battery and an aerial. When attached to a vehicle it allowed the vehicle's position to be checked every thirty seconds.

He remained crouched by the window until he heard a shout from Lemaître announcing Jenny's escape, followed by the sound of running foot-steps and more shouting. Taking advantage of this confusion, he ran over to the blind side of the Mercedes, switched on the transmitter by removing a protective tape and pin, and attached the magnet to the underside of the front mudguard. He then retired discreetly, and by the time the three inmates emerged, he was safely hidden behind a clump of laurel.

Annettte Barry was in a furious temper and screaming at Lemaître, who was cursing and waving his arms about. Marcel Masson was following behind, looking almost as though he had nothing to do with them.

When she reached the car she flung open the driver's door, took the keys from her handbag, then rounded on the others.

"Don't stand there, get in the car," she screeched. "Mon Dieu, am I always to be surrounded by idiots? First Boscawen and now you, my little man. You had the girl in your power and you've lost her. And how did that happen? I'll tell you how. Henderson's been watching you and you didn't have the wit to look out for him. Yes you've got the jewels, and I'll bet he knows you've got them! He's probably here listening to us, so watch out for following cars – if you're capable, that is."

Lemaître looked for a moment as though he might attack her, but thought better of it. Then, as Masson had already got into the front seat, he threw the jewel box into the back and got in after it. Annette slammed her door, started the engine and roared down the drive in a shower of mud and gravel, barely stopping as she turned onto the road in the direction of London.

Andrew emerged from his hiding place and went into the cottage to see if there was anything of interest. Finding nothing, he closed the sitting room window, locked the front door and dropped the key through the window by which he'd entered.

He'd originally thought of ringing Wilfred to come and pick him up, but then he'd remembered the bicycle. Retrieving it from where Jean had left it, he rode down the lane, over the river and up through the wood to the Hall, where he found them having tea.

"A splendidly English scene," he said, walking into the drawing room. "Whatever happens – people imprisoned, jewels stolen – it doesn't matter, nothing must interfere with tea!"

"Would you like some?" Mary asked.

"I'd love some," Andrew replied, "and, if it can be done, something to eat. I've just realised I've had nothing since our early tea and toast."

"Of course, we'll get Steven to bring you something," said Wilfred ringing the bell. "And now tell us what you've been doing since we left you at the cottage."

"Just hang on a moment while I get something from my room," Andrew said. When he returned he was carrying a leather case, about the size of a mobile telephone, and with a somewhat similar keypad and display.

"Now let me show you one of the latest wonders of science with which we baffle our enemies," he said, and pressed a couple of keys, resulting in a small section of map appearing on the display. "Now, if you watch, you will see a red dot flash every fifteen seconds, showing the position of their car." After some ten minutes of watching the progress of the car towards London, Andrew switched off the device so that he could describe how he'd followed Jean to the island and watched the recovery of the jewels.

"Did you know there was an old ice house on the island?" he asked Wilfred. "Because that's where the jewels were. Thomas's cold place, you see."

"Can't say I did, but it's an obvious place if you come to think of it. Water and a convenient hole in the ground," Wilfred replied.

"What happened then?" Jenny asked. "Did he go back to the cottage, and what happened when he found that I wasn't there?"

"Yes he went back, and I followed by a rather roundabout route, and when I reached the cottage there was another car parked in the front," Andrew continued. "Then somebody obligingly opened a window and I managed to crawl over to it and the first thing I heard was Annette's voice. Then I managed to get a quick look into the room and found there was another man there as well. Someone we haven't seen before. They'd just opened the box Jean had found on the island. It contained the jewels right enough, but I only got a very brief look before I had to duck down out of sight. Shortly after that I heard the Barry woman saying they ought to clear out and return to London, and then telling Jean to fetch you, Jenny."

He then described Annette's fury when it was discovered that Jenny was not there and how, in the ensuing confusion, he'd managed to fix the bug to the car and remove himself from the scene.

"Annette was still cursing Jean when they drove off," he said, "and such was her rage that she barely stopped to look as she turned onto the road. She was lucky there was nothing coming. Then, as soon as they were out of sight, I shut up the house, which they hadn't bothered to do, and came here by bicycle. Perhaps, Wilfred, someone could in due course return it to the cottage?"

During this conversation, Jenny had been unusually subdued, and apart from asking what had happened when they discovered she was missing, had kept quiet. Now she looked up and asked, somewhat nervously, what Andrew proposed to do next.

"Whatever it is," she added, "please, please don't leave me alone. I could not stand being attacked again. Just let me show you this," and she pulled up her skirt to show her bandaged left thigh. "And up here too, Andrew," and she pointed to the bruises on her neck.

Andrew, faintly ashamed of himself for not having asked after her injuries, now made an adequate show of sympathy and promised that in future she would be kept well out of the line of fire.

"I must get back to London as soon as possible," he added finally. "Now we know about the jewels, I think that the police will have to be involved. I must also talk to the Bank of England and possibly the Foreign Office about the King's money. If it still exists, hidden somewhere in the UK, it almost certainly belongs to France. The jewellery may have been the Queen's to leave, but I think the money would be state property. Most important of all, though, I must find out where Annette and her friends hang out, and then recover the jewels."

"Must you go tonight? Couldn't you please stay now and go as early as you like in the morning?" Jenny pleaded. "Wilfred, can't you persuade him?"

"Alright, I'll stay tonight," Andrew conceded after a good deal of arm twisting, "but first I must ring Norrie as I need some help on contacts. Also, my staying here is a bit dependent on what the bug tells me. At present, by the look of it, they are still on the road. If they settle somewhere in London – fine, we'll know where the jewels are. The danger will be if they go drive-about."

Norman Colquhoun, when Andrew spoke to him, was more than helpful. He agreed that it was essential to contact the police, for apart from any money that might be involved, the jewels were now technically stolen property, and therefore a police matter. He undertook to contact the appropriate branch and then ring back.

"It's fortunate," he said, "that this sort of international operation is within the orbit of the one area of intelligence work where I am still employed."

True to his word, about an hour later he reported that he had talked to various parts of the security services, and that a Superintendent Wilkinson would shortly be in touch with Andrew.

Wilkinson, when he rang, also proved to be extremely helpful. The first thing he told Andrew was that the Bank of England security people were already aware of the King's treasure: apparently, the French authorities had been in touch with them.

"They asked me to tell you to contact them tomorrow," he said and gave the name of the security man, then added, "And now how can I help?"

"I had already intended to talk to the Deputy Governor, who is a friend of mine," Andrew replied, "and also to the Foreign Office, but here's what needs to be done tonight. How it's done, of course, I leave to you."

By the end of their conversation, it had been agreed that if and when the bug showed the Mercedes had ended its journey, and they were assuming that would be in London, Andrew would inform the police. They would then put it under observation and, if opportunity occurred, they would remove the bug and install a tracking device of their own. Finally Andrew described Annette, Jean and the third man, and said that he would be in his office by seven thirty the next morning and would contact the police as soon as he arrived.

CHAPTER 23

THE MERCEDES PARTY REACHED ANNETTE'S FLAT IN Somerley Gardens, Bayswater, just after six in the evening, by which time she had more or less recovered her equanimity.

"We've lost the girl, which is perhaps not a bad thing after all. Keeping her could have been a little bit of an embarrassment," she said suddenly after they'd been driving for about half an hour, "and at least we've got the jewels."

Having said that she again relapsed into silence until, as they neared London, Jean asked where they were going and what she proposed to do next.

"For the moment we will all keep together and use my flat as our base," she told them. "I don't want any more disasters, so I want you all where I can see you. As for what we do next, that can be decided later this evening."

When they got to the flat Annette told Jean to organise some dinner and suggested that Masson went round to the local off-licence for some wine. She then retired to her bedroom to think what to do next. They had the jewels; that was good. However, she was more than ever convinced that they were not the end of the story and that somewhere there was something infinitely more valuable. What or where, she did not know, but she was fairly sure that Andrew did. How to extract this information was her problem, particularly now they had lost the girl.

"Listen, my friends," she said later as they were finishing dinner, "I have been thinking about our next step and here is what I propose. First the jewels; they cannot stay here, for we must assume Henderson knows we've got them. Marcel found this place easily, in which case so can our friend. Tomorrow you, Jean, must take them to a railway station and put them in a left luggage locker; that's as safe a place as any."

"Yes I agree, but which station, and how do I get there?" Jean asked. "And how do I carry the jewels? We can't use that old tin box. It's too heavy and very conspicuous."

After a moment's thought, Annette answered, "I think Watford will be the best place. I caught a train there once and it's big and busy with plenty of lockers. I don't think using the car's a good idea – too conspicuous. Get a bus at the end of the road here, one going to Euston Station. There you can get a train to Watford. You can take a small suitcase and you'll look the complete traveller, mon Jean!"

"That is good. He will do it well, I agree," Masson said. "But now what about the other thing? What do you know about it and how are you going to find out more?"

"I know very little about it, and there's nothing in any family records that I've seen," Annette replied. "However, in a museum in South Africa, I found some papers that Thomas Saddler must have deposited there before he died. I did not study them closely, but they appeared to suggest that there was more to the Bourbon legacy than Marie Antoinette's jewellery. What it is I don't know, but I'm sure it's of great value. Coins, perhaps? Bullion, perhaps? Who knows? Well maybe Henderson does, for I discovered that he had borrowed those papers and had kept them for twenty-four hours. Furthermore we know he was looking for something and we believe he found it."

"What was it?" Masson asked.

"We don't know, but we think it was some sort of clue," Annette said. "We've tried to find out, but have had no luck. Our best chance lay with the girl, but now we've lost that."

"We really need to try and get hold of her again," Jean said, "or Henderson. I wonder where they are?"

"I believe the girl is still at Passford, and he could be too, although I suspect he's come back to London," Annette said. "I think I might go down there again."

"They won't tell you anything. They didn't last time when we went to that farm near Paarl, so why should they this time?" Jean said.

"I shall not be myself – a wig, perhaps, and different clothes. Yes, and a strong French accent. I shall have come from the Embassy, perhaps. At least I can find out who is there and, with a bit of luck, they might give away something."

"And when will you do this?" Masson asked. "Soon, I hope, for I must make a report to Le Grand Homme."

"Not tomorrow, for I need a little time. Let us say the day after," Annette replied.

As he had promised he would, Andrew arrived at the brewery just before seven thirty and went straight to his office, followed by Tom carrying a wire document tray full of papers.

"Miss Richardson thought you might be in early today and asked me to give you this," he said.

"Thank you, Tom; though how much time I'll have to look at all this, I don't know."

In fact, he had a quick look at the first dozen documents and scribbled instructions on them to various members of the staff. A couple of other items he put aside for further consideration then, seeing it was just after seven forty-five, he pushed the remaining papers aside, and using his private line, dialled the number Superintendent Wilkinson had given him. Almost immediately, the superintendent himself answered.

"Wilkinson here. Is that Mr Henderson? ...Yes, the news is good. That map reference you gave us turned out to be Somerley Gardens. Quite a fashionable street just north of Bayswater Road. Big turn-of-the-century houses, mostly turned into flats, and we think they are in number twenty. Car's still there and we have it under observation."

"Good. So now we know where they are, we should be able to keep track of what they are up to, anyway for the next few days," Andrew said. "Now listen, – I'm in my office at the brewery and you can ring me here on my private line – I'll give you the number in a moment. If I'm not available you can leave a message with my secretary, Miss Richardson, who knows all about this little affair and is entirely reliable."

The policeman grunted an acknowledgement and asked to know Andrew's plans for the rest of the day.

"Well let's see; it's now about eight, so in an hour I'll ring the Bank of England and try to fix an appointment for this afternoon and until then I shall be working here. I suggest, therefore, that you ring me at lunchtime and update me on what's happening at the flat."

With that agreed, Andrew devoted himself for an hour to the business of running the brewery. At ten to nine Angela appeared and he explained to her what was happening. When she heard about Jenny, she was horrified and told him in no uncertain terms that in future he must treat her with more respect.

"You may enjoy your little games of cops and robbers," she said, "but just remember that most girls don't. They expect to be looked after and cherished!"

"Alright, Angela," he said in a suitably chastened voice. "I've already told her that will happen in future. Now can you please get me Jock McCracken, the Deputy Governor at the B of E, and are the sales figures for World Wide Wines in that basket?"

"Of course," replied Angela, handing Andrew a blue folder.

Five minutes' perusal of the figures convinced Andrew that, unless the first month's sales were a flash in the pan, they were onto a good thing; and he was about to send for Tony to discuss progress, when the phone rang.

"Mr McCracken's in a meeting and will be all morning," Angela said, "but I've spoken to his secretary. They were expecting you to ring and her words were 'that they would be obliged if you could attend at the Bank to see the Governor and Mr McCracken at two thirty this afternoon.' I assume that means that you fail to attend at your peril, so I've told Jim to be ready from one thirty."

"Well done, Angela. Bit pompous though, are they not? But then bankers always do have illusions of grandeur! Now could you ask Mr Tony to come and see me?"

The rest of the morning was taken up with discussions on the progress of Three Ws and also on briefing his cousin about the management of the brewery for the next month or six weeks.

"I think I'm going to be pretty occupied with this Saddler business," Andrew said. "It's rather passed beyond the family and taken on an international flavour. You, therefore, will have to take charge here. I will try and come to the next board meeting and I'll keep in touch through Angela." Then, with a grin, he added, "I'll also try to remember to have my mobile switched on so either of you can contact me. If it's not switched on, it'll be for reasons of security. Now I'd better..." and Andrew paused as the telephone rang. "Hang on while I answer this."

"I've got Superintendent Wilkinson for you," said Angela's voice.

"OK, put him through... Yes, Superintendent, what news?"

"About ten o'clock the small man, Lemaître I think you said his name was, left the flat on foot carrying a suitcase. In Edgeware Road he caught a bus to Euston. The man following him then reported that they were on a local train, but we've heard nothing further as yet."

"I'll bet he's gone to hide those jewels somewhere," Andrew said, "and if that's so, with any luck your man will be able to report where they are. I'm going out now, but ring me after six on my home number." Never a man to waste words, Wilkinson said he'd do that and rang off. Andrew then turned to his cousin.

"I think you got the gist of that," he said, adding, "Now I'd better attend on their lordships at the Bank, after which I'll go straight to the flat."

"Good luck, dear boy," Tony said, "and see you take better care of that girl of yours!"

At exactly twenty-five past two, the Jaguar drew up at the side entrance to the Bank in Bartholomew Lane, and Andrew was ushered in by a doorman resplendent in top hat and pink tailcoat.

"If you would come this way please, Mr Henderson," he said. "The Governor is upstairs and I'm to take you straight to him." And he was led across the magnificent marble-floored hall to a discreet lift which took him to the first floor, where he was met by a good-looking, grey-haired woman.

"The Governor asked that you go straight in," she said, knocking and opening one half of a massive mahogany double door. "Mr Henderson's here, Sir Marmaduke," she announced, and closed the door behind him.

Andrew had not met the Governor before and so looked with interest at the man who walked towards him, noticing the compact figure, the dark wavy hair with just a touch of grey, and the light, almost athletic, step. Sir Marmaduke Austin was indeed a most impressive man.

"Come in, Mr Henderson," he said, shaking hands. "I regret not having met you before, but it's a pleasure to do so now." Then he turned to the other man in the room. "But I think you do know Jock," he said.

"Yes indeed," Andrew replied as the two men greeted each other.

It was a large, beautifully furnished room with two big windows over-looking the Bank's famous inner courtyard. By one of the windows was a desk, bare except for a telephone and a blotter, but it was to a sofa and two chairs by the other window that Andrew was ushered.

"It's a most intriguing story you have to tell, Mr Henderson," Sir Marmaduke said, "and you may be interested to know that just before you got in touch with us, we had been contacted by the French Finance Ministry. They had discovered papers, it seems, suggesting that early in 1792 various items of value had been smuggled out of France by Bourbon agents, including a considerable sum in gold bullion which has not been heard of since. It could be that you have found a clue to its whereabouts. That, however, is something I'm going to have to leave Jock to discuss with you, as I have been summoned to an urgent meeting with the Chancellor. But I wanted to meet you and assure you that the bank will give any help it can in finding and clarifying the ownership of the missing valuables." Sir Marmaduke then got to his feet and held out his hand, before escorting them to the door.

"Come down to my office," Jock McCracken said as the door closed behind them. "I've got Bill Shankland coming to join us. He's the Deputy Chief Cashier, but he has another little-known job. He is responsible for dealing with any mysterious appearance or disappearance, or rumour thereof, of national funds; either our own or belonging to other countries. And of course he works closely with all the national and international security agencies."

"Janet, would you ask Mr Shankland to join us now, and perhaps we could have some coffee? Oh, and no interruptions, please, for the next hour," McCracken said to his secretary as he showed Andrew into his office.

"What I'd like to do, if you agree," he said, sitting down at a small conference table and inviting Andrew to do the same, "is ask you to tell what you know about any treasure, money or anything else, which may have been removed from France at the time of the Revolution, and also how you came by this information. We'll then tell you what we know and we can discuss the next steps."

A knock at the door announced the arrival of Bill Shankland, and when the introductions were completed, Andrew was invited to tell his story. He described the family connection with the Bourbon monarchy and the series of coincidences that had resulted in the discovery of the Saddler papers in South Africa, and how these had suggested to them that the jewels were hidden at Passford. Finally he explained how Thomas's diary had led them to the monument and how what they found there resulted in the discovery of the box, originally deposited at Peascod and Murray, and now in the vaults of the United Counties Bank.

"So the situation now is that the jewels have been found, and in addition to them we have an indication that somewhere, presumably in the British Isles, further treasure, probably bullion or specie is hidden, and that this was intended for Louis and his Queen when they escaped to England – which, of course, they never did. We also, as I said, have the added complication of the French party led by the ex-wife of another descendant of the Chevalier de la Tour du Lac. She, according to my erstwhile commanding officer, Brigadier Colquhoun, whose forbears incidentally were partners of the Saddlers in the Far East, may well be associated with the criminal fraternity in Paris." Here Andrew paused and thought for a moment, then looked across at the other two.

"That, I think, is all I can tell you, Jock, at least for the time being," he said.

"And a very clear exposition it was too," Jock remarked, turning to Shankland. "Don't you agree, Bill? And now let's see if you can do as well. So, before we get down to questions and possible action, perhaps you would describe what we, on our side, know about what we'd better refer to as the Bourbon treasure?"

"Of course," Shankland said, "and I'll try to keep it as short as possible. Well, about three weeks ago the Governor received a letter from a senior official of the French Finance Ministry, backed up by a call from the Banque de France, asking if we knew anything about a cargo of gold bullion which recently-discovered records suggested had left France for somewhere in the British Isles, probably in 1791 or 1792. The letter was passed to me for investigation, and as far as I could ascertain there was nothing in the Bank's archives about such a shipment."

"Did the French give any indication of where the money came from, or for what reason it had been sent?" Andrew asked.

"Apart from mentioning that the French Rothschilds, and a firm of lawyers in Paris acting for clients, would lodge claims if anything were to be found, both the Ministry and the Banque were as non-committal as only the French can be. Since we had no information here, I got on to the Foreign Office, who were unexpectedly helpful. Said they could not answer at once but they'd come back to me, which they did within twenty-four hours."

"And what did they have to say?"

"Well they produced an extraordinary story, and why it has never come to light I don't know. It appears that shortly before the arrest of the French Royal Family, there were plans for them to escape to England, and secret negotiations were taking place between the French Court and a group of well-wishers – a euphemism, I think, for the British Government – using the fifth Earl of Strathconon, who had been our ambassador in Paris in the 1770s, as the go-between. It seems everything was ready for the escape and arrange-ments made with Lord Strathconon for money to be available for the King and Queen on their arrival. It all came to nothing, however, for before they could escape, they were arrested, imprisoned and executed."

"Was the money sent, and if so what happened to it?" Andrew asked.

"That is a question to which we have no definite answer," Shankland replied. "The only further information the FO have is that in the spring of 1792 a French brig, the *Candide,* sank in the Minch in mysterious circum-stances. It appears that a man from Kintail called Macrae, a tenant on one of Strathconon's estates, was friendly with the captain of the brig and shortly after the wreck he too vanished, never to be seen again."

"What do you make of that, Andrew?" Jock asked.

Andrew smiled and felt in his briefcase. "Have a look at this," he said. "It was in the box that was deposited in Murrays Bank," and Andrew produced the letter and poem. "Ties in nicely, doesn't it?"

"Extraordinary. It seems to confirm everything," Jock said, and passed the papers to Shankland. "The letter in particular is quite explicit. Do we know, Andrew, who this Chisholm was?"

"No, but I guess he was an agent or factor; or possibly a lawyer who had been sent to Paris to finalise the arrangements there."

"Does the poem mean anything to you?" Shankland asked.

"I have to admit – no," Andrew replied, "but again my guess, based on what we now know, is that it is a clue to the location of the treasure. The evidence, such as it is, suggests that that place is somewhere in north-west Scotland, but I need to talk to people familiar with the area. But what I really want to know is what happens next? Do we continue the search, and what do we do if we find something?"

"What do you think, Bill?" Jock said. "I personally feel that knowing what we now know, we must make a serious search for whatever may have been sent to Strathconon. The Governor will expect to say as much in his reply to the French."

"I agree, and here is what I suggest," Shankland said. "The searching and finding is a matter for the police. Obviously Mr Henderson, as the person with background knowledge, must be involved. I suggest, therefore, that he and Superintendent Wilkinson get together and formulate a plan, and I think Brigadier Colquhoun and his links with France could also be helpful. We must be kept informed and anything that is found must be handed over to the Bank. Any bullion or specie almost certainly belongs to France, and we will be responsible to them for it. The jewels are a different matter, and ownership is probably a matter for the lawyers. You say you know where they are?"

"No, I don't but I hope that by now the police do. If that is so, then I hope we can recover them in the next couple of days."

"Well, if you do," Shankland continued, "I think they should also be kept by us until the question of ownership is settled. All negotiations with the French will be conducted by the Bank and we will keep the FO informed. By the way, if I understood my French colleague correctly, it was Annette Barry who in some way started their interest in the matter, and I have a suspicion that they may have sent an agent over here to check on her."

"Interesting," Andrew said. "Could be the third man I saw up in Suffolk. He was certainly not with her in South Africa."

"Well if you find out, let us know," Jock said. "Now, are we agreed on this plan? If so, I will put it to the Governor. If he is happy, I'll let you know, Andrew, and you can get cracking with the police."

"In that case, if there's nothing further," Andrew said, "I'll leave you, because I must find out about the jewels and I must talk to Norman Colquhoun."

CHAPTER 24

AS SOON AS HE GOT BACK TO his flat Andrew rang Norman Colquhoun in Scotland, only to discover that he was in London.

"Yes, he went south last night. A meeting somewhere to discuss NATO security, I think he said," Barbara Colquhoun told him. "He's staying at the Rag and I know he's dining there tonight."

Andrew gave a short laugh. "That is very convenient of him," he replied, "for I really need to see him, rather than just talk. I'll ring straight away, so love to you, Barbara, and thanks for your help."

He found Norman Colquhoun in his bedroom at the Rag and in a somewhat uncertain temper.

"Can't get this bloody black tie to tie properly," he said. "Had a very tiresome time this afternoon with the CGS and an American general from Fontainbleu and now I've got this dinner. Stag night for my nephew. At the age of thirty-five he's finally taking the plunge, though why anyone should want to marry a major in the SAS search me! Now what can I do for you?"

"Sorry about the tie, Norrie; you should try one of those made-up velvet jobs. Anyway, just put the bloody thing down and listen to me for a few minutes," Andrew said, and gave his friend a quick update on the discovery of the jewels at Passford. "But as well as the jewels, I've discovered something else," he continued, "and I believe it's something even more significant. You remember that you found a mention of a bank called Murrays in your family archives. Well, I discovered that their records are now with the United Counties Bank." And he went on to describe, in some detail, his visits to both United Counties and the Bank of England, ending by saying, "So now what I'd like to do is to review the whole operation with you. I particularly want you to see the papers I found in the box that was deposited at Murrays, and then to get your advice on what we do next. I'm hoping to drive over to Passford tomorrow. Can you come with me?"

"I'm sure I could," Norman replied. "I did say I'd go home tomorrow, but I've got nothing urgent waiting there, and I'm sure Barbara won't mind. Won't have to, will she!"

"Right, that's fixed then. I'll just have to confirm with Wilfred, but I'm pretty sure he's there and that there won't be any problem. So unless you hear to the contrary I'll pick you up at eight thirty. Goodnight, and have a good party!"

No sooner had Andrew put down the receiver than Superintendent Wilkinson rang. "Got some news for you," he said. "We tracked the Frenchman, Lemaître, to Watford Station, where he put a small suitcase in a left luggage locker. He then very conveniently went to the toilet, so our man was able to get the number of the locker. He then caught the next train back to London and went straight to Somerley Gardens. The flat there has been under observation all day, and apart from a woman – a daily cleaner, I expect – arriving and leaving, and our friend going to Watford, there has been no movement."

"Can you continue the observation?" Andrew asked. "And I think you'd better tell me who's paying for your services."

"Don't worry," Wilkinson replied with a laugh. "With the Bank, the Treasury and the Foreign Office all involved, it's now an official enquiry."

"Thank God for that," Andrew said. "Now what do we do about the jewels? I would like to retrieve them, and so would the bank."

"I think we can arrange that," Wilkinson said. "We have a man who's very experienced at that sort of operation. I think you should be there too, but not directly involved. Then once he's got them he can hand them straight to you and they become your responsibility. So when can you manage? The sooner the better, I think, for we don't want to find they've gone before we get there."

"I can't do tomorrow, but the next day would be fine. Look, we're having a family conference in Suffolk tomorrow to try and work out where we've got to. I'll ring you tomorrow evening when I get back here. We can fix up about the jewels and I can bring you up-to-date on what we know and what we think we should do. I imagine that anything we decide will have to be cleared with you, the Bank and heaven knows who else."

"I'm afraid so," Wilkinson replied. "Anyway, I'll arrange for your call to find me, wherever I am. Oh, and by the way, we've changed the bug on their car. It's easier for us to use one of our own. I'll let you have the brigadier's back."

On the way down to Suffolk the following morning, Andrew gave Norman Colquhoun a more detailed account of the happenings at Passford earlier in the week.

"You're sure the jewels were in the box that Lemaître found?" Norman asked.

"Yes, Annette very helpfully opened the window so I was able to hear all that went on in the room," Andrew answered, "and I also managed a quick look, and what they had on the table was undoubtedly jewellery."

"Well that seems fairly definite," Norman said. "Incidentally, now I've seen him, I'm sure that Lemaître is the chap I knew as Pascal Nero. A nasty bit of work, and what he did to Jenny is typical of the man. I shall consider this operation a success even if all we achieve is to put away Monsieur Nero!"

There was then a short interval while Andrew overtook a string of slow-moving traffic.

"I suppose you did see that bus coming towards us?" Norman said when the manoeuvre had been completed. "I don't know what the driver felt, but I did just wonder if my last hour had come."

Andrew smiled and said, "Nerve not failing, is it, Norrie? Common sign of increasing age, you know." The brigadier scowled at him, but Andrew continued unperturbed. "Now, if you look in my briefcase, you'll see an envelope marked 'Strathconon papers'. They are what I found in the locked box that was deposited in Murrays Bank by we don't know who. Have a look at them."

"Your friends do go in for riddles," Norman remarked after a few minutes' perusal of the two documents. "I presume the poem gives a clue to the hiding place mentioned in the letter. If the name Macrae is anything to go by the place will be somewhere in Wester Ross and, if I'm not mistaken, there used to be a Strathconon estate in that part of the world."

"Exactly so," Andrew commented, "and if we want to make progress we've got to find the place described in the poem. Incidentally, when I went to the Bank of England, I discovered that the French authorities had already been in touch with them about a valuable cargo shipped to Britain in the seventeen nineties. The Bank, in turn, found out from the Foreign Office about a plan to finance the escape of the Bourbons to England which involved Lord Strathconon and a French brig called the *Candide*. Why none of this had come to light before, no one seems to know."

"Why have the French suddenly become interested?" Colquhoun asked.

"Apparently through our friend Annette," Andrew replied, "and the bank believes they have sent an agent over to keep an eye on things. He could be the new man I saw at the cottage in Suffolk."

"Very interesting," the brigadier said, lying back in his seat and studying the poem. Five minutes later, when Andrew looked round at him, he saw that his friend was sleeping peacefully and remained so for the rest of the journey.

"Wake up, Norman. We've arrived," Andrew said as he pulled up outside the front door of Passford Hall.

"So we have," and Norman sat up with a start, "and there's Wilfred. How are you? It must be five years at least since I last saw you," he said, getting out of the car and shaking his host's hand. "And Mary too. You look wonderful, my dear, and not a day older," he said, kissing her, as she led the way into the house.

"And you must be Jenny," he added, seeing an attractive girl standing by the fireplace in the drawing room.

"I am indeed," Jenny replied, leaving Wilfred's attempt to effect the introduction stillborn, "and I imagine you're the famous Norman Colquhoun I've heard so much about. Trust Andrew not to be around to introduce us."

"Sorry, sorry!" said that person, hurrying in clutching a briefcase and a pile of maps and bending down to kiss Jenny. "I was just collecting all these bits and pieces." Then adding as an afterthought, "How are you, darling? Are the wounds healing?"

"I thought you were never going to ask!" the girl said with a laugh, while the other three grinned at Andrew's discomfiture. "Yes, darling, they are, and thank you for asking," and she kissed him again.

"Now come on, you two," Mary said. "Sit down everybody and I'll give you coffee and then leave you to get on with whatever it is you're going to do. I've got to see someone down in the village, but I'll be back for lunch."

While the rest were still drinking their coffee, Andrew put down his cup and got to his feet.

"It's alright," he said, "I'm not going to make a speech, but I must just stretch my legs while I talk. I've already told Norman a good deal of what I've been doing for the last couple of days, but so we all know where we are, here's a brief summary."

As he'd never had time to tell Jenny and Wilfred about it, he first described his visit to the United Counties Bank and what he'd found there. Then he told them what the police had found out about Annette's flat and the depositing of the jewels at Watford, and finally he summarised his meeting at the Bank of England.

"So you see," he ended, "I've been fairly busy and I seem to have made quite good progress. To capitalise on this, what we now have to do is to see if we can find out the meaning of that poem. Assuming we are successful in this and if, as I think, it tells us where whatever was sent to Strathconon is hidden, then we have to decide what we do with the information. I am convinced that we must try and find this unknown treasure and I have a very personal reason for my belief." And he told them of his dream on the plane from South Africa.

"Are you saying that Marie Antoinette was willing you to search for the royal legacy to the Chevalier?" Jenny asked.

"I think so, but as I say, I remember little of the dream," Andrew replied. "But the more I think of it, the more convinced I am that someone was trying to tell us to continue looking for what they had given us. So do we agree that that is what we should do?"

Having obtained their agreement on this, Andrew went on to explain that there was another matter that had to be considered and that was what to do about Annette and company.

184

"We might get a better idea of how to handle them," he said, "if I can manage to meet the third man I saw at the cottage, particularly if he is the agent the French authorities have sent to England, which is something the Bank want to know too, so I'll see what I can do."

"Let's have a think about the poem," Wilfred said when Andrew sat down. "Come on, Norman. You know Scotland better than any of us, have you any ideas?"

"Not much, apart from what I told Andrew in the car. If the brig sank in the Minch, that's north of Skye. If a man called Macrae was involved, well, Macraes still come mainly from Kintail – and in those days, they certainly did. So we're probably looking at the area between extremes of, let's say, Gairloch and Knoydart. Do we have an atlas?"

Wilfred left the room and returned with the large Reader's Digest atlas. "This should do," he said, turning to the appropriate page. "There, that gives a pretty good picture of the area." And they all crowded round to look.

"Never having been to Scotland, other than Edinburgh, I can't help much," Jenny said, "but 'confluent seas' – that suggests somewhere where two lots of waters meet, like there," and she pointed to Applecross, "or there," pointing to the Kyle.

"Not Applecross," Norman said. "Sea's too wide there. If we're going to stand on one shore and line up something on the other, we're looking for a set of narrows. The Kyle or Dornie look the most promising." And he tapped the map with a pencil.

"It says 'The western shore you there must land'," Andrew said. "Western shore? If we look at the Kyle, then that would be on Skye. Surely our poet would have mentioned that. Also, wasn't there a ferry there even in those days? Hardly a promising place for landing secret treasure!"

"I agree. So no, I don't think it's the Kyle we should be looking at," said the brigadier, who was now studying a one-inch map. "Here, this shows the area much more clearly. Supposing one was somewhere there," he went on, pointing to the end of the western shore of Loch Duich. "I know Letterfearn, and at the end of that road there are both trees and rocks at the water's edge. Then what about 'With steps across the wave'? Have a look at what's on the opposite shore."

"Looks like '𝕮𝖆𝖘𝖙𝖑𝖊', and written in Gothic letters," said Jenny, squinting at the map, "and also some words in an unpronounceable foreign language."

Andrew laughed and said, "Eilean Donan. It's the name of the castle and, my dear, that foreign language is Gaelic! They speak it in those parts, so treat it with respect!"

"Yes, it's Eilean Donan Castle. It's belonged to the Macraes on and off for years," Norrie said. "I know it well and, what's more, it has some steps leading down to the shore. Looks like we're on the right track, but I don't know about these 'ice cold maidens'."

Jenny, who had now got the bit between her teeth, clapped her hands and pointed again at the map.

"Look there, at the end of that bit of water. What's it called? *Lock Jewick* – I suppose that's Gaelic too – and what do you see?" she demanded, then immediately answered her own question, a note of triumph in her voice: "'Five Sisters'. I don't know if they are ice cold, but they sound quite like maidens."

"Well done, Jenny," Norrie said, adding quietly, "Of course, The Five Sisters of Kintail. They're mountains. Big ones too, each one around three thousand feet. So for most of the winter ice cold would be a good description of them. And they look straight down the loch – Loch Duich it's called – to the narrows at Eilean Donan where it joins Loch Alsh."

"Well it certainly seems as if this place, Letterfearn, is where we should be looking," Andrew remarked, "but what about the 'monster's back' and the 'noble head'?"

"I think they'll have to wait until we can have a closer look," Norrie said. Then, looking round the group, added, "So what do we do now?"

"I suggest we have lunch," said Mary's voice from the door. "It's all ready, so come along. You can continue with your discussions afterwards."

"Excellent idea," Wilfred said. "We could all do with a break and, I'm sure, a drink. What are we having? Fish pie, you say; then in honour of Jenny we'll have some of that South African Sauvignon Blanc." And he added with a grin, "Comes from a place with an unpronounccable foreign name! So just give us five minutes, my dear, to tidy ourselves and we'll be with you."

After the hard work of deciphering the poem, the conversation at lunch was decidedly light-hearted. Jenny was given a mini-lesson in the history and geography of Scotland by the brigadier. In return, she instructed them in the pronunciation of the Afrikaans language and the finer points of the white wines of her country.

After lunch, while they were drinking their coffee in the drawing room, Andrew looked up from his notes of the morning's proceedings and tapped his cup for silence.

"I think we did very well this morning," he said. "Now assuming that all the information we have is genuine, we know that something of value was landed on the west coast of Scotland in the seventeen nineties and is probably still hidden there. What I suggest happens now is that Norrie and I discuss possible courses of action. I'll then have to agree any proposals we have with all the various authorities who have now got themselves involved. I'll also deal with the jewels and see if I can find the mysterious French agent. That's quite a deal of work, so I suggest that Norrie and I return to London and get on with it."

Norman Colquhoun nodded. "Yes, I'm sure that's the best plan," he said, "and I'll be happy to stay on in London for a few days. Apart from this little lark, I know the Ministry would be pleased if I did."

"Everyone happy with that?" Wilfred asked.

"What about me? I suppose I'll be left out as usual," Jenny said.

"I think, darling, it would be wiser if you stayed here," Andrew replied. "London is rather too full of the enemy at present. As soon, though, as we know our plans, you will definitely be part of them."

Jenny gave her best theatrical groan and made a point of saying a very reluctant goodbye when they eventually left for London.

CHAPTER 25

As SOON AS ANDREW TURNED OUT OF the Passford gates and headed towards London, Norman Colquhoun leaned back in his seat, closed his eyes and remained apparently asleep until they crossed the North Circular Road and joined the queue of traffic crawling towards the City, when he sat up and looked round at Andrew.

"You just keep driving," he said, "I'll do the talking. Now, you may have thought that I've been asleep for the last forty miles. Well I haven't. In fact, I've been doing some hard thinking. We have agreed that unless the bank or some other set of busybodies stop us, we continue our search for this mysterious Bourbon legacy. We've already got the jewels, or rather we know where they are. We also believe we know that the other part is hidden somewhere in the general area of the Kyle of Lochalsh. We can only find out if it really exists by going there and following the instructions in the poem. Agree?"

Andrew, who was trying to force his way through the crowd surrounding a Bangladeshi street market, nodded.

"Good; so now listen carefully. Exactly what we do next depends on two things, both of which must be your responsibility. First we need the OK from the various authorities involved; secondly we need to know what's happening in the enemy camp, and I agree that the best bet for that is this third man. If he really is an agent of the French Government, then he ought to be on our side. I suggest therefore that your first move on reaching home should be to ring the police and see if their watchers can tell you anything about his movements. Don't bother about me, when we get to central London just drop me somewhere near the club."

The brigadier had never lost the habit of making suggestions as though they were orders, and Andrew could not resist replying in the same kind. "Yes sir!" he said, and was rewarded with a ferocious glare.

"No cheek, young man," Norman barked, then relented and added, "Here's Trafalgar Square. Stop when you get into the Mall and that'll do me fine. Good luck, and let me know how you get on."

He smiled at this instant obedience to a senior officer's orders; then, when he reached his flat, Andrew rang Superintendent Wilkinson and caught him just as he was leaving his office.

"Any news from the Bayswater front?" he asked.

"Nothing at all," the policeman replied. "Apart from the little Frenchman going to the local supermarket, they all appear to have stayed put."

"Well we've had quite a successful time," Andrew said, "for we now know, or think we do, where the money meant for the French Royals was hidden." And he explained the meaning of the poem and how the directions it contained tied in with the other information they had.

"So what do you propose to do?" Wilkinson asked.

"According to the poem we have to look for a place in Kintail – that's opposite Skye on the west coast of Scotland," Andrew explained helpfully, "but we can only find the exact spot by going up there. That, we think, needs your agreement, and that of the Bank, because we might find something."

"Indeed it will," Wilkinson replied. "It will also need the consent of my superiors and of the local police who, I'm sure, will want to be involved. I'll have to come back to you on this. What about the Bank? Will you contact them?"

"Yes, but I want some more help from you first. As I told you, the Bank want to know if the other man who has joined Mrs Barry is an undercover agent of the French Finance Ministry. The only way to find out is to ask him direct. He doesn't know me, but if I can get him on his own, I can probably do that. If he goes out alone, can your boys somehow point me in his direction? I think this takes precedence over recovering the jewels, so we'll have to risk putting that off for twenty-four hours."

"We'll see what we can do," Wilkinson said, adding, "I doubt much will happen tonight, so where will you be tomorrow morning?"

"Here; but if I do have to go out, you've got the number of my mobile and I'll try and remember to have it switched on."

Annette Barry had spent most of that day in her bedroom trying to work out what to do next. She was now quite certain that there was something more to be found than just the jewels and that Andrew Henderson either knew, or had the means of finding out, what and where that something was. Her problem was that she did not know where either Andrew or Jenny were, nor was she sure how to find out what they knew if she did find them.

What she was certain of, however, was that her companions were tired of sitting around doing nothing. She therefore decided that she could no longer delay taking the first obvious step. At about five-thirty, therefore, she went down to the sitting room where she found Lemaître and Masson playing a complicated variation of rummy.

"Well, have you decided what we should do?" Jean asked. "Because we're getting bloody fed up stuck in here."

"Yes, my friends, I have decided what we should do," replied Annette, "and I agree we can't stay in here for ever like rats in a sewer, particularly as I don't believe that Henderson knows where we are. He knew we were at that cottage because he must have freed the girl, but I don't believe he knows we found the jewels. Why should he? What we have to do is to find out if he really has discovered that something other than the jewels was entrusted to the Chevalier de la Tour du Lac."

"And how, ma chère Annette, do you propose to do that?" Jean asked.

"As I told you before, I am going to visit the family home and I shall go in disguise," Annette replied. "I believe either Henderson or the girl, or possibly both, are there, and if I can tell a good story I should find out something. I shall drive down there tomorrow."

"I too must go out tomorrow," Masson said. "I have one other little job to do for Le Grand Homme while I'm in London."

"Very well," Annette said, adding, "In that case, Jean, you'd better stay in. You are our biggest danger. After what you did to that silly little bitch the police might just have been informed, and we mustn't forget you are known to Interpol."

At ten o'clock the next morning, the telephone rang in Andrew Henderson's flat.

"Mr Henderson?" a strange voice asked. Andrew hesitated for a moment before acknowledging.

"Sergeant James here," the voice said. "I'm in a house overlooking Somerley Gardens and Mr Wilkinson asked me to let you know if anything unusual happened in a house we both know of."

"I take it from your tone, Sergeant, that something odd has happened," Andrew said.

"Indeed, sir, it has," the sergeant replied. "About ten minutes ago a strange woman came out of the front door. We can't be sure which flat she came from, but the odd thing is that she got into Mrs Barry's car and drove off."

"When you say a strange woman, Sergeant, you mean someone none of you watchers has seen before and who has not been seen entering the house?"

"That is correct, sir. No one we can't account for has gone in during the past twenty-four hours. The only thing I can say is that there is a back way in, and from our vantage point, it is difficult, in the dark, to be sure of what's happening there. Someone could have got in without our noticing. The car is bugged and we are tracking it."

"Well, thank you for letting me know," Andrew said. "There's obviously nothing I can do, so keep me informed. I should be here for the next two hours at least."

"Odd," Andrew said to himself when the sergeant had rung off. "I suppose she could have sent for reinforcements but why? And indeed who? And could they have got in unobserved? Well, we shall doubtless find out in due course."

With that he put the matter out of his mind and rang Jock McCracken at the Bank of England. To his surprise he was put straight through.

"Morning, Andrew," McCracken said. "Thought you might ring. How are you getting on?"

"Quite well," Andrew replied and explained that they now thought they knew the general area where the Bourbon treasure had been landed, and was presumably still hidden. "The thing is," he continued, "that we can't make further progress without actually going and looking for it. Can we do that, and do we need your permission? And what happens if we find something? I have spoken to the police and they have gone off to take advice from higher authority."

"I think I shall have to do the same," McCracken said. "Apart from the Governor, I'll have talk to the FO. But really the key player is this elusive French agent. Any sign of him?"

"Not yet, but the police and I have a plan which may enable me to contact him."

"Let me know if you have any luck, because either I or someone on my staff, Bill Shankland probably, need to talk to him if we're to allow you to continue your search. I'm loathe to let you do so until I know the French attitude."

"Fair enough. Well, I hope I'll be able to let you know something before the day's out."

Some ten minutes later, just as Andrew was settling down to study some urgent papers that had come by courier from the brewery, the telephone rang again.

"Sergeant James here again," the voice at the other end said. "Sorry to bother you, sir, but you asked me to let you know if the bigger of the two men went out. Well, he has; he left on his own about twenty minutes ago and we've tracked him to a place off Charles Street – back of Shepherd Market – seems to be a club of some sort, so my man tells me, and full of foreigners."

"Of course," Andrew said half to himself, "Le Petit Club de Paris. I know it; great meeting place for Frenchmen in London; in fact I'm a member. Thank you, Sergeant. Very helpful. Just keep an eye on it and I'll get down there as soon as possible."

Le Petit Club, as it's always known, is a favourite haunt of French businessmen and professional people visiting London. It also has a number of English members, most of whom have either lived in France or have close family ties with that country and, more importantly, are friends of the somewhat eccentric owner.

Elizabeth de Selincourt, known to everyone as Madame Lise had, for a well-born English girl, led an unusually romantic and adventurous life. Some years before the Second War she had eloped from her Swiss finishing school and married an officer in the French Army. In May 1940 his unit was surrounded by the advancing Germans, but he managed to escape capture, joined up with a retreating English unit and was eventually evacuated via Dunkirk.

Elizabeth was not so lucky. She was trapped in Paris, but in the confusion following the fall of France she managed to assume the identity of a recently deceased neighbour and escape to the farm of some friends in Normandy. There she joined the Resistance. In 1943, she was wounded during an arms drop that went wrong, but the next night was fortunate to be taken on board, as an extra body, by an RAF rescue plane.

After the war, she followed her husband to Indo-China, where he was killed in a skirmish with communist guerillas. Back in England, she looked for some means of supporting herself and her young daughter. It was an inspired move to open Le Petit Club and now, into her eighties, she was still running it and looking after what she referred to as 'mes enfants'.

Andrew walked down the narrow alley off the market, and through a door with depressed-looking bay trees in tubs on either side. He glanced into the bar which was still fairly empty and there, sitting alone at a table with a half-empty glass in front of him, was a man who looked very similar to the one he had had a glimpse of in the Suffolk cottage. Then seeing Mme Lise alone in her tiny office, he squeezed in and was greeted effusively.

"Andrew! You may kiss me," she said, taking his hand in both of hers, "but you have not been to see me for a long time, so why this sudden visit?"

"Yes I know," he said, straightening up from the white head, "and I'm very sorry, but I've been abroad and then involved with my new company, which you may have heard about."

"I have," she replied turning her still vivid blue eyes on him, "and I did not like what I heard. Why you people have to go messing about with these foreign wines I don't know. Aren't the French ones good enough any more? And that's not the only thing I've heard. They say you have a girl – should I be jealous?"

"I don't know," he said with a laugh. "I'll bring her to see you and you can judge for yourself. But the cause of my coming here today is that man sitting in the bar – yes, over by the wall – him with the wavy hair and the light grey suit. Do you know him?"

"Yes, but not well," Mme Lise replied. "His name is Charles Morey, although he sometimes uses other ones, and he's some sort of civil servant. He comes here quite often if he's in London; uses the club as a sort of office – indeed he's just made a couple of telephone calls. Why do you want to know?"

"That's a long story," Andrew answered, "which one day I'll tell you, but if he's who I think he is, then I believe we can be of considerable help to each other. I think I'll go and have a word with him."

The bar was now much fuller. All the stools and most of the tables were occupied, but the Frenchman was still alone. Andrew got himself a glass of wine and looked vaguely round, nodded to a couple of acquaintances, and made his way over towards the far wall.

"May I join you?" he said in French to the man whom he now knew as Charles Morey. "This seems to be about the only chair left."

"Mais oui, monsieur, certainement," Morey replied with evident pleasure, then added in good English, "You are one of the English members?"

"Yes I am, and have been for quite some time," Andrew said. "I'm a brewer, and as we own quite a lot of hotels and pubs, my father thought I should learn about wine as well as beer. So I spent a year in Bordeaux and another in Burgundy, and apart from that I have known Madame Lise for many years. And you – you are here on business?"

"I am; but not, unfortunately, anything to do with wine or beer, although I do have a cousin in Rheims who works for one of the champagne houses, but only as an accountant," Morey said with a smile. "Me, oh I'm just a civil servant and I'm here on very boring business to do with missing goods."

Andrew looked at his watch. "What about some lunch?" he said. "Would you perhaps join me?"

Their conversation remained general throughout the meal, but when they reached the coffee Andrew felt sufficient confidence in his companion to broach the subject he really wanted to discuss.

"Tell me, Monsieur Morey," he said, looking straight at the Frenchman, "these missing goods; would they by any chance have a royal connection?"

"It's possible," Morey replied. "After all, almost anything can have a royal connection if you search hard enough for it."

"Let me ask you something else," Andrew said. "Does the name Dulac mean anything to you?"

This time his companion showed a definite flicker of interest. "If it does," he said, "and I'm not saying it does, let me ask you a question. How do you know the name?"

"That I cannot tell you until I know for certain who you are," Andrew answered. "At present I can only guess, and my guess is that you have some connection with the French Government, probably in the area of finance."

"My friend, that is a good guess," Morey said, "and now let us stop fencing and establish some bona fides. I think perhaps you may know Mr Bill Shankland at your Bank of England. If you wish to you may contact him and he will vouch for me."

Andrew thought for a moment, then decided that if they were going to make any progress he was going to have to trust this man.

"Monsieur Morey," he said, "that will not be necessary. Bill Shankland has already told me that he believes that an agent of the French Finance Ministry is in this country and I, in turn, have told him that I believe I have seen such a man." At this Charles Morey looked across with a surprised expression.

"Yes," Andrew continued, "I saw you, fleetingly I must admit, with someone called Annette Barry, at a cottage in Suffolk. Am I right?"

"Indeed," Morey replied, "and now let us stop talking in riddles. Tell me how you know of Dulac and Madame Barry and what your connection with them is. I, for my part, will then tell you what my interest is."

"It's quite a long story," Andrew said, "but I will make it as brief as I can. Dulac, or more properly the Chevalier de la Tour du Lac, was an ancestor of my late wife. The Chevalier, according to family history, had quite a reputation in Court circles, for as well as being Marie Antoinette's page, there were rumours of a more intimate relationship. Anyway, for whatever reason, legend has it that at the time of her imprisonment, she gave him some of her jewellery, and although he escaped the Terror, he was banished to India taking the jewels with him. An interesting story, you will say, and one that lends a bit of excitement to the usual dull run of family history; and you would be right, until a month ago that is."

"And what happened then?" Morey asked.

"Quite by chance, while I was on holiday in South Africa," Andrew continued, "I found some papers belonging to a member of the Chevalier's family, which had lain hidden for a hundred and fifty years, and which suggested that the legend of the jewels was true and gave a clue as to where they had been hidden. The rest you know."

"I do. I also know who found them and where they are now. Surely it was rather careless of you to let that happen?" Morey said.

"I agree, so perhaps I should explain how it came about," Andrew said. "As I'm sure Annette Barry has told you, her ex husband is another descendant of the Chevalier's through the Saddler family. Aware of the legend, somehow she discovered that Thomas Saddler might have hidden the jewels in South Africa and went searching for them, only to find that I had got in first. She made several attempts to find out what, if anything, I had discovered, including one in which her boyfriend came to a very sticky end after trying to rape my fiancée. What I had discovered was that the jewels were hidden at the Saddler home in Suffolk. Annette somehow guessed this, and the little man, Lemaître I think he's called, went there, and I think you know how he found the hiding place and recovered the jewels. What he did not know was that I saw him do so and, what none of you knew was that when he showed them to you and Annette in the cottage, I was watching through the window."

"Do you know where they are now?"

"Yes. Having bugged your car, I tracked it to London, where the police found it in Somerley Gardens. They subsequently followed Lemaître to Watford where he deposited something, presumably the jewels, in a left luggage locker. I intend to recover them tomorrow."

"You'd better do it first thing," the Frenchman said, "for Lemaître is to fetch them tomorrow afternoon. Incidentally, Lemaître's real name is Pascal Nero and he's a very nasty bit of work. Your girl is lucky that all he did was the little beating. Monsieur Henderson, may I give you some advice? If you are going to continue in this game, you must take more care of those you love. Madamoiselle Jenny has suffered twice, and there has to be a limit to love."

Andrew acknowledged the rebuke and said that the lesson had been learned. He then went on to say that they already knew that Lemaître's real name was Pascal Nero.

"Yes, a friend of mine told us," he said, "and he also told us that he thought Annette Barry was someone who, back in his days in Military Intelligence, he knew as Annette Duvalier, nicknamed La Chérie."

"That is correct; and so who is this friend who seems to know everything?" Morey asked.

"Brigadier Norman Colquhoun," Andrew answered, "and he certainly does seem to know everyone of importance in the Security Services and, apparently, in the international underworld. Very useful that's been, but now let's change the subject." Here Andrew paused and looked his companion full in the eye. "I think you are here on the track of something far more valuable than jewellery, even royal jewellery. That, at least, is what our mutual friend Bill Shankland told me."

"You are aware, then," Morey said, "of the gold bullion that was shipped to the Earl of Strathconon in Scotland for the benefit of Louis XVI and his Queen should they escape the Terror, and of which nothing has been heard since."

"I am not only aware of it, although I did not know for sure that it was bullion," Andrew replied, "but I am reasonably sure that, if it still exists, I know where it is. You see, in the event of the escape failing, it too was to go to the Chevalier." And Andrew described the discovery of the notebook, the copper tube and the papers deposited at Murrays Bank, finishing by saying, "So, having solved all the puzzles, we are fairly sure that the bullion is hidden on the west coast of Scotland. Now we want to know two things: first, to whom do all these valuables belong, and secondly, what do we do next?"

"Those are very interesting questions," the Frenchman said, "so let me tell you a little of how I come to be involved. As you correctly surmised, I work for the French Finance Ministry, doing much the same job as your Bill Shankland, although perhaps not at such a high level. Like you with the papers in South Africa, we came on the 'affaire Dulac' by accident. A minor official in another department stumbled on some records and, despite a warning to secrecy, talked to his wife, who passed the information to her lover, one Pascal Nero. Nero mentioned it to a certain fence known as Le Grand Homme who agreed to finance a search. This came to nothing until Nero chanced to meet La Chérie, whom the police were watching for quite different reasons. Conversations were overheard, two and two put together, and I was told to investigate. Now the South African police had, by good fortune, done a little checking with the Sûreté when they realised who Annette Barry might be and kindly tipped us off when she left for England. I picked her up at Heathrow, lost her but then found her number in the directory, rang her and introduced myself as an agent of Le Grand Homme."

"And what is your brief from your masters?" Andrew asked.

"Although it was a mention of the jewels that started our enquiry, it was when we unearthed the papers referring to the bullion that we became really interested," Morey replied. "It was then that our ministers got in touch with yours; so far to no avail. It seems that it was not until you came on the scene that anything useful was discovered. I came here today to telephone Bill Shankland and he suggested that you and I should meet and he would arrange it. Then – marvel of marvels – you walked into the bar. Now to answer your two questions about who owns what and how to proceed, I suggest that we meet again as soon as possible, and this time I think you should bring Mr Shankland."

"I agree, so just leave it to me," Andrew said, getting to his feet. "One o'clock, here, tomorrow. As I obviously cannot communicate with you, come here anyway. If there is any alteration I will leave a message with Madame Lise. Now I must go as I have some matters of normal business to attend to."

"Au revoir, monsieur; until tomorrow, then," the Frenchman said and resumed his seat.

CHAPTER 26

ANNETTE BARRY HAD TAKEN CONSIDERABLE TROUBLE OVER her disguise. Her fair hair was hidden under a severe black wig. She had plucked her eyebrows and this, together with a subtle altering of the lines round her eyes and nose and a pair of steel-rimmed glasses, contrived to make her appear both plainer and older. A high-necked white shirt and a severely cut black suit, the skirt rather longer than the current fashion, added what she hoped was a faintly academic air.

All the way down from London she had been convincing herself that if she used a thick Belgian accent and stuck to her chosen identity as a genealogist working for the University of Liège, she would be unrecognised even by Henderson and the girl. Researching English families who had ancestral links with the French Revolution would be her line, and her hope would be that judicious questioning would extract some inadvertent information.

"Maintenant, ma chère, le moment arrive," she said to herself as she drove slowly along the Passford avenue and parked on the gravel sweep opposite the front of the Hall. A quick look in the mirror to make sure her wig and make-up were undamaged, then she got out of the car, walked across to the front door and rang the bell.

While she waited for a response, Annette turned to look at the smooth sweep of gravel backed by lawns and trees and, for a moment, wished that James Barry could have inherited such an estate. Her reverie was interrupted by the sound of the front door opening and she turned to see Steven standing in front of her.

"Good morning, madam," he said, "and can I help you?"

"Bonjour; non, non, good morning, I mean," she replied. "You must forgive me – my English, it is not so good. I am Anne Marie Albert – Doctor

Albert of the University of Liège – and I was given the name of Mr Saddler as a person who might help with my research. It would be possible to see him perhaps – yes?"

"I don't know about that, madam. Mr Saddler would normally expect an appointment for something like that. I would have to ask him. If you would like to come in and sit down, I will go and see if he's about."

"I make my apologies for not telephoning," Annette said. "My programme, it is altered and I find myself near here and I wondered..."

"If you will wait for a moment, madam, I will see what I can do," Steven said, turning and walking down a passage to the left.

Five minutes later he returned. "Mr Saddler has to go out in half an hour but says he would be happy to meet you and see if he can help. So if you would like to come this way."

Steven led the way down the passage and after knocking on the door at the end, opened it and stood aside to let Annette in.

"Doctor Albert to see you, sir," he said and closed the door.

Annette found herself in a pleasant book-lined room with windows on two sides giving views over the lawn and shrubbery. The tall man standing in front of the desk walked towards her, holding out his hand.

"How do you do, Doctor?" he said. "And tell me, how can I help you?"

"Ah, how do you do, Monsieur Saddler?" she replied. "It is most kind of you to see me. It is my sorrow that I have not made an appointment, but I pass your house and decide to come in, as you say, I think – spur of moment!"

"I quite understand," Wilfred replied, "but time is short, so perhaps you could explain what you want to see me about."

"Ah yes, I understand, I must not waste time. We at Liège have a project..." and she started to explain about the descendants of victims of the Terror.

When Annette drove up, Jenny was walking along the gallery that runs the whole length of the first-floor front of the house. Hearing the slam of a car door, she looked out of a window to see a woman walking towards the front entrance. Now she would not have expected to recognise someone visiting Passford, but having a very good memory for people, she felt there was something familiar about the figure below who had now reached the three steps leading to the front door and was ascending them in a slightly laboured manner.

"Of course, the built-up shoe," Jenny said to herself. "I know where I've seen one like that before." Then, as the woman looked round for the bell push, Jenny got a better look at her face and continued with her thoughts. "That is definitely Annette Barry, and what on earth is she doing here in disguise?"

She walked quietly to the top of the stairs and looked over to see Annette sitting in the hall. Then, a few moments later, she saw Steven lead the visitor off in the direction of the study.

As soon as she heard the door close, she ran down to the hall and stopped Steven.

"Who was that woman and what did she want?" she asked.

"She's a Doctor Albert and she's come over from Belgium," Steven replied. "She wants to see Mr Saddler. On some historical matter, I believe."

"Well she's not a doctor and she's not called Albert," Jenny said. "I must warn Mr Saddler. I must write a note." She looked round vaguely.

"Here, Miss Jenny," Steven said, producing both paper and pencil from his pocket.

"You must take him this immediately, Steven," she said when she'd finished writing. "Make sure he reads it, then make any excuse to get him out of the room. I must see him, and without the woman. What's more, she must not see me."

"Very good, Miss Jenny, just leave it to me," and he walked back to the study door and knocked.

"Excuse me, sir," he said, "but Mr Williamson of Brocks Farm is outside. He's in a terrible state and asked me to give you this note. He says he must see you urgently."

"Well he can't. Tell him I'm busy," Wilfred said to the butler.

"I think, sir, you should read the note. The poor man's almost in tears," Steven replied.

After a moment's hesitation, Wilfred tore open the envelope and turned to his guest.

"Will you excuse me for a moment, Doctor Albert?" he said. "This man is a very old tenant and has been having trouble with his farm drains. I think I should just see what he wants."

"But of course, monsieur. I cannot stop your business, non," Annette said.

Wilfred nodded his thanks, looked down at the paper in his hand and just managed to keep the astonishment off his face as he read it.

> *'You could not know it, but that woman*
> *is Annette Barry. I don't know what story she's*
> *told but I can guess what she wants. You must*
> *come out and talk to me. Make any excuse, but*
> *she must not know I'm here.*
> *Jenny.'*

He folded it carefully and put it in his pocket, then thought for a moment before turning to Steven.

"Tell him I'll be out directly and we'll see what can be done," he said then, when the butler had left, he asked Annette to excuse him for five minutes while he found out more about his tenant's problem. "If it's really serious I may have to ask you to come back another time," he added as he left the room.

He found Jenny walking towards the drawing room and when he followed, she grabbed his arm, pulled him in after her and gently closed the door.

"How on earth do you know that's Annette Barry?" Wilfred asked. "She says she's from Liège University and doing research on descendants of aristocrats who survived the French Revolution. Very interesting she is. Knows all about the Chevalier."

"I recognised the built-up shoe and the very slight limp," Jenny replied. "I managed to get a good look at her face when she was talking to Steven in the hall, and despite the make-up, there's no doubt. Of course she knows all about the Chevalier, and I can see exactly what her game is. She's got plenty of charm, even with that awful wig, and she's going to lead you along until you forget what's happening. Then with a cunningly placed question, she'll hope that you get talking about what we've discovered. Then... bingo! And thank you very much; and she'll be off to her maps of Scotland. What excuse have you made to come out?"

"Steven said a tenant with a problem wanted to see me and I told him to ask the fellow to wait," Wilfred answered. "Then when I read your note I changed tack and said perhaps I should see what the problem was. I did warn the professor that I might have to ask her to come back another time."

"Good. Well now you've got to get rid of her." Jenny was at her most decisive, and forgetting who she was talking to, continued: "We can't risk a slip of the tongue or her seeing me. Tell her the tenant's problem is more serious than you realised and you've got to go with him to see... etcetera, etcetera. You know the sort of thing. Then add your apologies and say how interested you are in her work, and you'd be delighted if she could come back some other time and so on. I'm sure you can tell a great story."

Wilfred looked doubtful. "Well, I'll see what can be done," he said, and walked slowly down the passage to the study.

As soon as she heard the door close, Jenny ran up the stairs and took up her former observation post on the landing. Ten minutes later she saw an apologetic Wilfred escort his visitor out of the front door, followed by the sound of a car's engine and the scrunch of wheels on gravel.

"That all worked very well. She went off good as gold," said Wilfred, in a voice filled with relief.

"I just hope so," Jenny said, "for that woman has a nasty suspicious mind and I think that I too am rapidly developing one. She's drawn a blank here, but that won't stop her—" but before Jenny could finish what she was saying the telephone rang.

As soon as Andrew Henderson got back to his flat he rang his office and talked to his cousin Tony. Finding that all was well at the brewery, he suggested to his cousin that he'd better keep it that way, for he was likely to be on his own for the next few weeks.

"I've found out some interesting new facts," he said, "and it looks as though I shall have to go to Scotland, and possibly other places, and I may be difficult to get hold of. I will keep in contact – I think through Angela would be best; so now, if there's nothing else we need to talk about, put me through to her. Oh, and good luck!"

When his secretary came on the line he gave her instructions regarding various matters that she raised, and then told her what he'd just said to Tony.

"I think, Angela, if you don't mind, I'll leave messages at your home," he said. "It's a bit more secure than the brewery. Your answering machine's always on, isn't it?"

"Yes, Mr Henderson, and nobody's going to listen to it except me," Angela replied.

"Good. For the time being you can get me here, at the flat," Andrew said, "but if I go away, I'll warn you, and I'll have my mobile on most of the time. If you can't get it, try again later."

Having dealt with his office and future methods of communication, he rang Jock McCracken at the Bank of England and told him about his meeting with the French agent.

"He's from the Finance Ministry, as you guessed, and his name is Charles Morey, although I gather he's in England under the name of Masson," he said. "His bona fides appear to be good and he knows Bill Shankland."

"Yes," Jock replied, "that's who I thought it was. We've worked with him before. What did you find out?"

"That the treasure or whatever, referred to in the letter to Strathconon, is in fact gold bullion, and recovering it is Morey's main objective," Andrew replied. "He was interested to hear about the jewellery, but said he thought that was probably a family matter. As regards the other, he wants to talk to you boys. I have provisionally arranged to meet him again at the French club for lunch tomorrow, and to bring someone from the Bank."

"Right, and that had better be Bill. Just hold on a moment," Jock said. "OK, here's Bill, and he'll come with you. I'll leave the two of you to fix the details. Bye."

"Bill, you there?" Andrew asked, and when he got an affirmative, he went on, "I've arranged that we meet Morey at one at the Petit Club de Paris. Can you meet me first at Parks's in St James's Street, say twelve fifteen? I think we need a short chat before we see Morey."

When that was agreed Andrew rang off, and almost immediately the phone rang again.

"Wilkinson here, Mr Henderson," the voice on the line said. "You remember that earlier today Sergeant James reported a strange woman driving off in Mrs Barry's car? Well, we tracked the car to a house in Suffolk called Passford Hall. Our people thought it best not to follow it up the drive, but they did make a short reconnaissance on foot and saw the car parked outside the house. I believe you have some connection with the house."

"Yes indeed, Superintendent," Andrew replied. "It belongs to my wife's family, and was the home of the chap who left all those clues in South Africa. Anyway, I think we now have the answer to the mysterious woman, though why Annette Barry should drive there in disguise I'm not sure. Hoping to pick up an unconsidered trifle, I suppose! I'll ring them straight away and find out what happened. And by the way, while I've got you on the line, you might be interested to hear about a gentleman I met this afternoon." And Andrew related the gist of his meeting with the Frenchman. "I'm meeting him again tomorrow with a man from the Bank of England. I'll let you know what happens."

When he got through to Passford it was Jenny who answered the phone. "I think, darling, that you've had a visitor?" he said.

"We have," Jenny replied. "The wicked Mrs Barry has been here, hideously disguised as some sort of researcher from the University of Liège, and pretending to be looking for descendants of French families."

"What happened? I suppose she was hoping to wheedle something out of one of you?"

"As she drove up I was in the long gallery, and being nosey by nature, I looked out of the window and saw this woman walk towards the door. 'That's funny,' I thought, 'there's something familiar about you.' Now do you remember that Annette Barry had a built-up shoe and a slight limp? Well so had this woman. Then, as she waited by the door, she turned and raised her head and I could see that, for all the wig and make-up, it was definitely Annette."

"Good for you. What happened then?"

"Steven and I managed to get a message to Wilfred who was talking to her in the study. He came out and I told him that he must get rid of her, so Steven and he cooked up some story about a tenant in trouble and, somewhat reluctantly, off she went."

"Did she discover anything, do you think?" Andrew asked. "And, most important, did she see you?"

"No and no. I caught Wilfred in time – and I kept well out of sight."

"She is obviously a daring, not to say ruthless woman who does not give up. I wonder what she'll do next? I'm going to be busy all tomorrow, but I will try to ring in the evening. For God's sake, all of you... be on your guard, for we don't want any more kidnaps. And you, darling, look after yourself and I'll see you soon."

When Annette got back to Somerley Gardens she was again in one of her savage moods.

"I got nowhere," she said. "I thought I was doing well with that silly old cousin Wilfred – God, I can't stand these English gentlemen – but then some bloody peasant had a problem and off he went to help him. I was politely sent away with an invitation to return another time."

"Were you recognised?" Jean asked.

"No, I don't think so."

"Did you see Henderson or the girl?"

"No. They could have been there but I don't think they were," Annette replied in a slightly calmer voice. "I have the feeling that Henderson is in London. I'll try a little deception on his office and see if I can find him. Now look, if I discover anything we may have to move fast, and I think we must have another car. The Mercedes may be known. Marcel, you will attend to that tomorrow morning. Get a big one, a powerful one. We may need speed."

CHAPTER 27

A<small>T SIX THIRTY THE FOLLOWING MORNING, JUST</small> as Andrew was finishing his coffee, the door-bell rang. A youngish man with a freckled face, wearing a smart blue denim workcoat with a logo on the breast pocket and a cloth cap set at a jaunty angle, stood at the door, carrying a bucket filled with dusters and brushes in one hand and a small plastic attaché case in the other.

"Mr Henderson?" he enquired and when Andrew nodded he said, "I believe there is a job to be done at Watford Station?"

"Yes indeed," Andrew answered, adding, "I take it you've come from Mr Wilkinson?" When the other agreed, he said, "Well just hang on a moment while I get my jacket and lock up. The car's outside with my chauffeur. He'll get us through the traffic much quicker than I could – and don't worry, he's not in uniform and the car's an inconspicuous Ford. By the way, what's your name?"

"Just call me Bert, sir," the man replied. "And remember, I represent the security company responsible for the lockers. One other thing, sir – bring a hat and a light coat of some sort with you. I'll tell you why later."

Once they were in the car, heading north through the early morning rush hour and following one of Jim's complicated and apparently trafficless routes, Andrew asked what the procedure would be once they approached the station.

"Quite simple, sir," the young man said. "You see, we have an arrangement with the company that when there's a job to be done in a station somewhere, one of us takes the place of the normal man – you know the sort of thing – sickness or Granny's funeral or whatever. It happens quite often; it's usually drugs we're after but sometimes it's jewels and once I had to recover a missing head! The railway people don't know, so keep it to yourself."

"I most certainly will. So what do you want us to do?"

"Just drop me where I tell you, then go on to Watford Station and get Jim to park somewhere convenient for a quick getaway, but don't go near the main car park. You, sir, get out and go into the station, buy yourself a paper and find a seat where you can observe the locker area. It's at the back of the Booking Hall on the left beyond the refreshments. Eventually you'll see me there. I'll be checking some of the empty lockers and giving 'em a clean. I have a passkey for that purpose. In due course I shall move to the one we want and unlock it – don't ask me how, that's a trade secret. I'll then close it so it looks shut. Okay so far?"

"Sure," Andrew acknowledged.

"Good; so when I signal to you, you get up and go to it – I suggest by a route which I'll explain in a moment; one that'll make it look as though you'd just got off a train and don't forget which locker it is – number 26. When you reach it, go through the motions of unlocking it with this dummy key" – he handed Andrew the key – "take out whatever it is you want and walk out of the station and back to your car. Don't worry about me. I shall shut and lock the cupboard and then I'll make my own way back after I've done a further spell of maintenance."

"What happens if the station staff decide I'm a suspicious character?" Andrew asked.

"They won't. I'll see to that. Your biggest worry is if the bird has already flown."

"The bird is under observation," Andrew said with a smile, "and is reported safely in the nest!"

Just after they'd crossed the North Circular Road and were negotiating a series of small roads between Wembley and Harrow, Bert turned to the chauffeur.

"Do you know Hatch End station, Jim?" he asked, and when Jim replied that he did, he said, "That's fine, then you can put me down there," and turning to Andrew added, "I think it's best if I appear off a train – more natural like, if you get it. So I'll catch a local at Hatch End."

Five minutes later Jim was told to slow down. "The station's in here," Bert said. "Drive into the yard and park for a minute or two. You, sir, come with me."

Once inside, Bert went straight to a ticket machine and bought a ticket to Watford.

"You do the same, sir," he said to Andrew, "and when you get to Watford buy another ticket. One to Berkhamsted will do fine. When you see I've opened the locker, go through the barrier using that ticket. On the platform, put on your coat and hat and when a train from the south comes in, walk back down to the concourse using your Hatch End ticket and collect what you want from the locker. Got it? Good, then I'll see you in about forty minutes."

When they arrived at Watford Junction Andrew went straight into the station, leaving Jim to deal with the car.

"You go ahead, sir," he said. "I'll find somewhere which will allow a quick departure. When you've got the goods just walk out of here; I'll be waiting for you and will take the bag, like I was meeting you off a train."

Inside the station, Andrew's first task was to find the left luggage lockers and then to find a place from which he could keep them under observation. With this accomplished, he bought a ticket to Berkhamsted and a paper and settled down to read it on a bench some twenty yards from the lockers.

This he found difficult to do, for he kept searching the Booking Hall for a sign of the maintenance man's blue coat and cloth cap. He knew this was thoroughly unprofessional, for if there was anybody on the lookout for him, they would not have much difficulty in picking out the agitated man who kept peering round the edge of his paper, then putting it down and looking closely at everyone who walked past.

Eventually, finding an article on the consolidation of the brewing industry in Bavaria, he became so engrossed that it was only when he glanced down at his watch that he saw, out of the corner of his eye, a man in a blue coat washing out the interior of a locker.

Folding his paper and stretching out his legs in what he hoped was a natural manner, he watched the man move on to another locker, open it and do something to the hinges with a screwdriver. After more cleaning and work with the screwdriver on several lockers, the man arrived at one which he opened and peered inside. He appeared to hesitate, then closed it and picking up a duster, shook it out, polished the door with it and then shook it again and moved away, nodding his head.

Andrew got to his feet, tucked his paper under his arm and walked through the barrier and up the steps to the platform. He found a cloakroom and put on his coat and hat. Then, as he came out again onto the platform, a train came to a halt opposite him and he joined the crowd of people getting off it. With them he went down the steps and out through the barrier, taking the dummy key from his pocket.

There was no sign of Bert, but once through, he went straight to the lockers and found 26 without difficulty, inserted the key and pretended to turn it.

Then, just as he was about to open it, he heard a woman's voice and felt a tap on his elbow. "Excuse me," the voice said, and for all his experience in clandestine operations, he could have sworn that his heart stopped beating, "but I wonder if you would help me. You see, with this bandage I can't turn the key and I daren't let go of the boy."

He forced himself to look round calmly and saw a young woman at a locker about three away from his. One of her hands had a heavy plaster cast and the arm was in a sling. In the other hand, she held reins attached to a small, restless, red-haired boy.

"Yes, you do have a problem," he said, in what he hoped was a reasonably calm voice. Then he took the key which protruded from the plastered hand and unlocked the door.

"Thank you so much; that's very kind," she said. "Now there should be a parcel inside. Yes, that's it. Would you drop it in my shoulder bag? Lovely, thank you so much." And she wandered off, the child pulling strongly on the reins.

"I suppose these things are sent to try us. I now know what dying of fright means," Andrew said to himself as he turned back to his locker. With a shaking hand he opened the door, felt inside and pulled out a cheap imitation leather suitcase. Having checked that there was nothing else there, he closed the door, leaving the key in it, and made his way to the main exit.

Jim took the case and led him to the car which was only about twenty yards away. "Yes, I persuaded them that I was meeting someone with a damaged foot," he said, "so we'd better move fast, before they see you." Then, as he opened the door, he looked at Andrew, and in a horrified voice said, "Sir, you're shaking like a leaf. Are you all right?"

"Yes fine, Jim, but I've had a bit of a shock. I'll tell you about it in the car."

As they drove off Andrew lay back in his seat, took two or three deep breaths and closed his eyes. After some ten minutes, he sat up and looked at the chauffeur, who was aware of the reason for the journey.

"You know, Jim, I'm afraid my nerves are not what they were," he said. "Just as I was opening the locker I felt a tap on the elbow and a voice saying 'Excuse me'. Ten years ago I wouldn't have turned a hair, but today was different. My heart stopped and my legs nearly gave way. I thought of every-thing from the police to Mrs Barry." He paused and gave a short laugh. "I just about mustered the strength to look round, and what did I see? A young woman with a plaster cast and a recalcitrant child, asking for help with her key! Oh well, all's well that ends well I suppose, but let's just hope that we've got the right case!"

A few minutes later he looked at the dashboard clock. "Nearly half past nine," he said. "I think, Jim, we'll call in at the brewery first."

At the brewery Andrew took the suitcase off the rear seat, at the same time saying to the chauffeur, "Be ready in half an hour to take me to the flat – yes, in the Jaguar. I'll do a quick change and then take me on to Parks's, and I'll want you to pick me up from there between half two and three."

Inside, he waved to the commissionaire and receptionist and went straight up to his office.

"Angela, would you please find me a good strong cardboard box?" he said to his secretary. "A twelve-bottle case would do fine. Then I don't want to be disturbed for half an hour. After that I'll want to see you for a few minutes, and Mr Tony, if he's around."

While his secretary was finding the box, Andrew rang Passford and Jenny answered the call.

"Yes, darling," she said, "they've gone in to Colchester. And yes, I'm quite safe. I feel more secure with Steven than with any of you."

Andrew gave a somewhat unenthusiastic grunt and then said, "I went to the station today and collected the goods – at least I hope it's the goods. I'll know in about five minutes. Then I'm busy until this evening, when I'll ring again from the flat. Look after yourself." And he rang off leaving Jenny looking at the receiver and thinking, once again, how odd Englishmen were.

"They sent these two up from Despatch," Angela said, coming in with two substantial cardboard boxes. "They said they were the best they had."

"That one looks just what I want," said Andrew, picking up one and inspecting it, "but you'd better leave me both. I'll shout when I'm ready."

As soon as his secretary left the room, Andrew walked quietly to the door and locked it. Then he picked up the suitcase, looked at it closely and tried the catches. As he had suspected, it was locked, but the locks looked pretty flimsy. "Better try and force them first," he said to himself, "and if that doesn't work we'll just have to cut it open."

In the bottom drawer of his private filing cabinet, amongst other odds and ends, he found a fairly hefty screwdriver. This he slipped between one of the catches and the body of the lock and gave it a sharp jerk and, at the second attempt, the catch flew up. He then repeated the process on the other lock, lifted the lid, and there, well padded with newspaper, were two soft leather bags.

He took one of them over to his desk, opened it and drew out a square, blue box from which he removed a magnificent diamond-and-ruby tiara. More like a coronet, was his private thought. Another box produced a diamond pendant almost as big as a breastplate, and loose in the bag were rings, brooches and bracelets. All of these he carefully replaced and turned his attention to the other bag.

First out was another, smaller tiara of the sort used to secure piled-up hair or a high wig. Next came a pair of superb emerald sprays with long matching eardrops, and then a multi-strand pearl choker from which depended a circular gold pendant containing a single, perfect sapphire. These again Andrew carefully replaced and secured the bag.

"Well, we've certainly found the jewels," he said to himself, "but obviously they must be properly sorted and listed and, I suppose, valued."

He bent down and picked up one of the two boxes then, after looking at the bags, picked up the other. He carefully placed one bag in each box, padding them with the newspaper from the suitcase. Then, from the bottom drawer of the filing cabinet, he produced a roll of sticky tape and some sealing wax and closed and taped the flaps of both cases, leaving a small space, in the middle of the top, untaped. This he secured with a liberal amount of sealing wax and, taking the King's seal from his pocket, sealed both cases with the running hound. That done, he put his head round the door and asked his cousin and his secretary to come in.

"I'm sorry to have been so secretive," he said, "but we have now found the Bourbon jewellery that I told you about. It's there, in those two boxes."

Tony drew in his breath sharply. "Who does it belong to, I suppose is the only sensible question to ask, as I imagine its value is incalculable," he said.

"At the moment, we don't know for sure who owns it. It's a matter for the lawyers. As to value? As you say, Tony, probably incalculable. Not only is there the value of the stones, there is also the fact that it is of great historic interest. I'm sure that, regardless of ownership, the main pieces are museum stuff."

"What are you going to do with it?" Angela asked. "I hope you're not expecting me to guard it."

"No, I'll spare you that," Andrew replied. "For the moment I'm going to put it in the safe in the strong room and I want you both to come down with me as witnesses. Later this afternoon I'm going to hand it over to the Bank of England for safe-keeping. Tony, could you please collect the keys from Security and then come back here and help me carry down the boxes? Once they are safely locked away, I want you to keep the keys until I collect the boxes this afternoon and take them to the Bank. Until that time, no one is to enter the strong room unless accompanied by you. I will sign the necessary authority and talk to Finance and Legal. If anyone else asks what's going on, say that I have been asked to help the Bank on a confidential matter."

"What about you? What are you going to do?" Tony asked.

"First I've got a lunch appointment with the Bank and a Frenchman. After that, I don't know for sure. It depends on how certain other people react," Andrew said, "but after this afternoon don't expect to see much of me for a week or two, although I will try to keep in touch."

Once the boxes were safely locked away, Andrew was driven to his flat, where he had a quick shower and changed his clothes, and just after midday he was chatting to a friend in Parks's club and awaiting the arrival of Bill Shankland.

When Shankland was announced, Andrew led him to a quiet corner of the Morning Room.

"We're better here than in the bar," he said, "unless you're panting for a drink. The early lunchers are just arriving but we'll be alright here for twenty minutes or so."

"No, this is fine," Bill replied. "And now tell me, what do we hope to achieve at this meeting?"

"All in good time, but first let me tell you something interesting: we have got the jewels. I retrieved them from a left luggage locker at Watford this morning and they are now in the safe at the brewery."

"Are you sure it really is Marie Antoinette's jewellery? Have you looked at it?" the banker asked.

"As sure as a non expert can be. I've looked at the main pieces and it's obviously no ordinary collection. How did you come here? By tube? Excellent. Then I suggest that you come back to the brewery with me after lunch, collect the loot and then my chauffeur will drive you back to the Bank. Perhaps you could have it listed and valued. That ought to be done as soon as possible, and I imagine you can do it under conditions of secrecy."

"That can easily be done. And now, about today," Bill said, looking at his watch.

"We've plenty of time, only takes about seven minutes to walk to the Petit Club," Andrew said. "At our last meeting I told Morey that I needed to know two things – the ownership of the various valuables and what's to be done next. Do we continue the search for the French gold? And I need to know that the answers are acceptable to the Bank, the Foreign Office and the French authorities."

"The ownership may take some sorting out. A lawyers' beanfeast, I imagine," Shankland said. "But on the search for the gold, the Bank and the FO are agreed: it should go on and should be conducted by the police and yourselves – you taking the major part, which with any luck will keep it out of the hands of the media, at least to start with. Obviously our French friend has to agree to this." Andrew nodded, and looking at his watch, led the way out of the club and up St James Street.

They found Charles Morey in the bar of Le Petit Club de Paris, sitting at the same table as yesterday.

"I got in early and grabbed this table," he said. Then, having greeted Andrew, he turned to Bill Shankland. "It's good to see you again, Bill. And how is le Petit Banque Anglais? Not flooded with euros yet – non!"

"We manage, Charles, we manage," Bill replied.

While this exchange had been going on, Andrew had collected a bottle of white wine, filled their glasses and suggested that they look at the blackboard and order. While they ate their salade niçoise and waited for the sole in a shrimp sauce, Andrew described the recovery of the jewels and what he proposed should be done with them.

"Indeed I think that is the best plan, that the Bank of England should hold them for the moment," Morey said. "I have spoken to the Ministry and to the Banque de France and they are making arrangements for a lawyer and an expert on the personal and public property of the Bourbons to visit London."

Then, when the sole arrived, Andrew led the conversation round to ownership and what was to be done next.

"As I said, these experts are coming to London," Morey continued, "and no doubt, Bill, when they arrive, you and your lawyers and, I expect, people from your Foreign Office will get together with those representing Mr Henderson's family interests and, one hopes, come to some conclusions. For now, I do not believe we can speculate."

"That is what I thought you would say," Andrew remarked, "and I have already discussed the matter with Dick Wentworth at Hoopers and asked Jock McCracken to contact him when he's ready. But now what about the gold? I understand from Bill that, on our side, we want to continue the search and settle the matter one way or the other. So what is the French position, Monsieur Morey?"

"Yes," Morey replied, "if the bullion still exists, we think it should be found. If it is, and subject to the lawyers' opinions, my Minister hopes it may be returned to France. It must be understood that this is a police matter, but we accept that Mr Henderson must be involved, provided his side is led by the General Colquhoun, of whom the Ministry has the highest opinion."

"Do you agree to this, Bill?" Andrew asked. "Because if so, we have no time to lose. As Charles here is well aware, there are others determined to find the treasure, if possible before we do. I therefore suggest I go home and contact Superintendent Wilkinson and the brigadier and make plans to move to Scotland. You will go back to Annette Barry, Charles?"

"Yes. I cannot do otherwise," the Frenchman said. "I shall, as you say, run with the hare and hunt with the hounds. I shall do my best to keep in touch. Do you have a mobile telephone number? Good, I have noted that and your home number. Oh yes, and I almost forgot. We have a new car; another Mercedes, but newer, faster, and it's silver grey. I expect your watchers have noticed it. Now I must go or the good Annette will become suspicious. Au revoir, mes amis."

On the walk back to Parks's it was agreed that, unless Andrew heard to the contrary, he should assume that the Bank and the Foreign Office agreed with their proposed course of action.

"But," Bill Shankland added, "please let me know your detailed plans before you set off for Scotland."

"Jim, Mr Shankland has to collect some things for the Bank of England," Andrew said when they reached the brewery, "and I want you to drive him there. When you've done that, that will be all for today. I'll get one of the others to take me home in the Ford. As for the next week or two, Angela will let you know if I want you to do anything."

Inside the office, Andrew told the receptionist to ask Mr Tony to meet him outside the strong room.

"There you are," he said to Shankland when they'd opened the safe, "two very valuable cases of wine. Let's take them up to the car." Then with the banker and his cargo safely loaded, he added, "Mind you don't lose them."

216

CHAPTER 28

THE FIRST THING ANDREW DID WHEN HE got back to his flat was to telephone Norman Colquhoun, whom he was fortunate to find at his club.

"I've got a lot to tell you," he said, "starting with the fact that we've got the jewels. More important, though, I've just had lunch with people from the Bank and from the French Finance Ministry and have agreed with them what we do next. I therefore need your help. Can you come round here? Yes, to the flat. We'll need about an hour and it's now just after half-three. OK, see you in about twenty minutes."

Next he rang Superintendent Wilkinson and thanked him for his help in retrieving the jewels and put him in the picture on the lunchtime meeting.

"I've already heard about that," the policeman said. "Had Mr Shankland on the phone. Both the Bank and the FO have been on to my superiors and I've been told to discuss your plans with you and, if I approve them, to agree what support you need and who will provide it."

"That's excellent," said Andrew, "for I've got Brigadier Colquhoun on his way round here now. We should have some sort of plan worked out by five o'clock because the brigadier's got another meeting at half past. Can you come round here sometime after five and I'll tell you what we propose? You can? Good, see you then."

Norman Colquhoun, when he arrived, asked if there was a good-sized table in the house, and when Andrew led him into the dining room, he opened his briefcase and dumped a bundle of maps and a notebook on the table.

"That's fine," he said, "and now let's get cracking for I haven't a lot of time. Due to see the CGS at five thirty – more NATO security problems. Only one proper army left in the world and that's ours, although I will say

217

that the Americans and the French try hard. However their politicians can be even more difficult than ours. Now you say you've got the jewels. Where are they?"

"Safely locked up in the B of E."

"Good, and you say everyone is keen for the search to continue for better or for worse?" Norman said.

"That's right," Andrew replied, "as long as the police are ostensibly in charge, and as long as you are our lead man. The French were very definite about that."

"Decent of them," the brigadier grunted, "considering I spend a good deal of time trying to do them down. What about the police? You say Wilkinson's coming round later to hear our ideas. Well now, here's what I've been doing in the past twenty-four hours." And he paused, spread out a map and opened his notebook.

"First," he continued, "I rang Tommy Macdonald. Do you remember him when you were on my staff? A Gunner – rose to Major General and retired just after me. Lucky chap, his mother was called Kern, daughter of a Swiss banking family, so he was able to buy Knockbain. Nice deer forest between Glenelg and Ratagan. Nothing much but mountains, deer and eagles, but as those are his three interests in life, he spends his time either watching them or sitting on committees and talking about them! Naturally he knows the area we're interested in like the back of his hand, so was the obvious chap to ask."

"And what did he say? Did you tell him about the letter and poem?" Andrew asked.

"Yes – and our interpretation of them. He was very interesting about it. First he confirmed that in the eighteenth century the Strathconons owned land in the north-western part of Kintail. Then he told me something I didn't know, and that is that there have always been rumours in that area of a mysterious ship landing treasure somewhere on the coast, possibly from the West Indies." Here Norman consulted his notes. "Yes, that's right; he said the rumours were vague and no particular place was mentioned. However, when we got to the details of the poem, he was much more definite. He said that if you go on beyond Letterfearn, to a place somewhere about here," he said, pointing on the map, "there's a little bay there dotted with rocks, and one of them – almost a small island, I gather – is known as the Dragon or the Monster or something and, moreover, is exactly opposite Eilan Donan."

"It sounds as though we need to go there – and quickly," Andrew said. "Annette is quite capable of finding out about it and getting there first. So, what do you suggest?"

"That we drive up the day after tomorrow," was the brigadier's answer. "As I've already been stuck here for longer than I planned, I got Barbara to send me some more clothes so I'm set for a long haul. I've fixed with Tommy that we base ourselves on him. Now, who's in our party? You, me – anyone else?"

"I must take Jenny," Andrew said, adding with a short laugh, "She'll come anyway. I don't think anyone else; the smaller the party, the better. What I don't know is how the police will want to play it. I don't imagine they'll want anyone actually with us, but I assume Wilkinson & Co will involve the people in the highlands, and possibly others along the way. So I'd better know what route you're proposing."

"Oh, straight and simple. M6, M74, round Glasgow to Stirling, then west to Fort William and Shiel Bridge. It'll be up to Wilkinson what he wants to do and I'll leave you to discuss that. Now I must go; ring me at the club after nine – no, better first thing in the morning."

After the brigadier left, Andrew remained sitting in the dining room with the maps and the Strathconon papers all over the table, trying to work out the best route from Suffolk to the M6 when, twenty minutes later, Superintendent Wilkinson rang the bell.

"Got some news for you," he said as he came in. "Apparently the little Frenchman left Somerley Gardens at about ten this morning and went to Euston. We decided that he must be going to Watford for the jewels so we thought it best not to follow. Now it's just been reported that he has returned, so I guess your friends have now discovered their loss. The only other news is that the cleaning lady has arrived but has not yet left. Now, Mr Henderson, have you decided on your plans?"

"We have, and they are very simple," Andrew said. "We understand from a friend of the brigadier's, who lives near where we think the bullion may be, that our interpretation of the poem fits in with the local landscape. He also says that there are many stories of local buried treasure. Our plan, therefore, is that Brigadier Colquhoun, Miss Stanley and myself should drive north the day after tomorrow and stay with a General Macdonald – he's the friend – at a place called Knockbain. From there we should be able to reconnoitre the supposed site. More than that I can't say until we get there. Obviously we'll keep in touch. Will you give us a contact in the police up there?"

"Yes, I'll talk to them this evening. I'll also alert my little group who are attached to the force in York. They cover the whole of the north of England, so it's essential they know what's going on. I'll give you a special number for them; just say 'Is that group 101'? That identifies you as someone who needs their help. We'll keep in touch via your mobile, so for God's sake keep it on and charged!"

"I will," Andrew said. "Now about our friends. I gather they have a new car. Is it bugged?"

"Yes, it's a grey Mercedes. I expect Morey told you that, and we managed to change the bug without being seen. Whatever they do we'll be able to track them and report to you. Let me know before you leave and I'll confirm that everything's in place. Also remember that my superiors require you to be under my control, so any change of plans, however slight, you must tell me about. Now I'll be off and do some planning of my own. Good night, Mr Henderson."

A very unhappy Lemaître returned to Somerley Gardens at about three o'clock. The whole way back from Watford he had been wondering what to say to Annette and now the moment had arrived.

He let himself in and walked past the sitting room where Masson was reading a French newspaper.

"Eh bien, mon ami, how did you get on? Any problems?" the latter called, but Lemaître walked straight on towards his bedroom without answering and Masson smiled to himself.

Just as he reached his door, he heard a shout from the kitchen. "Come here, Jean, and tell me that you have the suitcase safe and sound," Annette cried, and Jean knew there was nothing for it but to obey, so he turned and sidled round the door to see Annette standing by the table slicing carrots. She looked at him, opened her mouth to say something. Then, seeing his empty hands, her voice rose to a scream.

"Mon Dieu, where is the suitcase? You haven't got it! Merde! You mean they got there before you?" And she advanced on him, raising the knife.

"You've failed me once too often, little man. You're useless," she yelled. "You're an encumbrance and I shall kill you. Kill you, d'you hear!"

Lemaître dodged round the table and she leaned across and slashed at him, missing his arm by inches. As she stood back and looked to see how she could get him into a corner, she felt her knife hand held, and a powerful arm round her waist almost lifted her off her feet.

"Prenez garde, idiote que vous êtes," Masson's voice hissed in her ear. "Remember the maid is still here. Getting us arrested will do no good." His grip on her hand tightened. She cursed and dropped the knife. Masson picked it up and pushed her into a chair, while Jean cowered against the wall.

She glared at Masson. "Do you realise what this wretch has done?" she said. Then her voice rose again. "He's lost the jewels!" she yelled, before slumping back in the chair and saying, in a voice now barely above a whisper, "First he loses the girl and now the jewels." Changing mood yet again, she started towards Lemaître. "Just let me get my hands on him," she snarled.

At that moment Masson, who had left the room, returned carrying a glass. "Here, drink this, it's cognac," he said, giving it to Annette, "and calm yourself. Let's hear from Jean what happened and then think what we do next."

Annette sat sipping the brandy and finally looked across at Lemaître. "Yes, little man, tell us what you found when you went to the locker."

"I went up to it and everything seemed normal," he said. "I put my key in and the door was certainly locked. So I unlocked and opened it and what do I see? Nothing – rien – the cupboard is bare. What did I do, you ask? I did nothing."

"Did you not complain? Send for the manager?" Annette asked. "It might have been a mistake. There had been an emergency possibly, and things got moved."

"Chère Madame Annette," said Jean, in a tone both whining and whee-dling, "you are experienced in these matters; you have been at it a long time. You know and I know that when you have lost a case full of stolen jewel-lery you do not call the management and you do not hang around. No, you do what I did. You leave the key in the lock and catch the next train back to town."

"He's right," Masson said. "Tell me, Jean, do you think you were watched?"

"I could have been. I didn't particularly notice. I certainly wasn't chal-lenged and I'm sure I was not followed back here. Because for that, I kept a special look out."

"Well, one good thing at least has come of this," said Annette, who by now had got her emotions under control. "We can assume that Henderson is in London and that he knows where we are. He must have had you followed, Jean, when you hid the jewels, and it would have been he, or one of his minions, who would have retrieved them. Damn him! We've underestimated him, he's cleverer than we thought."

"And what are you going to do?" Jean asked.

"As I said before, I'm going to visit him. I now know the address of his London flat and I'm going to find out what he knows about the other thing and what he's doing about it. Don't ask me how, but I just feel we're due a little luck. However, there is a problem: as we must now assume that this house is watched, how am I going to get out without being followed?"

Jean gave her an appraising look. "You are about the same size as the maid and she will be leaving shortly."

"You mean I will be leaving shortly?" Annette said after a moment's thought. "Yes indeed, it might work. I leave as the maid, go to my friend's flat and change. Then I visit Henderson, spend the night at the other flat and come back here tomorrow at the maid's normal time. Only one problem that I can see: how do we fix the maid?"

"Leave that to me," Jean said. "In half an hour you will have the clothes. And you, Marcel, you will perhaps go to the cinema."

Lemaître walked through to the hall where he found Bessie, the daily maid, just closing the door of the cupboard where she kept the cleaning things and about to collect her coat and shoes and go home.

As she walked across the hall, he gave her his most dazzling smile and asked her if she'd mind waiting for a moment before putting on her coat, as he had a most important request to make.

"What is your name?" he asked.

"Bessie," she replied, overcome by being asked such a question by he whom she had come to think of as the charming foreigner.

"Ah Bessie! Mais oui, Bessie! Indeed a most beautiful name for a beautiful lady," he said. "You see, Bessie, your mistress Madame Barry has a problem. She believes she is, how do you say it? Yes, being spied on – she is being spied on and she needs to leave the house without these spies realising it is her, and we think you can help."

"Ooh, I don't know about that," Bessie replied, reaching for her coat. "I wouldn't want to get caught up in doing anything wrong, anything criminal like, if you get me."

"It is nothing criminal, we promise you," Jean said. "It is just that madame has a friend, a very good friend, comprenez? I think you say an affair, and there are people who want to follow her and find out more about this affair. Now you have noticed perhaps that you and madame are about the same size, and so we thought if she was to wear your dress, coat and shoes and cover the hair she could slip away for a couple of hours and no one would know."

"But what about me, what will I do?" she asked.

"Have you anything to do tonight? Does anyone wait for you at home?" When she shook her head, Jean continued: "Well, I will find one of madame's dresses for you and I will cook you a special French dinner and we await madame's return. You will help now, I'm sure."

"Well alright," Bessie said. "Mrs Barry has been good to me; so if she needs help, I will do my best."

"Good, then come to my room and I will ask your mistress for a dress and you can give me yours."

Five minutes later, when the exchange had been effected, Jean took Bessie's slightly grubby print dress to Annette, having first told the maid to wait in his room.

"How do I look?" Annette asked as she prepared to leave the flat.

"Toute comme la belle Bessie," Jean replied, and Masson nodded.

"Well, let us hope I come back with something useful," she said, and gently closed the door.

"No doubt, mon Jean, you also will find something useful," Masson said with a grin, as he too left the flat.

"And now, Bessie," Jean said, going back to the bedroom, "let us go to the kitchen and have a glass of wine while I cook something. Do you ever drink wine? It is part of life in France but not so, it seems, in England."

"Oh yes, we drink it when we go to Spain on our holiday. It's alright, but I really prefer Coke. The wine makes my head spin," she said with a giggle.

"You say 'we' – you are married then, Bessie?" he asked, handing her a glass and adding, "This is good French white wine, so your head will not possibly spin."

"I was married, but my husband left me five years ago. I go on holiday with my friend Shirley and sometimes with my sister. This is very nice, this wine Mr... there now, I don't even know your name," Bessie said, taking a sip, then a bigger mouthful.

"Come now, let me fill your glass," he said, reaching over. "And you can just call me Jean. Tell me, Bessie, do you like spaghetti? I make it well, with a special sauce I learn from my mother who was Italian."

By the time Jean had cooked the spaghetti and they had eaten it, Bessie had drunk considerably more wine than she meant to and had become distinctly garrulous.

"Dear me," she said, getting rather unsteadily to her feet, "I think I must go down the passage. That wine does funny things to one," and she gave another of her giggles.

As soon as she had left the kitchen, Jean picked up the bottle and glasses and moved into the sitting room. Five minutes later Bessie appeared in the doorway, to see Jean just replacing the telephone.

"That was Madame Barry," Jean said. "She cannot get back tonight, so you'll have to wait until tomorrow for your clothes. She says that of course you may go home in hers or, if you want to, you can stay here in the flat."

Bessie stood in the doorway, steadying herself with one hand, while the other hand went to her mouth.

"I couldn't possibly do that, not with a man in the house," she said. Then she dropped her hand from the wall, straightened herself and smiled, perhaps a little lopsidedly. "Or could I?" she asked, adding somewhat inconsequentially, "It's been a long time since."

She walked firmly across to the sofa but when she reached it she subsided, laughing, onto the cushions.

Jean looked at her with an expert eye and reckoned that with one more drink, two at the most, she'd be out until the morning. He walked over to the table where he'd put the bottle and filled two glasses; then when he turned to walk back to the sofa he got the shock of his life.

Bessie had got to her feet and was trying to struggle out of Annette's dress. When she eventually succeeded in doing so without falling over, she stood before the astonished Jean holding out her hand for the glass and wearing nothing but an ill-fitting bra and thick dark brown tights which, together with an improbably sexy pair of black panties, she was struggling to take off. The effort was too much; she staggered towards him and tried to speak but all that came was an idiotic giggle; then her eyes glazed and without a word, she slid to the floor and lay there snoring loudly.

Jean bent down, picked her up and carried her to his room, where he laid her on the bed, pulled up her panties, slipped off the tights and gently covered her with the eiderdown. He then closed the curtains and walked quietly from the room, turning off the lights.

As he crossed the hall, he heard the front door open and Masson walked in, closing it behind him. He had spent a somewhat uncomfortable evening wondering whether he should try to warn Andrew of the impending visit. In the end he decided it was too risky. If Annette had any reason to think that Andrew had been forewarned, it seemed likely it would be him she'd suspect, and he felt his position in the enemy camp was too valuable to compromise.

"Well, how did you get on?" he asked Jean.

"Better than I could have hoped," Jean replied. "I persuaded her, I think against her better judgement, to have a drink. But after she had two – mon Dieu, she was away. She started undressing but fortunately she passed out. So now she sleeps it off in my bed. She'll be out until Annette returns. Now I shall borrow the bed of la belle madame – unfortunately without her in it! So goodnight to you." He went into Annette's room and closed the door.

Shortly after Wilkinson left, Andrew had a call from the team watching Somerley Gardens to say that the cleaning lady had just left.

"Later than her usual time," the officer said, "so the Super thought you'd like to know."

Andrew thanked the man and, having other things to think about, he put the matter out of his mind. Picking up the map of Wester Ross and the Strathconon papers, he moved into the drawing room and poured himself a whisky and soda and sat down to ring Wilfred Saddler and tell him all that had happened that day.

"So there you are," he ended by saying. "Norman and I drive up to Scotland the day after tomorrow and we'll take Jenny with us – if she wants to come, that is, which I'm sure she will, and if that's the case we'd better spend tomorrow night at Passford, if it's alright by you."

"Fine," Wilfred replied, "and now I suppose you'd like to speak to Jenny, so I'll hand you over."

"Yes, my darling," he said in response to Jenny's greeting and comment about his earlier call, "I'm sorry about that but I have had a very busy and successful day, so perhaps I can be forgiven." And he then gave her a summary of his doings and explained the plan proposed by Norman Colquhoun. "So, darling, we leave for the north at dawn on Wednesday."

"Who's we?" asked Jenny, interrupting him. "Does it include me?" she added in a voice that made clear that she assumed it did.

"Yes it does. The party will be you and me and Norman, so get your bag packed and don't forget warm clothes, waterproofs and proper footwear! The west coast can be cold and wet... Yes, Wilfred will advise you... And yes, we're coming down tomorrow evening, so see you then. Must stop now, there's someone at the door. Look after yourself."

Opening the front door, he was more than a little surprised to see Annette Barry standing there.

"Mon cher Andrew, do not look so surprised! I won't eat you," she said. "And now aren't you going to ask me in?" She walked forward, leaving Andrew no alternative but to stand aside.

"Forgive me," he said closing the door, "but you rather took me by surprise. You were about the last person I was expecting to see here."

"Why?" she said, turning to face him. "We are, after all, sort of cousins." She put a hand on his shoulder and looked up into his eyes. "You and I are stupid to fight each other over this Saddler legacy. Why don't we work together – forget my French friends and your little South African girl." And she pressed herself against him and looked up into his eyes. "If we pooled our knowledge, instead of fighting, we would get on much faster and, mon ami, we could have lots of fun." He felt her hands wandering over his body.

Catching her wrists, he gently disengaged himself and guided her towards the drawing room, on the way picking up the evening paper off the hall table.

"Mrs Barry, as I've told you before, I don't know what this knowledge is that you think I've got," he said dropping the paper on top of the maps, "but since you are here, please sit down and let me get you a drink."

"Why so formal, Andrew? My name is Annette," she smiled at him, seating herself on the sofa. "Yes, I would love white wine if you've got some."

"Of course," he replied, "but I'll have to get it from the kitchen."

"Andrew, you know exactly what I'm asking for," she said when he returned and handed her a glass. "You have the jewels. I know they exist because I had them and only you could have taken them from me and I intend to get them back. More important now, however, is the fact that I believe there is more to the Saddler legacy than the jewels, and I believe that you know what it is. You found out something in South Africa. I don't know what, but you do, and you are going to tell me."

"Mrs Barry, you say I found out something in South Africa but you don't know what it is. Well that makes two of us, for I didn't find out anything," he said, and sat down. He looked vaguely round, picked up his glass and squinting at it, added, "God I feel tired, but your good health anyway."

"Merci, à votre santé." she said, walking round behind his chair and putting her hands on his shoulders. He raised his arms to remove the hands but found he couldn't. He tried to get up but his legs wouldn't move. He felt her bend down and kiss the top of his head and from a great distance he heard her voice.

"You poor little man, you and your foolish friends thought you could compete with La Chérie. But now I shall get what I want." And she took a small camera from her bag.

Through the mist that appeared to drift before his eyes, Andrew could just make out the woman turning over the maps and papers. Then everything went blank and he never heard her valediction.

"I said I'd get all I wanted – but no! Although I've got this." She waved the camera. "I really wanted you too, but perhaps there'll be another time for that." And she leaned over and kissed him full on the lips.

CHAPTER 29

WHEN SHE LEFT THE CHELSEA FLAT, ANNETTE went first to an all night shop in the King's Road where, as she walked in, a somewhat portly Indian came out from behind the main counter.

"My goodness, Mrs Barry, why this honour? What can I do for you?" he asked with a broad smile.

"You can help me, Mr Bedi, as you did once before," she replied. "You developed a film for me overnight. I want you to do the same with the film in this camera." She held it out.

"Dear lady, yes indeed we have a same-day service but not, I fear, a same-night service," the little man said. "It would mean starting the machine and it is expensive. Other people, if they see it, might be asking..." He paused and shrugged. "There is not the staff here so I could not oblige. It is my sorrow not to help the Chérie."

"But, Mr Bedi, I think you will help. I will pay, and anyway you would not like me to talk to the police... No, I thought you wouldn't." Again she held out the camera. "There are six exposures and you will enlarge them as big as you can. At eight tomorrow morning I will collect them." And she turned and walked from the shop.

In the King's Road, she hailed a passing cab and was driven to an address in the Notting Hill area.

"How very convenient of Carla to be away and to have left me her keys," she thought as she walked into her friend's flat.

Finding some eggs and some bread, butter and cheese she made herself a light meal. Deciding there was nothing further she could do that day, she undressed, bathed and even found a new and unused toothbrush. She then lay down naked on the bed and wondered what the films would produce.

She'd had no time to look at what she was filming and could only hope it would be useful.

Her final thoughts before drifting off to sleep were of Andrew. "He's a very attractive man – I wonder what he'd be like in bed."

The next morning, at eight o'clock precisely, Annette arrived at Mr Bedi's shop, to be greeted by the owner, who bent down and took a large unsealed envelope from under the counter.

"Dear lady, this, I think, is what you wanted." He gave her the envelope.

Annette took it from him and had a quick glance at the contents. There were six coloured prints, each about A4 sized. Three showed papers covered in writing, the remainder showed sections of a large-scale map and there was also another envelope containing normal-sized prints and a strip of six negatives. She nodded and slipped them back into the envelope and sealed it.

"That is excellent," she said. Then she tapped the envelope and added with a grim smile, "I hope these are the only copies. It would not be good for your business, or indeed for yourself, if I was to discover this was not so."

"No! Oh no, most definitely there are no copies and you have seen that the negatives are there. I would not be so stupid," he replied.

"That is good. And how much?" Annette asked.

"Forty pounds," the Indian said, averting his gaze.

Annette glared at him, opened her bag and thrust two twenty-pound notes at him. Then she turned, walked quickly from the shop and hailed a cab to take her back to Notting Hill.

Reckoning she had no time to look at the photographs there, she took off her friend's coat and skirt and hung them in the wardrobe. The shirt she dropped in the laundry basket. She then dressed again in Bessie's clothes, checked that she had everything, locked the front door and took the tube to Lancaster Gate.

"How did you get on?" she asked Jean as she walked into the Somerley Gardens flat. "Incidentally, I hope the watchers did not notice my limp. Nothing we can do if they did."

"The good Bessie has, I think, a big hangover," Jean replied. "She sleeps it off in my bed."

"I'm sure!" was Annette's sarcastic comment. "Now I'll just change and then both of you" – and here she nodded to Masson – "come into the dining room and we will see what I've managed to get."

"So! I will now tell you what happened last night," Annette said, sitting down at the table and emptying the envelope. "I arrived at the good Henderson's flat, and to say he was surprised to see me would be an understatement, but he let me in. He led me to a very elegant sitting room and tried to hide some documents that were lying on a small table by dropping a newspaper on them. Very amateur! We exchanged some pleasantries and he offered me a drink. While he was getting it I was able to drop the powder in his drink. It was thoughtful of you, Jean, to give it to me."

"It's usually most effective. I hope it was last night," Jean said.

"Very much so," Annette replied. "Two minutes after taking a mouthful he was out cold and I was able to photograph the papers he tried to hide. I took the film to a little Indian who I know many things about, things he would not like the police to know. His shop is just round the corner from Henderson's flat. I persuaded him that it was in his interest to develop the film at once and here is the result. Let's have a look."

"Well, these three seem to be part of a map," Masson said, placing them together. "A map of a coastline with mountains and very few roads."

Annette looked closely at the map, tracing part of the coast with her finger and finally pointing to two places.

"I think I know where it is. You see here," she said, pointing to the first place, "here is the Kyle of Lochalsh – very difficult to pronounce, is it not. It's in the west of Scotland. Now let us see – yes, here," and she pointed again, "on this little bay, what they call a *lock*, is the farm of my friend Calum."

"What are these papers?" Lemaître asked. "I cannot understand them."

"Well, one is a letter, obviously to someone important. The other seems to be a poem," Masson said.

"Now this is interesting," Annette cried, picking up the letter. "It talks of the Chevalier Antoine, and it is he who was my husband's forebear. Then it mentions a cargo, and patrons who may be overtaken by fate. Now, if the chevalier is to be a beneficiary, the patrons must be Louis and his Queen and the cargo must have been something for their benefit – bullion perhaps." And she gazed out of the window, a faraway look in her eyes.

"Yes, these papers are indeed a find," she said, coming down to earth again. "They suggest that Henderson will have worked out that the bullion, or whatever it is, was hidden somewhere on this map. Now, since the King and Queen both lost their heads, this cargo, according to the letter, should belong to the Chevalier and his descendants. So it could be ours if we get to it first, therefore we must move fast. Henderson's no fool, even if he was a bit naive last night, and he's not going to waste time."

"What about this poem?" Jean asked. "I don't understand it."

"I don't understand it either," Masson said, "but it could be the directions to where the cargo is hidden."

"Probably is," Annette replied, "but I'm not going to waste time on it. I guess Henderson must have worked out what it meant, so we'll just watch him when he gets there, but to do that we must get to the area no later than he does."

"Well then, what's your plan?" Masson asked. "Where are we going and when do we start?"

"We're going first to an hotel I know in Yorkshire. It's called The Packhorse," Annette said, "but I'll give you details later. You, Marcel, you go and fill up the car and also buy some maps of the west coast of Scotland; the part opposite the island of Skye is what you want. I'm going back to my friend's flat to do some telephoning, as I don't think it's safe to do it here. I'll be a little time as I need to make sure I'm not followed. Pick me up at this address at one o'clock." She scribbled something on a piece of paper and gave it to Marcel.

"And what about me?" a rather dishevelled Bessie said from the door.

"Oh, Bessie, I'm sorry," Annette said, looking round, "I rather forgot you, but thank you for lending me your clothes – yes, they were very helpful. Now could you leave us for a few minutes as we're busy, then Mr Lemaître will come out and tell you what's happening and pay you. Thank you, Bessie, that'll be all." As soon as she'd left the room, Annette turned to Jean and said, "Here's some money. Pay her for the week and a bit extra for last night and explain that I'll be away for a few days. And now let's get going." She swept the map and papers back into the envelope and went to her bedroom.

Fifteen minutes later, she emerged carrying a small attaché case and walked across the hall.

"Jean," she said as she reached the front door, "there's a suitcase on my bed. See you put it in the car."

As she reached the street, Annette noticed a man walk up the steps from the basement of a house opposite. Then as she turned towards Lancaster Gate, she saw that he was following her. Again, as she bought her ticket for the tube, she could see him waiting just outside the station. On the platform he took up a position about ten or twelve yards from her. "Now I've got you," she said to herself.

When the train stopped, Annette waited while a woman with a child and pushchair got in, and then followed her slowly. As the doors started to close she could see that the man had got into the next carriage, so thrusting the doors with her elbows, she stepped smartly back onto the platform and joined the last of the people heading for the exit. Then, instead of leaving the station, she went round to the eastbound platform and caught a train to Marble Arch and a taxi to the Notting Hill flat.

It was a shaft of sunlight shining straight in his face that caused Andrew to open his eyes, and then to shut them again quickly. A few minutes later he pulled himself upright in the chair and opened his eyes again, this time more slowly, and looked round the room. The top of his head appeared to be bouncing up and down and there was a filthy taste in his mouth, but gradually his memory returned.

He remembered Annette at the door, getting her a drink and then not much more. He looked down at the table and saw that the maps and papers were still there. Then he noticed the empty glass on the floor and the stain on the carpet. With an effort he bent down and picked it up. There was still a little liquid in the bottom which he smelt and, dipping his finger in, put a drop on his tongue. Of course, he thought, the bitter taste. His last mouthful of whisky had tasted all wrong.

"So she drugged me," he said out loud. "A good old Mickey Finn, idiot that I am. And there was a camera. Now I remember it; it was the last thing I saw. So she photographed this lot." He looked again at the papers on the table. "The poem won't mean much, but the letter and the map will tell her what she wanted to know."

Having reached that unhappy conclusion, clutching his head, he staggered to the bathroom and reached for the Alka Seltzer and then went to the kitchen and made himself some coffee. Feeling now that he might live, he was making his way to his bedroom, when the telephone rang.

"I thought you might like to know," Superintendent Wilkinson said, "that the cleaner has just arrived at Somerley Gardens, but that's not what I rang about." But before he could say anything else he was interrupted by a shout from Andrew.

"Of course!" he cried. "That's how she did it."

"How who did what?" Wilkinson asked.

"Annette Barry. I've been had for a mug," Andrew said. "She visited me yesterday evening and slipped something into my drink which put me out cold. I've only just come round and I've got one hell of a head. She now knows, though, that Kintail is the place to be, that is if she's got any imagination at all, for she photographed my maps. That was the last thing I remember before passing out."

"But how did she get out without my chaps seeing her?" Wilkinson asked.

"That's what I was about to tell you. She went out and came back as the daily," Andrew replied.

"Yes, I guess that's just what she did," the superintendent said. "It seems we have somewhat underestimated her. So what are you going to do now?"

"First, before I do anything, I'm going to have a bath," Andrew said. "Then, hoping I shall feel a bit more human, I'm going to get hold of Brigadier Colquhoun and Miss Stanley and advance all our plans by twenty-four hours. Assuming I get the brigadier – perhaps I'd better try him before the bath – I would hope we'd be able to leave for Suffolk by noon. Then, as soon as we've collected Jenny, we'll head north. We ought to be somewhere in North Yorkshire by dinner time, so we'll stop and eat and decide what to do about the night. That's what I propose to do, so can you bring your plans forward?"

"I'm sure I can; just give me an hour or so, then ring me when you're ready to go. And now I'll leave you to it." He rang off.

Andrew was lucky and caught Norman Colquhoun just as he was leaving the club. When he had explained the situation, the brigadier, after castigating him for being an unsuspecting idiot, agreed that they should leave that day, and as soon as possible.

"That woman's no fool," he said. "We've underestimated her twice and we can't afford to do it again. Now you go and get that hangover sorted and pick me up here at about ten to twelve."

About half an hour after Annette had left the flat in Somerley Gardens, and just as Masson was preparing to go and deal with the car, he heard a tremendous row going on in the hall. Peering down the passage, he saw the maid, Bessie, standing in front of Lemaître and gesticulating and shouting.

"What's this extra money for?" she screamed. "There's me wages, but what's this extra ten quid? I suppose you think you're paying me off for 'aving some fun on me when I was pissed."

"Non, non, Bessie," Lemaître said, trying to calm her. "No one did anything to you. You drank a lot of wine and started to take your clothes off. Then you collapsed and you were asleep on the floor, so we put you to bed."

"Put me to bed?" Bessie shouted. "D'you think I'm that stupid? I know your sort. I wake up with a hangover, in your bed, in nothing but me bra and knickers. You been in there too, you with your interfering fingers at my parts and now you're trying to pay me off."

"Non! It is not so," Jean snapped. "I did not touch you – I did not fancy... Non, the money is from madame for lending her your clothes."

"Did not fancy! I like that," Bessie said. "I bet you fancied like anything. You want to pay me off, then I want another twenty quid."

Masson walked down the passage, taking a note from his wallet. "Bessie," he said gently, "what monsieur says is true: he did not touch you. But you had an unfortunate time last night, and it was kind of you to help madame. So here is twenty pounds and perhaps you would now leave us. We ourselves shall be going soon and we'll lock up – and you will look after things while Madame Barry is away, won't you?"

Bessie looked at the money, then stuffed it away in her bag and, without another word, marched out of the front door, slamming it behind her.

"It was best," Masson said, "for we do not want her causing trouble. Now I will go and get the petrol and the maps."

Masson drove first to a garage off the Edgware Road and filled up and checked the oil. Then, using the knowledge of London that he had acquired in the course of his many visits, he drove back to Marble Arch, along Park Lane and Piccadilly to St James's Square. There he parked on a meter and walked to a shop that he knew sold maps and bought the ones Annette wanted.

Back in the car, he sat for a moment and considered his position. Lemaitre, he felt, was becoming increasingly suspicious of him, so he must be even more cautious in his actions. With this decided, he picked up his mobile telephone and rang Andrew Henderson.

"Charles Morey here," he said, "and I must be quick. You will realise now that we know that something valuable was shipped to that place in the west of Scotland. We start heading north at one o'clock, making first for an hotel somewhere in Yorkshire called The Packhorse. The plan is to get to Scotland before you and then see what you do. She has a friend in that area. When I know more, I will try to contact you again, but I have to be careful. Keep your mobile on in the car. Have you got that?"

"Yes," Andrew said, "and we too are heading for Yorkshire... Are you still there Charles?" But the line had gone dead.

After he'd spoken to Norman Colquhoun, Andrew retired to the bathroom, shaved and had a bath. Then, feeling somewhat more human, he dressed in sweater and flannels and packed a small suitcase. That done, he sat down and rang Passford.

"Listen, we're going to have to change our plans," he said when Wilfred answered, "for I had a visit from Annette last night and made a complete fool of myself." And he explained about the drugging of his drink and the photographing of the maps and papers.

"So," he continued, "we must assume she now knows the general area where the Bourbon treasure is likely to be and that she'll not waste any time in getting there. That means that we must set off for the Kyle today... Yes, more or less at once. I'm picking up Norman just before twelve so, depending on the traffic, we should be with you around half one. Now I'd better speak to Jenny. See you later... Thanks, yes, a quick lunch, and I mean quick, before we go would be lovely."

"Now look, darling," he said when Jenny came on the line, "there's been a complete change of plan and I'll explain why later. But the fact is that Annette has stolen a march on us and is probably already on her way to Scotland."

"And I suppose you want us to follow her immediately – starting now!" Jenny said, interrupting him. "So I'd better go and pack my bag... You say you're picking up Norman at twelve... Yes, I'll be ready to go as soon as you get here. Drive carefully. Bye, darling."

Andrew put down the receiver, glanced at his watch and saw it was eleven fifteen. He collected his suitcase and put it in the hall, adding cap and waterproof to the pile.

"I think we'll take the Range Rover," he said to himself. "It's fast and comfortable and could be useful. Boots and anorak are in it I know. Now, I'd better have a word with Marg."

He found her in the kitchen and explained to her what was happening and what he wanted her to do.

"I've no idea how long I'll be away," he said, "or, come to that, where I'll be. The mobile will be on the whole time so you can get me on that. We'll leave the answer-phone on and I can collect any messages. Don't give the mobile number to anyone, just tell me who rang. If anything sounds like business, tell them to ring Angela at the brewery. Now I'd better go... Yes, I'm picking up Miss Jenny at Passford and they're going to give us lunch."

As soon as he got back to the hall, the telephone rang and he answered it in the drawing room.

"Wilkinson here," the superintendent said. "Thought you might like to know the daily has now left. Seemed in a bad temper apparently. Just before that, Mrs Barry went out. She was followed but they lost her in the underground. Sorry about that. Also your friend Morey went off in the car about an hour ago and has not yet returned. As far as we know, the little man is still in the flat. Now, are you about ready to go?"

"Yes, I pick up the brigadier in about half an hour and we drive to Suffolk. We should leave there between two and three and be on our way north. I think we'll probably head for Knaresborough. It's quite a good place for dinner. After that I'm not sure."

"Okay. Well remember to keep your phone on and I'll let you know if anything interesting happens down here," Wilkinson replied. "Now, one or two things you need to know. First, I've alerted the boys in York and they will give any assistance you need. Don't forget: 'group 101' – and refer to yourself as 'Fido'... Yes, 'Fido' – sorry about that. Secondly, the Northern force know you're on your way. I don't have a group there but the Assistant Chief Constable is a good friend of mine. Cameron is his name. He'll be your contact and he knows General Macdonald at Knockbain. That's all for now. Go carefully and don't do anything stupid – ask a policeman first."

No sooner had Wilkinson rung off, than the telephone went again. Andrew picked up the receiver and listened to the voice of Charles Morey. He acknowledged the information Morey gave, but before he could say more the line went dead.

He looked thoughtfully at the phone for a minute or two, wondering whether he ought to ring Wilkinson. Reckoning that the police would anyway follow the bug, he decided not to waste the time, so shouting goodbye to Marg, he grabbed his luggage and went down to the basement garage.

CHAPTER 30

JUST AFTER TWELVE THIRTY THE MERCEDES, WITH Masson at the wheel, left Somerley Gardens and headed west along the Bayswater Road.

"How well do you know this part of London?" Lemaître, who had been looking out of the rear window, suddenly asked. "We're being followed, so I think we should take a roundabout route."

"Fairly well," Masson replied, and swung left at the next traffic lights and drove down towards Kensington High Street.

"Magnifique! The lights changed as we went round and our pursuers, they are stuck," Jean said with almost childish glee.

Masson turned east into the High Street, and again they were lucky with the lights. In Queen's Gate, he asked Jean what he wanted to do next.

"Should we go on a bit further or head back to collect Annette?" he asked.

"Turn into one of these little streets and stop for a moment," Jean replied, and when they pulled into a space in front of one of a row of pillared Victorian front doors, he produced from his pocket a device resembling a television remote control.

"I have been watching carefully," he said, "and have not seen anything since we turned into that great wide street. But if we are being followed, may we not also be bugged? Now watch." He pressed a key. Immediately a red light appeared.

"Aha, I thought so. Now quick, and we disable you." He pressed another key. The little device emitted a series of high-pitched bleeps and the red light first blinked and then went out, to be replaced by a green light. "It is good. Our bug no longer transmits, so let us go quickly and round a few more corners and we should be safe."

Masson turned into Gloucester Road and made his way back to Bayswater Road by the park and Marble Arch. Ten minutes later, they were outside the address Annette had given them.

"No, I never saw the following car again after the bug was switched off," said Jean, after explaining why they were late.

"Then all we must decide is which way we go," Annette said. "I think the A1 would be best; we can always get off it, which we can't with a motorway. If the police did spot us, then Henderson would know where we are, and I'd rather he didn't. So, Marcel, turn right at the end here, then left and we're on our way. Just follow my directions."

Andrew pulled up outside the Rag at five to twelve, and hoping there were no wardens about, went in and found Norman Colquhoun talking to the hall porter.

"All ready?" he said to Andrew. "Then let's get going. See you in a couple of weeks, Barker."

"Any further problems?" the brigadier asked.

"Not exactly problems," Andrew replied as they drove along the Embankment, "but I had a call from Wilkinson, who said the daily, presumably the real one, had left, and that Annette Barry had also gone out. She was followed but managed to give them the slip. Morey also went out in the car and had not returned – but more of that later. He then told me what he'd done about alerting other forces and who to contact if we needed help. Now to go back to Morey. I also had a call from him, I think on a mobile phone, and he seemed to be in a great hurry and unwilling to say much. What he did say was that they were off north at one o'clock and heading for an hotel in Yorkshire called The Packhorse, and would ring again when he could, with more information."

"Sounds a bit as though he's worried about being discovered," Norman said, "and in my opinion rightly. Pascal Nero has a nasty suspicious mind and may just know about Morey."

The lunch hour is not a bad time to drive through suburban traffic, and also on busy main roads, so it was just after two when they drew up at the front door of Passford Hall. Wilfred was as good as his word and lunch was waiting for them.

While they ate, Andrew described in more detail the events of the past twenty-four hours and then went on to outline his plans.

"We know from Charles Morey that they are heading for an hotel or pub called The Packhorse and that it's somewhere in Yorkshire," he said. "I therefore suggest that we make for Knaresborough. There are a couple of decent hotels there, where we can have dinner. Then, depending on what further information, if any, we get from either the police or Morey, we can decide what to do next. Either sleep there or, as we've got three drivers, drive on through the night."

"I don't recommend that," Norman said. "No point in arriving exhausted at the other end, particularly if urgent action may be needed."

"I agree," said Jenny.

"Well, we'll see. As I said, we don't have to decide now." Then turning to Jenny, Andrew asked her if she was ready as he would like to get away by two thirty.

"Yes, as soon as you like," she replied, "for I hope Steven has already put my things in the car."

"Yes, madam," the butler replied, "all done."

As they stood on the steps some ten minutes later, Wilfred pointed at the Range Rover. "Why on earth are you taking that clumsy great thing?" he asked.

"Useful for Scottish terrain and weather," Andrew replied. "It's also very comfortable. We can even sleep in it if necessary."

"God forbid!" said Jenny and Norman in unison.

"Come on and stop nattering," said Andrew, getting in and starting the engine. "Au revoir, Wilfred, and we'll keep in touch."

Prior to Annette's visit the previous night, Andrew had spent some time studying the map and now put his researches to good use. First he took a twisting cross-country route to Sudbury then, just before they reached the town, he asked Norman to look at the map.

"Sudbury is a mass of roundabouts," he said, "and I don't want to go wrong. There should be a short cut that will take us out to the main Cambridge road. Got it?"

"Yes. Go easy though, for the turning's just coming up," Norman said. Then, after a quick glance at a sign, he went on: "Take the second left at this roundabout and after about four or five miles we should hit the road you want."

"Now, Jenny, I seem to remember you're a Shakespeare scholar," Andrew said when, some fifteen minutes later, he turned onto the main road.

"Just because I found a quotation from Macbeth, that doesn't make me a scholar," Jenny replied. "Anyway, what's the question? I suppose you've thought of something clever just to show up my ignorance!"

"No, I'd never do anything like that. Just a good general knowledge question," he said. "Remember false, fleeting, perjur'd Clarence?"

"Yes, Richard III. Why?" Jenny said.

"Do you know the origin of Clarence? It's the name of a royal dukedom that has appeared several times in the last five or six hundred years."

"No, and I've often wondered about it," the brigadier said, and Jenny agreed.

"Well, look around you now," Andrew said. "It comes from this village, Clare, and its royal castle."

"Very interesting. I shall add it to my stock of useless knowledge," Norman said, "and I hope this history lesson is not going to continue the whole way north. We pass an awful lot of battlefields!"

With Andrew's assurance that there would be no further intellectual exercise, other than what might be required in the course of their business, the rest of the journey, round Cambridge and Huntingdon and up the Great North Road, was uneventful. There was the inevitable hold up on the Doncaster bypass, one of those maddening stretches of motorway with only two lanes, but despite that they reached their hotel near Knaresborough just after seven.

"Now, what does anyone want to do?" Andrew asked as they were finishing dinner. "I've checked that they have vacant rooms, so we can sleep here if we want to. That would mean an early start and a long drive tomorrow. The alternative is to press on; in which case we really want to cross over towards the west, don't we, Norrie?"

"The west coast route is certainly the shortest, so the sooner we're on it the better," Norman replied, looking at his watch. "It's now just after nine thirty, so what about Barnard Castle? It's only about an hour further on, it's in the right direction and there's a good hotel there. Or there's Appleby; it's about another twenty miles on, so it would be after eleven before we're there. The hotel might not appreciate that."

Further discussion was then cut short by the shrill buzz of Andrew's mobile phone.

"I'll take it outside," he said, and walked out of the dining room towards the main entrance.

"Andrew Henderson speaking," he said as he stepped out onto the porch.

"This is Charles Morey. We're at the hotel I said and I must be quick as I think Nero is suspicious—"

"But where is it?" said Andrew interrupting.

"Never mind that," came the reply, "the main thing is we're on our way to—" Andrew heard what sounded like something being hit, followed by a groan and a crash and the line went dead.

"What's happened? Are you alright...? Charles, can you hear me?" But there was no reply. Then suddenly he heard a short laugh and the connection was broken.

He hurried back to the dining room and beckoned to Norman Colquhoun to join him.

"That was Morey," he said, "and something's happened to him. Something serious by the sound of it." And he described what he'd heard.

"Sounds as though he was attacked," Norman said, "and then someone switched off the phone. Did he say where he was?"

"No, that's the problem. He just said they were at the hotel he'd told me about. I asked him where that was but he said that didn't matter, the important thing was to tell me where they were going to next, but before he could give me the name of the place, I heard the sound of the blow."

"So he wants to tell us something important and is being forcibly prevented from doing so," Norman said. "We can't help him because we don't know where he is, except that he's at a pub called The Packhorse. I think the best thing to do is to ring Wilkinson and see if his boys in York can help – or even ring them direct—" But whatever he was going to say next was again cut short by Andrew's telephone and the voice of Superintendent Wilkinson came on the line.

"Before I say anything else, I owe you an apology," he said. "Soon after I last spoke to you the two Frenchmen left the flat and were followed by one of our cars. They lost the Merc in the Kensington traffic and then the bug failed. I've only just discovered this, so I'm afraid no call was put out to watch out for them, so I don't know where they are. Now, however, I've got some better news for you—" But before he could go any further, Andrew interrupted him.

"And we've got some news for you. Serious news, and we were just about to ring you for assistance," he said, "but tell us your news first. It may have a bearing on our problem."

"Well we'll see, but either way it is important," Wilkinson answered. "About a couple of hours ago the cleaner from Somerley Gardens turned up at Willesden Police Station. According to her, she'd been assaulted and swindled by a bloody Frenchie, and so had it in for her employer. Also she thought that all of them at the flat were up to no good. She'd seen Mrs Barry looking at a map and saying something about an hotel: 'The Ackus at Oars', she said it sounded like, and she also heard her say something about getting help with the gold."

"Did she say where this Ackus place was?" Andrew asked. "Or anything about who or what could help with the gold? Incidentally, how did you get to hear of all this?"

"By sheer coincidence. One of my men had been interviewing someone out in Brondesbury and called in at the station for some local information," the superintendent replied. "The sergeant, who was a bit of a friend of his, showed him the report of Bessie's interview and asked him what he made of it. Of course he recognised Somerley Gardens at once and rang me—"

Andrew again interrupted him. "Hang on a moment, Superintendent, because I think now's a good time to tell you what's happened here." And he described the call from Morey and their suspicion that there had been foul play at The Packhorse. "But as we don't know where that is, we can't do much to help, and so we were about to see if your boys in York could help."

"Well, they can, for I've just been talking to them," Wilkinson replied, "and what Morey said about a pub called The Packhorse fits in nicely. I told them about the Ackus nonsense, and as you'd told me they were going north, I wondered if it could refer to somewhere in Yorkshire; and then one of the chaps had a brilliant idea. Apparently there's a town in the Yorkshire Dales called Hawes – Oars, you see – and some five or six miles from Hawes, out on the moors, there's a small hotel called The Packhorse – and that's the Ackus for you. So now perhaps you'll believe that the police are sometimes quite clever!"

"Oh, we believe it," Andrew said; then remembered his last call in London. "I'm afraid I too owe an apology. Morey told me about The Packhorse before I left London, but I was in a hurry so never told you. But now we need to think of the present and what's happened at this hotel. What do we know about it?"

"It's quite well known and used to be popular with tourists," Wilkinson replied, "but I understand the present landlord is a pretty unpleasant character, and that, together with its remoteness, has given it a rather sinister reputation. That being so, we must get people there as soon as possible. Where are you now? Knaresborough, you say. How far's that from Hawes?"

"Brigadier Colquhoun's just looking at the map," Andrew replied, "and he says it's about sixty miles along a winding, hilly road which I don't know – oh, and I see it's just started to rain. It'll be after midnight before we could be there."

"Right then, I'll get onto York and get them to do something urgently," Wilkinson said, "and I'll ask them to contact you and let you know what's happening there and also give you directions, because I think you should go there as quick as you can." And he rang off.

The Mercedes crew had an uneventful journey until they stopped for petrol and a rest at a service area near Wetherby. Annette, who had eaten nothing except a biscuit and a cup of coffee since her rather scrappy supper the previous evening, decided she must have a proper meal, so she and Marcel went to the coffee shop. Jean said he wasn't hungry, so bought a sandwich and a copy of *Men Only* and retired to the car.

He had just settled down with his magazine when something made him look up and then hurriedly down again, for a police car was cruising slowly along the front of the line of parked cars. At the end of the row it turned and drove back along the next row. In the mirror he watched the two policemen carefully scrutinise each car as they passed it.

Opposite the Mercedes they slowed down, but to Jean's relief appeared to be more interested in the car behind. After a moment they drove on, but Jean continued to keep his head well down, buried deep in the over-exposed body of an astonishingly well endowed young blonde.

When, some forty minutes later, Jean told the others about the police car, Annette said that she did not believe its appearance had anything to do with them. The police had lost them in west London and so with the bug disabled, the only way they could have been picked up again was if their number plate had been spotted, and that would surely have happened much earlier.

"Nevertheless," she said, "we'd better get out of here and push on north as fast as possible. We can't get off the main road for a bit or we'll get tied up in Leeds and Harrogate. We'll have to go on to Ripon. I think I remember the road, so I'll drive."

There was no sign of the police on the long stretch of road that passes Wetherby and Boroughbridge, and after thirty minutes they were round Ripon and heading for Leyburn.

In Leyburn they turned left towards Wensleydale. After a couple of miles, at the top of a steep hill, Annette braked sharply and pulled in to the side of the road. Ahead of them were three or four stationary cars and at the bottom of the hill they could see the flashing blue lights of police cars and ambulances and other signs of a major accident.

"This is not for us," said Annette. "Help me turn, Marcel, and we'll go back into the village. There's a road I know which will take us round and back onto this road further up the valley."

Their new way, which Annette seemed to know quite well, took them past a ruined castle, its grey stone walls standing four-square above the road, and then down through woods to a narrow bridge over tumbling falls and finally up a winding hill and back onto the main road.

"You know this country very well – how is this so?" Marcel asked.

"My husband used to come here shooting – what we in France call hunting," Annette replied as she turned out of the side road. "Now, thank heavens, we're on our original route again. It's about twenty miles from here to the hotel, so let us hope we are done with the police."

Outside Hawes, they stopped for petrol. "Always best to keep the car full," Annette said. Then it was on through the attractive old town, where every other building seemed to be a pub, and out onto the open moor. After about five miles they turned right towards a range of much higher hills and then left up a short, steep drive to the hotel.

Behind the building was a small pine wood, giving some shelter from the incessant wind, and in front there was an ill-kept lawn, in the middle of which were bedraggled roses. Beyond the lawn was a clump of birch and rowan and fronds of encroaching bracken. The drive led round the side of the hotel to a car park, its surface cracked and pitted with weeds. Annette, however, stopped in front of the door, marched into the hotel and banged on the counter. After a minute or so a tall, thin woman, her grey hair swept back in an old-fashioned bun, appeared and greeted Annette in a quiet, rather hesitant voice.

"Good evening, Liza, and yes, I'm well, thank you," said Annette, returning the greeting. "And you and Silas, you too are well? And the hotel? Ah, not so busy, I can tell, but you have our rooms?"

"Yes, they are all ready for you," the woman replied, "and you are the only people here tonight. It's still early for the tourists; and now the wind's getting up and the rain's just starting, so I doubt there'll be many in the bar tonight."

"They'll not come these days, rain or no rain," said a gruff voice and a huge man, six foot six and seventeen stone, came into the room through a side door. "But we'll look after you. The rooms are warm and the food's still good. And these are your friends?" he asked as Marcel and Jean came in with the cases.

Annette effected the introductions, then looked at her watch. "It's now just after seven, so let's have dinner at eight fifteen."

"That'll be fine," Liza said, "and now I expect you'd like to see your rooms." And she led the way up the stairs while Silas stumped off to the back regions.

Outside her room, Annette took her case from Jean. "We'll meet in the lounge in a quarter of an hour," she said and closed the door.

Despite its outside appearance, inside, as Silas had said, the hotel was comfortable and well managed, something Marcel realised as soon as he walked into the lounge. For, with the wind increasing and the rain battering against the windows, he was pleased to see that a fire was burning in the old stone hearth and that an opened bottle of red wine and three glasses stood on a table.

He poured himself a glass of wine and walked over to the fire, wondering what was the right thing to do. Although they were now aware of the general area where the Bourbon gold might be hidden, Marcel knew that tomorrow Annette was hoping to pick up Henderson's car somewhere along the route, then to follow it and find their base. Her exact plans he hoped to find out in the next hour or so, then somehow he would have to find a moment to ring Andrew and warn him to take a different route. His problem was to escape from Jean, who seemed to have become increasingly suspicious of him.

A short time later Annette came into the lounge and walked over to a chair by the fire. Marcel poured her a glass of wine and sat down opposite her. Jean then appeared and stood by the table, staring irresolutely at the bottle and the one remaining glass.

"Go on, have a drink, Jean," Annette said. "It might cheer you up, and I can't stand you looking like this all through dinner."

Jean scowled at her, reluctantly poured some wine and took a sip from his glass, then reverted to watching the rain lashing against the darkening windows.

"I've been looking at the map again," Annette said, "and trying to guess what Henderson is doing. He must know that we are heading north, but he can't know when we started – or even if we have yet started. Therefore he's unlikely to be in any hurry. Like us, he's probably dining in some hotel and will shortly be tucked up in bed with Madamoiselle Stanley."

At this remark, Jean's thin mouth twisted into a grin. "That's better, my little man," Annette said, smiling at him and getting a vicious glare in return. "Enough of this," she continued, "we must be serious. Wherever Henderson is now, tomorrow I think he will head over to the west. We will do the same and drive slowly up the motorway in the hope that we will see him. If we don't we'll just have to go on to Calum's. Now let's go and have dinner," and she led the way towards the dining room.

Despite the excellent food, dinner was a far from happy meal. Annette did her best to make conversation but Marcel was occupied with his own thoughts, while Jean, who, after a slow start, had now been drinking steadily for over an hour, was making little sense.

The general air of gloom gave Marcel a reason for leaving the table early. So at about nine thirty, refusing coffee, he made his excuses and retired to his room.

"Madame Barry," Jean said in a far more sober voice than his appearance warranted, "I do not trust that man. This morning, while he was getting petrol, I made a little telephone call to Paris. They told me that Le Grand Homme had sent no one to England. So who is he and where has he come from?"

"Damn him. Of course, I see it now! That bloody office that you got the information from would have informed the Government, Le Banque de France, tout le monde." Annette, again in one of her rages was shouting and swearing. "And this bloody shit's been sent over to find out what's happening. He'll have been to the financial people here, probably the police, and he's certainly in touch with Henderson. He's probably now telling Henderson exactly what our plans are, sod him. Find out, Jean. Find out what the bugger's up to!" Then in a calmer voice she added, "Be careful, though; you're not as sober as you might be."

As soon as he got to his room, Marcel looked out of the window. The rain had eased to a light drizzle and the night was pitch dark. "Not safe to use the phone in here," he decided, "so it'll have to be the garden." He closed the curtains and picked up his dark blue raincoat, slipped a torch and his mobile phone into the pockets, then turned out the light and walked towards the door.

Now, earlier in the evening, before going down to the lounge, he'd done a quick reconnaissance of the hotel and noticed that there was a side door facing towards the small wood beyond the car park. This door was reached by a short passage that led off the bottom of the service stairs.

When he opened his door there was no one in sight. He made his way unobserved to the back stairs and, in semi-darkness, started a cautious descent. He had reached the halfway landing when he heard heavy footsteps approaching the bottom of the stairs. Seeing a door in the wall to his right, he quietly turned the handle, pushed open the door and stepped through, closing it silently behind him. He stood absolutely still while the footsteps came up the stairs, passed his door without stopping and went on up to the next floor. Risking a quick flash from his torch, he discovered that he was in what was evidently a servants' lavatory. Hearing no further movement, he left his hiding place and went quickly down the remaining stairs and out into the car park.

The drizzle had almost stopped and he made his way across the tarmac to the shadow of the trees. After pausing to check that there was no one in sight, he took the telephone from his pocket and rang Andrew's number.

Bypassing Andrew's request to know where he was, he was about to tell him their destination in Scotland and to warn him about tomorrow's route when there was a slight rustle in the trees behind.

He lowered the handset and turned in the direction of the noise. Something surged towards his head and he felt a sharp pain across his right ear. He tried to raise the phone but his arm would not move and his head felt as if it would burst. The breath rattled in his throat, then everything went black and he crumpled to the ground.

Jean Lemaître turned the heavy torch downwards so that it shone on the inert body at his feet and knew instinctively that Marcel Masson was dead. He bent down and looked at the eyes. There could be no doubt; he'd seen that glazed appearance often enough. He sniggered, switched off the phone and then turned and walked slowly into the hotel lobby.

"Well, what did you discover and what he was doing?" Annette asked.

"Yes – and you were right, he was talking to Henderson," Jean replied, "and was just about to tell him where we were going, so I tried to knock the phone from his hand with the torch. It was dark; I could not see properly and instead of hitting his hand, the torch caught him below the right ear. I think he heard me and dropped his hand as I struck."

"He is unconscious, yes? So what do we do when he comes round?"

"He won't," Jean said; "that blow below the ear is often fatal, as indeed it was in this case."

"Merde! You killed him, fool that you are!" Annette screamed, seizing him by the shoulders and shaking him like a terrier with a rat. "I told you to be careful, you drunken wretch, and again you've let me down; but that we can see about later. For now, we must deal with the body." And she marched over to the desk, rang the bell and yelled, "Silas, come here at once."

The big man listened in silence as Annette recounted what had happened and explained its implications.

"You do not need to know what we are doing or why," she said, "but that man was talking to what, for a better name, we'll call our enemies. We don't know what he may have told them, whether they know where we are and whether they may have told the police. The body must be hidden and we must leave here at once."

Silas scowled at them. An experienced criminal himself, he disliked amateurs and particularly foreign amateurs, but he dare not let down La Chérie. That woman knew too much about him.

"We are building a new cesspit." Silas was a man of few words. "We will dig a little deeper for the foundations. Tomorrow the concrete arrives and your friend will never be seen again." He turned to Jean. "You will come and help me." And to Annette: "Liza will look after you. Luckily the rain has started again, so we shouldn't be interrupted."

Such was Silas's strength and expertise, that in little more than twenty minutes, he had lowered the hole by some two feet. They wrapped the body in an old blanket, eased it into the makeshift grave and covered it with earth. Jean crossed himself and muttered a brief prayer.

"That is all done?" Annette asked and Silas nodded. "Good, then we will get away and head for a place where we can change the car, for it's not safe to stay with this one. I've looked at the map and we can drive cross-country and over the border into Scotland. There I noticed several towns and one of them should surely provide us with a new car."

Silas, who had left the room, returned carrying two number plates. "I think you'd be best to change to these even before you change the car," he said. "From what you've said, your present number might be known. Just give me ten minutes."

"That's done," he said, returning with water dripping from his cap and jacket. "It's a dirty night and the wind's near a gale, so go careful if you're going over the hill; there's some nasty drops up there."

He looked down as Annette thrust a roll of bank notes into his hand. "Thanks, and that should cover everything," she muttered, getting into the car.

"It'll have to," Silas replied in a low, rather sinister voice, "for I'll thank you, Mrs Barry, not to come back here again. Not ever. Understand?"

Annette nodded and drove slowly down the drive and turned left towards the high hills and into the teeth of the gale.

CHAPTER 31

"WELL THAT SETTLES WHAT WE DO TONIGHT," Andrew said when Wilkinson rang off. "First, we go to The Packhorse. What we'll find when we get there heaven knows, and I don't even know what good it will do us, but we must find out what's happened to Morey."

"And having got Wilkinson all excited, we must make our number with the police," Norman said. "If you want my opinion, I think we'll find that the birds have flown, taking Morey with them as some sort of prisoner. What do you propose when we've finished at The Packhorse?"

"Whatever it is, will it involve a bed of some sort?" Jenny asked. "I'm beginning to feel the need for my beauty sleep."

"Yes, darling," Andrew replied. "I don't know exactly where this pub is, but it can't be far from Sedbergh. There's a good hotel there and I know the people who run it and I'm sure they'll help, however late we are. Now into the car everybody, and Norrie, you'd better have the map handy because I'm not at all sure of the way."

"Well, start by going back to the A1 and then straight up to Leeming and turn left. From then on it looks pretty straight, but I'll direct you if need be," Norrie said.

The rain was still only a mild drizzle when they left the hotel, and on the dual carriageway they made good progress. However, by the time they'd turned off and reached Bedale, the rain was coming down in earnest and the wind rising. Beyond Bedale the road became a series of sharp bends and sudden short, but sometimes steep, hills.

Not knowing the road, Andrew found this combination, together with the worsening weather, extremely trying. What made it worse was that such traffic as there was obviously knew the road and this, with the approaching

253

lights and the desire of those behind to overtake regardless, made progress slower than he would have liked.

Then, as they were negotiating a bend at the top of the steep main street of a small town, the telephone buzzed and the brigadier answered it.

"No this is Brigadier Colquhoun," he said. "Mr Henderson's driving. Who's that speaking?" And then with a brilliant burst of memory he added, "Is that group 101? ...Yes, and we are Fido."

"Right, sir," the voice at the other end said, "this is Sergeant Mellor and we're at The Packhorse, and a nasty mess there is here. Where are you now? ...Leyburn – that's about twenty-five miles. How soon d'you think you'll get here?"

"It'll be at least forty-five minutes, perhaps an hour," the brigadier said. "The weather's terrible and it's a bad road. Anyway, where is this hotel? ...Hawes, yes... six miles on, then right and signed Kirkby Stephen... and it's up on the left in the trees. We'll be with you... no, don't tell me about it now. Goodbye, sergeant."

About ten minutes later, with the rain easing off a little, Andrew pulled into a convenient lay-by.

"Now you know where we're going, Norrie," he said, "would you mind driving for a bit? It's now after eleven and I think I'd better ring the people in Sedbergh before they go to bed."

"Okay, that's fixed," Andrew said, laying down the telephone. "There's a night porter who'll let us in whatever time we arrive and there'll be rooms ready for us."

Thereafter they drove in silence, and apart from a few stray sheep, they reached The Packhorse without further incident, and just as it started to rain again. As they drove into the car park, the headlights picked out the yellow waterproof of a policeman who walked across towards them.

"Sergeant Mellor, sir," he said to Andrew through the open window. "We've got a very serious situation here, sir, and I think it's best if we go into the hotel."

In the lobby, they found a grey-haired woman in tears being attended to by a young policewoman, and while the sergeant led the others through to the lounge, Jenny paused to talk to the policewoman.

"Right, Sergeant," Andrew said, "you'd better tell us what's happened here."

"Well, sir, when we arrived," the sergeant said, "there were just Silas Black, that's the landlord, and his wife here. We explained that we believed they had recently had three visitors and that friends of theirs had reason to think that all was not well with them and where were they? Yes, that's right, we were told, and they went off a good half hour ago. Yes, all three and they were quite all right. No, they hadn't made any calls – can't think what all the fuss is about.

"Well, sir," the sergeant continued, "a few minutes later one of my men came in carrying a mobile phone; found it by the back door, he had. When I looked at it, I saw it had a label on the back with something written in French. Knowing your friends were French, I asked how this come to be there. Big Silas was just saying something about he must have dropped it when the woman started screaming. 'No, they killed him, and he's buried out t'back,' she yelled."

"Let me see the mobile," Andrew said. "Yes," he said, turning it over, "this belonged to Charles Morey. I recognise it from yesterday."

"Well, then Silas rushed towards his wife," the sergeant continued, "but the man who brought in the phone was quick. He tripped him, sat on him and we had the cuffs on in a flash. Then the story all came out, and we found the body in the bottom of a new cesspit they are building. It's now in the laundry and I'm afraid I'll have to ask one of you to identify it."

"Do you work for Superintendent Wilkinson, Sergeant, and if so have you spoken to him?" Andrew asked.

"Only, sir, to say that we had found a body and that you were on your way. And of course, sir, I've had to inform the local CID," Mellor replied.

"In that case we'd better now tell him what's happened, because there'll be a lot of people to be contacted," Andrew said. "I'll have to go and see the body because I'm the only one who knew Morey. Therefore would you, Norrie, get hold of Wilkinson? He'll have to contact the Bank and the FO – I guess it'll be their job to report to the French what's happened."

"There's a phone in the back office, sir," Mellor said. "You'd best use that. Jenks here will show you the way." Then to Andrew he said, "If you'd come this way please," and he led him along a stone-flagged passage to a room full of various items of laundry equipment.

On a long table in the middle of the room was something covered with a sheet. Sergeant Mellor walked over and rolled back the sheet.

"Yes, that is Charles Morey," Andrew said, and at that moment there was a commotion at the door and a tall man in a tweed suit walked in, shaking the rain from his cap.

"Good evening, Sergeant," he said to Mellor, unceremoniously dumping his case on the body's legs. "What have we here? And incidentally, Inspector Robins, the photographers and the rest of the gang have arrived."

Mellor introduced the police surgeon and then, leaving him to get on with his work, led Andrew back to the office. There they found Detective Inspector Robins and Norman Colquhoun having a three-way conversation with Superintendent Wilkinson.

"Here's Mr Henderson," Norrie said and handed over the handset.

"Yes it's him all right," Andrew said grimly, "and a bloody mess it all is. Can you take the necessary action with the various bodies involved...? Good, I'll leave that to you... yes, it seems the others have gone off in the car... cross-country as far as I can make out and presumably heading for you know where... What's that you say – the daily said something about an oblong? ...No, can't say it means anything to me. Anyway, we'd better follow them but I'll have to talk to the people here first... Right, here's Sergeant Mellor."

Leaving Wilkinson to talk to the policemen, Andrew and Norman went back to the lobby, and finding the women no longer there, they retired to the lounge.

"What I would like is a large whisky and soda," Andrew said, throwing himself into a chair, "but with the place crawling with police and us going to leave here by car, I suppose that's out of the question."

"I'm afraid so," Norrie agreed, leaning against the mantelpiece.

"Let's therefore think about Annette," Andrew said. "As well as having stolen the jewels, she is now a murderer, or at the very least an active accomplice. If you were her, what would your next move be?"

256

The brigadier thought for a moment. "I think the first thing I'd do is get rid of the car. Its number and appearance are now known." And when Andrew looked puzzled, he added, "Yes, I gather the Blacks have told all, and so every policeman in the United Kingdom will soon be on the lookout for it. If I was her, I think that early tomorrow, or rather today, I'd find a nice hidey hole on the outskirts of a town; then I'd get Lemaître or whatever his name is to drop me near an hotel, before he goes back and hides the car. Annette is nothing if not plausible, so she should have no difficulty in persuading the hotel to organise another car for them. She then nips back, picks up her friend and off they go into the wide blue yonder."

"And where's all this going to happen?"

"That we don't know," Norrie said, "but probably somewhere in the Borders. There are several towns there where one should be able to rent a car. It's a popular holiday area after all. Having done that, I think I'd head for the motorway and then Glasgow, Stirling and the north-west. Nobody except you and Jenny really knows them, so once they've changed cars they'll be difficult to pick up, unless they have a crash or something. And now here's Inspector Robins, who, I fear, is going to ask a lot of questions, are you not?"

"I'm afraid so, gentlemen," the inspector replied, taking a notebook from his pocket, "for regardless of other things which may be involved, the investigation of the murder itself is a matter for the local force."

For the next hour, therefore, Andrew and Norman did their best to explain the background to the events at The Packhorse and the murder of Charles Morey.

"So you see, Inspector," said Andrew, summing up their conversation, "the most likely sequence of events is that Morey made some excuse to slip out and telephone me with their plans. We think that he was already worried that Lemaître had rumbled him and this seems to have been the case, although why he did not take more care I'm afraid I can't explain."

After further discussion and another conversation with Superintendent Wilkinson, who had also talked to the Chief Constable, it was agreed that once they had signed statements, they could continue their journey north in the hope that they would find the others. They would keep in touch with Wilkinson, and once in the north, with the Northern Police.

"And don't forget," were Wilkinson's final words to Andrew, "your responsibility is, and always has been, to find the Bourbon treasure and now, if possible, Barry and Lemaître. All other action is the responsibility of the police."

"What will happen here?" Andrew asked.

"Black and his wife will be taken into custody, and I imagine his solicitor will have to make arrangements about the hotel," Robins replied. "I think it likely that the woman will be bailed or even released without charge. There will have to be a post mortem but after that, I understand, the diplomats will arrange for the body to be returned to France."

At that moment, Jenny walked into the room. "The doctor has given Liza Black a sedative and she has been taken away in a car," she said, then she turned and looked at the inspector. "I hope you won't be too hard on her. Although she knew of her husband's previous dealings with Mrs Barry, I don't believe she had anything to do with the night's happenings." Robins inclined his head in acknowledgement.

"Well, I've learned quite a lot tonight," Jenny said as they drove off in the direction of Sedbergh, "and mainly about how your police got their reputation. In South Africa, Liza and her husband would have been chucked straight into a van and driven off for interrogation in the privacy of the station, and just for good measure, Silas would probably have been beaten up. Here every consideration was shown to the woman and Silas, once he'd calmed down, was quite well treated, although they did keep the handcuffs on. God, I'm tired. What's the time?"

"About one thirty, and try to stay awake for a few more minutes for we're just arriving at the hotel," said Andrew as he turned through a narrow entrance and into a secluded courtyard.

No sooner had they pulled up, than a side door to the hotel opened and a tall, lugubrious looking man in an old-fashioned green baize apron appeared.

"They said you'd be late, but you're not – it's not yet two," he remarked somewhat inconsequentially. "Well, you'd best come in. Is that the luggage?" And he picked up two suitcases and led the way in. "You made it just in time," he added. "The rain's starting again and there'll be another storm likely."

"Now just sign here," he said, opening a leather-covered register, "and will you go straight up or will you be wanting a drink? They said you were to have whatever you want."

"I'm going to bed," Jenny said. "And what time in the morning?"

"We must leave by seven thirty at the latest," Andrew said, "and I'll arrange calls. Goodnight, darling. I don't know about Norrie, but I must have a drink." Then to the man, whose name was Frank, "Please show Miss Stanley her room, Frank, and then bring a bottle of whisky and some soda water."

"What about tomorrow, Norrie?" Andrew asked once they were settled in a corner of the bar with their drinks.

"I don't think we've much alternative but to carry on up to Knockbain," Norman answered. "If my theory's right and they've changed cars, there's not much chance of us finding them en route or, come to that, of them finding us. No, I'm sure the right thing is to press on and then see what happens when we get to the other end. Now I'm for bed – see you about seven fifteen then. I suggest we just have tea before we start and stop somewhere for breakfast."

Andrew, having arranged with Frank for them all to be called at six thirty with tea, retired to bed and drifted off to sleep wondering how Annette would set about finding the gold without being arrested for murder.

Chapter 32

To say that Annette was unhappy as she drove away from the hotel would be an understatement, for she was more than unhappy – she was in a truly savage rage, the cause being Silas Black's parting words. His demand that she should never come near him again had brought home to her both the seriousness and the discomfort of her present situation.

First of all, she was travelling with someone wanted for murder, and she herself, at the very least, was an accessory. Secondly, the rain was such that the wipers could hardly cope with it so she was having difficulty seeing the road, a difficulty aggravated by the constant buffeting of the wind. She glanced down at her companion and, seeing him asleep, her anger boiled over.

"Dear God," she screamed, "can't you even keep awake and help me watch the road? You lost the jewels and the girl and now – now, you wretched little piece of crap, you've got us wanted for murder." And she took her left arm from the wheel and smashed it into his face, catching him across the mouth. He screamed and grabbed her hand and pulled her towards him.

The car lurched as the front wheel climbed the verge and then careered across the road towards a sign indicating a sharp left-hand bend. Beyond the sign, the road appeared to vanish into blackness.

With the strength that fear could give, Annette jerked her arm downwards, forcing Lemaître to release her as he grunted and clutched at himself. She wrenched the wheel round with both hands and just made the bend, the rear wheels dragging along what she could see was the edge of a precipitous drop.

"Damn you, you bloody whore," he gasped, wiping the blood from his face. "Keep your hands on the wheel before you kill us. And stop blaming me for everything that goes wrong. You picked up that bastard Masson and you should be thankful that I disposed of him before he did any more damage. He's dead and buried and only the man Black knows where. We're out in this devilish wilderness in a fearful storm and no one else, least of all Henderson or the police, knows where we are and you may be sure Black will keep silent. All is well, ma chère Annette, and tomorrow we have a new car. Then nobody recognises us, so we find Henderson and see where he goes. Then we take the gold – mais oui, it is so, n'est-ce pas?"

Annette did not reply immediately, and for the next five or six miles concentrated on keeping the car on the road. The weather was showing no signs of improving and their recent near disaster had made her very conscious of the fact that, at all costs, they must avoid any form of accident or breakdown. Eventually, however, her anger, which cooled as quickly as it flared, had subsided sufficiently for her to realise that they must take stock of their situation. Seeing a convenient track, she turned off the road and drove cautiously along it until she found a ruined building in the lee of a clump of trees where they could park out of sight of the road and sheltered from the worst of the storm.

"It is curious, you know, mon Jean, how Masson attached himself to us," she said turning to Lemaître. "I would have thought, if he was a French Government agent, he would have gone for Henderson rather than us."

"Mais non, for I do not believe the French knew about Henderson," Lemaître replied. "How did they know about us? I remember you saying something about the bloody office where I got the information. Well, I think they traced me through that little clerk and his sexy wife, and then perhaps enquiries by the South African police would have put them on to you. As to Henderson, I do not know. If Masson really was a government agent, he may have found Henderson through the authorities in England."

"Well, that is all past history. What matters now is that he is dead and you killed him," Annette said. "We are safe for the moment for, as you say, only Silas and his wife know that. But it cannot last, for we know he was in touch with Henderson. Henderson is bound to be in touch with the police, so eventually the murder will come out. How long we have before that, I don't know – perhaps two or three days. That may give us time to find the gold and escape with some of it. Once I find Calum I can arrange that. But first we must have a new car. Now where's that map?"

Lemaître lent over and from the back seat produced a road atlas and handed it to Annette. With the aid of the rather inadequate overhead light she eventually found what she wanted.

"I think we're about here," she said, pointing to a spot on the map. Then she turned over several pages and eventually nodded and turned to Jean.

"What we've got to do is to find a town where we can rent a new car," she said, "and it's got to be somewhere that we can get to without using main roads and it's got to be a place where they will not think of looking for us. Now, as I said, we are here," pointing at the map, "about seventy miles from the border with Scotland; and here," pointing again, "is a town called Hawick. I went there once with my husband. It's very much a local centre and has a couple of hotels. It must, I think, be possible to rent a car there."

"How do we get there?"

"Just look at the map while I explain. Oh, and by the way, can you read a map?"

"Mais oui, but of course; in the military service they taught us," Lemaître replied in a slightly injured voice. "Just show me where we go."

The next thirty minutes were spent in tracing a route over the sparsely populated Cumbrian Fells and through the border hills to Hawick.

"That should do us," Annette said, handing the atlas to Jean. "We do touch two small towns and bypass another, but in the middle of the night that should not pose a problem. We do have about fifteen miles of main road and, unless we're very unlucky, that again should be no problem. Now, mon Jean, do you think you can guide us over these mountains?"

"Yes; but it will not be easy," Jean replied. Then he looked out of the window. The rain had stopped and, although the gale was still blowing, a pallid moon showed through occasional breaks in the cloud. "The weather is clearing a bit. With the moon it will be not so bad, perhaps."

"Well, let's hope it doesn't get worse again. Now, what's the time?" Annette said, looking at her watch. "Nearly midnight, and I reckon it'll start getting light around five, so by then we must have found somewhere to hide this car; somewhere that's about six or seven miles from Hawick, say eighty miles from where we are now. That can't take more than three and a half hours, even allowing for getting lost. So as we're well hidden here, let's get a couple of hours' sleep."

"Good idea," Jean said, "and why don't you get in the back? You'll be more comfortable there."

The faint pinging of the pocket alarm she kept in her bag woke Annette and she leant over and shook her companion. "Come on, time to move," she said. There was now no sign of the moon and the night was inky black, but at least the wind had gone down.

"Now, do you know where we're going?" she asked, getting into the driving seat, starting the engine and driving slowly down the track.

"Turn left when you reach the road," Jean said, "and keep going till you get to a town and then I'll tell you what to do."

With the improvement in the weather, the first part of the drive was comparatively easy. The open moorland eventually gave way to a more enclosed country as they dropped down a hill and into a small town. Apart from street lamps and the odd shop window, there was not a light to be seen. Beyond the town, a narrow country lane took them past a darkened village and several isolated houses, until eventually they reached a main road, where they met the first traffic they'd seen since leaving the hotel.

They were some two hundred yards behind an articulated lorry when they rounded a corner to see the yellow jacket and white cap of a traffic policeman, his red torch waving them down. Annette, fearing the worst, for the lorry had not been stopped, pulled into the side behind the police car and wound down her window, as another policeman shone a light into the car.

"Where have you come from?" he asked.

"Darlington – and we go to Glasgow," Jean, who had had a quick look at the map, replied.

"Have you seen any other cars since you left the A1?" the officer asked.

"Perhaps three or four," Annette replied. "Two passed us and you must have seen them," she added, taking a gamble. "There were two others, I think, who turned off. Oh yes, and then one who stopped in a little town."

"Did you notice the colour or make of any of them?"

"I'm afraid not. I'm not very good at cars," Annette replied, gently kicking Jean and hoping the police would not ask him.

"Can I see your driving licence?" the officer asked.

"Of course," she said, searching in her handbag and producing the document.

"An English one I see, but you're not English, are you?"

"No, but I used to be married to an Englishman and I live in London with my brother," Annette said, indicating Lemaître.

"I see," said the policeman, obviously not believing a word. "Well, it's not you we're after, so you'd better get on." And he stepped back and waved them away. As they drove off they heard the radio in the police car crackle into life.

Some five miles further on, just after they had passed another two lorries, they heard the sound of a police siren behind them.

"Vite, Annette – quick, down there to the left," Jean shouted and Annette just managed to swerve into a road with houses on either side, obviously the approach to a small town. "Now turn out the lights and stop here. I don't think they saw us and there was a car in front so they'll follow that for a bit."

"What on earth do you mean – they didn't see us? Who didn't? And why have we come down here?" Annette asked.

"Didn't you hear the siren? That radio in the police car – I'll bet they were being told about us, but we're alright. Just hold the torch." Jean looked at the map. "Eh bien, I see what we do. We go on to here," he said pointing at the map, "and take this turning to the right, then if I can find the way, we go on these little roads and meet our proper route here. Yes, you can use your lights again now. Even if they come back, we should be well away from them."

Despite Jean's optimism, finding their way in the dark, along narrow, twisting roads and through unlit villages with inadequate signs, was no easy task. So it was nearly an hour before they dropped down into a straggling village and rejoined their route, and there they ran into further difficulties. The road climbed steeply out of the village and, with the weather worsening, Annette found negotiating the sharp hairpins and steep ascents in driving mist and rain by no means easy.

"Ugh! I'm glad it's dark for I wouldn't want to look down on some of those corners," Jean said.

"And I wouldn't want to live there," Annettee commented as, at almost the highest point, a building loomed out of the cloud on their left.

A few more hairpins and then they started the long descent into another small town. After that they crossed a main road and found themselves in another maze of small roads and misleading signs. An hour later, with the weather improving and the sky lightening in the east, they finally drove through Newcastleton and turned up the Hermitage Water towards Hawick.

"Go slow here," said Jean as they descended a narrow defile towards a thickly wooded area, "there should be a turning to the right. Yes – there, let's try it."

Again, the road started to climb and then on the left there was a track, almost concealed by the trailing branches of the firs.

"Wait! I will look," said Jean, jumping from the car and running up the track. In less than two minutes, he was back. "It's fine. There's an old quarry and it doesn't look as though anyone goes there. I can't see any tracks."

"It's now five thirty," Annette said, having parked the car, "and I don't think I can go to the hotel before seven, and even that may be too early for Hawick."

"What about the tracks?" Annette asked as, an hour later, they drove out of the quarry in the direction of the town.

"Do not worry, chère Annette," Jean replied. "I will deal with them while you're away."

Ten minutes later, he dropped Annette at the Cornet's Arms and as soon as he saw her wave, he swung round and drove back to the quarry. There, having concealed the car as best he could in the remains of an old shed, he spent an hour obliterating their tracks. Not being a countryman he found this hard work, but by eight o'clock he thought he'd done a pretty good job. So he carried the two cases down to the road, hid them in the trees and sat down to contemplate the situation while he waited for Annette. Jean Lemaître had been in trouble with the law so many times, and for so many crimes, that he was not really worried by what had happened the previous night. No one knew where they were or where they were going and there was little to identify them, so why worry?

Shortly after eight thirty he heard a car approaching and a few moments later Annette, in a white Toyota, stopped just past the end of the track. Two minutes later, with Jean and the luggage on board, they were heading back to the town and then west towards Langholm and the main road north.

"You were very quick," Jean said. "How did you manage that, and can this car be traced to you?"

"The night porter was very obliging and gave me a room and a cup of coffee," Annette replied, "so I had a quick bath and then, when I came down to the hall, I found a charming lady at the reception desk. I enquired about rental cars, and would you believe it, someone she called her partner had a taxi business and also hired out cars to tourists. Well, twenty minutes later this car appeared. I produced a driving licence and credit card in the name of Mrs Gabrielle Johnson, signed a form and drove off."

"Did they not ask where you came from?"

"Yes, and I told a long story about being on holiday with friends who were suddenly called away, but offered to drop me somewhere where I might get a car. Flimsy, but it appeared to satisfy them. And now," she said, pulling into a lay-by, "let me have a look at the map."

"Here," she said eventually. "Here's where we want to join the motor-way. I'm sure that's the way they'll be going and we must still be ahead of them. What we'll do is get onto the motorway and then find somewhere to stop for breakfast."

On the motorway, they had no problems, but once they got near Glasgow they found themselves in a maze of roundabouts and roadworks where wrong turnings were only too easy. So it was nearly eleven before they got clear and Jean started to complain.

"We must stop soon," he said. "I've had nothing since dinner last night, not even a cup of coffee, and I'm starving."

"Yes of course," Annette said. "We've got to get off the motorway soon and head west, so let's see what we can find."

Some ten minutes later, she slowed and pulled into a service station. "How about this place? It's got some sort of café," she said. "It's not exactly Paris standard, but it'll do, and it has the advantage of overlooking the road."

They found a table right in the window and ordered and paid for their meal. "Just in case we have to leave in a hurry," Annette explained.

"The eggs and pommes frites are good," was Jean's comment, "but the English sausage I cannot understand. The bread, though, it is good."

"Not English, Jean," Annette explained, "Scottish. You are in Scotland now, and they don't like you to call things English. You are right, though: they make bread like the French." And she paused and looked at a line of slow-moving traffic.

"Mon Dieu!" she cried. "Look there – that big Land Rover thing – the brown one. It's them. There's the Stanley girl in the back."

Annette was already picking up her bag and moving towards the door as the lights changed and traffic moved on.

"Quick! We must get after them!" Moments later they were out on the road heading north. "It's a brown Range Rover, that's what it is. Watch out for it. I don't want to lose it, but I don't want to be too close."

CHAPTER 33

IT WAS JUST BEFORE SIX THIRTY WHEN Andrew awoke to the persistent ringing of his alarm clock. He reached up and silenced it, then lay back trying to think where he was and why. The effort was almost too much and he was just dozing off again when he was brought back to consciousness by a knock on the door and Frank appeared, turned on the light and put a tray on the bedside table.

"'Morning, sir," he said. "It's just after six thirty. Stopped raining and not a bad morning – could stay fine, too. Lizzie will be taking the others their tea and Mr Maynard said he'd be pleased to see you in Reception about seven." With that, he turned on his heel and marched out, closing the door behind him.

Andrew sat up and swung his feet out of the bed, then poured himself a cup of tea and while he drank it, considered what was the best thing to do. "Seems to me we want to press on as fast as possible. Leave as soon as everyone's down and then stop somewhere for breakfast in about an hour," he decided.

Thirty minutes later, having shaved and bathed, he was down in Reception greeting Charles Maynard who, with his wife, owned and ran the hotel.

"Hope they looked after you properly last night?" Charles said.

"Indeed yes," Andrew replied. "Frank could not have been more helpful, particularly as we didn't get here until after one. We got involved in some nastiness at The Packhorse. It's a long story which you'll no doubt read about in the local paper, and one day I'll tell you what really happened. Now, though, have you got a bill for me?"

"Yes, all ready." He pushed the document across the counter. "But you'll stay for breakfast, won't you? Jane would love to see you."

"No, honestly we must push on. I want to get up to Wester Ross this evening for reasons that are all part of the same story," Andrew replied, producing a credit card from his wallet and handing it over together with the bill.

No sooner was the payment complete than the brigadier appeared, closely followed by Jenny, and Andrew effected the introductions.

"Well I'm sorry you can't stay," Charles Maynard said. "Our breakfasts are generally thought to be excellent! But you always were one for tearing about." Then he called for Frank, who seemed never to go off duty, to take the cases to the car, and five minutes later Andrew drove out of the yard and turned in the direction of the M6 motorway.

"I'm sorry about breakfast," he said, "but I think we must get north as soon as possible. Annette and Co. must be well ahead of us and if they've changed cars as you think, Norrie, then even if we catch up we may not identify them and, what's more, we won't even be able to describe their car to the police. No, we must get on for I don't want them messing about up there without our being around. However, we must eat, so I suggest we drive for an hour or so while the traffic's still comparatively light, then stop for breakfast."

And it was an hour or so later, as they approached the border at Gretna, that Andrew turned to Jenny and, pointing to a large sign said, "I think you told me you'd never been to Scotland. Well, you're there now."

Jenny gazed round at this new country and tried to look suitably impressed, when another sign caught her eye.

"What's the significance of the 'Famous Smithy'?" she asked. "And what is a smithy?"

"Scottish for blacksmith, or what you'd probably call a farrier," Norman said, before Andrew could answer. Then with a wicked grin he added, "As for the 'Famous' part of it, perhaps Andrew will tell you one day."

Fortunately Andrew's blushes were spared, for at that moment he saw that they were approaching the entrance to a service area and so hurriedly turned in.

"How about this for breakfast?" he said.

Jenny, who was feeling decidedly hungry, forgot her curiosity about Gretna Green.

"It'll do very nicely," she said. "Dear Andrew, I thought you were never going to stop. You must remember that we colonials value breakfast as an important meal. You Brits seem nowadays to disregard it."

"Not me," said the brigadier. "Always have breakfast – never know when you may get your next meal. Come on, Jenny, we'll leave him to park the car."

While they were eating, Norman Colquhoun could not resist telling Jenny about Gretna Green and weddings solemnised over the forge. "Yes, my dear," he said, his voice booming round the little restaurant, "the dashing, well-born but impecunious young man would sneak to his beloved's home. She, heiress to ten thousand spreading acres and a fortune to match, but forbidden by her wicked guardian to marry our hero, would be waiting at her window. Up goes the ladder and our hero spirits her away to where his faithful servant awaits them with the horses. Then up the North Road and across the moors to Gretna. Once in Scotland the guardian cannot touch them and the blacksmith does his stuff. Guardian has an apoplexy in the night and they return to take possession of her inheritance!"

"I don't believe a word of it," Jenny said, barely able to suppress her laughter. "It's not true, is it, Andrew?"

"Well, yes, darling, it more or less is, that is if you cut out the worst of Norrie's embroidery," he replied. "And now, before he starts another of his Tales of Ancient Britain, I think we'd better get going. Norrie, would you like to drive while I study the maps and get the lie of the land in the Kyle area?"

A couple of hours later, somewhere between Stirling and Callander, Jenny happened to look out of the rear window and noticed a white car at the far end of a straight stretch of road. A few minutes later they rounded a bend to find roadworks and temporary traffic lights. As they waited for the lights to change, Jenny, who was still looking out of the back, saw the white car come fast round the bend and brake sharply. The fact that it did not close right up to them as they pulled away made her look at it more closely and realise that the driver looked familiar. "Once again I'm recog-nising Annette – or am I?" she thought, but for the moment decided to say nothing.

Twenty minutes later, though, as they ran in to Callander, she had an opportunity to confirm her suspicions. They were stopped in a traffic jam and she saw the white car about four behind them. Suddenly a figure darted out of the passenger door and vanished into a newsagent's. Moments later the man emerged and jumped into the car as the traffic started to move, and the man was Jean Lemaître. No doubt about it, for his was a face Jenny was unlikely to forget.

"Listen," she said as they drove out of the town, "Annette and Jean are in a white car behind us."

"Are you sure?" Andrew asked.

"Yes, quite sure," Jenny replied. "I thought I saw Annette in the car six or seven miles back. Then in that town we've just left, Jean got out of the car and went into a shop. Absolutely no doubt it was him... No, I can't see them now but this bit's pretty twisty and I guess they're not going to risk closing up again."

"Well, assuming they are still following, what are we going to do, Norrie?" Andrew said.

"Yes, they are following," Jenny said as they neared the end of a straight bit of road. "They're quite a way behind us and there's two cars in between. Can you see them in the mirror, Norrie?"

"Yes, just about," he replied. "Now, two important questions. Are they following this car knowing we're in it? If so, do they realise we've seen them?"

"The answer to your first question I'm sure is yes," Jenny said, "because when I first saw them at those roadworks they deliberately hung back. So, do they realise we've seen them? No, I think not, for Jean would never have risked getting out if they did."

"I agree," the brigadier said. "Well now let's think what's the best thing to do. What's the time? Hmm – twenty to twelve, so we should be in Fort William by one thirty."

"If we assume they are following us because they hope to find out exactly where we're going," Andrew said, "then if they were to lose us, they'd probably go on to the general Kyle area, but at least our base would still be secret. So, Norrie, can we lose them and is there an alternative route we could take?"

"Yes there is, but it involves two ferries and so is time-dependent," Norman replied. "What we have to do is to cross to Skye from Mallaig and then back to the mainland at Glenelg, which incidentally is on Tommy's doorstep. If we're not held up I think we'll just about make it, for I know all the roads pretty well, and as I'll have to drive fast, you'd all better hang on tight! And you, Jenny, try to keep them in sight."

"And also watch the scenery," Andrew added. "This is one of the most beautiful drives in Scotland."

They were lucky with the traffic and it was just after one when they descended Glencoe and saw the loch ahead of them. The brigadier, who had been silent for a long time, suddenly spoke.

"Jenny, in a moment we're going to come to a bridge," he said, "and I want to be sure they see us cross it. After the bridge, the road becomes very twisty and I'm going to try and drop them before we get to Fort William. We'll just have to hope that even if they can't see us, they'll keep on going straight."

The next twenty minutes were some of the most terrifying Jenny had ever spent in a motor car. The road was indeed nothing but a series of fairly blind corners, and there were a number of very large lorries using it in both directions. A Range Rover is not the ideal vehicle for those conditions but Norman swung it about with considerable skill and somehow managed to avoid hitting anything, although there were some very close calls.

At one moment they were passing between a gigantic articulated juggernaut and a vertical cliff face with a blind corner fast approaching, when round the corner came a very ancient tractor towing a trailer full of sheep. They made it, but only just.

"If that had been anything faster than a tractor," Norman said, "they'd be preparing the funeral now."

On another occasion, passing a cyclist, they kissed wing mirrors with a van and caused a flurry of horn blowing. Finally, partly by luck, partly by the driver's skill, they reached the end of the long straight that leads into the town.

"Any sign of them?" Norrie asked.

"No, and there's quite a lot of other traffic behind us," Jenny replied, adding rather spitefully, "including several furious truck drivers."

"Good, that's excellent," Norrie said. Then, when they were a mile beyond the centre of the town, he added, "We'll just nip up here and see what happens." And he turned up a steep hill leading to a housing estate.

At the top of the hill he turned left and stopped by a grassy bank above the main road and asked Jenny to get out and watch for the white car.

"You got the best view of it, so let's hope you can recognise it," he said. "There are traffic lights just ahead so, with any luck, they'll stop in your sight."

It was twenty minutes before there was a shout from Jenny. "There they go!" she cried. "They've just passed the lights and they're fairly moving."

"Okay. Back in the car now," As soon as Jenny was on board they drove round a block of houses and back down the hill onto the main road. "Now for the road to the isles," the brigadier said, whistling the first few bars of the famous song.

It was about twenty minutes later, and once they were well on the way to Mallaig, that Norman Colquhoun pulled into a lay-by, stopped the engine and asked, "Did anyone think of taking the number of their car?"

"Now I come to think of it, yes, I did, and quite by accident," Jenny replied. "I just happened to notice it when they stopped back at those road-works, for it contained my initials – JES. It was Y344 JES and the car's a white Toyota."

"Well done! I must say that was very quick of you," Andrew said. "And now let's pass the information to Wilkinson." He picked up his mobile telephone. "Quite a good signal," he remarked with some surprise.

"That's why I stopped here," Norman said, "for I don't think you'll get any sort of joy out of a mobile once we're into the hills."

Wilkinson himself answered and Andrew told him how they'd found out that they were being followed by Annette Barry and the Frenchman.

"Yes, in a white Toyota." He gave the number. "No, I don't know how or where they picked us up. We first noticed them just north of Stirling... No, we managed to drop them and the last we saw of them was heading north out of Fort William... You'll tell the Inverness people? Good... Yes, we'll contact them when we get to Knockbain. We're on our way there now by a rather roundabout route via Skye and should arrive between five thirty and six. Don't try to contact us till we get there... No, the mobile will not get any signal on this road – too many high hills."

By the time they got to Mallaig the weather, which for most of the day had been dull and damp, cleared, displaying the whole magic panorama from Rhum and the distant peaks of the Cuillin in the west to the rugged mountains of Knoydart to the east.

"I'd no idea that you had views like this in Britain," Jenny gasped.

"Not Britain, darling – Scotland," Andrew reprimanded gently. "Norrie doesn't approve of Britain getting the credit for something uniquely Scottish."

"Alright, Scotland then!" Jenny said. "And it's not only the view, it's the light. I've never seen anything like it. We always say that there isn't any view more beautiful than the mountains of the Cape in the summer dusk, but I confess – reluctantly – that this beats it."

"The light is a Highland speciality," Norrie said, "and it's certainly put on a full dress display for you."

Despite an unscheduled stop at the hotel at Eilean Jarmain, they caught the last ferry to Glenelg without any bother and then drove up the glen and over the old stone bridge to the great front door of the Castle of Knockbain, to find the laird standing there in a faded Macdonald kilt and a much-darned jersey.

Again Jenny gasped with excitement. "A real castle!" she cried. "You never told me that's what we were going to." And as she surveyed her host from the car, she whispered to Andrew, "I thought you only wore kilts on special occasions, and can't your generals afford new jerseys?"

"Behave yourself, young lady," Andrew hissed. "Remember you're in tribal country now." Jenny assumed a suitably contrite expression.

However, moments later, she was completely disarmed as the general came forward, opened the door and handed her down from the Range Rover.

"You must be Miss Stanley," he said, smiling at her with every ounce of his very considerable charm. Major General Tom Macdonald was a man of around sixty and big in every way; tall and broad-shouldered, his square-jawed, clean-shaven face topped by a mane of wiry grey hair. This somewhat intimidating appearance was redeemed by a ready smile and a pair of brown eyes in which lurked both humour and an undoubted air of command.

"And Norrie, how good to see you," he said, shaking hands with the brigadier. "Something told me you might come by the ferry, and we picked you up with the glasses as you left the village. Now here's Janet," he added, as a slim, fair-haired woman, considerably younger than the general, came down the steps. "So introduce your friends and then we'll all go in. I expect you'd like baths before dinner – need them after a day in the car." He grinned. "Now let's have the cases and darling, you take Miss Stanley and I'll show these boys their rooms. Meet in the library at a quarter to eight and no shop this evening. That can wait until tomorrow."

"Oh, please not, Miss Stanley," Jenny said to her hostess as she led the way up the stairs, "my name is Jenny."

CHAPTER 34

O N A LONG STRAIGHT BIT OF ROAD some five miles beyond Fort William, Annette, who had not said a word since they left the town, stopped by the entrance to a muddy track and turned to Lemaître.

"Well, little man, you've done it again, haven't you," she said, barely suppressing her irritation. "There's not a sign of them and we can see more than a kilometre ahead."

"It's not my fault," he replied. "They were already out of sight when we came into the town, and if I might say so, you won't find them if you hang around here."

"Don't talk to me like that!" she snapped. "They must have turned off and now we shan't know where they've gone. You weren't watching, were you?" she cried, her voice rising. "Here, give me that map."

"This is the only road they could have taken and it seems to end in the sea," she said, pointing. "Oh, I suppose they could have turned off here. No, but none of those lead to where I think they're going. Perhaps they are staying the night somewhere perhaps... Merde! There's nothing for it but to go on, and perhaps Calum will have some ideas."

Perhaps with the vague hope of catching the Range Rover, or perhaps it was just a means of venting her anger, but for the rest of the journey Annette drove like a maniac. That was fine until they turned off towards the west, but from there on the road is not suited to high speeds, particularly if the driver is not familiar with it, and Annette certainly was not.

Jean dropped the map, leaned back in his seat and closed his eyes. "If you want to drive like that," he said, "you can find your own bloody way. I'd rather not watch my approaching death."

After a bit, Annette looked at him thoughtfully, nearly putting them in the ditch in the process, and it was fortunate indeed for Jean that his eyes were closed, for the look on Annette's face would have scared him more than her driving.

She risked another glance at the reclining figure and wondered how she could ever have been so stupid as to take him on. He'd bungled every job he'd been given. Until he'd killed that man they were clean, for it seemed that Henderson, having recovered the jewels, was not going to pursue the matter of their theft or the assault on the Stanley girl. But now they were wanted for murder, and that could mean not only the British police, but also Interpol.

No, there was no longer any doubt about it, Jean would have to go. Calum would arrange it and then somehow she and Calum – well, maybe not Calum, that would depend – would get the gold and escape to France. The decision made, her temper cooled and she drove down the steep, winding pass to the shore of Loch Duich at a more sedate pace.

It was nearly eight and just beginning to get dark when they finally reached Clovulin, Calum Macrae's farm on the east shore of Loch Long.

"Aye, well you've arrived," he said, "and it's guid to see you, Annette. And this'll be your friend Mr... I'm afraid I didna catch your name."

"Just call him Jean," Annette said. "And now, Calum, mon cher, do you have some wine? We've been on the road all day and I badly need a drink."

Calum Macrae was a tall red-haired man whose gaunt face, tanned by a life on the hill, was fringed with a neatly trimmed beard which gave him a somewhat unlikely, but in fact well-merited academic air, for Calum had a good degree in zoology and agricultural science from Aberdeen University. He was dressed in a tweed suit which, despite his academic air, somehow seemed incongruous on a remote hillside farm.

"Aye, I've been over at Dingwall at the sales," he said in answer to their looks. "And now come in and we'll see what we can find. I could do wi' a dram myself," he said, then added, "I'm sure you'll be hungry too, and there's a wee bit of dinner all ready."

Calum was the third generation of his family to occupy Clovulin, his grandfather having taken the tenancy at the turn of the last century and then bought the property cheaply when the estate was sold up. His father, a shrewd dealer in both sheep and cattle, and also a noted breeder of the sturdy high-land ponies known as Garrons, had prospered during the war and its immediate aftermath and had left Calum a substantial holding and a considerable amount of money.

Calum himself, although a successful farmer, realised the uncertainty of hill life and had wisely diversified. He owned a helicopter which he hired out to stalking parties and others who were too lazy to walk up the hill, and also to wealthy tourists who wanted an unusual view of the highlands.

As well as the helicopter, he had several boats, including a well-appointed and fully staffed motor yacht which took parties on week-long cruises around the Western Isles. It was said in some quarters that these leisure activities were a cover for more sinister operations. Drugs and illegal immigrants were mentioned, but the police had never been able to pin anything on him.

Annette knew about this background, for she had made use of his marine services in a job involving the Basque country and Ireland. So during dinner she watched him carefully and decided he was the man she wanted.

"You're looking very prosperous," she said, "so last year's tourist season must have been good. Still doing the flights and cruises, are you?"

"Aye, I've still got the chopper and the gin palace," he replied, "but there's no' the money about there was. This high pound's killing both tourism and farming and last winter was bad, verra bad – and the lambing's no' looking too good – but we manage. And what about yourself? You mentioned you might need some help, so what are you at?"

Annette looked at her watch. "It's late now and I've been driving all day. Let's talk about it tomorrow when I'll make more sense."

So it was at six the next morning that Annette, who had been awake for more than an hour and had finally decided on her plan, slipped on her dressing gown and tiptoed across the passage, tapped on Calum's door and gently opened it. The curtains were not closed and by the cold grey light of the highland dawn, she could see Calum's eyes were open.

"I thought you might be about early," he said as she came over and sat on the bed. "You'll be wanting to talk wi'out the wee mannie being around.

You need'na worry – he's down the other side, he canna see or hear us. So, what can I do for you?"

"Listen, Calum, and I'll tell you a story," she said, and explained about the reputed treasure and how she came to hear of it through the Saddler family, and that she was not the only member of the family to show interest in it. She then described how she'd found out that the treasure was probably hidden somewhere in the Kyle area.

"There's a man called Henderson and both he and I have family connections with the Saddlers. I visited him one evening and found him studying a mass of maps and papers. I slipped a little something into his drink, and while he was out I managed to photograph the maps, and also a letter and a rather cryptic poem. The maps were of this area, and here are the letter and poem." And she gave him the two photographs.

"Doubtless 'My Lord' would be the Earl of Strathconon," he said after studying the letter. "He had estates about here and many Macraes worked on them; and there have been many stories of a ship loaded with gold sinking in the Minch. Aye, and now I mind it there's the strange story of the death of one of the earl's servants, a certain Rorie Mor Macrae. Now, what about the poem?" He read it several times, then lay back on the pillows and stared at the ceiling.

"Well, what about the poem?" Annette asked after some seven or eight minutes had passed.

"What about it indeed?" Calum said with a grin. Then he leant forward and picked up one of the maps. "Just look here," he said, pointing. "It'll be easier wi' a proper map but this photo will do for now. See this castle? It has steps that lead down to the shore; and here, in this wee bay there's a rock they call the Dragon – it looks a bitty like one. So the poem seems to say that if you line up the steps and the rock, somewhere up the hill, and it's gey steep there, there's maybe your treasure hidden. We'd have to go up and look a bit closer."

Annette got to her feet and walked over to the window and looked more closely at the map. After a few minutes, she put it aside and turned to Calum.

"That's certainly a start and we can talk more about it later," she said, "but now we have a more important matter to consider. What do we do about

Jean Lemaître? To my mind, he has outlived what little usefulness he had. Give him anything to do and, in the English metaphor, he cocks it up. Also there's his master, Le Grand Homme. He'll want his cut, but without Jean, I'd risk forgetting him. No Calum, Jean Lemaître must go – but how?"

"In your words, I can 'slip a little something' in his breakfast coffee. Then we tie him up and leave him to sleep it off in the cottage. Nobody will look in there. How's that for a grand idea to be going on with?"

Annette walked over and kissed the top of his head. "You're a good boy, Calum. That'll do fine. C'est très bon!" she said. "And now I shall go and have a bath. You do have a bathroom in this primitive country, I suppose?" And she vanished before he could reply.

Just after eight, Jean came into the kitchen to find Calum drinking tea while waiting for an egg to boil.

"Bonjour, Monsieur Jean. I'm having tea mysel', but I expect you'd rather have coffee," Calum said, getting to his feet, and Jean nodded. "Then there's eggs, there's bacon and there's sausages. Whatever you fancy."

"Non, non; just bread, butter and perhaps some confiture, that is the jam, n'est-ce pas?" Jean said. "But not the toast, non, jamais!"

"There's good Scots bread on the side there, and those buns are what we call baps," Calum replied. "I think they'd be to the French taste. And here's your coffee."

Jean helped himself to the bread and covered it liberally with butter. Then he sat down and stirred his coffee, while he tried the bread.

"It is indeed good, this bread; better than in England. And you make good coffee too," he said appreciatively, taking another mouthful. Then he picked up his bread, dropped it and looked down stupidly at it as his eyes glazed over and his head slumped forward sending the coffee cup flying.

"That's you out for a bit, laddie, but I think we'd best make sure you stay that way," Calum said and walked over to a large cupboard in the lobby by the back door. A minute or two later he came back with a hypodermic, and he'd just finished injecting the contents into Jean's arm, when Annette walked into the kitchen and looked down at the unconscious Frenchman.

"That's him fixed till after lunch," Calum said, and at that moment there was the sound of an engine outside. "That'll be Seumas – Jimmy to you. He'll just have been up round the ewes. I'll get him to give me a hand shifting the wee mannie. No, you need'na worry," he said, seeing Annette's dubious look. "Jimmy's used to these odd happenings. He'll no ask questions. Or, come to that, answer any."

Calum went to the back door and let fly a torrent of Gaelic. Seumas, who followed Calum into the kitchen, proved to be a giant of a man with a shock of yellowish hair and piercing blue eyes. He smiled briefly at Annette, then bent down and picked up Jean and carried him from the house.

"I'll just go and see to the prisoner." Calum smiled. "Help yersel' to whatever you want. I'll no' be long and then we can decide what happens next."

Annette made herself some toast and coffee and sat down to consider her present position and future plans. As far as Jean was concerned, she had no doubts; he had served his purpose and it would be dangerous to have him around any longer. Calum was altogether different and without him it would be impossible to recover any of the treasure. Besides, she thought, she had always been quite fond of him. Nevertheless, the more she thought about it, the more attractive the idea of finishing the operation with no partners and all the gold was becoming. She sighed, and thought momentarily of Andrew, then shook her head and consoled herself with the thought that whatever action she decided upon, she had the means to carry it out. For there were some things about her that that neither Calum nor any of the others knew of, certain skills she had acquired in a career involving drug smuggling, illegal arms dealing and the procuring of young girls for prostitution. These skills she felt could be put to good use in her forthcoming activities and might surprise both her friends and her enemies.

"Are you sure that what you're doing is quite safe?" she said as Calum came back into the room. "I thought you had a housekeeper or someone? What's she going to think?"

"Aye, I did," he replied, "but she left, and now there's just a lassie comes in by the day. It's fortunate indeed that she has three days off to go to her brother's wedding in Brechin. So you need not worry, we'll no' be disturbed whatever we do."

"Good. Now then, listen to me," Annette said, "and I'll tell you what I think we should do. The first thing is to locate this treasure, assuming, that is, that it's still there. Then we've got to find out what it is – gold bars, coins, even possibly precious stones – and how we can move it. Thanks to your understanding of the poem, we know where to start looking and what we have available, I hope." And here she looked enquiringly at Calum, who nodded. "Your helicopter and a boat. So here's how I think we should proceed."

During the next two or three hours they considered Annette's ideas which Calum, with his local knowledge, refined. They considered fallback plans to deal with such eventualities as discovery by the police, equipment failure or human error. They even looked at a couple of completely different alternative plans.

Finally Annette rose from her chair saying, "Right, then that's what we'll do. Now I would like to get an idea of the geography of this place." Calum glanced up at the clock.

"It's now nearly one o'clock," he said, "so I suggest we have a bite to eat and then I'll take you for a drive around. Just give me ten minutes and I'll have a piece of some sort ready. Aye, and you might just take a look at the prisoner."

"And I might have a glass of wine too," she added over her shoulder, as she walked towards the back door.

An hour later, they set off towards the Kyle of Lochalsh in a rather battered, long wheelbase Land Rover with a pick-up body.

"Sorry to take you in this jalopy," Calum said, "but it's good and high and you'll see more from it."

From the Kyle they went on round the corner where he stopped and pointed across the water to a distant shoreline. "You see yon wee cluster of houses? Aye, the ones by the trees. That's my cousin lives there. He has fishing boats and sheep on the hill. And way up behind him, right out in the wilds, I have a place I land the helicopter. It's an arrangement I have wi' the laird and his stalker that I can take parties up there. There's an old bothy

I've done up and we spend the night. Oh, they think it's grand and pay good money to try their hand at living with nature."

Then they turned and went back to Eilean Donan Castle so Annette could look across at the Dragon rock and the hills above it. Then finally right round the other side of the loch to have a look back at the castle.

"Now if you turn round," Calum said, pointing up through the trees at the bare hillside above, "somewhere above that crest. That's where your gold will be. We'll do a recce, but we'll do it from the other side where it's a lot less steep."

When they eventually returned to Clovulin, Calum said that he'd better go and deal with Jean.

"He should be awake by now, so he'll need to wash and have something to eat. We'll not be wanting him to die on us yet! Would you perhaps cook us some dinner? You'll find chops in the fridge and there's vegetables there in the larder. And there should be cheese and some apples."

When he came back, some twenty minutes later, he found Annette drinking wine, and a very good-looking meal well advanced.

"He'll live," he said, "and when you're ready I'll take him some food. But he's no' in a very good temper, so I'm going to hobble him and keep him locked in. You canna escape from the back room o' that cottage; and now, before I do anything else, I'm going to have a dram and then we'll eat."

"Is there somewhere more comfortable than this kitchen?" Annette asked as they finished dinner.

"Sure, there's the sitting room. It's just I get used to not using it when I'm alone."

"Then I'll make some coffee and we'll move in there," Annette said. "And have you got any cognac? I can't stand those drams of yours."

"Aye, I'll bring you some, but first I'd better see that your friend's okay."

The sitting room was a delightful room with two large windows giving sensational views over Loch Alsh and the Skye hills, and displaying a fine collection of furniture and pictures, all acquired cheap when two local estates were sold up in the late nineteen forties. Annette put the tray down on a table between the two windows, turned on the lights and drew the curtains, then took her cup over to a sofa and sat down.

"He's quietened down a bit now," Calum said, coming into the room from the kitchen carrying a bottle and two glasses which he put down on the coffee tray, "so I've taken off his hobble and told him the place is surrounded by dogs and there are wild animals in the hills. I dinna think he's much used to the country! Now here's your brandy." He picked up the bottle and looked at it. "It's the genuine article, brought back from Cherbourg only last month." And he poured two glasses, gave one to Annette and took the other over to a chair by the fireplace.

"Tomorrow," he said, "I suggest we take the boat out in the morning and see if there's any activity across the loch. Then, if necessary, we can take the helicopter and have a closer look. It's the sort of thing I'm always doing so it'll no' arouse any suspicion."

"Très bon," Annette said looking up and smiling at him, and leaving him wondering if she was referring to the brandy or tomorrow's plans. "But now let's talk about something nicer than business. Do you remember that time in Brittany? You were little more than a boy and you'd been sent to work on that farm with all the artichokes. It was called Saint Pol and belonged to my sister's brother-in-law. It was before I married the Englishman and I had an office job in Morlaix, but I was really arranging shipments of arms and other illegal items from Roscoff to Ireland. We had a lot of fun, and I taught you a few things, didn't I?"

"Aye, you did that," Calum replied with a grin.

"Well, now you can get me some more of this cognac," she said, "and then we'll see if you need more lessons or perhaps we'll find, will we, that you are now so advanced that you can even teach me a bit!"

"I doubt that," he said, picking up her glass. "There's not a lot to practise on round here."

"Mon pauvre Calum," she said, as he put her glass back on a table beside the sofa and stood looking down at her, "all alone on his mountain with only his sheep for company. But what about Cherbourg? There are pretty girls there I'm sure!" And she reached up and took his hands, catching him off balance and causing him to collapse on top of her.

As he fell, her arms went round him and her mouth found his. The kiss seemed to last forever, but eventually she released him and he found himself kneeling between her legs. He bent down and unbuttoned her blouse, slipped it free of her skirt and gently massaged her breasts. Then he lifted her skirt and ran his hands up her thighs and felt under her knickers for the thick bush of hair. She looked up at him, smiled and gave a gentle tug to his beard.

"I'm not sure I really like making love to a little red clothes brush," she said, and he was still trying to think of an answer when she suddenly rolled him over and before he knew what was happening, she was standing above him, stepping out of her skirt and dropping it and the blouse on the floor.

"I think you do need more lessons, my Calum," she laughed. "Just look up at me, mon cher, for I'm almost naked" – and she shed her bra – "while as for you – you are still fully clothed! If you're not careful I'll have come before you even reach me." And she slipped down her knickers, kicked them aside, then bent down and started to unfasten his belt.

Then she stopped. "No, it's too uncomfortable here," she said and pulled him towards the door. "Come on, you can finish undressing upstairs for I think a bed will make a better school room for the rest of our little lesson."

CHAPTER 35

THE NEXT MORNING ANDREW WALKED INTO THE dining room at Knockbain at five past eight to find Norman Colquhoun helping himself to kippers and coffee.

"Morning, Andrew," he said. "Tommy's already had breakfast and gone out to look at some cattle. Said we'd meet at ten and discuss plans. Now, you must try these kippers. Straight from Mallaig. Some of the best there are."

Andrew complied with this advice and acknowledged the excellence of the kippers. Then, having finished his breakfast and saying he needed some fresh air, he picked up a stick and set out to explore the policies.

The Castle of Knockbain stands on a bluff above the river, some three-quarters of the way up the glen from the village. Beyond the castle the main road climbs steadily to the top of the pass and then drops down in a series of vertiginous hairpins towards the loch shore and the mountains of Kintail. Another smaller road follows the river to a farm, beyond which are a series of tracks leading to the formidable jumble of hills that form the southern marches of the estate. To the north and west, the castle is sheltered by woods containing many fine specimen trees, and to the south the terrace and lawn command outstanding views of the mountains and the distant Sound of Sleat.

Andrew returned from his walk to find the others assembled round a table in the library on which was a large-scale map of the entire area. General Macdonald, who was pointing out various significant places, looked up as Andrew walked in.

"Enjoy your walk?" he said and when Andrew nodded, he continued, "Splendid, it's a wonderful situation, isn't it? And now, if you're ready, shall we get to work? I think it's probably best, Andrew, if you give me a quick run down on what you're after."

"Well, to cut a long story short, we're trying to locate some gold bullion," Andrew said. "At least, that's what we think it is. It was shipped over here for the benefit of Louis XVI and Marie Antoinette when they escaped from France – which, of course, they never did. As you will see from this letter," and he gave it to the general, "if they failed to make it to England, they wished the money to go to someone who had already escaped the Terror. That someone was an ancestor of my late wife. Now, although it seems clear that the gold belongs to France, as we have done all the donkey work, we have been authorised to try and locate it. The clue as to its whereabouts is contained in this poem."

"Very interesting," Tommy Macdonald said after he'd studied the two documents for several minutes. "I gather from Norrie that you have established that 'My Lord' is the Earl of Strathconon and I'm sure you've been told that there were Strathconon estates in this part of the world. I'm equally sure you've been told about wrecked ships and buried treasure and mysterious deaths. There are any amount of stories about them round here."

"Indeed yes," Andrew said, "even the Foreign Office seemed to have heard of them! But now we need your help. We think the poem indicates that we should align some steps at Eilean Donan with something on the opposite shore of the loch and then somewhere on the same line there should be a funny-shaped hill or rock or something."

"The monster's back is the Dragon, that's obvious," Tommy said. "It's a large rock or small islet and it can certainly be aligned with the castle steps. Don't know about the rest. We'll have to ask Charlie Noble if he can help. He's the local laird; family's been there for years and he knows everything there is to know about this area. I'll ring him and see if we can go over this afternoon."

Charlie Noble indicated that he would be very happy to see the party from Knockbain for tea that afternoon and give what help he could. Tommy Macdonald therefore suggested that after lunch they drive first to Eilean Donan and have a look across the loch from the steps mentioned in the poem. They could then drive round and look at the Dragon and 'The rocks beneath the trees', Charlie's house being only some five minutes from there.

"Sounds splendid," Andrew said, "but now, before I do anything more, do you think I could ring the police?"

"Certainly," Tommy replied. "Who do you want and where is he?"

"Our chap in London, Superintendent Wilkinson, gave us the Assistant Chief Constable in Inverness, Cameron by name, as our contact."

"Dougal Cameron! Know him well," the general said. "Come along to the study and we'll see if we can get hold of him."

Mr Cameron was fortunately in and was expecting a call from Andrew. "Aye, I had a call last evening from Jack Wilkinson saying you were on the way to Knockbain and giving us details of the car with Mrs Barry and the Frenchman. We kept the best lookout we could on the roads from Fort William to the Kyle, but there's been no sign of it. Probably arrived wherever it was going just in the darkening and is now securely hidden somewhere. We'll need a bit of luck to put us on the track."

"If I get that bit of luck," Andrew said, "I'll let you know... Will you do the same? ... Thanks, and keep in touch."

Janet Macdonald, who had been at a National Trust meeting all morning, excused herself from the forthcoming expedition, so just after two the four of them set off in the general's Subaru.

It was a fine afternoon, and as they came over the pass and started the descent to the loch, Jenny let out a gasp of astonishment, for the whole panorama of Kintail, lit by the westering sun, was displayed before them.

"There's your ice cold maidens," Tommy said. "The Five Sisters of Kintail, and you may never see them better."

There was further excitement when they reached Eilean Donan. "It's wonderful," Jenny said, "like something out of a fairy tale."

As they walked round to the loch side and stood at the head of the steps, looking at the opposite shore, Tommy was explaining to Jenny something of the history of the castle.

"It was a ruin for many years. Then a major restoration was put in hand before the war, and the family have continued it ever since," he was saying, when he was interrupted by Norrie.

"Just look over there, above the tree line," he said, pointing across the water. "Do you see that knoll with the pointed rock on the top? Looks like a bird – an eagle perhaps – could that be our 'noble head'?"

"Could be. We'll have to put it to the laird," the general answered and turned and started to walk back to the car, then suddenly stopped.

"Speaking of lairds," he said, as a small, sprightly woman walked towards them across the bridge, "here comes the lady of Eilean Donan. How are you, my dear? And let me introduce my guests. We won't bother too much about the men, but this is Jenny Stanley from South Africa. Her first visit to Scotland and she'd never seen a real castle before. Now we must go because we're due at Charlie's for tea. Lovely to have seen you."

"Really, Tom?" the lady of Eilean Donan said. "Can't I tempt you away from Charlie and I'll show Miss Stanley the castle? No? Oh well." She turned to Jenny and said, "They're always in such a rush, these men, but enjoy the rest of your time in Scotland."

Charlie Noble could not have been more helpful. When he was told the story of the French gold, he agreed with his neighbour that, over the past two hundred years, there had been many rumours of treasure landed from a ship and buried in the area.

"You're obviously right about the castle and the Dragon," he said, "but I don't know about the noble head. Sounds as though it's something above or behind the line of the castle and rock."

"When we looked back from Eilan Donan just now," the general said, "Norrie pointed out quite a high hill with a rock face which, from our angle, made it look like the head of a large bird."

"That's Sron na h-Iolaire, literally The Eagle's Nose." Charlie paused, then banged his hand on the table. "Of course, that'll be it, that's your 'noble head'!" he exclaimed. "It's one of our higher hills, around two thousand feet, and I must admit that although I've been walking over it all my life, I've never seen or heard of a mossy grave. There's a sort of plateau at the base of the rocks and a mass of peat hags and lochans; altogether a pretty wild sort of place. It's a bit late now, but tomorrow morning we could go up and have a look. I'd like to take Jock, that's my stalker. It's okay, he's absolutely reliable."

"Sounds a splendid arrangement, Charlie. The only snag is that I won't be able to come. Got a Timber Growers' meeting in Fort Augustus," Tommy Macdonald said, "but I don't see that that matters, provided Andrew and Norrie are happy."

"Fine by me," Andrew said, and Norman Colquhoun nodded his agreement.

"Good, then that's fixed," Noble said. "I suggest we meet at the farm half a mile down the road at nine thirty."

When they arrived at the farm the next morning they were met by a cheerful-looking young man in well-worn plus fours.

"Which one of you will be Mr Henderson?" he asked, and when Andrew stepped forward the stalker shook his hand and said, "Pleased to meet you." Then he held out a hand to each of the others. "And this'll be the brigadier, and this Miss Stanley. Aye, Major Noble briefed me well," he said with a grin. Then he led the way over to a low, green, eight-wheeled vehicle.

"The major said we were to go on in the Argo and he'll follow on on the bike. He's been held up by a man from the Hydro. Terrible nuisance they are. Always wanting to do something to their lines. Now you'll all be having good boots? Fine, and we'll maybe put the waterproofs in the back. Aye, better to be safe than sorry."

On the way up the hill, despite the clatter of the engine, he managed to establish from Andrew where it was they wanted to go and what they wanted to do.

"The major gave me a rough idea," he said, "so I've put in a spade and a crowbar. A strange place to be going looking for valuables it is, so we'll just have to see."

The first part of their route was up a well-established track through woods, but once on the open hill they started to climb steeply and the going deteriorated as they switchbacked over burns and zigzagged round rocky spurs. Finally, the track petered out and they had a tricky climb across a slope dotted with pools, ragged boiler plates and great boulders.

Eventually Jock stopped on a large flat area relatively free of either peat hags or boulders at the foot of a towering grass slope topped by a vertical cliff with a menacing overhang.

"There ye are," he said, "the eagle, Sron na h-Iolaire. So what'll you be wanting to do?"

"Well, the first thing I want to do is to look at the view," Jenny said, "so can Jock tell me a bit about it?"

So while Jenny received a lesson on the geography of Scotland from Knoydart round to Applecross, Andrew and the brigadier set about exploring the ground. The flat on which they had parked yielded nothing. Despite an hour of prodding the ground with their sticks, and on one occasion using the spade to explore further, they found nothing to indicate any sort of grave or burial chamber.

Halfway through their endeavours the noise of an engine indicated the arrival of Charlie Noble on a four-wheel ATV.

"Wonderful machines these, can't think how we managed without 'em," he said. "And how's it going? Have you found anything?"

"Not down here," Andrew replied. "Do you think it's worth going up a bit? It looks too steep to me, but maybe there are some flat bits."

"Let's ask Jock." He called him over.

"Aye, it looks steep enough, but no hill's entirely smooth," and he started to climb. What he said was indeed true, for what appeared a smooth slope proved to be a mass of dips and steps, and when they moved round to the right below the cliff they found themselves on quite a wide platform.

Jenny, who was walking along the edge, with a steep drop below her on her right, suddenly tripped and cried out, and Jock only just caught her before she would have vanished down the slope.

"Are you okay?" Andrew asked, rushing across to her.

"Yes, fine," she said, rubbing her ankle. Then she moved carefully towards the edge and tested the ground with her foot. "Here, look at this," she said. "The whole ground moves if you tread here. That's why I nearly went over."

"Get the spade, Jock," Charlie shouted to the stalker, "while we have a closer look."

While this was going on Norman Colquhoun had already started testing the ground with his stick.

"We seem to have some sort of stone slab here," he said, "for there's an edge along this side – yes, another at right angles here, only about six inches from this steep drop."

"And the same at this end," Andrew cried. "If this isn't a 'mossy grave' then I don't know what is!"

"Aye, it likely is," said Jock, who was scraping away the grass and peat with his spade, "and look here where it's broken. It could be in several pieces, and that's why it moved when the young lady trod on it. Aye, that'll be what's in it; and just as well, ye'd never move it if it was all one block."

"And there's something else here," exclaimed Jenny, who was standing to one side of the main slab, "and it's only just below the surface. It makes a sort of dull noise when Charlie prods it. No, it's not a rock; look, you can see a curved edge here."

"We seem to have discovered quite a lot this morning," said Andrew, standing back and surveying the scene, "but if we're to make any further progress we'll need some more tools and possibly manpower. Isn't that right, Jock?" The stalker nodded, and Andrew turned to Charlie Noble.

"Would it be alright if we came back this afternoon and tried to lift the slab and see what's underneath?" he asked. "I hate to impose on you, but this looks like the culmination of our efforts. I must go back to Knockbain now, for I need to make quite a few telephone calls to report progress."

"Of course," Charlie replied, "and Jock and I will assemble the necessary equipment."

As they were going down the hill, Andrew suddenly turned to Jock and pointed towards the loch.

"You see that boat? It's been buzzing around there all morning. I've noticed it several times."

"That'll be Calum Macrae," Jock replied. "He has a farm up above Dornie there, where the big glen comes down to Loch Long. He takes the tourists out as well as running sheep, cattle and ponies; oh, he's in quite a way of business, is Calum, for he has a helicopter for the stalkers that cannae walk the hill."

Andrew looked up at the sky. "Loch Long, of course, that's what she said, not 'oblong'," he said out loud, then added to the surprised Jock, "Don't worry, but you've just helped solve another piece of the jigsaw."

The first thing that happened when they got back to Knockbain was that Janet apologised for the fact that her husband would not be back for lunch and asked if there was anything they needed.

"Of course, and use the study. You know where it is," she said in answer to Andrew's request to use the telephone.

His first call was to Superintendent Wilkinson in London to whom he explained that they had discovered what they believed to be the hiding place of gold.

"No, we don't know if the gold itself is there but I hope we'll know a bit more by this evening." When Wilkinson asked if there had been any sign of Mrs Barry and the Frenchman, Andrew had to say that neither they nor the police had seen anything of them since the previous afternoon.

"Yes, I have talked to Dougal Cameron, and I'm just about to do so again, for I now think I know where they are... That's right; and I hope, with police assistance, we'll find them this afternoon... I'm going to leave Brigadier Colquhoun to check whether there is anything actually in the grave... Yes, I'll ring again tonight when I hope we'll have a bit more to tell you."

The Assistant Chief Constable, when Andrew rang him, said that he'd been trying to get them, for he'd just heard from the crew of a patrol car that a man called Calum Macrae had been seen disembarking from one of his boats with a stranger who they thought fitted the description of the woman they were looking for. Andrew then explained what they'd been doing that morning and that he'd become suspicious about a boat that had been patrolling the loch.

"When I asked about it," he said, "I was told it belonged to a Calum Macrae who had a farm on Loch Long. This was an interesting coincidence, for I'd been told that Mrs Barry had been overheard saying they were going to a place that I'm now sure was Loch Long. I would like to have a look at that place this afternoon."

"That's fine," Cameron answered, "I told the car to hang on at the Dornie Hotel. Meet them there – what time shall I say? ...Two fifteen. Okay, and it's a Sergeant Matheson."

It was just before two fifteen when Andrew drew up beside the police car in the hotel car park to be greeted by Sergeant Matheson. After a short consultation, he and Andrew set off in Andrew's Range Rover through the village and up the road to Clovulin, leaving the police car and driver at the hotel.

"There's mebbe one thing I should tell you," Matheson said. "We'll not find the helicopter there. It took off about ten minutes ago and headed northwest towards Skye." Then three minutes later he told Andrew to slow down, and then to stop.

"You can park there, in the shelter o' that wee shed," he said. "I'm no' sure what we'll find at the place. Calum and his visitors will surely be away in the chopper, but there's Jimmy, he's the shepherd. He'll most likely be out on the hill, but he could be about the steading, so we'd best go careful."

The first building they came to was a pair of cottages standing right alongside the road. Sergeant Matheson, who seemed to know a lot about the place, explained that the first of the pair was kept furnished and used for casual labour at lambing and clipping times. They tried the door and found it locked, and a quick look through the front windows suggested that the place was unoccupied.

"The other cottage is not used at present," the sergeant said. "It used to be Jimmy's, but he's now got his own house and a wee bit o' land the other side o' the bridge."

Moving on from the cottages, they turned into the square and searched the various buildings surrounding it, but found nothing, and when they reached the house they found both back and front doors locked.

"Aye, as I thought, they're all away out, so we'll just have a look at where they keep the helicopter." The sergeant led the way round the back of the steading and into the mouth of the glen. Some three hundred yards up a well maintained gravel track, they came to a flat, open field of rough grass that was obviously kept mown. At one side of the field was a large prefabricated barn and a couple of smaller sheds.

The door of the barn was closed but not locked, so Andrew walked in and wandered round looking at workbenches, store cupboards and a fuel pump.

"It's where he keeps it in bad weather and if he's away," Matheson said, "and there's a mechanic comes every month, from Aberdeen they say, for the maintenance."

Andrew nodded and moved on to the larger of the two sheds. Finding the door locked, he walked round and peered in at a window.

"Now that really is interesting," he said. "There's a car in there that looks exactly like theirs. I can't actually see the number plate from here, but it looks as if there's another window at the back." He walked on round. "Yes, that's it alright, S344 JES."

There being nothing further to see, Andrew and the sergeant walked back along a track that brought them down to the road at almost exactly the place where they'd left the car.

"Now that we know they arrived at the farm and are presumably out in the helicopter," Andrew said, "let's think what's the best thing to do. As two of them are wanted for murder, I suppose that's a matter for the police, but let me make a suggestion. Once they get back that'll be the ideal opportunity to arrest them, and it may be the last one you'll get, for they're not going to hang about here longer than necessary. However, it will be a difficult and dangerous operation, for Mrs Barry is a ruthless woman and Lemaître has already committed one murder, so you will need men. What are the chances of getting another three or four men here in the next hour or so?"

"Just about nil, sir, I would say," Matheson replied. "They'd have to come from Fort William or Inverness and that would take two hours or more. Dingwall might be a wee thing quicker, but I doubt there'd be enough men there. No, the only hope is if there's men out on the road for some reason. I'd need to go back to the car and get on the radio."

"Right then, do that, and quick as possible. Take this car." Andrew threw him the keys. "I'll stay here and keep the place under observation."

"Well, sir, it's worth a try," said the Sergeant, getting into the Range Rover. "Aye, and now, mind you, no heroics. I'm no' wanting to be finding a corpse when I get back. Leave the arresting to the polis."

Andrew walked round the back of the cottage and, in a shed full of straw bales, found an excellent observation post from which he could watch the landing field without, as he thought, himself being seen.

It was unfortunate, therefore, that Jean Lemaître, watching from the back window of the cottage, had seen them searching the steading. Then, when he saw Andrew take up his position in the shed, realising what was likely to happen, he redoubled his efforts to deal with the lock on the door of his room.

When Calum had brought him coffee and bread that morning, he had said that he and Annette would be going out for the morning, but that Jimmy would be there, so not to try to escape, for Jimmy was a very violent man. That warning he took with a pinch of salt and so, as soon as he heard the car leave, he started to consider possible means of escape.

The massive oak door of his room was obviously part of an older building and was fitted with a lock to match. A lock which Jean, who knew something about locks, could see no simple way of forcing. There was, however, a chance that if he could expose the plates, he might be able to manipulate the levers so as to release the tongue. It was a question of whether his flick knife, which Calum had not bothered to remove, was strong enough to tackle the oak.

What he would do if he managed to escape he had not really worked out, but he knew that if he remained where he was, he would be in considerable danger. Being unsure when they would return, he thought it best to leave the lock for the moment, but a little hacking at the base of the door did suggest that his scheme might work.

His caution was rewarded some two hours later when he heard the car return and, shortly after, Calum brought him some soup and cheese.

"We'll be out again shortly," he had said. "You'll hear the helicopter; and mind now, dinna try to escape."

As soon as he heard the helicopter's engine and saw it lift off in the direction of the glen, he whipped out his knife and started work on the wood around the lock. It was hard work, for the wood was old and very solid, but after an hour he had exposed the bottom of the lock plate and was working forward so that he could see the tongue. It was then, happening to look out of the window, that he spotted Andrew.

Seeing Henderson was with the police, he guessed that they must be planning a raid on the farm, probably as soon as they were sure that the helicopter had returned and that they were all in the house. He therefore reckoned that, if he could disable Henderson and then warn the others, they could all get away before the police could act.

He had just managed to expose the whole lock mechanism when he heard the beat of the rotor. Looking out, he saw Annette and Calum walk towards the house and open the back door. Moments later Andrew left his hiding place and, under cover of a wall and a straggling beech hedge, reached the kitchen window. Jean looked round the room for another implement but all he could find was the knife that had come with his cheese. However, it was enough and, after a further five minutes' work, there was a click followed by a rasping sound and he was able to withdraw the bolt from its hole in the door frame and push open the door. The cottage door was not locked and Jean was out in a flash and dodging across the square towards the house.

When Andrew reached the kitchen window, forgetting the sergeant's warning, he raised his head for a quick look. Annette was sitting at a table, while Calum was pouring coffee and talking earnestly. The window, however, was shut and, try as he would, Andrew could hear nothing. He moved to the back door, and finding it unlocked, edged his way cautiously into the lobby. Here he had a bit of luck, for the inner door had been left ajar.

"You saw where they were digging," he heard Calum say. "Well, we need to get a closer look at that. See what they were at and possibly whether we can land there. If it's the gold they've found, then the chopper's the only way we'll get it out. I'll see if I can organise my cousin for a dawn recce."

Then he must have moved, because his words became indistinct and the next thing Andrew heard was Annette's voice.

"...assuming we get it. What then?" she said. After which Andrew heard Calum say something about a pier, and then in a louder voice, "Aye... the gin palace, it's alongside at..." And that was all he heard for there was a crash behind him, the back door was flung open and a heavy object whistled past his head.

"What the hell...?" he exclaimed and whipped round to see Jean leaping towards him, knife in hand.

Now one of the things Andrew had learnt during his athletics days at Cambridge was judo. Indeed he had represented the University at that sport, and with some distinction. So the next thing the advancing Lemaître knew was a sensation of flying, followed by a surprisingly soft landing as he collided with Calum, and they both went backwards through the inner door, landing in a heap on the kitchen floor.

Not waiting to see the result of his throw, in one lightning move Andrew turned and left the house. As he went, he grabbed the key from the outer door, slammed and locked it and threw the key into the hedge. He then ran as fast as he could in the direction of the village.

In the kitchen, Annette rushed forward and seized the badly winded Jean by the collar and yanked him to his feet. Then she altered her grip to the front of his jacket, pulled him towards her and kneed him in the groin.

"You really should be more careful, mon pauvre garçon," she said. "That's twice I've tickled your testicles. The next time, if there is one, the damage could be permanent." And she pushed the groaning Frenchman into a chair.

As she did so there was the sound of a shot as Calum blew out the lock of the back door, and she saw him rush out in the direction of the road. Then there was another shot and after a couple of minutes Calum appeared, swearing.

"I bloody missed him," he cried. "Yon bugger can fairly run, and he was just too far for me. And what the hell's going on? How many others has he got with him, d'you think?"

Jean staggered forward. "He has the police. They've been here all afternoon and when I saw them I cut my way out to warn you. We must go! Vite! For he'll be back with many. I heard them saying it. There, listen! What did I tell you?" And there was the sound of a siren from the direction of the village and, to the left, the noise of motorcycle engines.

"Quick! The helicopter!" Calum yelled. "And take this other pistol," he said thrusting it into her hand, adding as an afterthought, "You'd best come too, Jean, and mind you do what you're bloody told."

Then he ran towards the landing field, the others panting behind him. He flung open the door, told Jean to jump up and over into the back, and when Annette arrived he almost threw her in and himself jumped up behind her.

"Over into that seat," he shouted, "and both of you, get your belts fastened." Then he slammed the door and started the engine. The blades began to rotate slowly at first, then gradually gaining speed until, as the first of the police motorcycles appeared from behind the hangar, Calum lifted the machine into the air and headed up the glen and out of the view of the two patrol cars which were pulling up in front of the steading.

CHAPTER 36

A NDREW HEARD THE SOUND OF THE SHOT as the lock was blown out, followed by the crack of a bullet passing over his head, and then he was round the corner, to see a police car racing towards him and sliding to a halt opposite. Sergeant Matheson wound down the window.

"Are you all right?" he shouted then added, as they heard the helicopter's engine start, "Ach hell! That'll be them away, and I doubt Bethune and Kennedy will have been in time. Quick, sir, jump in while we see what's happening."

"Yes, I'm fine," Andrew said, scrambling into the back as a constable held open the door, "although that last shot was a bit too close for comfort. The helicopter arrived back about fifteen minutes ago. Mrs Barry and the man, Calum, went straight to the farmhouse. I managed to get into the back lobby, I thought unobserved, when I was attacked from behind. It was the Frenchman, Lemaître. Somehow, Sergeant, we must have missed him during our search."

Moments later the car pulled up at the start of the track to the landing field, but there was no sign of the helicopter. Sergeant Matheson, who was driving, turned to the inspector sitting beside him.

"I'm afraid they've got away, sir," he said. "Yon Calum Macrae knows these hills like his own home. He'll be away round the glens and keeping low. Illegal and gey dangerous, but it avoids the radar. We can check with Air Traffic Control but I doubt they'll know where he went. Anyway, here's Bethune, we'll see if he saw anything." One of the motorcycles pulled up beside them and while the rider took off his helmet, Matheson turned to the inspector.

"Sir, I'd best introduce you. Mr Henderson, this is Inspector Sym from Dingwall."

"Pleased to meet you," Inspector Sym said. "And now let's have some action. Matheson, while I talk to Bethune, you get the whole place thoroughly searched. No overlooking anything this time. You've got six men between the two cars, so it should not take too long. Oh yes, and tell someone to get onto Inverness and have them check with the Air Traffic people. Now, Bethune, tell me, what did you see?"

"Not verra much, sir," the constable replied. "As we came over the crest we saw three people, it would be two men and a woman, running for the plane. Then as we came down towards those sheds there, the engine started and they were away off. There was nothing we could do to stop them."

"Which way did they go?"

"Up the glen there," said the constable, pointing. "Verra low they were, sir. Gey dangerous it looked, and when they jumped yon ridge I was looking for them to crash. They'll have gone down that big corrie and round the head o' the loch. After that I dinna ken, for we couldn'a see them."

"Very good, Bethune, that'll be all for now," said Sym and then turned to Andrew. "It seems all three escaped. A great pity that was, and it's always the same with helicopters, you canna stop them like you might an aeroplane. But I wonder where the hell they've gone. Any ideas, Matheson?" he asked, as the sergeant appeared from the direction of the house.

"No, sir," Matheson replied, "and it's always the same wi' yon Calum Macrae. You'll mind that we thought we had him over the picking up of those Irish, but he vanished and reappeared at the farm two days later with a ready-made alibi about taking Yanks from about Dunvegan down to a place in Fife. He'd been to Fife right enough, but not wi' Americans, of that I'm sure, but we could prove nothing."

"He's got a hiding place somewhere and no one's letting on," Sym said. "We'll just have to do a bit of searching, for it canna be that easy to hide a helicopter. Perhaps, Mr Henderson, you heard something that could help?"

"Well, one thing I know for sure," Andrew said, "and that is that when they were out earlier this afternoon they saw our party at the Eagles Nose or whatever it's called, and they think we've found the gold. Calum wants to do a recce, with his cousin I think he said, tomorrow morning. On foot, I imagine, because the object is to see if they can land the helicopter up there."

"Sounds right," the sergeant said. "The cousin will be that fisherman laddie from about Kishorn way. He'll pick them up in his boat wherever they may be and take them across to the Letterfearn side. We could mebbe ask the Customs to watch for them, sir."

"Aye, we could," Sym said, "but did you hear anything else, Mr Henderson, anything that might suggest where they've gone?"

"Not anything that would suggest where they are now," Andrew said. "The trouble was that Calum either moved or lowered his voice, for the next thing I heard was Mrs Barry asking what they did if they got hold of the treasure. Then Calum said something about a pier. Where it was supposed to be I don't know, but the gin palace is alongside it, whatever that means."

Again it was Matheson who answered. "That'll be yon big motor cruiser, the *Ariadne* or some such name, that he has for the tourists. He sometimes keeps it over at the back of Knoydart – Inverdoran I think they call the place, it's where the track along the shore runs out. You can just about get a vehicle along to the old pier and there's a ruined bothy beside it. Outside o' the stalking season the laird allows Calum to fly his clients in there. They get an easy look at the high hills and then a trip across to Skye and down to Mallaig. He has a skipper, Jakie I think they call him, looks after the boat."

"Aye, man, that'll be it and I mind the place fine. It's where we got the Mackay gang with those four stags," Sym said, then added, "Did you find anything around the farm, Bill?"

"Nothing, sir, except that the lock of a bedroom door in one of the cottages had been forced. I'm thinking the Frenchman had been locked in there. We'll need to talk to Seumas when he gets back."

"Yes we'll surely do that," the inspector agreed grimly, "and I'll need to report to Mr Cameron and find out if there's any news of the helicopter. What about you, Mr Henderson, what'll you be doing?"

"I need to get back to Knockbain and see how they got on up at the grave and what they saw of the helicopter. Then we'll have to try and guess what Mrs Barry is going to do, and consequently what our next move should be," Andrew replied. "Then I must report to London and Inverness and tell them what's happening and, I hope, get agreement on the next step and how it should be implemented. So now, if you don't need me, I'll push off, and thanks for all your help."

When Andrew got back to the castle, finding his host in the hall, he apologised for his late return and said he would, in due course, explain the reason.

"Doesn't matter a bit," the general said. "The others have gone to have baths, so why don't you do the same then we can have a drink and hear what you've all been doing."

Andrew, never one to hang about in a bath, was the first down, and found Janet Macdonald gathering up an assortment of caps, waterproofs and boots preparatory to taking them out to the back regions.

"Tom has never mastered the art of living without a batman," she remarked, laughing. "For a man who is irritatingly precise in most things, he is quite unable to understand that clothes, casually discarded around the place, will not automatically make their way to their proper home, there to be ready when he next wants them. No, don't bother," she said when he picked up a tweed jacket and two odd shoes, "I can manage very well. You go on into the drawing room and help yourself to a drink; you should find everything on the table behind the big sofa."

The next person down was Jenny, who put an arm round Andrew's waist and kissed him, almost causing him to drop the heavy cut-glass whisky decanter. Having asked for a glass of wine, she enquired what he had been doing all afternoon.

"We had a wonderful time," she said without waiting for a reply. "We got the stone moved and underneath found a mass of bones and two skulls. It was quite creepy! Then Norman had a closer look and found that they were lying in an iron tray – a sort of false bottom. He and Jock managed to lift it out and underneath we found..." and here she paused as the brigadier came into the room, then added, "Here he is so I'll let him finish the story himself."

"You had a successful time, I gather, Norrie. So what was under the bones?" Andrew asked.

"There was a small tin deed box which I've got upstairs," Norman replied, helping himself to whisky and soda, "and rows of gold bars. Thirty in the top tier, and I don't know how many tiers. Didn't like to move them without some official observer to see fair play. But it's a lot of gold. There was a helicopter buzzing round and I didn't like the look of that. It makes me think that our friends may have got the idea that we've found something."

"I'm afraid that's just what they have done," Andrew said, and explained what he'd heard at the farm. "As far as I could make out they propose to do a recce early tomorrow morning to see if they can land the helicopter up there, but I'll tell you the whole story during dinner, for here's Tom."

With the arrival of the laird, followed a few moments later by Janet, the conversation became general, and remained so for the first half hour of dinner. Eventually, with the arrival of the cheese, Tom Macdonald turned to Andrew and asked what, if anything, he'd discovered, and where the enemy were now.

Andrew then described his meeting with the police, the search of the farm at Clovulin and his decision to remain there while Sergeant Matheson went to see if he could raise reinforcements.

"When the helicopter returned, I made a mistake," he continued. "Only Annette and the farmer, Calum Macrae, got out and walked to the farmhouse. Of course I should have wondered what had happened to Lemaître, but I completely forgot about him."

He then described how he managed to overhear Annette and Calum disussing both the proposal to reconnoitre the area of Sron na h-Iolaire and also the use of the pier and the gin palace, and finally the arrival of Lemaître on the scene.

"God knows where he came from. The police think he may have been locked up and escaped. Be that as it may, he very nearly got me. I managed to throw him and run for it, pursued, as I once heard an American say, by hot lead. They had a shot at me and then I was round a corner and meeting the police. They'd sent a couple of motorcyclists round in a right flanking, but they were just too late. The chopper was off and away up the glen with all three of them onboard, and it's not been seen since."

"Someone must know where they are, surely. Helicopters can't just disappear. In the vastness of South Africa possibly, but not in little Scotland," Jenny said.

"It's not so little up here, you know," the general remarked. "There's mile upon mile of mountains separated by hidden glens. No, if you know your ground and are brave or foolhardy enough, you fly beneath the radar, keep clear of habitation and have arrangements with friendly keepers, you can vanish quite easily. Macrae will have these sort of arrangements for his tourist business. Probably even has the lairds organised."

Andrew nodded. "That's more or less what the police said. I'll have to ring both Wilkinson in London and Cameron and perhaps we'll get some news then."

"So what do you propose to do?" Norman asked.

"The first thing is to find out if Annette and Co. really do know where the grave is," Andrew said, "and that, I think, means you and I, Norrie, must be up there at dawn to see if their recce does actually happen. The rest of my plan depends on the agreement of the police – and probably also that of the Bank, the Foreign Office, possibly even the President of France. I want to keep the details secret for the moment, but my idea is roughly this." And he gave a very brief outline of what he proposed to put to the authorities and finished by saying, "I have just one worry and that is security. Telephones can be tapped."

"Funny you should say that," Norrie said, "for I thought before we left London that secure communication might be required. So I spoke to my people and they had a word with Wilkinson. As a result I have a little box of tricks upstairs which, if I may, Tom, I will attach to one of your phones and then we can talk to Wilkinson without anyone understanding a word we're saying. Yes, and Cameron has the right black box too."

With this plan agreed, Norrie left the room, returning some five minutes later with a small leather case and also the tin box from the grave.

"Now, Tom, if I may use the study telephone I'll get this gismo set up," he said. "And you, Andrew, had better have a look in this box and see if it contains anything of interest."

The box was locked but the metal was brittle with age, and after a little work with a stout chisel the whole lid split open disclosing three or four neatly folded papers tied with blue ribbon. Andrew opened one and found it intact and the writing legible. He read it quickly and then opened and read the remainder.

"Nothing new," he said, "it's all in reasonably modern French. There's one letter from, I assume, the King's private secretary. It's addressed to Strathconon and is instructions about the gold. Then there's an inventory. That'll be handy for checking. There's also a personal note from Louis hoping all will be well and telling the earl that he knows what to do if the worst happens. What I don't understand is why he apparently didn't do whatever it was he was supposed to do when the worst did happen."

"I think," said Norrie who had come back into the room, "it was because Strathconon died – very suddenly, I seem to remember. He got up to tell the House of Lords about the latest reports from Paris, and had what in those days was described as an apoplexy. So I suppose in the ensuing excitement the whole thing was forgotten; furthermore, all those who had been involved had either been disposed of or were keeping their mouths tight shut."

"Of course – Rorie Mor Macrae – I had forgotten, but it all fits in," said Tom Macdonald.

"What fits in?" asked Norrie. "Tom you're talking riddles, and that's not like you."

"Listen, and I'll tell you a story. It's one of the many tales of the supernatural common to this part of the world," the general said. "One winter's day around the 1790s, an overseer on the Strathconon estate, Rorie Mor Macrae, left home without saying where he was going. The next that was heard of him was when a horse was heard galloping up to the inn at Shiel Bridge. When the innkeeper went to investigate he found the horse in the last stages of exhaustion and lying beside it, the body of Rorie Mor. He was stone dead and they say there was not a mark on him. Now it was known that he had hired a gang of Macdonalds from Skye for some job. They left Skye but never returned – except for one. He was found on the shore, quite mad, and for the rest of his life unable to say what had happened to him. As for Rorie, legend has it that he saw a Kelpie, and no man survives that."

"What is a Kelpie?" Jenny asked.

"The terrible highland water horse that lives in the lochs of this part of Scotland," Tom replied. "Now, I hate to spoil a good story, but I think, as well as everything else, we may have solved the mystery of the death of Rorie Mor and the disappearance of the Skye men. The only thing I would say is that perhaps Rorie was not supposed to have died, and it was he that would have dealt with matters when the worst did happen. How did he die? That we will never know. Perhaps he did see a Kelpie – who knows?" and he looked round and grinned, while his audience gave him a gentle round of applause.

"Well done, Tom," Andrew said and then asked if he could now use the telephone and did he have to do anything special?

"Yes, go ahead. The study telephone's all ready," Norrie said. "All you need do is dial Wilkinson's or Cameron's number and the box'll do the rest, but you can't ring any other number while it's connected. Okay? Well then, we'll leave you to it. Tom, did I see a bottle of twelve-year-old Dalmore on the side there?"

Andrew's first call was to Superintendent Wilkinson to confirm that they had indeed found the King's treasure and that it was gold bullion. He then explained about Calum Macrae and his helicopter.

"Yes, I'm afraid he and Annette Barry saw us from the helicopter and so they now know where the hiding place is," he said, "but what's worse is that we missed an opportunity to capture them." And he described the events at the farm.

"No we don't know where they've gone," he said in answer to Wilkinson's question, "but it's possible that by now the Inverness people may know something."

"So what are you proposing to do?" was Wilkinson's next question. "I hope you've got some sort of plan, because I've got a lot of high powered people, including both the Foreign Secretary and the Home Secretary and also the Scottish Office, wanting to know what's going on."

"Yes, I've got a proposal to make. Whether it's acceptable to the great and good you'll have to find out. If it is, then I'll need quite a lot of help from Cameron's boys, so he'll presumably need some sort of authority from on high. Anyway here's what I want to do."

Then, for the next fifteen minutes, Andrew described his ideas in detail, finishing by saying, "Of course, what I've suggested depends on their deciding they can land the helicopter up the hill. I think they can and that they'll make the attempt tomorrow evening at about eight thirty. That would give them about two hours of daylight to load and get away."

"It all sounds feasible," Wilkinson said, "and I must admit I can't think of anything better, although I expect Cameron will have some operational alterations. Give me a couple of hours while I tell the powers that be and get their authority and then talk to Cameron and probably also his boss. I'll try to get back to you by eleven."

Having rung off, Andrew returned to the drawing room and told the others in a little more detail what he was proposing.

"So, assuming we get the necessary authorisation," he said, "Norrie and I will need to be in position at the grave by five tomorrow morning. Then at a time to be agreed with Cameron, you, Norrie, accompanied by a police representative, will take a party up to count the gold. You must have completed your inventory no later than six and you will leave a guard there. That is assuming Cameron agrees. Exactly what I shall be doing depends on a lot of things, and I want to keep quiet about it."

"You're not proposing to do something dangerous, are you?" Jenny asked. "And what part am I playing in all this? After all, if I hadn't suggested going to the museum in Franchhoek none of this would have happened."

"No, nothing dangerous," Andrew replied, "just rather complicated. You, my darling, I suggest should go with Norrie. Your acute business sense will be invaluable in taking an inventory of the King's treasure." And he ducked swiftly as a cushion came flying towards him.

"Now, I expect all of you want to stay up until we hear again from your policeman in London," said Tom Macdonald, "so I thought it might amuse you to watch a video that we had made last year about the natural history of this whole area."

It was some ten minutes after the video finished, while Tom was telling Jenny about the eagles and red deer of the highlands, that Wilkinson rang back.

"Okay, tell him I'll be with him in a minute," Andrew said and walked across the passage to the study.

Wilkinson had obviously worked quickly and effectively, for he had got agreement to Andrew's proposals from all the necessary organisations. He had also talked to both Cameron and his Chief Constable, and aided by a request from the Secretary of State, they agreed to provide all the required assistance.

As soon as he had finished talking to London, Andrew rang Cameron in Inverness, and at the end of forty-five minutes they had agreed the detailed plans for the following day.

"Right then," Cameron said, "one of my men will be at Knockbain at eleven tomorrow morning. Can't say yet who it will be; probably a sergeant with a knowledge of gold and other valuables. Then I'll meet you at the Kyle about midday. Aye, and one last thing. The Chief Constable would be verra grateful if General Macdonald would have a wee word with the Convenor of the Police Authority. Satisfy his curiosity, you know."

When he got back to the drawing room only the two men were there, discussing the merits or otherwise of the various Arab levies of the Gulf region.

"Yes, the girls have gone to bed," Tom said.

"And so had we better," Andrew replied. "It's now midnight, and Norrie and I will need to leave here at three. We should be back by eight unless anything disastrous happens. I hope it won't for this is a recce, not a fighting patrol, and that's something I've promised Cameron. Details for the rest of the day after breakfast. Oh, and by the way, there's been no sign of the helicopter. It seems that once again it's vanished into the hills."

CHAPTER 37

"GOD, THAT WAS A NEAR THING. AND where the hell did he spring from, for Christ's sake?" Calum asked as, at three hundred feet, he turned the helicopter east into a narrow corrie and then north through a gap in the hills at the furthest end of the loch.

"He came with a policeman soon after you left," Lemaître said, "and they searched the place. Then the policeman left, but Henderson, I think you call him, he stayed to watch. What can I do? I wondered. I am locked in, but Jean, he can pick locks. Not this one though, so I have to cut into it. Then I hear you land and see him go towards the house. The lock gives and I run over to find him listening at the door. I try to hit him with a stone but this time I miss."

"What will he have heard? Will he have any idea where we've gone?" Annette asked.

"No he'll not that," Calum said, "but he'll mebbe have heard me mention going to look at where they were digging, aye, and possibly also about the gin palace. It all needs a wee bit of thought, but not now, for I've some tricky flying to do."

He continued heading north and for the only time on the flight had to climb in order to clear a high ridge, before dropping down to Loch Carron. He then skirted Kishorn and appeared to be flying straight for a cliff face. At the last moment, however, a gap appeared and they were heading up a glen into the wilds of Applecross, and Calum gave a quick glance at his passengers.

"It's kinda scary this, I'm afraid, but we're nearly there," he said.

The glen narrowed into a corrie with a sheer rock wall at its head. They just cleared this, then circled a boulder-strewn plateau and landed beside an old stone bothy under the lee of a steep scree-covered slope.

As soon as they had disembarked, Calum threw Annette a key and told her to go into the hut, while he and Jean hauled upright and locked in position a scaffolding frame consisting of three vertical poles joined by a horizontal roller, the whole being some fifteen yards in length. Telling Jean to stay where he was, Calum scrambled some thirty feet up the hill, threw down two ropes and slithered back again. Throwing one rope to Jean and taking the other himself, they unrolled a grey tarpaulin sheet, pulled it over the frame and then secured the ropes to rings in the ground.

"I can tell you this machine's now quite invisible from the air. I've flown over and checked it," he said, leading the way into the bothy. This was surprisingly large and comfortable, the adjoining outhouse having been re-roofed to make a washroom and a storage shed. The bothy itself now consisted of two rooms with bunk beds, and a living room with cooking facilities.

"You make yourself very comfortable here," Annette said. "Who knows about it and how did you fix it?"

"As I think I told you, I have an arrangement with the laird and the stalker," Calum answered. "Out o' the stalking season I bring parties up here. Mainly Yanks who think they're living like Bonnie Prince Charlie, but not so's to be uncomfortable. There's bottled gas for the cooking and lighting and running water. No," and he smiled at Annette, "we canna just manage the WC, but there's the chemical wi' a proper seat so you'll be quite comfortable."

"But what about the helicopter?" she asked.

"No one knows about that but the stalker. The tourists come up in the Argo from my cousin's place on the shore," he replied. "The chopper's for special. Air Traffic seem unable to track it up the glen and you'll see it's now camouflaged. It's a grand place. Walkers and the like never come this way, and to a stalking party, if Wullie ever brings one about here, it's just an old bothy. Now let's have a wee bite and some tea, or coffee if you'd rather, while I think what we do next. Yon police raid was a fair nuisance, I'm telling you."

Leaving Annette and Jean to prepare the meal, Calum went out, returning some fifteen minutes later.

"I've been to have a look at the weather and I believe we'll have a fine evening, so here's what I think we should do," he said, and while they ate he explained his plan. On the assumption that Henderson and the police now knew that they might go to the site of the grave early the next morning, they should bring forward the recce.

"We must go tonight," he said, "and we'll just have to hope that my cousin can manage. I daren't use the radio, so we'll go down on spec. I've only the quad bike here, so I'll just take Annette. It's about five miles and it'll be a rough ride. You, Jean, will have to stay here until we get back and that'll be tomorrow morning – and dinna try to escape. It's terrible country and we might never find your bones."

Ten minutes later Annette and Calum set off on the Yamaha down the edge of a burn. There was no proper track and they were in constant danger of plunging into the water or of missing the way and hurtling over one of the many mini precipices. It was some three miles down the burn before they joined a genuine path and Annette decided it was the most uncomfortable – and terrifying – three miles she'd ever met. There was nowhere proper to put her feet and she found herself alternately clinging to odd bits of metal and Calum's belt. However, once they were on the track, things improved, except that they increased speed and she was bounced up and down on the not very soft seat.

Another three miles on and they descended a steep brae and came to a cluster of buildings by the shore. Tied up at a pier were two boats. One, a fishing boat with a small upright wheelhouse and a pile of nets at the stern. The other, a rather clumsy-looking boat with a covered area for'ard, an open cockpit aft and, unusually for such a craft, on the stern was a very powerful-looking outboard. As they stopped by one of the outbuildings, a youngish man with a mass of black curly hair and a weatherbeaten face came towards them.

"Well now, Calum, man," he said, "it's good to see you, and what can we do for you? Aye, and for your leddy," he added, smiling at Annette.

"Aye, Sandy, and how are you?" Calum replied. "And this is Annette Barry. Annette, meet Sandy the Fishing, an unruly member of the clan." Then having made the introductions, he continued, "Sandy, we have a wee small problem and we think you can help us."

"Come on up to the house then. Cathy's away to her sister in Portree but the Blocker's here." Sandy turned and shouted through the door, "Hey, Blocker, we've Calum here and he's wanting some help."

A tall stringy-looking man with very pale blue eyes emerged from the building, nodded to Calum and Annette and then walked on with Sandy towards the house.

"That's another cousin. His real name's Patrick but he's always known as Pat the Blocker, or sometimes just the Blocker," Calum said as they followed behind the other two. "He used to work for the forestry and also had a firewood business. Could be useful because he was once a ghillie on the estate where the gold is. He's dangerous though. He's done time for poaching with violence."

"Well I don't understand half what you've said," Annette replied, "but I leave it to you to decide what we do. For me, this is a foreign country."

Once they were settled round the kitchen table, Sandy asked what their problem was and Calum gave a brief outline of the story that Annette had told him.

"So you see," he said, "we need to go up to this place tonight and see if there is anywhere there I can land the helicopter, and the only way I could think of that we could do that is if you could put us across to Letterfearn and then we climb up."

"Ach, ye'll no' do that, it's gey steep that side," Pat the Blocker said. "I ken fine the place ye're talking about; it's called Sron na h-Iolaire, the Eagle's Nose. You could probably land there, but if you must see it you'll need to go up from the other side. Sandy, hae ye a map? Aye, that'll do fine. See here, we go into this wee bay and it's a much easier climb up. I can take you up, Calum, but it's no' suitable for the leddy though – not in the dark."

After considerable further discussion, it was agreed that the four of them would go across in the launch and that Calum and Pat would go ashore, leaving Sandy and Annette on guard.

"It'll take an hour and a half to get there," Sandy said, "for we'll need to go careful. You'll not be wanting to meet the Customs boys. Then how long on the hill?"

"A good two hours," Pat said.

"Then ninety minutes back. It'll be a long night, so we'd best have something to eat," Sandy said. "It's now just after seven, so we'll start at eight. Okay?"

At exactly five minutes past eight, Sandy eased the launch, *The Maid of Kintail*, away from the pier and headed out into the loch. It was a fine night with a light wind from the north-west and a calm sea. However, once they cleared the shelter of the land the wind freshened, and in the Sound there was a considerable sea running. Since, in the interests of time, Sandy was unwilling to reduce speed, the next two miles were fairly uncomfortable. Once past the Kyle, though, the wind dropped and the loch surface was barely ruffled and, as they passed the harbour the Blocker, who was standing beside Sandy, pointed to a police launch.

"Now what'll he be doing there? Not usual for the polis to be at the Kyle," he said. "Engine running too. Aye, but there's a bit o' luck," he added, as any view of them the police boat might have had was blocked by a large motor yacht which was in the process of mooring and by the time it was safely tied up the *Maid* was well over to the far side of the loch.

An hour later they were gliding quietly into a small bay, where a narrow pebble beach was backed by a steep grass slope that vanished upwards into the gathering darkness. One end of the bay was formed by a high rocky bluff, on part of which was a narrow shelf that led along the cliff face towards the hill.

"In a moment I'll put the searchlight on so you'll see a bit better," Sandy said, "but you see yon shelf? Aye, well it's steep-to there and I can get alongside, and then when I say, you'll have to jump for it. As soon as you're ashore, we'll go down towards Kylerhea and wait there. We'll give you an hour and then we'll be back here. Now here's the light. Ready? Then off you go, Calum – now you, Blocker. Okay?" And the light was switched off and the *Maid* reversed away from the cliff.

Without the light, the ensuing blackness was absolute and Calum could see nothing at all and felt himself on the verge of panic.

"Come on, man, where's your torch?" said Pat at his shoulder. "Switch it on and you've only about ten yards before you're on the grass."

Edging his way along, Calum reached a narrow gap and jumped across onto the grassy slope. Pat had already scrambled further up the cliff and landed on the hillside ahead of Calum.

"Now out wi' the torch and follow me," he said. "Dinna worry, you'll soon get used to the dark. Just follow my boots."

The Blocker went straight up the face with huge strides and Calum, who kept stumbling in the tussocks, found it hard to keep up. Then suddenly his companion stopped and sliding back down beside him, put his mouth to Calum's ear.

"There's a path goes round just above us and there's people on it," he whispered. "It's a public path, but I'd no expect to find anyone there at this time o' night. We'd best wait in case it might be the polis. From what you say they could be looking for you."

Moments later even Calum could hear the footsteps and the occasional stone being dislodged, and soon they heard the sound of voices and saw the loom of a torch. The footseps passed them and then stopped and they heard a woman's voice.

"Do you have any idea where we are, Fred?" she asked. "Surely we must be nearly there." Then there was the rustle of paper and a flash from the torch. "Yes, the map's quite clear," a man's voice said. "We're here, and the place they said we could camp is just on a bit and down there." And they heard the footsteps shuffle on.

"Good luck to them. Queer though, it's kinda early for the campers," the Blocker said, getting to his feet and setting off up the hill with his great swinging strides.

Forty minutes later they reached a level place with a rocky peak looming above it. "There ye are – The Eagle's Nose," Pat said, "and here's your place. See where they've been digging and scraping." There were now a few stars out and Calum found he could see reasonably well. The outline of the grave was quite clear and so was the surrounding area.

"Aye, this is fine. We can land the chopper here no bother," he said. Then he turned to the grave again. "We should have brought a spade or crowbar or something. Annette'll be sure to ask did we see the gold."

"Aye, well I did just think of that mysel'," Pat replied, and produced from under his jacket an old army entrenching tool.

The Blocker managed to get the flat mattock-like end of the tool under the stone and lever it up enough for them to lift it to an angle of forty-five degrees.

"I can hold it," Pat said. "You see that stone slab over there, well slide it along to here... right, now stand it on edge." Calum just managed to do so. "There, that should hold it."

With the stone wedged up, they shone the torch into the grave and saw the tray of bones. "Sounds sorta hollow," Pat said, tapping it with the entrenching tool. "Let's see if it moves."

"Hey, man, look at that," he said, raising it six inches and peering in.

"Aye, it's gold right enough," Calum agreed, shining the torch into the gap. Then he looked at his watch. "No time to do more now, for we'll need to be getting back down."

Having carefully replaced everything so as to show no trace of their visit, they set off down the hill rather more cautiously than they'd gone up.

"We're no' wanting a broken ankle," Pat said, "and I'm no wanting to disturb deer. The keeper just might be out having a wee look-see."

In fact they saw nothing other than two hinds, which did not bother to move. "They dinna see well in the dark and the wind's in our favour," was Pat's comment.

"Aye, there's Sandy, and now hae ye the torch?" Pat asked. "For the jump across is a wee thing tricky."

"I canna find it," replied Calum, feeling in his pockets. "I put it down when we replaced the stone and must have forgotten to pick it up. Well anyway we'll not need it now," he added as Sandy switched on the searchlight.

"What did you find?" Annette asked with barely suppressed excitement, as soon as they were underway.

"The gold's there right enough," Calum replied and was just about to describe what they'd found when he was interrupted by Sandy.

"Quick! Up for'ard as far as you can go, while we cover you up. I see that bloody Customs boat – aye, the big one. Right, Blocker, pull that tarpaulin over them and pile the net and those ropes on top. Then bring those lobster pots aft – aye, and pile the boxes there and sit on them, that's fine."

Five minutes later the Customs boat hailed them. "*Maid of Kintail* there, come alongside."

As Sandy edged slowly along their port side, one of the excisemen who knew him well leaned over the rail and had a long hard look at the *Maid*.

"You're out late, Sandy boy. What have you been doing?" he asked. "We've Inspector Sym here and he's wanting to know if you've seen that cousin of yours, Calum Macrae."

"Not for a day or two, no," Sandy replied. "So, what's he been doing that the inspector's wanting him?"

"I'll tell you why we're wanting to see him," Sym said. "We believe there may be a man and a woman with him, French they are, and we want to talk to them about an attempted robbery, aye, and a murder too."

"No' like Calum to be mixed up in that sort of carry-on, and I've certainly heard nothing of it."

"Do you mind if we come aboard and have a look over your boat?" Sym asked.

"As you like," Sandy replied, and when a short ladder was lowered he made fast to it, and the inspector, a constable and the excisemen descended.

"Where did these pots come from?" Sym asked.

"Down Glenelg way. That's what I've been doing. I've been down there to collect them," Sandy replied. "Then we stayed for a bite of supper and syne we've been out to try a line, but nothing doing."

"What's up for'ard then? Mind if we look?" Sandy shrugged, then motioned to the Blocker to get out of the way. The constable pulled away the ropes and nets and the inspector crawled in and shone his torch all round the cabin space.

"Alright, Macrae," he said emerging into the cockpit, "sorry we kept you from your bed. But mind we're looking for Calum, so you'd best keep away from him." All three then went back up the ladder. Sandy cast off and backed away and the big boat moved off slowly in the direction of Mallaig.

"That was gey close," Sandy said and, as the Customs boat picked up speed, he moved for'ard, reached down and lifted a section of flooring and two wet and bedraggled figures emerged from the bilges.

"Here, you'd better get out of those wet things," he said to Annette, and after rummaging in a locker, threw her a pair of trousers and a donkey jacket. "They're a bit smelly but they'll keep the cold out – and dinna worry, we'll look the other way! Calum man, I'm afraid you'll have to stay wet, but that's nothing new to you. Aye, and just tell me how you came to be down there."

"When I heard them come on board," Calum replied, "I thought it was all up. Then I minded you showing me the false bilge and despite the ropes and things, we just managed to shift the planks, wriggle down, and then replace them, when we heard the hell of a commotion."

"Aye, that was them moving the nets and other gear. Luckily the inspector laddie didn't ask about the bilges. It was a nasty moment all the same. Now let's get away back home for a dram and a wee think about what we do next."

CHAPTER 38

THREE O'CLOCK IN THE MORNING IS NEVER the best of times to have to get up, and when your intention is to climb a rugged two thousand foot hill in the chill of a May dawn, the prospect appears even less inviting. So thought Andrew Henderson the following morning, as he dressed quickly and then made his way down to the boot room. There he found Norman Colquhoun, already equipped for the hill, pouring tea from the flask thoughtfully supplied by their host. It was the work of a moment to pour a mug for himself and to drink it while putting on his boots.

"All ready then?" he called, picking up his hat and coat, and walking out to the Range Rover, followed by the brigadier.

It was still pitch dark and all was quiet when, twenty-five minutes later, they parked in the farmyard at Fernfield and set off up the track towards the grave. Norman Colquhoun led them at a brisk pace, and with unerring accuracy, to the rocky face of Sron na h-Iolaire.

"Your man Calum is a local, and therefore hardly likely to come up the way we did," he said, "for even at this hour of the morning he might be recognised in the village or about the farm. Now yesterday afternoon, when they were exploring the grave, I had a little walk round and I noticed the north slope – that's over here" – and he pointed – "is less steep and, what's more, is easily approached from the sea. I think that's the way they'll come."

"If you say so," Andrew replied. "Not having studied the ground, I can't argue."

"Right. Then I suggest you cover the track we came up and I think you'll find good cover up amongst those rocks," Norrie said, pointing to the left. "And for God's sake mind you don't slip, for a broken ankle is the last thing we want. I'll be over there" – and again he pointed – "where there's plenty of dead ground and I can see without being seen."

Having taken up his position, Andrew found he could see little of his immediate surroundings, although far below, across the loch, he noticed an occasional light as some early riser prepared for the coming day. Then suddenly the jagged crests of the Kintail peaks appeared, silhouetted against the pallid glow of the rising sun, and gradually the grey light of dawn crept over the barren waste around him. A fox trotted across his front, paying not the slightest attention to him, and a raven croaked in the crags above him.

Not a sign was there of any human presence, and Andrew found himself dozing off. He had a packet of boiled sweets in his pocket and he tried to keep awake by sucking them, but even with their assistance his attention kept wandering. Then a rattle of falling stones to his left jerked him into full consciousness. A cough was followed by the sound of feet on rock coming directly towards his hiding place. He lay flat on his front, his face hidden in his folded arms, and hoped that in his grey tweed he would be invisible in the dim light.

The steps stopped about a yard in front of him. He risked a peep, not having the faintest idea what he would do if he found Calum looking down at him, but the eyes he saw were large, brown and filled with curiosity, and the muzzle was long and slender with a very black nose. They stared at each other for fully a minute, until suddenly the hind realised something was seriously wrong and, with a sound between a grunt and a cough, gathered up her calf and vanished round the face of the cliff above the grave.

It was now almost full daylight and as there was still no sign of the other party, Andrew decided there was no point in hanging about, so got up from his hiding place to see Norman Colquhoun walking up the hill to his right.

"I don't think they'll come now," Norrie said when Andrew joined him, "and what worries me is that I think we've been outmanoeuvred. I believe they thought you might have heard their plan, so they came last evening."

"I think that's exactly what they did," Andrew, who was poking about in a tussock, said. "Look at this." He bent down and picked up a torch.

"Pretty conclusive," Norrie agreed, "so now what do we do? I admit I'm not a helicopter pilot but I've been in a great many choppers, and I believe you could land one on this flat bit here, so I think we must work on that assumption."

"Yes, I'm sure we must," Andrew agreed, "so the first thing is to get back to the castle and do some telephoning."

They were halfway down the track to the farm when there was the sound of an engine and Jock and the Argo came over the ridge below them.

"Jump in," he cried, pulling up beside them. "I just thought you might be up here and wanting a lift. Aye, ye'll no have seen them, for I heard from the Customs that that cousin o' Calum's from Kishorn way had been out in the Sound last night. Na, na they didna see Calum or the Frenchies but I'm betting they'd been up here. Now hold on, for we canna turn here. I'll just go up a wee bit and then cross country. Great machine for the cross country, this is!"

Down at the steading they found Charlie Noble, to whom they explained what had happened that morning and when he asked what their next move would be, Andrew said he would ring when they knew their plans.

"And thanks for all your help," he added, "and for the free ride from Jock! But now we'd better get back to Knockbain, for there's a lot to be done."

It was just after seven thirty when they parked the Range Rover in the courtyard of the castle, to be greeted by Jenny standing by the gunroom door and wanting to know how they'd got on.

"Not very well! If you want the truth, we were had for mugs," Andrew said, taking off his cap and throwing it and his coat into a corner and bending down to untie his boots. When Jenny persisted in her questioning, he stood up, kicked the boots aside and replied in a rather petulant voice: "Listen, darling, I'm tired, hungry and rather cold and I'm sure Norrie is too. I therefore suggest we have a bath and shave and then we'll tell you everything at breakfast." And he stumped off up the stairs.

"Don't worry about him," laughed the brigadier, also heading for the stairs. "He'll be all right when he's had a cup of coffee."

Over breakfast Andrew continued to sulk, so it was Norman Colquhoun who described their abortive vigil on the hill, giving it as his opinion that it was far from a wasted operation.

"Poor old Andrew thinks it was, because all he had was a close encounter with a hind and calf."

"But are you sure they were there the previous evening? Couldn't they just have given the whole thing a miss?" General Macdonald said.

"They were there all right," Andrew said with a wry smile. "Proving it was my only contribution. I found a torch in the grass which could only have been there a few hours, for it was in full working order."

"So what now? Can they land their machine up there?" the general asked.

The two retired officers then decided that a full appreciation of the situation was called for, and when Norrie gave it as his opinion that the helicopter could land by the grave, the general suggested that that would be the place to catch them red-handed. The brigadier countered by explaining the difficulties of getting a sufficient force up the hill and achieving surprise. Without these two essentials, he felt, the whole crew might escape, never to be found.

"The helicopter vanished the other day, so could do so again," he said, "and don't forget we're not just trying to save our treasure. We must remember the police are dealing with a murder investigation, to say nothing of the fact that every banker and politician in Europe now seems to have an interest. No, we must not risk a fiasco."

"I agree," said Andrew, "and now I must use the telephone. Is your contraption still working, Norrie?" When the brigadier nodded, he walked towards the door saying, "I made some plans last night and I don't think they've been altered by this morning's events. I'll tell you about them when I come back."

It was getting on for two o'clock when the *Maid of Kintail* reached the pier on the Applecross shore, and a fine rain was starting to fall.

"You'll be trying to go back up now, Calum, will you?" Sandy asked. "With this rain the track will no' be very safe in the dark. We've plenty of beds here." And he turned to Annette and smiled. "I can even let you have one of Cathy's nighties."

"Merci, but that will not be necessary," she replied. "But I would like to go to bed now. I'm not used to these late-night adventures. Cuddling up with Calum in that smelly water to avoid les flics – no, that's not for me."

"Aye, well, I'll show you upstairs and I hope you'll be comfortable. You're sure you'll not take a dram? No? Well okay. You'll find the bottle and glasses in the usual place, boys, and I'll join you directly."

"Well, here's tae us, wha's wi' us?" said Calum, giving the old Scottish toast as Sandy came back into the room. "And I'm telling you it's not 'mony the few', it's two too many."

"How do you mean?" Sandy asked.

"This evening went better than I thought. There's no doubt we can land up there," Calum replied, "so we can load the gold and get it to Inverdoran and be away on the *Ariadne* easy enough. It's the police I'm worried about. Yon bloody Frenchie we've left at the bothy, he's wanted for murder and herself for an accessory. The police are closer to us than you might think. Why else was that Sym on the Customs boat?"

"What'ye going to do then?" Pat the Blocker asked. "I'm no' that keen on being involved in murder, and you heard the warning we had from Sym."

"We'll have to see in the morning," Calum said. "She told me yesterday that she wants to get the gold to the *Ariadne* and then tranship it somewhere. She was wanting to know all about the *Ariadne* and asked me a lot of questions. Then while I was out about the farm she spent a long time on the telephone. What with everything else, I never had time to ask what was going on. I have a feeling though that Jakie may know something. I wish we had him here, but it's a bit late now."

"Aye, and I'm for my bed," Sandy agreed. "See you the morn."

The next morning, despite the lateness of the night before, they were all about at an early hour. Annette, who was sitting at the kitchen table drinking coffee, had just announced that she had a plan to put to them, when there was a commotion at the back door and a squat, black-bearded figure in dripping oilskins entered the room.

"Ach, it's a dirty morn and it'll get worse yet," the figure said, struggling out of his soaking coat.

"Man, I'm glad to see you," Calum said. "But how did you come here?"

"I was about Arnisdale yesterday afternoon to collect the messages," Jakie replied, "when the keeper mentioned he would be going to Kyle the morn. Would I cadge a lift? says I. Man, I'd be glad o' your company, says he. So I stays the night and we drive over early. Then I got a lad going to Kishorn to put me over, ye see I was thinking you might want a word wi' me."

"You were right there, boy," said Calum and then remembering himself, he introduced Annette.

"Aye, I've heard of her. There was a radio message mentioning her name," Jakie said, then added, "Pleased to meet you I'm sure."

Annette acknowledged the greeting and then suggested that they should get on and consider her plan for removing the gold from the grave and getting it out of the country. Jakie pointed out that he had to be back in Kyle by one and Calum added that they should not be too much longer before returning to the bothy.

"That's good then," Annette said, "so here's what I propose." And she proceeded to describe in detail what she wanted done over the following twenty-four hours.

The plan was simple and was quickly agreed in principle. However, deciding each individual's part took more time, but by eleven o'clock everything was agreed, except for the matter of payment, and it was Sandy who put the question.

"Now this is all verra fine," he said, "but as far as I can see, you and Calum and the Frenchie maybe will be away off with the treasure. So what's in it for us?" There were murmurs of agreement from round the table.

"That's one of the things I arranged yesterday," Annette replied. "In a week's time, there's a man in Inverness will have received an amount in sterling equivalent to the value of a seven-pound gold bar for each of the three of you. I suggest he contacts Sandy and arranges how to get it to you."

"Sure, that'll be best," Sandy said and the other two nodded, "but just how much might it be?"

"Ah, my friends that will depend on a lot of things," was Annette's cautious answer, "but I believe you might each be richer by some twenty thousand pounds. It's good, n'est-ce pas?" The quick gasps of astonishment convinced her that it was indeed acceptable.

"You are sure now that this other boat will be there to meet *Ariadne*?" Calum asked.

"But yes," she replied, "I have told you already that that too was fixed on the telephone. It is indeed fortunate that the French Fishery Research ship is in Ireland and that it is often used for things other than looking for little fishes! And indeed that the captain owes me a favour." And while she was saying all this she was also thinking to herself how useful it could be that the ship had a helicopter pad.

"Then let's hope he keeps to it," Calum said, moving towards the door. "Come on, Sandy, let's have a look at the weather, for we'll be needing to get moving."

"It's moderating down here, so we'd best get away, Jakie," Sandy said when they came back in. "It does'na look so good up the hill, but I believe it'll clear by evening. Now a quick dram to wish us luck!"

So another dram was taken. Whisky for the boys and for Annette, a glass of the brandy that was kept for Sandy's mother. Then with handshakes all round, Sandy and Jakie departed for Kyle in an inflatable and Calum and Annette mounted the bike.

After the first few hundred yards up the brae, Annette, who had thought that nothing could have been worse than their journey down, decided that she was wrong. For they were now into low cloud and a persistent drizzle, and even with the waterproof and baseball cap she'd borrowed from Sandy, she was soon soaked through. On the track the going was not too bad, but by the time they turned off up the burn, the visibility had deteriorated further and even Calum, with all his experience, had difficulty in finding his way.

Then, at the bottom of a steep slope, their whole venture nearly terminated. Finding the path, such as it was, blocked by a boulder Calum, misjudging his position because of the mist, swerved to the left onto what he thought was a grassy flat, but which turned out to be a narrow ledge that sloped down to an area of pools and peat hags. Once off the ledge, the bike started to tilt as it slid across the slope. Annette, whose position was already somewhat insecure, was thrown off, and rolled down the hill into a shallow pool. Calum managed to straighten the machine but skidded on the wet grass and finished up with the front wheels stuck in a peat hag.

He got off and stood swearing and looking at the quad gradually sinking deeper into the quaking brown mud. Then, pulling himself together, he turned to see Annette crawling out of the pool on hands and knees. Helping her to her feet, he asked if she was hurt and she looked at him as only a Frenchwoman can.

"Non, my body is not hurt, my spirit is not hurt, but I am wet, cold and my clothes are ruined," she replied. "And now could you tell me – how are we going to get home?"

"Ach, we'll no get that bloody thing out wi'out a tow and as the Argo's down at the farm, we'll have to walk. Don't worry, it's only just over a mile from here," he said, and was rewarded with a vicious Gallic scowl.

"And now," she said when they eventually arrived at the bothy, "just tell me how I'm going to get dry."

CHAPTER 39

IT WAS SOME TWO HOURS AFTER HE left the rest of the party that Andrew returned to the drawing room to find Jenny alone, reading a magazine.

"You've been a long time," she said, giving him a faintly disapproving look. "The others all got bored with waiting for you. Janet's gone off to a meeting somewhere – something to do with local wifies, whatever that means. That woman seems to spend her life at meetings."

"Occupational hazard of being a laird's wife," Andrew replied, then added with a smile, "Just you wait, you may find yourself doing it one day. Anyway, from what I remember of your sister-in-law, it seemed much the same in South Africa. And what about the others – where are they, because I need to see them?"

"Oh! I suppose you don't need to see me. I know, I know – you don't need to tell me, it's the men you want to see and discuss all your secrets," Jenny said. "Well, they've gone to look at something on the river and said they'd be back by eleven. Just for a change, therefore, while we wait, you can tell me a little about what you're planning. I am, after all, probably going to be your wife."

Andrew, like all good executives, knew when he was beaten and so spent the next fifteen minutes giving Jenny an outline of what was going to happen in the next twenty-four hours. Then, before he'd quite finished, there was a noise of footsteps from the gunroom passage and the two soldiers appeared.

"Tom's been showing me his new fancy fish ladder. Very interesting. Given me something to think about," Norman Colquhoun said. "Now what about you, young Andrew? Got some orders for us, have you? Hope so, for you've been long enough on the telephone."

"Yes, I have," Andrew replied, "so sit yourselves down and listen carefully. The Bourbon treasure seems now to be a matter of significant interest to a variety of authorities and a whole gaggle of people are on their way here."

"And knowing 'authorities', I suppose I'm going to have to put them up," said Tom Macdonald in a resigned voice.

"Don't worry, Tom, they flew up this morning and will be based in Inverness," Andrew said with a laugh. "I understand there's a chap from the Foreign Office and another from the Bank and also a policeman from some group that deals with crimes involving precious metals. They are on their way over now and meeting Charlie Noble and his lawyer at twelve. As the stuff is on his ground, they have to sort out what rights, if any, he has to it, and also formalise the position regarding access."

"What about us?" Jenny asked.

"You and Norrie are to be at the farm at one, where you will be joined by a couple of chaps from some Mountain Warfare Unit who are currently testing equipment on Skye. They are bringing some new vehicle which will take you up to the grave."

"Who's 'we'?" asked Norrie. "And, more specifically, what is our job? Jenny's and mine, that is."

"The object of the exercise is to assess the amount and value of this gold treasure and also what will be required to bring it down. Specifically, to use your phrase, you and Jenny are there to represent the Saddler family. As to who goes up, I'm not sure, but I would think both of you, Charlie, the bank chap and the policeman and, of course, the two soldiers. Oh yes, and when you come down – and you're to be off the hill by five thirty – two policemen will be left to guard the site."

"What will you be doing?" Jenny asked. "Something far more exciting I expect – and probably dangerous."

"Well, I don't know about that," Andrew replied. "Your part, as I've just explained, is concerned with the treasure. My part is concerned with what happens to Annette and her friends. This is mainly a matter for the police, but I feel I have a responsibility to see that she is safely put away and I have been invited to go along as an observer."

"To observe what, and where?" Tom Macdonald asked.

"It seems," Andrew replied, "that you and Norrie made a pretty good appreciation. When the possibility of a helicopter attempt on the treasure was put to the Mountain Warfare boys, they agreed with you that the grave was not the place to attempt an arrest. We are therefore gambling on the fact that they will make an attempt tonight and that we know what they will do next and where they will do it. That is where I will be. And Tom, I have not included you in any of this. I hope that was right."

"Absolutely," the general replied, "for I've already told the Chief Constable that I do not want to be involved, at least not visibly so. Yes, I talked to him yesterday as requested, and some of the plans described this morning are based on my advice."

At that moment the butler appeared at the door. "Excuse me, General," he said, "there is a police car outside and they are asking for Mr Henderson."

"That's right, Tom," Andrew said. "They are taking me to Glenelg, where I'm going for a little voyage on a Customs launch." Then to the butler he said, "Tell them I'll be with them in a moment, as soon as I've got my things." And he looked round the group and added, "Here's good luck to us all."

Five minutes later he was down at the front door carrying an anorak and a small canvas bag, when Jenny came rushing out of the drawing room.

"Take care, darling," she cried. "I don't know what you're really up to, but just remember I've only got one of you." And she reached up and kissed his lips and then stood watching as the car vanished down the drive.

Just after half past midday, Norman and Jenny, in the Range Rover, drove over the Pass and down to the road junction at the head of the loch. There, parked in a lay-by, was an army truck and trailer, its load securely covered by a green canvas sheet, and standing by the truck were two soldiers studying a map. Norrie stopped, wound down the window and asked if he could help.

One of the two, a captain, walked over and, after a quick glance at the brigadier, saluted. "I'm sure you could, sir," he said. "We're looking for a farm called Fernfield, Major Noble's place."

"I thought you might be," Norrie said. "We're going there too, so follow us. Incidentally I see you're a Lomond, my old regiment."

"Yes, sir, I'm Edward Laurie..." and he hesitated before continuing, "and you are Brigadier Colquhoun, I'm sure. You interviewed me at Sandhurst when you were the Colonel."

"Did I? I'm afraid I've forgotten, but then one sees so many."

"Indeed, sir." Then he turned to the other man. "Staff, this is Brigadier Colquhoun. Staff Sergeant Jones, sir, our REME expert on mountain vehicles."

Jones saluted and indicated, in a strong Welsh accent, that he was pleased to meet the senior officer.

Norrie glanced at the dashboard clock. "We'd better get a move on if we're going to be there at one. Follow me."

There was no one except Jock in the farmyard but he said the major had just rung through to say they were on their way.

"I should go ahead and unload," Norrie said. "I'm sure Jock will give you a hand. He'll also give you the low down on the geography of the place."

Five minutes later Charlie Noble drove into the square followed by another Land Rover with a policeman at the wheel. By the time all the introductions had been effected, Jones was reversing an unusual-looking tracked vehicle off the trailer.

At a nod from the brigadier, who had been unanimously appointed leader, Captain Laurie explained that it had been developed as a load and personnel carrier specially for mountain and moorland use.

"This one has a windscreen and side windows," he said, "but with the glass removed and replaced by steel plates it is an effective armoured personnel carrier, but lighter and more easily manoeuvred than the usual version."

"How many can you take?" Norrie asked. "Eight – splendid, then we can all go up. Jock's going to bring on the other two policemen in the Argo, isn't he, Charlie?" The major nodded. "Right, so let's go."

Very soon after they reached the grave, and while Norrie was explaining some of the background to the discovery of the treasure to the civil servants, the Argo arrived with Jock and the two policemen and a selection of tools. Under the direction of Jock, who'd done the original excavation, the policemen and soldiers soon had the stone lifted and the top layer of gold exposed.

"Well, there you are, gentlemen. So what next, Major?" Jock said to the laird.

Charlie looked at Norrie, who looked at the man from the Bank. "How do you want to play this?" he asked.

"I think we'd better get it all out," was the reply, "or at least get it so we can see what there is there."

It took them two hours to empty the grave, and the contents produced one or two surprises. First there were two layers of gold bars and underneath them three large metal boxes. These were padlocked, but one of the padlocks had rusted through, and when opened, the box was found to contain gold coins, packed in orderly rows three deep.

"Time's getting on," the man from the bank, whose name was Taylor, said, "so I think we'd better leave the other two padlocks, but I'd like to replace the broken one and seal it." He turned to the Foreign Office representative. "Do you agree, Peter?"

"Yes," he replied, and the banker turned to the police sergeant.

"You've got the necessary kit, haven't you, Sergeant Alexander?" he said, and the policeman proceeded to lock and seal the box.

While everything was put back into the grave, Taylor asked Captain Laurie how easy it was going to be to get the contents of the grave off the hill and was told that it could probably be done in one journey.

"It depends on how heavy those gold bars are. If they are very heavy it might be better to make two journeys," Laurie said.

Taylor turned to Sergeant Alexander. "Two things, Sergeant," he said. "First and most important, did we get an inventory of everything we saw? Because I'll need to give everyone copies. Secondly, when we get the stuff down we'll need to transfer it to a Bank van, and we'll need a police escort."

"Aye, sir," the sergeant replied. "I've a full inventory."

"And so have I," said Jenny, interrupting him.

"And, sir," the sergeant went on, "the van's your business, but as soon as you're ready I will arrange the escort."

"And what about you, Captain Laurie, are you going back tonight?" Taylor asked.

"Yes, sir, they're laying on a special ferry for us," he replied, "but I'm to tell you that we'll be back whenever you need us. Just give us twenty-four hours' notice."

"Is that everything then?" the brigadier said, looking round the group. "So let's get back in the vehicle. The sooner we're away the better."

Then, while the rest were climbing on board, he turned to the two men who were to remain on guard and asked if they had everything they needed.

"Aye, thank you, sir. We've each got a piece bag and flask – and we've a sleeping bag. There'll always be one of us on duty, but the other will maybe get a wee bit rest."

As they drove over the Pass on their way back to the castle, Jenny turned to her companion.

"That was not the most exciting afternoon I've ever spent," she said. "Interesting to see all the gold though. How much do you suppose the whole lot's worth?"

"Hard to say," Norrie replied, "but it'll be millions rather than thousands – two or three million maybe for a guess."

"I wonder, will we get any of it?" And she gazed out of the window, a wistful look in her eyes. Then she turned back to look at Norrie and said, "I wish I knew what Andrew is doing. Do you know, Norrie? If you do, please tell me, is whatever it is dangerous?"

"Quite honestly I know little more than you," he replied. "You heard him say he hopes to be with the police when they arrest Annette and company. They seem to think they know where they are making for. As to danger – well, as always that depends on how the enemy reacts. Sorry to be such cold comfort" – he reached over and patted her hand – "but from what I know of Andrew, which is quite a lot, he's not likely to allow himself, or those with him, to come to much harm. As a young platoon commander in Borneo – that was just before he was seconded to my undercover operation – he led a patrol into the jungle to rescue the remnants of another platoon which had been badly shot up by insurgents. This he did, and sent the survivors back with his sergeant. He and a corporal stayed behind with a wounded soldier while they waited for a helicopter. Well, the soldier died and the helicopter crashed and they found themselves under attack from another rebel group. They managed to escape, but they were two weeks in the jungle before they got back to their battalion. Oh, young Andrew is well able to look after himself."

CHAPTER 40

In the police car that collected him, in addition to the driver, Andrew found Inspector Sym and a sergeant whom he had not seen before. On leaving the castle they drove down the glen to the village, and then along the coast for a couple of miles, before finally stopping at a secluded bay where a blue and white launch lay at anchor.

Inspector Sym led the way down an overgrown track at the bottom of which were the remains of a boathouse and a ramshackle wooden pier, tied up to which was an inflatable dinghy. As they approached the boathouse a man emerged from the shelter of the bushes.

"Just the three of you, is it, Inspector? Fine then, we'll manage with only the one journey," he said. "Just mind as you come on board; the pier's not that safe."

"It's a handy place this," the inspector said as they raced across the bay towards the launch, "and we thought it best to go on board where you and I are less likely to be seen. These Macraes have a fine intelligence network, and news of Inspector Sym and a stranger boarding a Customs boat at the Kyle would not be long in reaching them."

Once on the launch, which Andrew observed was called the *Kittiwake*, he was introduced first to the Senior Customs Officer, Mr Paterson, then to the other two members of the crew, and finally to a very sloppy springer spaniel.

"Okay, boys," Paterson said, "get the dinghy up and then we'll be off. Aye, head for Eilean Jarmain first and then we'll see how the time's going; and now if you gentlemen will come down below, I'll tell you what we're proposing."

"But first I was thinking you may not have eaten," Paterson continued, once they were seated in the cabin, "so I've got some tea, coffee and sandwiches here. Help yourselves.

"As I said, at the moment we're heading towards Skye, partly because that would be our usual course and partly to kill time. At about three we'll turn back and enter Loch Hourn and aim to be around Inverdoran just after four. I'm banking on *Ariadne* being alongside the pier. So with you boys out of sight, we'll tie up on the other side and I'll walk over to have a wee chat with the skipper."

"What about radio?" Sym asked. "And won't the skipper – Jakie, isn't it? – be suspicious?"

"I doubt it; we generally look him up every two or three weeks so he's no cause to be suspicious, and anyway, if what I've been told is true he's not likely to try the radio. Macrae only has radio at Clovulin and in the helicopter and it seems unlikely he'll be on either set at four thirty. Anyway, we'll have to risk it."

At the same time as the *Kittiwake* was making her way down the Sound of Sleat, an ex-army landing craft with two police Land Rovers onboard was heading for a slipway on the south side of the Knoydart peninsula.

Once there, and while the vehicles were being driven ashore, Sergeant Matheson, who was in charge of the operation, walked across the road to the Post Office, where he found the factor for that part of the estate with which they were concerned.

"All well?" he asked.

"Uh uh, it's working out fine for you," the factor replied. "As I expected, the laird went south last evening and I've a grand story to account for your presence. You see, everyone knows there's been trouble with sheep stealing, and cattle too, up about the head of the loch. So, once the laird had left, I put it about that there would be some police activity today on the other side of the high hills."

"And what about the boat?"

"*Ariadne*'s at the pier right enough. The skipper's been away, but Big John's just reported that he came across from Arnisdale half an hour ago. I suggest you go across by the estate road so you'll miss the crofts and John'll meet you and take you down to the shore. It's tricky there, for there's not much of a track. Okay? Well, take care then."

It took them nearly an hour to cover the six miles across to the other side. The track, never very good, had suffered badly both during the previous winter and in the recent heavy rains, and at one place, where a bridge had been washed away, they had to make a perilous detour via a rocky ford.

Then, as they negotiated the final descent towards the shore, a figure emerged from the trees by the side of the path. John Maclennan, the head stalker, was a big man in every way, not much given to talking, but with a fund of West Coast stories when he chose to tell them.

"Aye, Bill, so you're here," he said, getting in beside Matheson, who happened to be his brother-in-law, and then relapsing into silence and remaining so except for occasional directions, until they were just short of the crest of a ridge.

"Turn off now," he said, pointing to a clump of alders twenty yards away to the right. "Aye, you're alright, the ground's quite hard. You'd best stop here for a bit, for the pier's two hundred yards down from the crest wi' no cover. Na, na you're fine here, Jakie'll not come this way. Anyways he's no phone, so he'll not know what's happening."

"Well then, we'll just bide here till we see the launch, and that'll not be for an hour yet," Matheson said.

At about five o'clock the *Kittiwake* rounded a projecting headland and there, dead ahead, Andrew saw the anchorage of Inverdoran. A broad sweep of shingle was backed at one end by a rough meadow, and at the other by a rocky incline. In between was a steep grass-covered slope, and Andrew could see a track leading down past a building and onto the pier. Behind the building, at the bottom of the track, was a small wood.

Alongside the pier was a luxurious-looking motor yacht with a high bridge and spacious afterdeck. That was all Andrew had time to see before he and the two policemen were hustled below decks.

All appeared quiet onboard *Ariadne* until one of the Customs men jumped ashore with a rope and started to make fast to a bollard, when a man appeared from below and asked what they were doing.

"Just a wee visit, Jakie, and Mr Paterson will be across to see you in a minute."

"That's it, Jakie, just a wee visit," said Paterson, walking over to *Ariadne* and looking up at the skipper, "but I'd just like to come on board and discuss what you were doing the week before last. You and Mr Macrae were away for three days and I'd like to know where you went."

"Aye well, come on then," said the skipper somewhat grudgingly, and Paterson swung himself aboard followed by the other man. Jakie led the way into the cockpit and Paterson asked to see the log. While Jakie fetched this, the other man went down and into the saloon.

"Here, Joe, come and look at this," he shouted up to Paterson. "Aye, and bring Jakie. I think he's a bit of explaining to do."

Before Paterson could move, he was hurled across the table and Jakie took the companionway in one bound and had an arm round the man's neck and was squeezing the breath out of him.

"Ye've no right to be pokin' about down here, you and your bloody boss!" he screamed.

At that moment there was the sound of a whistle and Sym and his sergeant ran from the launch. "Down below!" the partially winded Paterson gasped, but the sergeant was already in the saloon to see Jakie opening a drawer.

"Put that away, you stupid bugger," he yelled and executed a forward roll over the table, his feet hitting Jakie's face and then pinning him against the bar. The skipper tried to get his arm down to aim the pistol, but the sergeant knocked it aside and the bullet smashed a porthole.

"Okay, I've got him," Sym said, running round the table and grabbing Jakie's wrist, forcing him to drop the gun.

"Now what the hell was all that about?" Sym asked the handcuffed Jakie as they hauled him up the ladder and into the cockpit.

"Aw, nothing. I just lost ma rag, that's all," Jakie replied, looking out over the water and avoiding Sym's eye.

"Come, man, you don't go shooting off pistols just because you've lost your rag," Sym said, but before the man could reply there was a sound of running feet and Sergeant Matheson vaulted over the rail onto the after-deck.

"We heard a shot and wondered what the hell was happening," he gasped, standing with his Heckler and Koch at the ready.

"It's okay, you can put that down," Sym said, then nodding towards the Customs Officer added, "That man went down into the saloon and Jakie here went off his head."

"Yes, Jimmy, what happened down there? Did you see anything suspicious?" Paterson asked.

"Not really," the man replied. "There were some boxes piled over by the bar. Aye, and the door at the far end on the left was locked. Then Jakie had me round the throat."

Matheson, who had been down to have a look in the saloon, reappeared in the cockpit saying, "I don't like the look of it. There's a wire coming from one of the boxes."

"We'd best get Moll then – that's the dog," Paterson said. "Drugs are really her thing, but she'll do explosives too, and that's what it sounds like we've got here." And he went off to fetch her.

Jakie, meanwhile, had relapsed into silence, replying to Sym's questions only with a surly glance. Deciding they were wasting time and having ascertained that one of the Land Rovers was equipped to take prisoners, Sym ordered him to be taken away and locked up.

"We'll deal with him later," he said, and turned to Paterson, who had returned with Moll. "So what's your dog going to tell us?" Moll looked at him and wagged her tail. Jimmy then took her down to the saloon, followed by Paterson and Sym.

Once let off the lead, the dog wandered round the cabin sniffing every piece of furniture and climbing onto the benches to investigate the porthole curtains, but showed no interest in any of it until she reached the polished mahogany bar at the far end. This she investigated carefully, her tail wagging enthusiastically. She then turned her attention to three cardboard boxes which someone had tried, not very effectively, to hide behind the bar. The tail wagging increased, then she sat back on her haunches and gave a sharp bark.

"There's something there, but I wouldn't care to say what," Paterson remarked.

"Just put her on the lead, while I have a look," Sym said. He then produced a torch and, crouching down, looked cautiously at the empty space under the bar. After that, he made a detailed examination of the boxes, but taking care not to touch them. Finally he stood up, and seeing Moll trying to scrabble at the door and squeaking with excitement, he turned to Paterson.

"Something through there, do you think?" he asked.

"Certainly looks like it," Paterson replied. "Do you want to have a look?"

"Definitely not, and we'd better evacuate *Ariadne* double quick," Sym said, urging Paterson and the dog up the steps. "There are wires trailing from one of the boxes but I can't see where they go. It looks like explosives, but what they are intended for I don't know. Scuttling her possibly, in the event of a disaster. But we can't discount a booby trap, maybe to stop us searching the rest of the cabins. Anyway, the only safe course is evacuation. We'll have to leave her tied up at the pier, but I suggest you move out as soon as possible."

Realising that there was not much he could do, Andrew had remained on board *Kittiwake* when the others went across to the yacht. Now, however, deciding that he'd better find out what had happened, he walked over to talk to Sym, who had just emerged from the cockpit.

"We had quite a bit of excitement," the inspector said, and told him what had happened.

"So you've got the skipper and you say the yacht's booby-trapped?" Andrew said, then, half to himself, he added, "Now just what is she planning? I wonder, could it be... Yes, I believe it could, for she's quite capable of it."

"What's that you're saying?" Sym asked, but Andrew decided to keep his thoughts to himself.

"It was nothing. I was just trying to remember if Mrs Barry had said anything that could help us, but I don't think she did," he replied. Then changing tack, he asked, "So what are you proposing to do next?"

By now there was quite a group standing around on the pier. Sym was checking with Matheson about the prisoner and asking how many men he had in his group. Paterson, having sent Jimmy and the dog back to the *Kittiwake* with instructions to prepare for immediate departure, was standing waiting for Sym to give his instructions, as was Andrew.

They did not have long to wait, for with a sign of acknowledgement, Sergeant Matheson set off up the track to where he'd left his vehicles, and the inspector turned to the others.

"Okay, here's what we'll do," he said. "Matheson has got two Land Rovers with five men and another sergeant. That sergeant and one man will take the prisoner back to the other side and wait there. You" – and here he turned to his sergeant – "will take one of the men and go with Mr Paterson." Then to Paterson he said, "Joe, it would be gey helpful if you were to lie off somewhere and prevent anyone coming up the loch. These boys will give you any help you need. Are you happy with that?" And after a few details had been sorted out, Paterson agreed to the plan.

By that time Matheson had brought the Land Rover with the rest of his men to the building at the foot of the track, where he parked it, before joining the group on the pier.

"Yes, Swanson will be here in a moment," he said in response to a question from Sym and, almost immediately, a constable came running past them down the pier and joined Paterson and the sergeant onboard the *Kittiwake*. The engines started and Andrew helpfully cast off the mooring ropes and the launch moved out into the loch.

"It's now eight fifteen," Sym said, "and I think we've agreed that the helicopter, assuming it comes, will not be here much before midnight. I suggest, therefore, that we have something to eat, then make our dispositions and await events. If we're lucky we may get some information from those boys on the hill."

CHAPTER 41

A T THE BOTHY IN THE APPLECROSS HILLS Calum and Jean were just finishing loading the helicopter when Annette, who had finally been able to change back into her own dry clothes, looked out of the door.

"It's nearly nine, Calum," she remarked. "Oughtn't we to be moving?"

He looked at his watch. "No great hurry," he said. "The boys will not be up there for another fifteen minutes and we don't want to be in before them. It'll only take us ten minutes once we're airborne, but we might as well get the cover off. Come on then, Jean, lend a hand."

As soon as the cover had been rolled back into its hiding place up the hill and the frame had been lowered and stowed, Calum went back into the bothy, telling Jean to get himself into the back seat of the helicopter. In the main room he found Annette, who had her back to him, pulling up her trousers and fastening the belt.

"Got a problem?" he enquired of a guilty-looking Annette.

"That is not a question you ask a lady in such circumstances," she replied furiously, and picking up her shoulder bag she stormed out of the building and got into the helicopter. Calum, after a quick look round, locked the door and followed her into the cockpit.

The rotor began turning slowly, then the engine sprang into life, and two minutes later they were rising gently above the scree.

Even though it was a reasonably fine evening, Sandy and Pat the Blocker had endured a cold, wet crossing in the inflatable dinghy, which was now pulled up and secured on the beach below Sron na h-Iolaire.

340

"Ready? It should be about dark enough when we get to the top," Pat said, and they set off up the hill. Just short of the final ridge before the grave, Pat stopped and motioned them to get down.

"D'ye hear them?" he whispered. "They'll be over by the big rock. We'll need to get round the back. Follow me, keep flat on yer belly and make sure the balaclava covers yer face."

It was a long, uncomfortable crawl, for they had to go down and then up again to get to the back of the rock, and they could not even risk hands and knees. There was too the constant fear of dislodging a shower of stones. It was also becoming increasingly dark and a thin drizzle was falling, so that by the time Pat pulled himself onto the narrow shelf at the base of the rock they could see very little. He got to his feet, and followed by Sandy, edged forward until, in the surrounding gloom, he could just make out the two men standing by the grave.

"Right then, Wullie," one of them said, "you'll take the first shift, so I'll get a wee bit rest, if that's possible in this weather." And he turned and started to walk away.

"Na, na, ye'll do no' such thing," Pat's voice came out of the darkness. "Ye'll just stand quite still and put yer hands up. Na, quite still, I said."

There was a crack, and a stone at the feet of the man who had spoken shattered into fragments. He stopped, and both of them raised their hands.

Pat's voice came again from the darkness. "Wi' one hand throw the handcuffs down behind, then both hands behind yer back." It took Sandy barely thirty seconds to handcuff both men. Then, from his pocket he took two canvas hoods, slipped them over the men's heads and secured them round the neck, leaving just enough room for air.

"Walk forward." The men stumbled some thirty paces down the hill. "Now stop and lie down." Sandy tied their ankles together and to each other. "Now dinna move or ye'll fall two hundred feet over the cliff – or maybe the chopper will land on top o' ye!"

Three minutes later they heard the beat of the rotor blades and the helicopter came over the crest of the hill above them and settled gently in the open space beside the grave.

As soon as the blades stopped rotating, Sandy ran forward and squeezed into the cabin beside Calum.

"Aye, they're safely tied up, and no, they didn'a see us," he said. "They just heard Blocker's voice, but it's no matter for I had a look at their IDs. They're from away about Aviemore, so they'd not know any of us. Now let's have the tools and we'll get the grave open."

This was no easy task in the dark and with the weather worsening and, after two hours' hard slog, they'd only loaded a little under half the gold bars. Calum, who'd been packing the bars so as to distribute the load evenly, beckoned Annette over to the plane.

"We've nearly enough weight," he said, "and I don't like the look of the weather. I'll give you another ten minutes, then we must go. Also I don't like the fact that we have na heard from Jakie. He should have come on the blower by now."

"Another ten minutes then," Annette said. "Me, I'm beginning to think we've been here long enough. Apart from the police perhaps coming, I've had enough of this weather."

Jock had meant to spend the afternoon and evening about the farm and at his cottage in case he was needed for anything. Unfortunately, however, because of the absence of a neighbouring keeper, he had been called away by the police to deal with three hinds, badly injured in a traffic accident some ten miles away. This took longer than he expected, for although he put all three animals out of their misery as soon as he arrived, there was difficulty in releasing one of the carcasses. The Fire Service had to bring in heavy lifting gear to move the vehicle and then had to get out the body of the driver, so it was nearly three hours before Jock had all three animals in the back of the Land Rover.

"Unless you'll be wanting these, I'll dispose of them for you," he said to the sergeant in charge, "and unless there's anything else, I'll be on my way."

"No, Jock, you deal with them and if we need you we know how to find you, and thanks for your help."

It was well after ten when he got back to the cottage and asked his wife if there had been any reports of activity up the hill.

"I've heard nothing except mebbe an engine out over the loch, but it's hard to tell wi' the wind the way it is, and no one's telephoned or anything," she said. "And here, Jock, here's a cup of tea and you must have something to eat."

"Aye, lassie, but be quick, for I'm thinking I'd better have a look up the hill. I don't like that bit about an engine over the loch and it's queer I've heard nothing from those policemen." Then while he ate, he tried to raise them on the radio. "Not a thing on the poacher's frequency. In fact it sounds as though they're no' switched on."

Then, with his wife's "Take care" ringing in his ears, he set off up the hill in the Argocat.

"What's that?" Calum cried, as the sound of an engine echoed up the hill.

"Sounds like an Argo," Sandy said. "Hell, do you think the police are coming?"

"Could be. Anyway, whatever it is, I think we should be away soonest," Calum replied. "You boys get away down the hill, for we're no' wanting you to be seen. The rest of you, in the chopper. Leave the grave, it's not our worry now!"

"Right, belt up," he shouted and started the engine and switched on the landing lights. "I'll have to risk them while we take off. I canna see a thing in this mist." Then, as Jock cleared the last rise, he saw the helicopter lift over the top of Sron na h-Iolaire and drop steeply down the other side towards the dark waters of the Sound.

He cut the Argo's engine and taking a powerful torch studied the grave. Always sensitive to unusual sounds, particularly at night, he thought he heard a scrabbling down the hill to his right and shone the torch there.

"Well, boys, you've a wee problem there," he said to the two policemen. "Now I'm going to free your legs, but don't try to get up until I tell you." And he cut the ropes. "Now one at a time, on your feet and turn round. Fine, and now let's have the gags off." He removed the hoods. "Let's come up to the grave now, and I wouldn't look where you were lying until daylight, and even then it'll scare you!"

Luckily one of the men had a spare key for the handcuffs strapped to his ankle, for Sandy had thrown the original one away.

"Always keep a hidden spare," he said as Jock freed them both.

"Very quiet they were," the senior man of the two said. "Came up behind us and we never saw them. When we attempted to move, one of them must have had a pistol for he shattered a stone right at my feet, and next thing we were lying there tied up. Gey quick they were, but we never saw a face."

"I ken fine who they'll be: Sandy Macrae and Pat the Blocker. Pat used to work here, and a grand shot he is."

"Well they left the radios at least, so we'd best warn them at Knoydart," the officer said, unhitching his from his belt.

"Mr Sym, sir," Sergeant Matheson shouted across to the inspector, who was sitting on a rock talking to Andrew, "we've Rogers on the blower. Seems they were surprised and tied up and then the helicopter appeared. It left in a hurry five minutes ago. That was when Jock, Major Noble's keeper, arrived and freed them."

"Five minutes, eh? That means, depending which way they come, they'll be here pretty soon," Inspector Sym said, running back towards the Land Rover which was now well hidden in the wood. "Quick now, let's have that searchlight ready. You say Rogers mentioned they were armed? In that case, Bill, one man over there with the carbine, and you'd better have a hand gun. And you, Mr Henderson, for God's sake have a care and don't go rushing in. Wait till I give the order, all of you."

"That's him now surely," Sergeant Matheson cried. "Aye, he's cutting across the hill there. Sounds as if he's going to drop down that steep bit to the edge of the field."

As soon as the helicopter had cleared the top of the hill above Fernfield, Calum switched off the lights and started descending towards the waters of the Sound, finally levelling off fifty foot above the waves.

Annette leaned towards him. "We'll do it now," she hissed in his ear, and as she swung back in her seat the plane gave a lurch to the right and rose a hundred feet.

"Merde!" she shouted. "Have a care! This door's loose and I'm slipping. Jean, Jean, help me. Pull on the door – quickly, or I'll be out." Jean undid his seat belt and plunged forward to Annette's shoulder. Annette held tight to the left arm of her seat. Calum again swung the plane to the right and down. Annette gave a push, the door swung open. Jean, losing his balance, toppled forwards, failed to hold onto the door frame, and assisted by a push from Annette, with a despairing cry pitched out into the darkness.

Calum swung the plane left, the door slammed shut and he levelled out at fifty foot above the water and flew on south until he could see a line of hills to port.

"That was good," Annette said. "You did well, mon cher écossais. Mais le pauvre Jean! He was useful, but a liability. He had to go; a pity, because he was quite good in bed," she added with a reminiscent smile.

"Nearly there," Calum said, and they turned inland over some low hills with the loch on their left. "I'll have to risk the lights again, for there's not a glimmer from *Ariadne* or any torch signal from Jakie. I canna understand it. It's not good but we'll have to risk it." And he took the helicopter down steeply, to land on the edge of a rough field, a hundred yards from the pier where the *Ariadne* lay, dark and silent.

He switched off the lights and cut the engine and sat silent for five minutes. When nothing happened, he opened the door, dropped to the ground and crouching in the shadow of the helicopter, carefully scanned the whole area. Finally he stood up and put his head in the door and beckoned Annette to come nearer.

"I canna see or hear anything," he whispered, "so I'm going to have a look at *Ariadne*. There's something wrong, but I don't know what. You stay here while I investigate. If everything's okay, I'll be back with the tractor and trailer we keep here and we can start shifting the gold."

Keeping to the bottom of the slope and avoiding the shingle, he reached the track and walked along the pier.

"Don't move," Andrew whispered as Calum passed within thirty feet of the Land Rover. "Let's just see what he does." Sym nodded his agreement.

The tide was high, so the deck and superstructure of the motor cruiser towered above the pier and, as a consequence, they lost sight of Calum in the shadows. They heard him shout to the skipper a couple of times, then they saw him silhouetted against the sky as he climbed over the rail onto the after-deck and vanished below.

A light came on in the saloon and a few minutes later was extinguished. Then they saw the outline of Calum's head and shoulders on the bridge. He walked from one side to the other as though looking for something, then he bent down and almost immediately a vivid flash, followed by a towering sheet of flame, tore apart the darkness of the sky and the sound of the explosion reverberated around the hills.

"Switch on the searchlight," Andrew yelled. "Quick now, shine it at the helicopter." They saw the blades begin to turn.

"She's a bloody helicopter pilot!" he shouted. "I knew she'd pull some sort of trick on us." And he jumped from the Land Rover and ran towards the plane, easily outpacing Sym, who lumbered behind him.

The passenger door, never properly closed, swung open as he reached it. He grabbed the frame with both hands, and as the engine noise rose to a crescendo and the machine started to rise, he half clambered and was half thrown into the cockpit.

Trying to control the plane, Annette reached between her legs, and from her open fly pulled a small pistol. As it swung round towards him, Andrew lunged forward, lost his balance and sprawled across, knocking both the gun and the controls from her hands. Then, even before the rotor smashed into the hillside, the engine coughed twice and died.

"The shit! He never filled up and I never looked," Annette screamed. "Look out! I can't control it!"

The whole machine hit the hill broadside on, bounced and rolled over. The weight of the cargo broke off the tail section which was left leaning drunkenly against the slope. Andrew was flung out through the gaping hole at the rear, landing in a peat hag, which probably saved his life. The rest of the fuselage bounced again and then landed, upside down, on the beach.

Andrew struggled to his feet, and apart from being winded, decided he was unhurt and so limped to where he could see the others clustered round the remains of the fuselage.

"Gently now," he heard Sym say, "she's badly injured. That's fine – easy now – bring her over here and lie her down. It's all right now, the air ambulance is on the way."

"What happened? And you, are you alright?" he asked Andrew.

"Yes, I think so. It seems they never filled up. So we ran out of fuel, the engine stopped and she lost control."

"So that's why there was no fire. Lucky for you." And he turned away as the dinghy from the Customs launch beached just below them.

Andrew bent down beside Annette and took the hand which she held out. Someone had produced a pressure lamp, and her face showed deathly white with a froth of pink blood around the lips. Andrew felt for his handkerchief and wiped it away.

Annette smiled at him, then coughed and more blood came from her lips. "I had no belt and so was thrown in the air and came down across the back of the seat," she gasped. "I have a terrible pain. I, I..." and she coughed again.

"I know – but keep still and we'll soon have you in hospital," he said, wiping her face.

"No you won't. It broke ribs and I've a punctured lung and maybe other things." She smiled weakly and clutched his hand tighter.

"Listen, Andrew dear," her voice was now much weaker. "I planned it all. I got the explosives to Jakie..." She paused, struggling to get air. "I got them; Jakie used to be in France – he did things for me. He arranged the booby trap. You were clever and I thought you'd be here," a note of triumph entered her voice, "and you were. So I blow up Calum and I get you on the heli. I had a gas gun and you would have gone to sleep. I had our escape plan... there was a boat and I would have had you and the gold. But... but you were too quick, I dropped the gun." Her breathing was becoming more and more laboured; she tried to sit up but blood gushed from her mouth and she almost choked; after another pause she summoned what remained of her fast-ebbing strength. Andrew bent down and she whispered, "Then I forgot Calum would not bother to fill up. It is always the little things... les petites choses."

She fell back, looked up at him, smiled and tried to say something that he could not catch; her breathing stopped and she was gone.

CHAPTER 42

Aᴺᴰʀᴇᴡ ᴍᴏᴠᴇᴅ ʜɪs ʜᴀɴᴅ ᴀɴᴅ ꜰᴇʟᴛ ꜰᴏʀ a pulse but could find none, then seeing one of the constables standing by the Land Rover, he waved to him to come over.

"I can find no sign of life," he said, "so can you see if you can find a rug or something to cover her?" As the man ran back to the vehicle, Andrew again bent down by the body.

He straightened the arms and legs as best he could and wiped the remaining blood from the nose and lips. He then gently closed the eyelids and stood for a few minutes looking down at Annette. In death, her face bore a look of complete serenity.

"She looks so peaceful," he thought, and then wondered what strange thoughts had really been going through her mind in those few final minutes of her life.

His reverie was broken by the return of the constable carrying a blanket. This they laid carefully over the body; then Andrew turned away and looked round the little bay with the vague feeling that there was something amiss. The area around him was illuminated by the pressure lamp and the beam of the searchlight, but everywhere else was in darkness.

"Of course," he thought looking towards the pier, "there was an explosion. Why then is there no fire? *Ariadne* should be a blazing wreck." But all he could see of her was what appeared to be part of the bow just visible above the water.

Seeing Inspector Sym walking up the beach towards him, Andrew pointed towards the pier. "What happened to the boat?" he asked. "After an explosion like that I'd have thought she'd be burning furiously."

"Aye, so would I," Sym replied. "Matheson has been down to look, and it seems that the force of the blast broke her back and ripped all the mooring ropes from the bollards. The stern, with the engines and fuel tanks, sank immediately, but the bow section, although flooded, appears to be still partly afloat. There was a bit of a fire there but it's gone out. We'll have to be a bit careful once the tide goes down, but the Customs boys reckon we're alright for four or five hours and we've a lot to do in that time." He looked down at the blanket-covered body. "Mrs Barry died of her injuries?" he said.

"Yes," Andrew replied. "I think when I was flung clear, she was tossed about inside the machine and must have suffered severe internal injuries. But no doubt there'll be a post mortem."

"Aye, and a fatal accident enquiry. And the same with the body of Macrae, or what's left of it, when we get it out of the wreck. Then there's the other Frenchman. I wonder what happened to him? We'll no doubt find out in time, but now we'd best go back to the Land Rover and get on the radio."

For the next two hours, while Sym and Matheson were occupied on the radio, there was little for Andrew to do other than answer questions and occasionally offer advice.

Sym had already sent the dinghy back to the *Kittiwake*, and as there appeared to be no further risk of explosion or fire, asked them to bring her in alongside the jetty. He had also radioed for the other Land Rover to return to Inverdoran, bringing Jakie with them.

Then, bit by bit, as relevant higher authorities gave their consent, action was put in hand. The gold from the helicopter was loaded into the two Land Rovers and Sergeant Matheson and three men took it back to the landing craft and thence to Mallaig where a van and escort would be waiting to take it to Inverness.

Jakie and his escort boarded the *Kittiwake*. A sergeant and constable were detailed to remain at Inverdoran to guard the wreckage of the *Ariadne* and the helicopter. They would be joined as soon after daybreak as possible by a police launch, and eventually, by various recovery crews.

Finally Annette's body, accompanied by Andrew and Inspector Sym, was taken on board the *Kittiwake* and they set sail for the Kyle of Lochalsh.

Arrived there, the full efficiency of the Northern Constabulary became apparent. An ambulance was waiting to take the body to Inverness. There was also a dark blue van, into which the police hustled Jakie and drove him off to the cells in Dingwall.

"I'll go straight to Inverness," Sym said as they walked towards a waiting police car. "I'll maybe get an hour's sleep and a shave and then I'll be seeing Mr Cameron. I'll drop you at Knockbain on the way, and you'd best hang on there if you don't mind, for we'll doubtless need to see you later in the afternoon."

It was almost six o'clock and broad daylight when the police car dropped Andrew at the castle. Having thanked Sym for the lift, he turned and walked towards the great front door, wondering whether it would be unlocked or whether he should ring the bell or even whether he should have gone to the gun room door. However, the problem was quickly resolved, for the door swung open and he was greeted by the general.

"No trouble at all," he said as Andrew apologised for disturbing them at such an ungodly hour. "Thought you might appear some time after five, and as I had some work to do, I thought I might as well get up and be ready for you. Now, what would you like to do? Bath, sleep, eat, or any combination thereof?"

"Quite honestly, Tommy, I think a couple of hours' sleep is the first requirement," Andrew replied. "It'll probably leave me feeling awful, but without it I'd probably feel worse. Then I think some breakfast, as I haven't eaten since about four yesterday afternoon. Then I'll tell you all the night's happenings."

"Right then, I'll leave you to it. Don't hurry yourself – and I mean that – for you look all in."

Once he was alone in the bedroom, Andrew threw off his clothes, flopped onto the bed, pulled up the eiderdown and lay back. But despite his extreme tiredness, sleep refused to come.

Round and round in his mind went the events of the previous night. Had they done anything wrong? Could the deaths have been avoided? Or were they perhaps, in a strange way, the best outcome for all concerned. And what of Annette's extraordinary outpourings? How true were they?

"Did she have some strange crush on me?" he wondered, and felt the tears starting down his cheeks. "Did she? ...It all seems so improbable, so out of keeping with her. Was I responsible for? ...I don't know." And at that point sleep finally overcame him – a sleep much troubled by strange dreams.

He awoke with a start to see someone standing by the bed looking down at him. Thinking he was still dreaming, he was about to shout when he realised that he was awake and that he was looking up at Jenny.

"It's alright, darling, it really is me," she said, seeing the fear in his eyes. "What on earth were you dreaming about? I came in earlier and you were shouting and yelling. I couldn't make out most of it – something about 'You'll kill us both' and 'No, you don't! ...Your plan can't work! It's only in your mind'. But now tell me what happened to you, you've got a terrible bruise on your shoulder?"

"What's the time? God, is it really eleven?" he cried, throwing back the cover. "Look, I'll shave and have a quick bath and I'll tell you a bit – the private bit – while I dress."

"You get on and shave, while I run your bath," she said and then, a few minutes later, added, "And now I'm going to find some things to deal with your wounds. You're covered in cuts and bruises."

By the time Jenny returned with sticking plaster, antiseptic and arnica, Andrew was drying himself somewhat gingerly, for the bath had stirred up his various injuries.

"Now just stand still and do as I say," she ordered. Then, some ten minutes later, she stood back, saying, "That's better. I think you'll live, and there's no need for the doctor that I can see. But now tell me, what on earth happened?"

"Well, as far as the injuries are concerned," he said, walking back into the bedroom, "in a nutshell, I was thrown out of a crashing helicopter."

Her hand flew to her mouth. "But how? ...Why?" she stammered.

"Listen, darling," he said, sitting on the edge of the bed and pulling her down beside him. "Annette tried to take off in the helicopter. I just managed to scramble in when she produced a pistol. I knocked it out of her hand and she lost control of the plane. Then, before she could regain control, it ran out of fuel and crashed into the hillside. The tail broke off and I was hurled out into a peat hag, but she was trapped inside and thrown about like a rag doll. They got her out and tried to make her comfortable. When I got to her, I could see that she had severe internal injuries, and she knew it too. Oh yes, she was conscious but how much she knew what she was doing or saying I don't know. And now this bit is for you only. I tried to comfort her but she was becoming delirious and I don't think she knew what she was saying. It was strange, almost eerie; she was saying she had planned it all... and that we would escape with the gold. She said she knew I would come – and then, a few moments later, she was dead. I think she thought she was in love with me – perhaps she was – we shall never know." And Jenny reached up and wiped a tear from his eye and kissed him gently.

"No we'll never know. So let it rest at that," she agreed. "Now come on, finish dressing and I'll go and organise some food for you, and then you can tell us the whole story."

The rest of the morning was spent in endless repetition of the story of the night's happenings. First to the party at Knockbain and then hearing from them about their activity at the grave on the previous afternoon.

Next, Andrew rang Superintendent Wilkinson, who said that he'd already been in touch with Cameron in Inverness and did Andrew know if Mrs Barry had any next of kin? Also, they'd better be prepared for it to be all over the papers the next day.

After dealing with several other matters with Wilkinson, Andrew rang Passford, spoke to Wilfred and gave him an outline of what had happened and asked if he could help over the next of kin and he said he would try and find out from James Barry. His next call was to the brewery. Again he gave a brief account and warned them about the press and, for his pains, got severe lectures from both his cousin and his secretary.

Then at about four thirty Cameron and Sym arrived and everyone assembled in the drawing room.

"First of all," Cameron said, "I've a few bits of news I'm sure you'd all like to hear. Those of you who were at the grave will remember that we left two policemen there. Well, two of the gang came by boat, ahead of the helicopter, surprised the men and tied them up. They were rescued by the keeper, who arrived on the scene just as the helicopter left. We tried to get a message to you, but I'm afraid we were a wee bit late! The two men involved were Macraes from Kishorn way. The keeper guessed it must be them and this was confirmed by the skipper of the yacht when we questioned him and, what's more, Inspector Sym had seen them acting suspiciously the previous day. They are now safely locked up in Dingwall. The gold from the helicopter has been taken to Inverness and they'll be up to deal with the grave tomorrow, but that need not worry you. No, we haven't yet got up Calum Macrae's body, but they'll be dealing with that and the various wrecks tomorrow. Now I'm afraid, Mr Henderson, I've a lot of questions to ask you, but I don't think the rest of you need wait."

Cameron had brought a shorthand writer with him and so the next two hours were spent getting detailed statements of exactly what took place at Inverdoran, from both Andrew and Inspector Sym.

"Aye, I think we're beginning to get the full picture," Cameron said, "but I'm afraid, Mr Henderson, we'll have to ask you to come back for the fatal accident inquiry, but until then then you're free to go. I'll also need to get a statement from Brigadier Colquhoun before I leave, but before I do, let me ask you a question. What do you think was Mrs Barry's real intention?"

"I've been wondering about that myself," Andrew replied, "and the best I can come up with is this. I believe the sinking of the yacht went according to plan. She always intended to get rid of Calum Macrae and I don't think he knew she was a helicopter pilot. It should of course have been Jakie who went with her, not me, and I think she also intended to get rid of him somewhere along the line; you remember she had that gas gun thing which she tried to use on me. But where she intended to fly to, I've no idea; and why she didn't check on the fuel I don't know."

"Aye, that's much the way I'm thinking myself," Cameron said, "and I think I can suggest what was to be her first stop. There's been a French Fishery Research ship out in the Irish Sea for the past few days. There has always been something odd about that ship, not least the fact that her skipper has a criminal record. There is one other interesting and very relevant thing about that ship and that is that it has a helicopter pad. We're making some further enquiries to see if there's any connection between the captain and Mrs Barry. It could be that that's where she was heading. We'll let you know. And now perhaps I could just have a wee word with the brigadier."

Later that evening they had a call from Wilfred Saddler to say that he'd spoken to James Barry and told him of Annette's death. He had been very helpful about next of kin. Apparently Annette had a brother, a highly respected industrialist who lived in Rouen and also had considerable property in Brittany. Andrew then told him their plans. He and Jenny and Norman Colquhoun would leave Knockbain the next day and drive to Barrs, where they would drop the brigadier and spend the night. They would then drive on to London and would like to come to Suffolk for the weekend.

Andrew then rang Cameron and gave him the address of Annette's brother. In return, Cameron told him that a body, believed to be that of the Frenchman Lemaître, had been washed ashore on a beach in Skye. Then, having finished his telephone calls, Andrew walked back to the drawing room, smiling broadly.

"Darling Jenny," he said, taking her hands, "shall we tell them now?" Jenny nodded, and the assembed company looked up expectantly.

"We are going to get married!" they said in chorus. Everyone got up and there were congratulations and kisses all round.

"Well now," said Tommy Macdonald, returning to the room after a short absence and carrying a magnum of champagne, "something just warned me that we might need this. Wasn't it lucky that I happened to put it on ice!"

And that is nearly the end of the story. There was more champagne at Barrs and from there Jenny rang her family in South Africa.

In London there were celebrations at Tony Henderson's house and a lot of 'Didn't I tell you...' from Phyllis. There was also a very special party for the staff of the brewery, to celebrate not only the engagement, but also the ever increasing success of World Wide Wines.

Finally there was a wonderful long weekend at Passford where Andrew was at last able to relax. He was also able to show them the old ice house where the jewels had lain hidden for some hundred and fifty years or more.

Andrew and his solicitors, as appointed representatives of the Saddler family, became involved in an endless series of meetings with English and French bankers and diplomats, the final outcome being deemed reasonably satisfactory to all parties.

The gold was returned to France and the French Government presented letters of thanks, beautifully inscribed, and signed by the President: one to Major Noble of Fernfield for his family's two-hundred-year guardianship of the treasure, and the other to Andrew for his part in enabling it to be returned to France.

After many hours of negotiation over the ownership of the jewellery, it was agreed that, with the exception of certain major items which were believed to be part of the French Crown Jewels and should be returned to France, the remainder could be considered as Marie Antoinette's personal property to dispose of as she wished, and was therefore handed to Wilfred Saddler as the senior direct descendant of the Chevalier. For his part, Wilfred agreed that most of the collection should be made available for display in certain English and French museums.

However, he did retain some of the smaller items for the family, three of which – a diamond necklace and pendant, an emerald ring and a very beautiful diamond, emerald and ruby spray – he gave to Jenny as a wedding present.

In December of that year, amid great family rejoicing, Andrew and Jenny were married in the Anglican Church in Paarl. Then later that same day, when they were at last alone, Jenny looked at her husband and asked a question that had puzzled her ever since the start of the adventure.

"I can understand the Queen giving a present – a memento perhaps – to a favourite courtier," she said, "but why, darling, should the King give such a person a substantial sum of his country's money? Money, moreover, which it seems to me he had stolen."

Andrew looked at his wife and smiled. "Louis the Sixteenth," he replied, "like nearly all eighteenth-century kings other than our own, was an absolute monarch and so could do, or try to do, what he liked with his country, its treasures and its people. In those days, to misquote a well-known saying, I think it could fairly be said that generosity really was the *prerogative of kings*. Favoured subjects benefited from such generosity, while kings who overstepped the mark lost their heads. How's that?"

ABOUT THE AUTHOR

ROBIN MACKENZIE WAS BORN IN LONDON IN 1926 and shortly thereafter he and his mother sailed for India where his father was serving in the Seaforth Highlanders. On returning from India, the rest of his childhood was shared between the family estate in Scotland and homes in London and Hampshire. He was educated at Eton and then spent four years in the army at the end of the second World War, including a year in Trieste. This was followed by a short time at Cambridge and then ten years farming in Scotland. Finding this not very profitable and having always been fascinated by anything automatic, he joined the computer industry where he spent the next thirty years. He is married to Jean and they live in Hampshire.

With a literary background on his mother's side of the family, in retirement he decided to follow a long felt ambition to write and *The Prerogative of Kings* is his second novel. The idea of a search for a mysterious legacy occurred to him after a visit to the Huguenot museum in Franchhoek as he has both Huguenot forbears and also an ancestor who was an eighteenth century French courtier.